THE COMPLETE ADVENTURES OF

THE GRIFFON

VOLUME 3

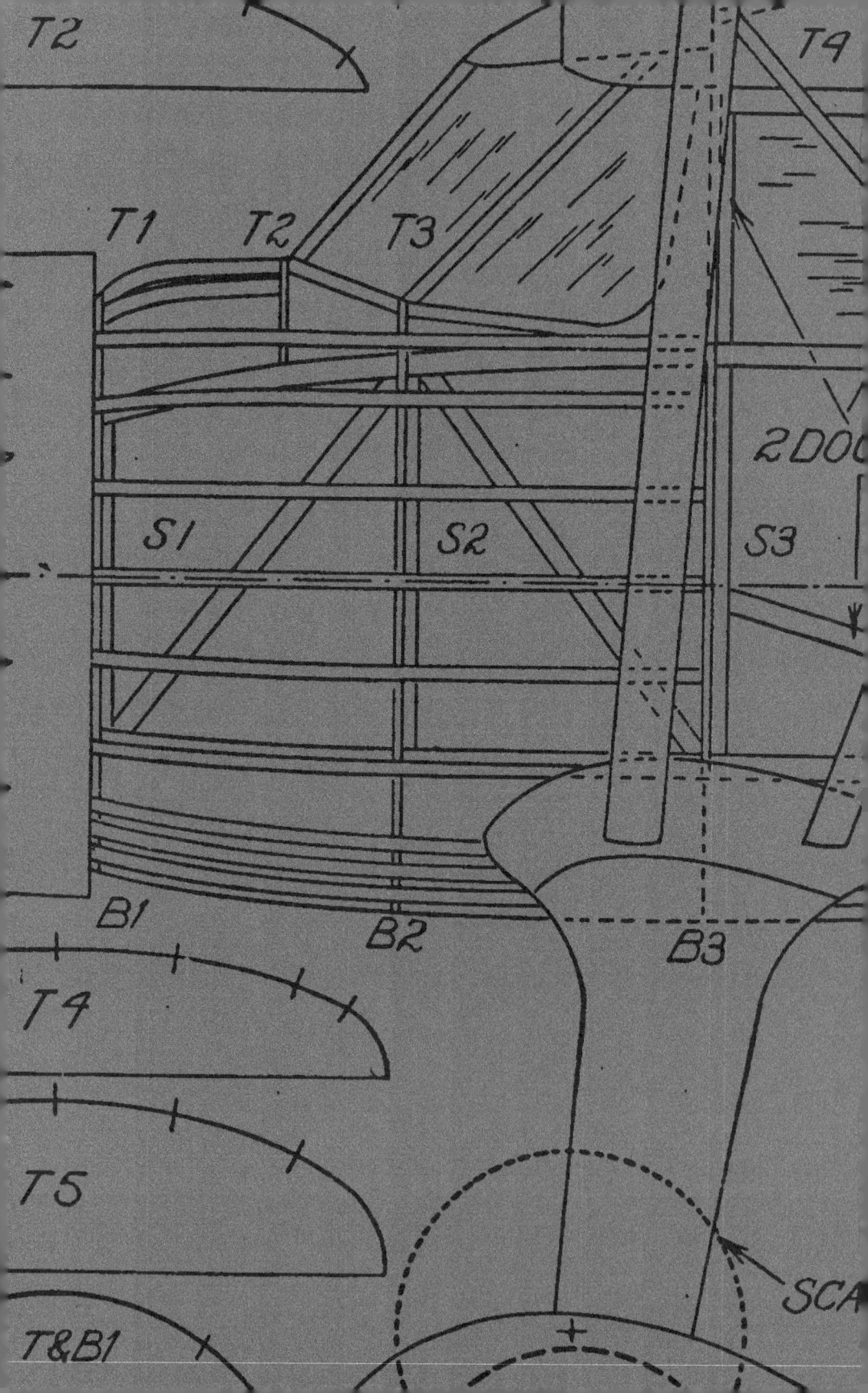

THE COMPLETE ADVENTURES OF

THE GRIFFON

VOLUME 3

BY

Arch Whitehouse

ILLUSTRATIONS BY
Alden McWilliams

ALTUS
PRESS

ALTUS PRESS

2016

© 2016 Altus Press • First Edition—2016

EDITED AND DESIGNED BY
Matthew Moring

ASSOCIATE EDITOR
Ray Riethmeier

PUBLISHING HISTORY
"Riddle of the Rocket" originally appeared in the January 1937 issue of *Flying Aces* magazine (Vol. 25, No. 2).
"Cavalry of the Clouds" originally appeared in the March 1937 issue of *Flying Aces* magazine (Vol. 25, No. 4).
"Twin-Engine Treachery" originally appeared in the May 1937 issue of *Flying Aces* magazine (Vol. 26, No. 2).
"Test Pilot Terror" originally appeared in the July 1937 issue of *Flying Aces* magazine (Vol. 26, No. 4).
"The Carrier Coup" originally appeared in the September 1937 issue of *Flying Aces* magazine (Vol. 27, No. 2).
"Scourge of the Sky Brood" originally appeared in the November 1937 issue of *Flying Aces* magazine (Vol. 27, No. 4).

THANKS TO
Everard P. Digges LaTouche

Visit *altuspress.com* for more books like this.
Printed in the United States of America.

TABLE OF
Contents

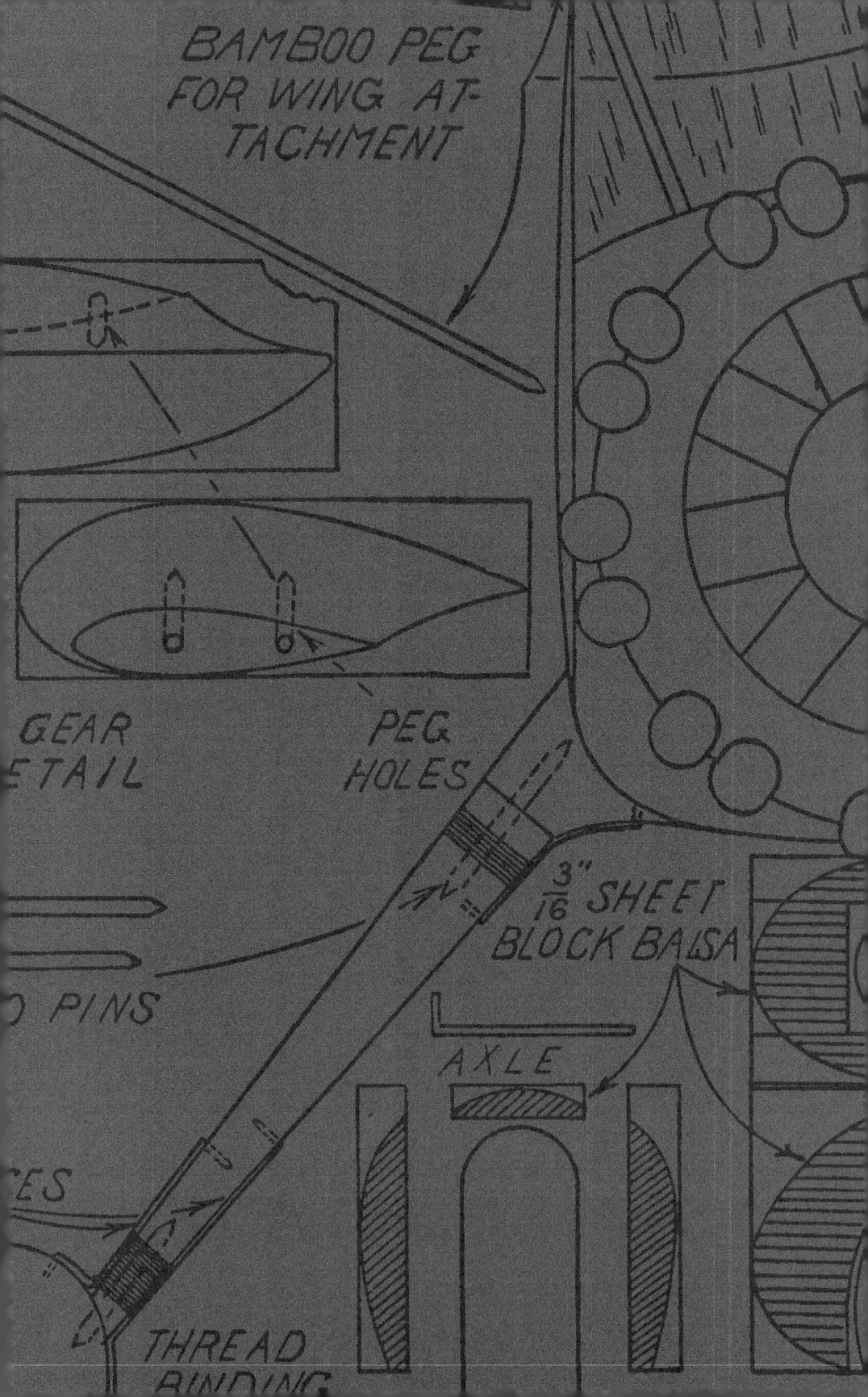

BAMBOO PEG
FOR WING AT-
TACHMENT

GEAR
ETAIL

PEG
HOLES

PINS

$\frac{3}{16}$" SHEET
BLOCK BALSA

AXLE

ES

THREAD
BINDING

Riddle of the Rocket

"**T**HERE'S** something screwy, somewhere," growled Barney O'Dare as he pressed the big black button which actuated the door of the camouflaged hangar at Graylands. "That guy Lang is up to something. He ain't quiet this long for nothing."

"I'm not worrying about Lang," Keen replied as he climbed up the pontoon of the *Black Bullet*. "It's that Milford *Monsoon* flying boat that has me worried."

Barney watched the doors open, saw the great steel prop slash silently as Keen applied the starter to the 1,000 h.p. Avia. The big eighteen cylinder power plant responded at once, for O'Dare had previously applied a heat-gun and warmed her from prop to carburetor gears.

He stood by while Keen rolled the ship clear, then he pressed another button that closed the great underground hangar. Outside, the layout looked simply like a well trimmed rock garden.

Barney moved swiftly then, folded down the great wings and held them in position while Keen jammed the king-pin levers down with his feet. Then silently, they rolled across the lush turf and eased down toward the water. Another lever was pulled and their sleek pontoons were sent down into position. Then Keen let her move silently out toward the open sea.

"You're not really taking that *Monsoon* thing seriously, are you?" O'Dare asked when he had made himself comfortable in the back seat.

"Scott and Lang will," replied Keen, preparing to take off.

"But I think that's a company gag—for publicity. An' as if they haven't had enough," Barney snorted.

"She's a great bus, Barney," Keen replied, now using the Gosport helmet phone to converse. "With things as they are for the trade on the trans-Atlantic run, they've got to put something out. The Germans have this catapult depot-ship business down to a science and they certainly have the dirigible business cold."

"Sure, but we got guys what have done that trans-Pacific show for nearly a year. All we need is to announce a schedule and we'll pack 'em in. Britain will be selling the *Queen Mary* for a show-boat on the Thames."

KERRY KEEN gave the Avia the gun and the *Black Bullet* hoiked up on her step, swished her tail, slapped at a roller, and was off. They were soon well aloft, circling for altitude over Block Island.

"It's not that easy," Keen warned when they were at 4,000. "The real competition will come when those new Short *Empire* boats start winging across. They're real jobs, Barney, and if we are to tie up with Imperial Airways, we shall have to put out something that will compare in comfort as well as speed."

"That's an angle," agreed Barney, "but you don't really believe anyone has swiped the Milford *Monsoon* do you? What the devil could they do with it?"

"No one steals things like that just for the pleasure of stealing."

"The British wouldn't—" began Barney, but he was tossed out of the conversation play before he could finish. Keen started to speak, but his voice suddenly broke.

He jerked the *Black Bullet* over with only a fraction of a second to spare just as a dark object flashed past with a roar. The swirl of

air caught the *Black Bullet* dead under her port wing. Before Keen could do anything the monoplane was swished over on her back.

"Watch that!" screamed Keen.

"I am," yelled Barney, scrambling about somewhere behind.

Keen had to let the *Bullet* fall away, and she lost plenty of altitude doing it. They fluttered and stalled, then finally Keen managed to pull her clear and ease her into a gentle dive from which she recovered with a tremble.

"What was that?" yelled Keen again.

"Cripes! I don't know. Looked like that guy in the Twenty-fifth Century. What's his name?"

"Stop gagging! What was that?"

"Something without wings, or I'm a Dutchman," Barney said hollowly.

"Have you been drinking again?"

"Not much. But you can say what you like—whatever that thing was it didn't have wings and it certainly was going like a bat out of hell."

"A rocket?" said Keen giving the *Bullet* the gun and heading speedily toward the Connecticut shore.

"Yeh, but there ain't any such thing—yet," Barney said.

"Hello!… Look!… Over there toward Black Point!" Keen cried. On the Connecticut shore ahead, they saw a sudden belch of flame. It looked like an explosion of some kind.

Keen turned, stared at Barney. "Did you see that?" he demanded. "Did that… that rocket thing head that way?"

"That's the way she was going," agreed Barney. "Funny, though—explosion, but no concussion. We should have heard or felt it by now."

"That's right," agreed Keen. "I'm going over that way and see what that was."

"You'll get nabbed, too. There'll be half a dozen Coast Guard tubs in the area in no time."

"I'll risk it," grinned Keen. "I'll run them ragged."

KEEN settled back, watched the plume of flame that had risen from a point about three miles southwest of Niantic. If that rocket—if it *was* a rocket—had hit there, it had been directed on the promontory known as Black Point, a colorless finger of land about a mile long and no more than a quarter of a mile wide. He reflected that if that "rocket" had been directed there, it had been dispatched by someone who certainly knew plenty about rockets.

As they raced on, Keen tried to rack his brain for anything that might give him a clue. He mulled over all the articles and books he had read on rockets, but could recall nothing equal to this. If it had come from anywhere within the area where they had first seen it, it must have travelled at least twenty miles to get to Black Point.

But a new glint caught his eye. The glare of the flame on Black Point had died down suddenly; and his vision now made out two glints of pennon-shaped flame hurtling toward them. Barney let out a yell, slapped Keen on the back.

It was a gray bullet-nosed biplane packed with plenty of "swift." It came on, glinting out of the two exhaust-port eyes—and then it added two more twinklers. The extra eyes were the spitting barrels of two machine guns set in the nose and firing through the airscrew.

The *Black Bullet* slammed into this storm, and Keen instinctively pressed his own trigger releases.

"What the devil sort of a bus is that?" yelled Barney.

"British 'Kestrel' engine, anyway," yelled Keen, holding his course.

The gray biplane whipped up, unable to hang on any longer. Keen drew his stick back slightly and let loose with the Chatelleraults fitted in the wings. Barney was ready, too, and as the gray raider swept over them he crouched under the grips of his Browning guns, let fly with everything.

The biplane wavered, staggered, then there came a metallic scream. That was the prop breaking up, ripping the motor out of the bearers. She rolled over, and Barney planted another wicked burst smack in her side as she started to boot-lace down. Keen rolled over fast as the raider fell into a sleezy twisting spin. They curled around and watched her, followed down carefully until she hit.

"What was it?" asked Barney.

"A Dutch Fokker fighter—C.X. type. A pip, too. They have daubed her all over with gray paint and blanked the insignia out. I'm going down to have a look-see."

Keen steadied his glide and let the pontoons down. He saw the wreckage of the Dutch Fokker bobbing helplessly below. They skirted her for a minute, then the *Black Bullet* dropped down beautifully and Keen taxied her in toward the wreckage. Barney stood up, kept a close watch on everything while Keen clambered out on the pontoon. He took a light line across and clambered along the wrenched wing of the gray Fokker.

"Make it snappy," warned Barney, the night glasses up to his eyes. "I can see a cutter heading this way."

"I'll be back," Keen cried, crawling to the cockpit hatch and ripping it back.

He found the pilot huddled over his belt. There was no one in the back seat. Keen fumbled fast, removed everything loose, then made a last hurried search through the dead man's pockets. He came away with a few letters, a leather pocketbook, a water-soaked map, and a small blue leather booklet. These he stuffed inside his coverall pockets and hurriedly returned to the *Bullet*.

He just had time to get aboard, let the *Bullet* ride clear, and head off. For not three cables' length away rode a Coast Guard cutter. There was a flash. Something crashed out over the cockpit hatch and made Keen move fast.

"Only the Coast Guard," snorted Barney. "They fire about five over to let you know they're coming. Then they try to hit you. Let's go!"

The *Black Bullet*, responding to the throttle, slammed across the rollers. With a flip of the stick she hoiked up and cleared. Keen held her down near the water and raced away toward Montauk light, zig-zagging all the way until the Coast Guard gave up the chase.

Barney was still fumbling with the stuff Keen had hurriedly handed him, trying to figure out what it was. There was a strange steel box from which emerged two heavy duty cables with quick release lugs on the ends. From it there also protruded three bright steel bars. The sides were dotted with bright-headed screws indicating that there was considerable intricate mechanism inside. It was all pretty puzzling to Barney and he put it down gingerly.

They climbed away, went out to sea for a short distance while Keen went over the unusual events of the evening. Then, as suddenly as he had started, Keen decided to return to Graylands.

Barney had sense enough not to ask questions.

The *Bullet*, silenced now, was brought down again, run gently up out of the water and into the arbor shelter while Barney opened the doors. Keen ran the ship in after the wings had been folded up and without a word, gathered up all the salvage and sauntered through the hangar, on through the wine-cellar, and up into the ground floor of his home. He slipped out of the black coverall and parachute harness, flipped off his mask and goggles, and wandered along with his plunder to his great study.

Barney came up in a few minutes with a bottle of Bollinger '28 under one arm and a stubby brown bottle of O'Doul's Dew under the other.

"Quite an evening," was all that Keen said when he raised his champagne glass.

"Well, we tested our new guns," grinned Barney, "An' that's what we went out for."

THE CLOCK on John Scott's desk disclosed that the New York Secret Service chief was half an hour later than usual. It was 9:30 a.m.

But he'd not enjoyed the extra thirty minutes. It had produced no rest. For the first time in his life he really missed his side-kick, Drury Lang.

He stared at the clock, then at his watch as if he could not believe his eyes. There was no sign of Lang anywhere. No scrawled notes on his desk. Nothing stuck under the telephone. Nothing folded and slipped into the leaves of the World Almanac which always rested on Scott's desk.

Scott stood in the middle of the floor, stared around. But there was no answer to his silent plea. "Gone since Monday," he muttered again for the tenth time.

He let his eyes rest on the telephone; then, like all men of his tribe, adopted the suggestion and took up the receiver. He was about to fumble for a number he had scrawled on the corner of his desk blotter when a voice caught his ear—

"Scott!"

The Secret Service man jerked the receiver away from his ear as though he half expected it to explode against his head. His right hand automatically reached for his shoulder holster. But the voice in the phone persisted—

"Scott! Listen to me, Scott. This is important... and get it straight!"

"Who is this?" asked Scott, still puzzled.

"You tell Lang to keep out of that Old Lyme affair, or he'll get his brains blown out."

"Who is this?" demanded Scott, enraged.

"The Griffon!"

"The who?" Scott floundered, almost biting his lip. But there was only a strange click and the voice was gone.

Scott pounded the bar of his telephone set, got the operator. "Get this," he stormed. "This is a G-2 call. I want the location of that call you just put through to me."

"Call?... You have received no call," the operator answered. "Are you sure?"

"Sure? Certainly I'm sure! I was just talking to a man who called himself— Oh, never mind," snarled Scott slamming the receiver down.

He sat down, stared across his desk at the map on the wall. Then he picked up the telephone again and started to call a number. Just then the door opened and Kerry Keen, the noted ballistics expert, sauntered in, trim and immaculate.

Scott set the telephone set down gently this time. "That's funny," he said. "I was just going to call you."

"Who shot who, and where?" beamed Keen, taking the best seat in the office.

"I just had the Griffon on the wire," said Scott slowly.

"Impossible," grinned Keen. "I just got off the top of a Fifth Avenue bus."

"No kidding Keen," Scott said anxiously. "I was actually speaking to him."

"Then I'm not the Griffon, this week, eh?" said Keen taking out a gold cigarette case. "I wish you'd get my status straightened out."

"Stop gagging. This is serious. I just picked up my phone to call you—"

"And there was the Griffon on the wire, I suppose," interrupted Keen with glee.

"That's right. How did you know?"

"I guessed it. You look as though you'd had some bad news. Besides, you told me when I came in."

"Let me talk for a change, will you?" growled Scott selecting a cigar half as big as a ferry slip pile. "This guy, the Griffon, was on the wire and told me to keep Lang off the Old Lyme business—or he'd 'get his brains blown out.'"

"Poor old Lang," said Keen with mock severity. "Still, it's an idea if you ever want to get rid of him."

"Shut up!" bellowed Scott. "Lang has been on the Old Lyme business since Monday, and I've had no news from him since he started. How do you like that?"

"Let's go out and celebrate!" cheered Keen.

"I'll brain you, Keen!" roared Scott. "Lang's missing, I tell you—on a smuggling show. And it's no joke. That's why I was about to call you."

"And got the Griffon, instead," laughed Keen, enjoying Scott's discomfiture. "What is this Old Lyme business, anyway?"

"Well, for about two months there's been a ton of ice slipping in somehow, and we've traced a lot of it to an old wharf on the outskirts of Old Lyme."

"Ice?" said Keen puzzled.

"Yes ice—diamonds," explained Scott, disgusted at Keen's apparent lack of criminal education. "Someone's been smuggling diamonds by the bushel into Connecticut, and Lang went up to look into it."

"And hasn't returned?"

"Not a word. And he was supposed to report every twelve hours."

"*Cherchez la femme,*" Keen smiled. "Diamonds? Look for the woman. Old Lang probably has a lady friend somewhere."

"I wish you'd come down to earth and act sane," stormed Scott. "I tell you Lang has been missing since Monday—three days."

"Lovely. Now I can rest," Keen said. "Of all the pests, that guy Lang was the worst. You'll be able to get something done now, Scott, old boy."

"I want you to help me, Keen. If anything happens to that guy, I'll go nuts. You may not appreciate him, but he's the best man on his job in the country. He's a bloodhound, a sticker, a guy who hangs on, and I couldn't replace him. I want you to help me."

"The Griffon told you to keep him off the Old Lyme business

or he'd 'get his brains blown out,'" reflected Keen. "You know, Scott, that would be a pretty neat job of marksmanship—considering the size of his br—"

"He's not so dumb," Scott cut in. "And now how about it?"

"What can I do? I'm not even sure where Old Lyme is."

"It's at the mouth of the Connecticut River near—well, it's right here," explained Scott, pointing it out on the map.

"Um," mused Keen. "That's queer. You know that's not far from where that meteor hit last night. Notice that in the paper, this morning?... Here, on page 3. It says that a meteor fell on Black Point. There's Black Point farther along the Sound."

"Meteor? What the deuce sort of a story is that?" slammed Scott. "We got a report of a *plane* falling into the Sound just off Black Point. I wonder if there is any connection."

"Too many strange things happening along there, Scott," Keen said, studying the map. "But what can I do?"

"I don't care what you do. I want you to work on this Lang matter and see if you can pick him up. I've got that damned Milford flying-boat mess to take care of. You heard about that, I suppose?"

"Sure, but I didn't get much sense out of it. How the devil can someone steal anything as big as that—and get away with it?"

"If I knew, I'd be going after Lang myself. As it is, the poor devil has to rely on you. Come on now, will you give me a hand?"

"I'll take a run up there and have a look around. Give me the full dope."

AN HOUR later, Keen left Scott's office, walked along the corridor, then suddenly darted into a steel doorway which led to the emergency stairway. He fumbled behind a heavy iron pipe and drew out a small but smart leather case. Then slipping off his hat and coat, he clambered up on a stairway window-sill and adjusted the small steel prongs of a lineman's telephone set to some wires that curled out of a light green box set high on the wall.

Had anyone come through at that minute, he would have accepted Keen for what he appeared to be—a telephone repair man.

He balanced himself there for several seconds, then got a response on the line he was ringing. In a low disguised voice he said:

"A monsoon should, he found, in the Indian Ocean—if you know your geography, Scott."

Then he quickly unclamped the steel clips, wound the wires around the hand set, and dropped down on the floor. The apparatus was quickly returned to its leather case. Then Keen slipped on his hat and coat, walked down three more flights of stairs, cut back into the corridors, and just caught an elevator car that was going down.

Outside in the street he hailed a taxi and ordered the driver to head for Grand Central Station.

BY THREE o'clock that afternoon he was back at Graylands, immediately darting back downstairs to where Barney was working on a long galvanized affair that looked like a bulbous torpedo.

Around him on the floor stood metal canisters of carbide and phosphorus. There were strange spring gadgets and coils of wire everywhere and there was every indication that the Mick had been working hard. Two empty O'Doul's Dew bottles were on the bench and Keen knew his man had been enjoying himself in spite of the amount of work he had completed.

Keen jumped into a pair of brown overalls, checked everything quickly, then picked up the strange steel box they had snatched from the Fokker fighter they had downed the night before. He went over it carefully while Barney babbled on with the day's news.

"What the devil have you been doing to old Scott?" Barney asked as Keen pondered on the steel box. "He called up here four times since lunch, barking something about monsoons in the Indian Ocean."

"Well," replied Keen without looking up. "That's where monsoons are to be found, aren't they?"

"I don't know. What is a monsoon?"

"Well, it's a periodic wind which during one half of the year blows from the southwest across the Indian Ocean and during the other half blows from the northeast."

"Funny. Old Scott seems to think it's something to do with that Milford *Monsoon* flying boat which has been swiped."

"Maybe he's right," said Keen with a noncommittal air as he set the steel box in a forward compartment of Barney's torpedo. "Did you know there's a second *Monsoon* over at the Milford plant awaiting a test flight?"

"Another?" gagged Barney. "When do they pinch that one?"

"That's what's worrying me. I was over there—in that general direction—today looking for Lang, and I found out that they are to test it tomorrow afternoon. I had a good mind to ask the guy what time he was swiping it."

"You... you mean you know who has his eye on it?"

"A good idea."

Barney decided to lay off that subject. He knew Keen's mood, so he turned to and helped fix the strange steel box into position. For more than an hour they toiled. They filled the rear compartments of the device with carbide and phosphorus, then bolted the chamber panels back into position.

"We'll put it on the bomb rack now, Barney," said Keen, surveying their work. "Then we'll be all set."

"What about Lang?" Barney opened again as they struggled with the heavy torpedo.

"Still missing. May be in a bad spot."

"Poor old Lang. I'll bet he's fuming by now."

"So would you if you'd been tied up somewhere since Monday."

"Where do you think he is?"

"I have no idea," replied Keen.

"You lie like a trooper," snarled Barney.

"I have to at times. Let's buzz upstairs. I have a book I must read. And in the meantime, lay off that Dew. We've got a big night ahead."

FOR TWO hours Keen sat in his study poring over shipping annuals and the *Aircraft Year Book*. He jotted down names of firms.

Then he opened his large atlas, went over a Mercator's map of the world, and worked out a series of charts and mileage plans. He also pored over a set of plane plans he had filed away in a large loose-leaf folder. Finally when finished he stared at two names that continued to bob up in his investigations.

He sniffed, shuffled all the papers together, and sauntered off to his bathroom for a shower. Later, as he dressed, the telephone rang and Keen took up the receiver and got John Scott who was in New York.

"Well?" Scott growled. "What did you get?"

"Nothing," replied Keen. "No trace of him even going up there. I checked with the police and he had not reported there or even been in."

"You go to the wharf?"

"Sure. Place looks as though no one had been in it for years. Just about falling down. Dangerous to walk about the floor even."

"Barney tell you I'd called?"

"Sure. Not much sense to it though."

"Well, this Griffon guy got through to me again soon after you had left and pulled a crazy line about monsoons being found in the Indian Ocean. What the heck does that mean?"

"He's right. That's where monsoon winds are found, aren't they?"

"But what the devil does that have to do with Lang and the smugglers?" pleaded Scott.

"You're the G-man in this act, not me. How should I know?"

"I don't think you're showing much interest in this thing, Keen. I'm telling you, I want that guy Lang back—right side up."

"Well, if you'd quit bothering me, maybe I could find some time to look for him. Now buzz off. I'm hungry and dinner is getting cold."

"Yeh? Well, maybe Lang is cold by now, too," moaned Scott.

"No such luck," replied Keen. "That guy'll be around to haunt me for years yet. Now let me alone. I have an idea, Scott."

"What is it?" cried the Secret Service man.

"A monsoon might be found in the Indian Ocean—if you wait

long enough," smirked Keen, hanging up the receiver and leaving Scott to splutter at the other end.

"I DON'T like lugging a thing like that around in the air," Barney suddenly barked as they prepared the *Black Bullet* for her night adventure. "A bullet in the right spot and we'd go up like a soda fountain."

"I'll take vanilla," gagged Keen, stepping into his black coverall and adjusting a scarlet mask over his face.

"It ain't funny," argued Barney sniffing at the galvanized iron torpedo that hung in the torpedo crutch under the black body.

"It won't be either for the guys who try to pick it up later," grinned Keen through his mask. "Come on, we're cutting it pretty fine. I see you put on those four small bombs, too. We'll need them, I'm afraid."

They clambered into their black parachute harnesses, checked their automatics; then Keen climbed into the cockpit while Barney doused the underground hangar lights and set the machinery in motion which would open the great doors. Keen started the big Avia motor and let her warm a trifle more while the big doors spread apart. Then he let her rumble out, completely muffled by the Skoda silencers.

The *Black Bullet* was soon surging across the easy swells still muffled. Then they cut clear of a mooring buoy, opened her up, and took off in the half-light of a first quarter moon.

Owing to the large torpedo, Keen could not retract the pontoons and they had to climb at somewhat reduced speed. Still they were at 4,000 in no time. Keen checked the clock and his wrist watch and continued to climb while Barney set out his armament store in the rear.

Keen watched his clock and carried out every move he had carefully planned the night before. Both watched eagerly for a trace of what they had come to intercept.

Suddenly Barney cried: "Here she comes!"

Keen stared out, saw a rocket-like form again approaching from far out to sea. It was coming from exactly the same direction. He turned the *Black Bullet*, opened the mufflers to get every ounce of power out of the Avia, and nosed down directly toward the hurtling object.

Their coup had to be timed perfectly.

"Now!" screamed Barney.

Keen pressed every trigger gear in his office. The Darns and Chatelleraults screamed, poured their withering wrath into the rocket.

There was a sudden flash. The rocket suddenly appeared to go haywire. It zig-zagged about, then swooped upward and seemed to be trying to sink its big nose into the whirling blades of the *Black Bullet's* prop. Keen just managed to yank the amphibian clear in time, for the rocket did a full loop, belched smoke, then continued on toward the water in a tremendous dive. She hit with a great chug and threw up a massive plume of water.

Without waiting to see what had really happened, Keen whipped the *Black Bullet* around and headed hell for leather toward Black Point. He gave the Avia all she had for several minutes, then suddenly slipped in the Skodas again and turned to Barney.

As though they had rehearsed the move a dozen times they changed places, Barney taking over the controls and holding the *Black Bullet* on Black Point. Keen huddled over a bomb sight set outside the cockpit cowling. Once they were over the outer tip of the Point he jerked the toggle handle and let their strange galvanized device slide away. They watched it start out. Suddenly it turned slightly and automatically steered itself toward a patch of woodland.

"It works!" gasped Barney.

"It was supposed to," replied Keen grimly. "There it goes toward that field beyond the wood. Get me over there."

Barney stopped, pondered on the strange little box with its three steel fingers. He knew the fingers had been attached to smooth copper cables that connected with the crude rudder and elevators of the torpedo device Keen had devised on such short notice. But his unimaginative mind could not visualize what was making the torpedo select such a definite path after leaving the crutch under the fuselage.

But Keen was acting fast now. He was clambering out of the cockpit and making his way to the wing root while Barney guided the *Black Bullet* toward the patch of open ground just beyond the woodland. The silenced Avia purred softly as Barney followed the road that wound around the wood and rounded off the northern side of the field.

"Now!" signaled Keen, with a glance through the cockpit hatch at Barney.

The Mick drew the stick back slowly, put the *Bullet* into a steep climb. With a cheery wave Keen dived headlong over the trailing edge and reached for his 'chute ring once he was well clear of the tail. He drew it out slowly and evenly, waited for the jerk. He twisted twice, then came a thunderclap of black silk above him. Almost at the same instant there was a low muffled thud somewhere below.

Keen steadied his 'chute, pulled away his scarlet mask, and stared down. In the center of the open field gushed a spurt of flame and then a bulbous cloud of white smoke where their rocket had hit. He smiled, tried to see beyond the wide ring of light that was given out by the burning phosphorous, hoping to get a full idea of what he might expect when he got down.

He reached for his automatic, then eased the shrouds on one side to slip a little closer to the field. He wanted to land inside, if possible.

Then to his amazement—and horror—a new menace swept into the picture. Keen instinctively raised his gun, fired. But it was like aiming a pop-gun against a battery of howitzers.

"Barney!" Keen cried, then clapped his hand over his mouth, amazed at the sound of his own voice. He wanted to cry out again, but instead he uttered a most unearthly laugh. The Griffon was trapped by the same snare he had devised for a man who should have been somewhere down in the Indian Ocean where monsoons blow!

A Dutch Fokker was plunging upon him! He looked again, waited. This was the end for Kerry Keen. Two blinking eyes flashed out of the mist and he waited for the thud of lead that would blast out his life. He could hear the leaden hornets zipping past him, plucking at his black coverall. He wondered what they would say when they found his lifeless body in the black parachute harness. But would they ever find him? Or would Barney, true to his trust, speed away and forever hide the secret of the Griffon?

He was near the ground now, less than a thousand feet to go. Would those swine in that Fokker ever get their gun eyes on him? The roar of the Kestrel was unmistakable now. The thud of the concussion from the guns pounded in his ears. Four seconds of terrific agony seemed like an hour.

The gray Fokker came on and then before it could complete its ghastly task, a black nemesis slammed out of the east with a screaming of wings and put a long wickedly-accurate burst smack into the Fokker.

Keen reached up quickly, snatched his shrouds, pulled. The big black 'chute slipped and just cleared the outer wing tip of the side-slipping Fokker. He twisted in his harness, stared into the gun muzzle of the observer, who, with one last effort to complete his mission, was drawing a careful bead on the swaying black figure.

Keen closed his eyes, instinctively drew in his stomach. Then there was a rattle of bullets and he opened his eyes to see the *Black Bullet* slamming at the Fokker. The observer was nowhere to be seen. The burst had caught a tank somewhere and the gray Fokker was rolling over with flames clawing at its tail from a great gash near the wing root.

"Good old Barney," breathed Keen, drawing his legs up for the landing.

DURING the last few hundred feet, Keen's mind worked like a high speed loom, weaving these strange events together. He asked himself a dozen questions, got no answers that really satisfied.

Where had this second Fokker come from? How did they know that he would be over Black Point at this hour? Would the trap still be open down below where the torpedo device still burned in the open field?

Before Keen could ponder further he hit the ground with a thud and rolled over, tangled in his shrouds. He lay still, then carefully slipped out of the encumbering harness and reached for his gun which had been fastened to him with a shoulder lanyard.

The burning torpedo device still emitted a great cloud of white smoke together with flame caused by the burning phosphorus. Keen eased around in the shadows, then saw that two men were working furiously in an effort to douse the fire with chemical extinguishers.

Adjusting his scarlet mask, he crawled as near to the burning torpedo as he could and still remain in the shadows. He listened, sensed at once that they were vainly attempting to retrieve something from the torpedo—just as he had known they would do. He could hear their anxious remarks.

One was a blond haired man, tall and heavy, who spoke with an accent. The other was a slim, dark, nattily-dressed man who reminded one, somehow, of a dagger.

"I tell you it's *not* one of our rockets," the slim dark man was shouting. "This is a gag of some sort. Didn't you see the Fokker go down. There's something going on... somewhere. That Griffon guy is in this somewhere."

The heavy blond man continued to use the portable extinguisher and vainly attempt to get near the torpedo. "But it iss, I tell you," he raged. "It iss vun—a new vun. They must be here."

"They'd better be, van Aller," the neat dagger-like man snarled, calmly lighting a gold-tipped cigarette. "There won't be any delivery tonight unless there is."

"But the *Monsoon* is up—waiting for the news," the big blond man pleaded.

"Maybe so, and the ice had better be delivered tonight, or that *Monsoon* does not go out. We're only risking our necks now. I tell you this Griffon guy is onto us and the quicker we get out of here the better. I don't like that business up there. Someone got Frolich in the Fokker."

"What vass he shooting at? What vass he shooting at?" the man named van Aller burst out, drawing back from the flames.

"That's what I want to know. I couldn't see anything, until that crazy black bus slammed in and got him. He must have been nuts, shooting at nothing. And now, what are you going to do, van

Aller? You've got the *Monsoon* up there on a night test; but where's the ice?"

"It must be in there. It must be in there," the big blond wailed staring at the blaze.

"If it is, there's no use looking for it now. They'll never stand phosphorus heat."

"But the *Monsoons* must start out tomorrow early if we are to make Batavia in time to cover the forfeit," van Aller moaned.

"If you think that is one of your old man's rockets—that piece of junk," the dagger man smirked, "you must be crazy. It's nothing like his outfit."

"But… but it came in perfectly when we put the control beam on it," van Aller pointed out. "How could that be? It came on under full control."

The dagger man rubbed his chin reflectively, pursed his lips. Keen knew that point had them all guessing. He was picking up plenty of hot information, but he still wanted more.

"I don't know, either," the dagger man now broke in. "But we haven't the ice, so what?"

"You've been paid plenty so far. We can get the rest to you as soon as the *Monsoons* are delivered to Batavia."

"Half a million dollars' worth of the best flying boat equipment in the world," stormed the other, "and we only got about $300,000 worth of ice, even if we can get rid of it. Where do you think we come off?"

"I know…. I know," pleaded the big blond Dutchman, "but we've done our best. Someone is… what you say… wise to us, eh? We must move quick, Blaine. We are taking long chances. You must let the second *Monsoon* out, or we'll all be trapped. We should let her through with the understanding that as soon as they get to Batavia they make arrangements to get the rest of the glass through to us—or."

Blaine, the dagger man, reflected a minute, then made a sudden decision. He looked around carefully at first, then turned back to van Aller.

"Okay! The *Monsoon* goes through to the *Waatlund* on schedule. But you stay here, van Aller, until the rest of the ice comes through. Get it? If it fails to get here on time, we'll put in the hooks, Milford will be tipped off—on who picked the special test crews for the *Monsoons*."

"But," gagged van Aller, his lower lip dropping, "they will need me aboard the *Waatlund* to tune the *Monsoons* for the trip. There's the changes to be made on the way. Motor numbers changed, new plates everywhere, on mags, radio sets and manufacturer's type plates."

"Yeh? Well, any guy with a hammer and a cold chisel can do that," smiled Blaine knowingly. "You're staying here, van Aller— just in case things don't work out just right."

"I can do nothing," shouted van Aller, throwing out his big hands. "You are the boss, I guess. There's nothing else to do. You will signal the *Monsoon* then?"

"Come on," snapped the big dark man. "Let's buzz."

Suddenly, Keen saw them stiffen. He had been quietly flipping a small flashlight on and off. Now he twisted in a new lens and the beam was flashing a bright green. But Blaine and van Aller had not caught the light; they were listening to an eerie wail somewhere above them. They stood still, tried to peer into the night sky. They cupped their hands around their eyes, listened intently.

"There it is again!" screamed van Aller like an hysterical woman. "The same thing—black and it wails. That's what poor Frolich was trying to get. It's a... ghost plane! We're caught!"

"Shut up, you Dutch fool!" snarled Blaine. "Come on, let's beat it to the car and get the *Monsoon* away. Come on, van Aller!"

THE MOVE caught Keen off guard; for they now turned and started toward him. Blaine had caught the final flash of the green light, and now he stumbled directly into Keen.

"Why you—" he started to say. But Keen had them all covered.

"Who the hell is that?" demanded the big man.

"And where is the *Waatlund*, gentlemen?" demanded Keen in his disguised voice.

"Who the devil are you, and where did you come from?" demanded Blaine.

"I'm known to my friends—and one or two enemies—as the Griffon. I'm sure you've heard of me," Keen replied, flashing the green light again. Overhead the *Black Bullet* droned in lazy circles.

"The Griffon!" screamed van Aller. "The Griffon! I knew it! I was warned to look out for him by that man Lang."

"Shut up, van Aller," yelled Blaine.

"Ah, yes, the indomitable Drury Lang," taunted Keen. "And where is Mr. Lang, may I ask? The quicker you answer, the sooner we can all get going. I'm sure you appreciate that fact."

"Lang's where you, or anyone else, will never get him," replied Blaine. "Just a dumb, nosey Secret Service man. He was easy. You'll be easier, Griffon, or whatever your name is."

"So you're getting the second *Monsoon* out tonight?" Keen went on in his Griffon role. "Mr. Lang wouldn't be aboard, would he?"

"Yes, he would!" almost screamed van Aller.

Blaine wheeled sharply, almost threw a punch at the Dutchman. But he controlled himself just in time, as the Griffon made a gesture that indicated that he would shoot on any pretext. Blaine scowled and stared up, trying to locate the eerie wailing that came from the *Black Bullet*.

"Thanks, van Aller," Keen taunted. "I presume your father, Waalart van Aller, of the Dutch East Indies Air Transport Company, is aboard the *Waatlund* expecting you?"

"No, he won't be there," snapped Blaine.

"Thanks," taunted Keen again. "So old man van Aller *is* aboard the *Waatlund*. Now where is the *Waatlund?*"

"You may have been smart enough to find out about Lang and van Aller, but you won't find out where the *Waatlund* is," Blaine snarled, glancing across at the Dutchman with a warning in his eye.

"You're in a tight spot, van Aller," Keen warned. "They are going to hold you here until the rest of the 'ice,' as Mr. Blaine so blithely calls Amsterdam rocks, is delivered. If those two *Monsoons* get clear, we can pick you up at any time, and there's been too many men killed to get off lightly. They may want you to sit in the big chair—just to make an example of someone, you know."

Poor van Aller stared from Blaine to the man in the scarlet mask, unable to speak or to even think straight.

"You may get the two *Monsoons* out and all the way to Java to cover your forfeit on the Royal Dutch government Batavia-to-Amsterdam air route contract, but *you'll* never get out to enjoy it," Keen continued.

"What can I do?" the lippy Dutchman pleaded.

"Tell me where the *Waatlund* lies and I'll put you aboard her so that you can make your getaway—but not with the *Monsoons*. They go back to the Milford ramp undamaged. That goes for Lang, too."

"But the *Waatlund* is out to sea about two hundred miles—"

"Damn you, van Aller, shut up!" screamed Blaine.

"Where?" snapped Keen. "Come on! Talk fast, if you want to get out of this the easy way."

"Two hundred miles out to sea, no matter how you figure it," van Aller gagged, fingering his lips like a haunted man.

"Two hundred miles from the Milford plant?" probed Keen.

"Two hundred miles from land," van Aller continued staring into space.

"What is she, a depot ship?"

"A copy of the German *West*—" van Aller tried to explain. But he never finished.

Crack!

A gun barked somewhere and van Aller toppled forward on his face.

Keen tried to figure out what had happened, but Blaine had been too fast for him. He had dropped van Aller while Keen was intent on getting the words from the Dutchman.

The dark man's gun spat again, clipped the air-pressure pad from Keen's helmet.

"Two hundred miles from shore, anywhere!" screamed van Aller rolling over on his back. "Two hundred miles, anywhere from shore. Like *West*—"

Keen tried to hold Blaine off, but the dagger-like man had now poured three shots directly into van Aller's head.

Keen fired again, blew the gun out of Blaine's hand with a shot. The dagger man stood holding his bloody hand, grinning maliciously.

"Not much information there, eh, Griffon?" he smirked.

"No, but enough. 'Two hundred miles from shore.' That's enough." Then Keen flashed the colored flashlight skyward again and waited, holding Blaine off.

For several seconds the two men stood there staring each other out. Blaine was plainly puzzled as to what would happen next. Then something swished past his head and he ducked as he would from the hiss of a wasp.

"Don't worry," smiled Keen, "it won't hurt you. Just my little idea of making a quick getaway."

Blaine was staring about trying to figure out what was going on. Above him wailed the wings of the circling *Black Bullet* and then that strange hiss came again and he stepped back, trying to determine what it was. But before he could come to any decision, Keen made a sudden snatch at something, gave the light a quick green flash, and—as far as Blaine could tell—simply disappeared into the swirl of smoke which still rose from the twisted debris of the torpedo.

"Damn you!" snarled Blaine, whipping around.

"Good-bye, Mr. Blaine," called a voice from somewhere in the darkness above. "I'll look for a ship masquerading as the German Luft Hansa depot ship, the *Westfalen*—two hundred miles from shore. Good night, Blaine."

But the frustrated Blaine whipped up his fallen gun, fired three times into the darkness, wondering by what means of magic the Griffon was able to escape so assuredly. He could not know, of course, that Keen had signed for Barney to drop their pick-up cable which had a weight on the end, and which moved in an easy ten-foot circle when lowered from an altitude of a few hundred feet while the *Black Bullet* circled lazily above.

Blaine finally threw the gun away and ran, still holding his wounded hand, toward a light truck which had been hidden in the bushes nearby. He leaped inside the truck, drove away for about three miles inland, then stopped and yanked open the cover of a radio transmitting panel. He barked quickly into the mike, got an answer, then gave an order for someone to proceed out to sea at once. Then he drove away into the darkness, cursing the man known as the Griffon.

KEEN clambered over the wing fillet and into the rear cockpit. Without much ado, he ordered Barney to head for the Milford plant farther down the Connecticut shore.

"When you get there," he ordered, "turn due east out to sea while I figure out something."

"What were you doing all that time," demanded Barney. "Taking fingerprints?"

"Shut up. They've got old Lang aboard the second *Monsoon*, so you can see where we fit in. This is a pip, this time. The plane is on its way out to sea by now, to join the other. Poor old Lang! A nice way of getting rid of him. Maybe they'll even hold him as a hostage."

Then Keen snatched out a Geodetic Survey chart, put a pair of dividers on the scale, and pinched them so that they marked the 200-mile measurement. Then he put one end of the dividers on Milford and marked the distance directly out to sea. He tried the same thing from a point off Falmouth on Cape Cod, which was the nearest point of land to the north, and checked that point on the arc he had drawn out from Milford. Then taking it from a point between Cape May and Barnegat Bay on the New Jersey coast, which was the nearest point of land to the south, Keen reached a cross-bearing that indicated that a ship lying 200 miles from shore must be somewhere in the vicinity of 38:42 N. by 70:58 W. This point was the only one that was exactly 200 miles from any point of the shore as well as from the Milford plant.

It had to be right.

All they had to look for now was a Dutch vessel masquerading as the German *Westfalen*, two Milford *Monsoon* flying boats worth about half a million dollars—and Drury Lang.

"Get out of your 'chute," ordered Keen, once he had completed his chart. "And your gun—I may need that, too."

"What the devil went on down there, anyway?" again demanded the perplexed Barney as he unsnapped the clasps of his 'chute.

"Things worked out very well, Barney," Keen explained into his Gosport headset. "A gentleman by the name of Waalart van Aller, a Dutch financier with a touch of Captain Cook in his makeup, decided to take a long chance on a big aviation line contract. It so happened that a man by the same name, evidently his son, was a trusted electrical engineer in the Milford aircraft factory."

"You can't beat the Dutch," grinned Barney.

"Be that as it may, our friend Waalart van Aller, bit off too big a chunk when he placed a large forfeit to produce at least two flying boats capable of regular service for the Royal Dutch government between Amsterdam and Batavia in the Dutch East Indies. This is a very important link of communication between Holland and her distant colony and there is a lot of money in it for the company that obtains the contract."

"But what was he doing trying to steal the *Monsoons?* I still can't get that angle."

"They were the only machines available to do the job. Van Aller tried to get the Fokker interests in Holland to build the planes for him, but they refused, mainly on the ground that they were not equipped to build flying boats of that size."

"So they came over and tried to swipe two *Monsoons?*"

"Well, hardly. They were prepared to pay for them—at least pay something for them—if they could get them. So they arranged for a gang to get inside the factory when the two planes were finished and ready for their test flights. Young van Aller was the brains of the business, of course."

"But the rocket racket?"

"That was the strange tie-up. They used that rocket idea to smuggle diamonds into the country to pay the gang for the *Monsoons.* You see, I learned from the foreign business almanacs that old van Aller had a neat tie-up in the diamond industry in Amsterdam, and he was able to get valuable stones cheap. If he could get a reasonable amount of them into this country without paying the duty on them, he could pay the gang a reasonable price for the ships. The trick was to get them in."

"So he had a rocket," grinned Barney.

"And what a rocket!" added Keen. "They first got a vessel which is fixed up to look like the German Luft Hansa depot ship, and by some means devised a rocket which could be directed by radio—which is a good idea, too. Old van Aller then sent the stones in small lots, and young van Aller waited at the other end with some sort of electrical directing device and brought it in. The rocket was fixed up to hit and flare up for a few seconds to give the impression that it was a meteor and thus put the inhabitants off the scent. Then they would open the rocket, take out the metal box of diamonds, and retrieve the radio homing device fitted inside for use again later."

"So that was what that guy in the Fokker was carrying back when we stopped him," mused Barney. "But that seems sappy. If they could get a Fokker back and forth, somehow, why didn't they let the guy in the Fokker take the diamonds."

"Any one but old van Aller would have done that. But he is a strange man. First off, he did not trust anyone but himself and his son. Secondly, this rocket is his own invention and he's childishly confident in it. As he was 'going in off the deep end,' so to speak, he decided to complete the exchange on his own hook and use his rockets."

"Which was the one mistake he made, eh?" said Barney.

"You mean we scotched his idea by swiping his homing device, putting it into a rocket of our own, and releasing it on gravity to trap them. But we took a long chance, too. I only *hoped* we had pinched their homing device. I was not certain, I had to take that chance."

"But think of all those rocks at the bottom of the sound," said Barney.

"I have, and I noted them particularly. You Barney, my boy, are going to take a short course in diving in a day or two and get them up. I checked the position. They are on Saybrook Ledge, only a matter of fourteen or fifteen feet down."

"Leave it to me, I'll get 'em," grinned the Mick.

THEY continued the wild flight for nearly half an hour more, checking their position and completing their amazing plans. Keen knew he had more than a job on his hands. For one thing he had to save Drury Lang and still retain his identity, which was a job in itself. Then he had to outwit Waalart van Aller and recapture the two *Monsoon* flying boats and still keep the *Black Bullet* for his own special use.

Even Keen wondered how he would get away with it, but like those of his tribe, he made plans as far as he could figure and trusted to his own ingenuity to complete the job successfully. He sat back and pondered on what was ahead, then suddenly decided that as Lang was mixed up in it somewhere, he might as well be put to work as soon as the situation arose. But Lang would have to be handled in such a manner that Keen could maintain his disguise.

He slipped into Barney's parachute and belted on two guns. Then he fitted his microphone speaker which would assist him in completely disguising his voice. He slipped off his shoes, put on a pair of rubber-soled sneakers, finally made certain that his scarlet mask fitted perfectly. His helmet and goggles completed the disguise.

They were ready now and Keen huddled over Barney's shoulder giving him the final word on his plans. They looked at the clock, timed their position.

Then they suddenly caught the outline of the second *Monsoon* flying boat, which was hurrying out to make its contacts with the *Waatlund,* still about fifty miles away!

"Get about 600 feet above her, dead on her tail," ordered Keen, "and then dive to go below the level of her tail and come up in a stall dead over her, giving her the gun just as she starts to flutter. Get it?"

"I get it," grinned Barney. "I hope you do."

"Give me any sort of a break and I will," growled Keen. "Okay, gear down!"

Barney nodded, let the pontoon gear down for a water-landing position, then took Keen's hand. They gripped, their eyes met, and Keen knew he could trust the Mick. He slipped outside onto the wing root, crawled along to the rear, then slipped down the metal tubing of the float legs. He crawled forward along the long pontoon and held on.

The *Black Bullet* had the desired height now. The *Monsoon* was plodding on at something well over 120 when Barney started his dive. The motor was silenced for the job, and Keen was steadying himself with the forward strut as he crouched on the pontoon.

The amphibian went below the tail of the big silver flying boat, then Barney cut the motor completely. He eased back on the stick and the *Bullet* with her flaps down seemed to flutter over the tail of the *Monsoon* and straddle the fin with her pontoons. Keen, staring forward, poised for the mid-air change, then gave a quick nod. Barney dipped the black amphibian gently, then rammed the throttle forward. Keen slipped down, hooked one arm over the nose of the pontoon, then dropped as light as a cat on the broad back of the *Monsoon*.

The *Black Bullet* plunged upward and away and Barney could see the faces of the two men in the pilot's compartment. It was obvious that they had not realized what had happened, so well had the contact been timed.

Barney let out a guffaw, curled away, and took up a position above and behind the *Monsoon*.

In the meantime, Keen had steadied himself on the broad back of the *Monsoon's* cabin. Then he crawled along, his legs and arms wide apart until he found the emergency hatch he knew must be somewhere in the roof. He fingered it and with two quick slashes of his knife, ripped the panel out and with one of the guns in his hand he dropped down inside.

ONLY on a ship the size of the *Monsoon* could Keen have gotten away with his contact. As it was, he was well inside the rear main cabin, and so far no one aboard even knew of his presence. He had dropped down in the aisle between two rows of cabin seats.

Before him was a wide bulkhead with a doorway leading forward. From the size of the cabin he sensed that the pilots were accommodated high in the nose. In all probability there were at least two more smaller compartments below the control pit.

He made certain that there was no one in the aft cabin before he went forward. Then he reached forward and twisted the lever latch handle of the doorway. He entered a square compartment and noticed that a dural tube ladder led up the side of the wall, evidently to an upper compartment which must be in line with the roots of the wide wings.

"Mail and freight compartments," he muttered to himself. Then he was startled to hear a voice—

"Who's there?"

There was a husky appeal to the voice, a strange pleading. But Keen took no chances. He darted to a corner, held his gun steady, and swept the small compartment quickly.

Then he saw a man huddled up in a corner on the floor. He nipped his small flashlight on, directed the beam on the figure.

It was Drury Lang, wild eyed and bearded, bound and shackled to a dural beam which ran from below the flooring to a point somewhere above.

Keen had to swallow his exultation, as he strode slowly across the floor. Could he maintain his disguise under the circumstances? Could he get Lang out of here and still get control of the stolen *Monsoon?* Could he get the *Monsoon* back to Milford plant and still escape to the *Black Bullet* and fool the redoubtable Lang?

This was his great test!

"Who are you?" he snapped into the voice-disguising mike fitted into the chest pad of his coverall.

"I'm a Secret Service man connected with the New York Division. Lang's the name. Where the devil did you come from?"

"Right out of the sky," replied Keen. "What are you doing in here?"

"Taking a one-way ride I guess, but the devil only knows what for."

"You know where you are, don't you?" Keen's metallic voice asked.

"I guess, from the feeling in my stomach every so often, I'm in an airplane. What's the game anyhow?"

"You are aboard a large flying boat which is being pirated and taken to the Dutch East Indies."

Lang allowed a particularly dumb look to soften his face as he tried to absorb all this information.

"But what the hell has a diamond smuggling outfit got to do with flying boats that are being pinched?"

"The diamonds were paying for the gang to swipe the *Monsoon* flying boats. You evidently got in the way somehow so that they decided to give you a ride and get you out of the way."

"Untie me, quick!"

"What for? What can you do about it?" Keen demanded.

"Well, you ain't going to leave me strung up here, are you?"

"I don't know why I should release you. You're nothing to me."

"No? Well, as an agent of the Department of Justice, I demand that you release me."

"And then, I presume, you'll go upstairs, shove a gun into the pilot's belly, and fly the *Monsoon* back, eh?"

"No, but I guess you can, can't you?"

"Sure, but again, why should I?"

"Because I'm ordering you to," snapped Lang struggling against his bonds. Keen had to admire the old cuss.

"Then when you get back with the ship and your two prisoners and get all the glory, you'll cook up some excuse to put me in the same brig and complete the job."

"I'm ordering you to release me, get me a gun, and help me get these mugs back to land," Lang barked again. Then he suddenly turned and glanced at Keen sideways and said: "Say, you don't happen to be a guy named Ginsberg, do you?"

For an answer, Keen slipped a small white card out of a small pocket in the waistband of his coverall and held it before Lang's startled eyes.

"The Griffon!" husked Lang, reading the card. "Holy Smoke!"

"So you see, Mr. Lang," Keen taunted, "you are in a tight spot, no matter what happens. What's the arrangements now?"

"Okay. Anything you say. Let's have it."

"I'll release you and you can help me nail the men aboard this bus. How many are there, by the way?"

"Only two, I think. A guy named Claggett and another called Wensley."

"That makes it easier," muttered Keen. "But you've got to give me your word that you'll pull no funny business with me. Remember, I've got a parachute and can step off any time and be sure of being picked up."

"Listen, you," Lang said in a confidential tone. "You get me out of this and let me get this bus back okay, and I'll forget there was ever a guy named Ginsberg—or the Griffon."

Keen smiled under his mask. He knew he had touched Lang on the only vulnerable point in his makeup. He knew the old devil would give his right arm to deliver the *Monsoon* and the two thugs into the hands of the authorities.

"It's a go, then, eh?"

"We'll shake on it when you cut these ropes."

In three minutes, Lang was on his feet again and gripping a big black gun, Keen had given him.

"One phoney move now," Keen reminded him, "and you hit the drink down below so hard, you and the *Monsoon* will come up somewhere outside of Shanghai."

"I'm a man of my word," growled Lang. "Let's go."

"You'd better be," said Keen, pointing outside where the *Black Bullet* coursed along convenient to receive any signal the Griffon might give.

TOGETHER now, they crept up the metal ladder and made their way into the upper mail compartment, eased along the gangway, and found the knob of another door. They stood, listened a moment, and heard the faint whine of a radio spark.

"One of them is in here using the radio set," said Keen. "Move fast now and get him when I open the door. Don't let him give a warning."

Lang nodded, moved over so that he could dart in when the Griffon opened the door.

Keen took a steady hold on the knob and turned it slowly. Then with a sure movement, he pushed it open and let Lang through.

The man at the radio panel was caught cold. He turned, one hand on a switch, and stared into the muzzle of the gun Lang held on him. He was a small stocky man with a warped face. His eyes were small and piggish.

"Cut it, Wensley," Lang ordered. "Reach!"

"How the—?" the man known as Wensley started to say, but Lang darted behind him, jerked his arms back quickly, and in no time had his wrists bound behind his back with a piece of the rope.

The Griffon took one look and saw that Lang had the situation in the radio room well in hand. Then he darted to the bulkhead and snatched at the small door that led into the control pit. He was in there like a flash and had the man at the big wheel covered before he realized that it wasn't Wensley returning from the radio cabin.

"Okay, Claggett," the Griffon, smiled, "You've hi-jacked your last bus. You've had a swell time since you first started this racket. It'll be rocks at Atlanta now instead of old van Aller's Amsterdam ice. Now then, we'll slip the robot pilot in, eh?"

Claggett didn't say a word. He sat there, holding onto the big wheel, his eyes small slits of bitter hatred. He was a man of medium build.

"I haven't seen you since the 1934 National Air Races when you managed to get that Renown Racer out of the country and sell it to a European aeronautical firm which wanted the 'inside' on that flush riveting idea. You've certainly stepped up some since then, eh. Picking up Milford *Monsoons* now."

"Who the devil are you?" Claggett asked finally.

"I'm known as the Griffon, Claggett. To my closer acquaintances, I'm a man named Ginsberg. Ever hear of me?"

"What's your split to get out?" said Claggett, still maintaining his icy calm.

"Nothing. I've got mine."

"Yeh? How do you figure that?"

"That last rocket didn't get through, Claggett. I know where it is. A little dough in that, eh, Claggett?"

"The devil!" gasped the hi-jacker pilot.

"Now do as I said," the Griffon ordered. "Shove the robot in while we re-arrange the seating accommodation."

And Claggett had to sit back while the Griffon set the throttles for a 60 per-cent power output, then rammed in the lever that brought that Sperry robot pilot into action.

"That's all," smiled the man in the scarlet mask. "Step back inside now and Mr. Lang will take care of you and see that you are made reasonably comfortable in the mail compartment."

"You damn fool!" raged Claggett, "you can't fly this boiler."

"I can fly anything from a barn door to a… a *Monsoon*," retorted the Griffon, "and if I can't, it will be just too bad for you. Get it?"

"And *where* will you fly it?" asked Claggett, regaining his composure a trifle.

"Out to the *Waatlund* to pick up the other," taunted the Griffon.

"Why, do you think you can get away with that?"

"They expect you, don't they?"

"Yes, but how the hell… you can't get two of them. They'll blow daylight out of you when you get over the *Waatlund*."

"Believing, of course, that they are blowing hell out of you," the Griffon said. "That doesn't seem to make sense, Claggett."

"Listen, if you get away with this, I'm willing to go to Atlanta for a stretch. A guy ain't safe with a mug like you around. I'll take Atlanta. Of all the damned fool ideas, yours takes the cookie."

For a reply, the Griffon simply bowed Claggett through the doorway and into the mail compartment where Drury Lang awaited him with one large gat and a length of manila rope.

BUT while Keen had been very optimistic before Claggett he was far from certain how he would make out. He began to wonder whether he would not be wise to be satisfied with what he had and turn back with the *Monsoon* and get Lang to safety.

He was pondering on this matter when Lang came into the control pit. The detective stepped a little gingerly, for he was amazed and completely overawed by the mad array of instruments and control levers. But he was jubilant nevertheless.

"Well," he beamed rubbing his horny hands together, "I took care of those mugs. They'll never move until we chop them apart. What's next?"

"You sit here," ordered Keen through his metallic phone. "Don't touch anything until I get back. I won't be two minutes."

He darted inside the radio cabin, swung the switch, and moved the wave-length dial around to the special band the *Black Bullet's* set was tuned to. Then he called a man named Pulski.

"Okay, Pulski," he spoke carefully into the hand-mike. "All set here. Now get everything straight. We're heading for the depot ship, you know. As soon as you see someone come out to us, you 'get' the vessel with the four small bombs. Remember, you've got to at least disable her. Take either the funnels or the screws."

He got a careful repeat of the order, then he ordered Barney to change the wave-length of his set to that the men aboard the *Monsoon* had been using for contacting the *Waatlund*.

"You'll be able to keep in touch with what's going on and act accordingly."

"Okey-doke," came back Barney, "but if you're going to do anything, you'd better work fast. There's the tub a short distance ahead of you."

"Right! Remember now, no busting things up until I get old van Aller." And with that Keen snapped the switch and ran forward into the control cabin.

"Hey you," bawled Keen toward Lang. "Get up there, through that hatch under the instrument board, and get into the marine gear locker. Get into the flag locker and get a 'V' flag."

"What the hell's a 'V' flag?" growled Lang. "I ain't no gob."

"No, you're just a dumb detective. A 'V' flag is a white square with a red St. Andrews cross on it. Go in and get it and run it up on that stub mast in the nose. You can probably hoist it from the marine gear locker nose hatch. Get moving."

"What's that flag for?"

"It's the international code meaning 'I require assistance.' We're getting old van Aller aboard... somehow."

"I get it," grinned Lang. "Say, by the way, you never knew a guy by the name of Keen, did you?"

"Sure," answered the man known as the Griffon. "His old man makes saws, chisels, and hatchets."

"No, I don't mean that guy, this bird—"

"I don't know any other. Now get down there and get that flag up. There's the *Waatlund* down there."

He booted Lang gently in the tail, hurried him through the hatchway, and took over the controls of the big *Monsoon*. He peered out of the streamlined windows and saw Barney easing away. Then he circled over the *Waatlund*.

He jazzed the throttles and made the big 1,000 h.p. motors spit and cough. Then he cut them off as he saw the small white signal flag run up the stub mast through the opening in the marine locker. He carefully let her glide down for her landing.

Lang came back and watched Keen with puzzled interest as he adjusted the flaps and let the big flying boat slither across the easy rollers for a soft landing about three hundred yards clear of the *Waatlund*.

"Now sit tight and don't move until they come out and board us. Let them into the main cabin entrance while I cover them. After that, watch what happens."

Keen slipped out into the marine locker, selected a sea-anchor, and tossed it overboard to hold them reasonably steady. Then they crawled back and watched out of the radio cabin porthole.

In a minute a searchlight swept across the water from the bridge of the *Waatlund* and caught the *Monsoon* full in its glare. The small white signal flag flapped in the breeze and indicated that they were in trouble. It was several minutes before there was any response, then an Aldis lamp twinkled and Keen watched it carefully.

"What do they say?" asked Lang.

"Just what I wanted them to say. They're coming aboard."

Lang stroked the blue barrel of his gun in anticipation.

A dory was put over the side and they could see four men going down the ladder. In a minute more, they were pulling away and heading for the bobbing *Monsoon* under the glare of the searchlight. Keen and Lang studied them closely.

"There's our man in the stern," the Griffon muttered. "He's the one we want."

The boat came well around the bow, then it eased in carefully under the wing and drew up to the cabin door which Lang drew open without being seen. Keen darted into the radio shack, snapped the switch, and called the man known as Pulski.

"Right!" he yelled. "Let 'em have it…. Hello! Look out, they're shooting something off a catapult. Get him, if he tries to block us off!"

Everything happened fast after that.

FIRST off, Keen suddenly remembered the other *Monsoon*, and while a Fokker two-seater leaped off the catapult and screamed into the sky, a big flying boat came churning around the stern of the *Waatlund* and taxied toward the ship Keen and Lang had captured.

"They're anxious," whispered Keen. "They've been waiting to get away. Something's worrying them."

But two men in greasy dungarees now came up the side and crawled into the half light of the cabin. Keen acted fast and tapped both of them smartly with a rubber-covered billy. He let them roll under the upholstered chairs. Another man, a flint-faced devil in shoddy ship's officer kit, came in and stared—stared into the black gun held by Lang.

"Come on in and sit quiet," Lang ordered.

The man started to whirl and yell, but Lang brought the gun up under his chin quickly and he went to his knees gasping. Keen then took care of the big Dutchman van Aller who came up puffing like a grampus, growling and asking questions.

"This way, please," said Keen shoving the man into the radio cabin. "Tie those guys up quick, Lang, then cut the painter on that dory they hooked up outside."

He rammed his gun into van Aller's back, stuffed him down in the operator's chair. Then he closed the switch.

"Now get this, van Aller," he ordered in no uncertain tones. "You tell those birds in the other *Monsoon* to follow us. We're damned serious about this, and these two ships are going back where they came from."

"Vass?... Vass?" gurgled old van Aller, still unable to comprehend what was happening. "Vere iss my son?"

"If you think anything of your son, you'll act nice and see that that other ship follows us. If it doesn't, we'll see that it's made to—or."

"Vere iss my son?" began van Aller all over again.

"Look here, van Aller. You've got to move fast. Your game is up and the easier you can make it for yourself, the better it will be. If these ships go back to Connecticut okay, they'll have nothing but smuggling on you. If they don't, you'll have plenty to answer for. Now, there's the mike and you can give your orders."

"But... but.... How...?"

"Never mind how or why. Talk!"

Lang came in grinning.

"Got 'em! The dory's free. Let's go."

"Go on, talk van Aller," ordered Keen again. "Here's the mike."

The big Dutchman took it and Keen held his gun up to the man's chest. There was a glint in his eye and the Dutchman knew the game was up.

"Allo, Heydemarck.... Allo, Heydemarck," he spoke.

"No Dutch now, van Aller," husked Keen. "Only English."

The Dutchman nodded in resignation.

He caught the reply from the other *Monsoon*.

"Heydemarck... this iss van Aller, Heydemarck. We are taking off at once for a hurried trip to Long Island Sound again. Hans iss in mooch trouble, and Claggett has an idea... no... no, this iss me—van Aller. You will follow us back.... You understand?... All right."

He put the mike down with the air of a very weary man and

threw out his hands. Keen leaned over, snapped the switch, and gave Lang the nod.

"Watch him," he said. "I'm taking off."

He charged into the control cabin, pressed the starters, and let the four big engines pick up. Then he eased her clear and watched the other *Monsoon* nose around into the wind. He wondered why things had been so easy.

He gave her the gun, let her zip over the waves and into the air. Almost at the same minute the *Black Bullet* shot across his bows and slashed toward the black hulk of the *Waatlund*.

Keen had his hands full figuring out the instruments and controls, but he managed to glance out and see the *Black Bullet* veer suddenly, hold her position, then slither across the two black funnels of the depot ship.

Keen waited anxiously as the big *Monsoon* climbed under his piloting. He turned her and watched the *Black Bullet*. There was a flash out of one of the *Waatlund's* funnels as the *Bullet* cleared, then two monstrous spurts of smoke and flame came up.

"Got him," beamed Keen as the *Waatlund* shivered. He knew the bombs had exploded down below and had blown the boiler room to atoms. There would be no escape now. He could call a Coast Guard unit at any time and have what was left towed in.

Then, as he turned the nose of the *Monsoon* around and headed northeast for Long Island, something else caught his eye. The gray Fokker, the third to turn up in this adventure, came thundering at him with guns flaming.

He huddled behind the wheel, felt the bullets patter about the big wings and thrum through the dural framework. Then out of nowhere came hope. The *Black Bullet* under the guiding hands of Barney swept into the picture again. With a splash of reddish yellow from her gun ports, she hammered down on the Fokker from an acute angle and pounded lead at her until she swung clear of the *Monsoon*. The Fokker was fast and wickedly maneuverable, but she was outgunned.

Barney waited his chance, displaying all the cunning of the Griffon. And then with a beautiful curving turn, he drew the nose of the *Black Bullet* up, poised a second, then plunged dead on the

Fokker which had dived for safety. Four guns flamed from the *Bullet*.

"Beautifully done, Barney," Keen muttered to himself, as he watched the riddled Fokker fly clean through her wings and hit the water below like a massive shark.

That was all as far as the Fokker was concerned, and Barney swung quickly and settled himself dead on the tail of the *Monsoon* flown by Heydemarck.

Keen set the gyro compass and the robot pilot and went back to where Lang sat with his legs crossed watching van Aller.

THE DUTCHMAN was now white and almost blubbering. His world had toppled about him in a shambles of torn wings and scuttled ships. It was all over and he knew that his best bet now was to play safe and cut his penalty as short as possible.

"Well," demanded Keen glaring at him. "Are you ready to play the game now? You saw what happened to your Fokker fighter. The same can happen to the other *Monsoon*, if they make one move. Do you want to talk to your gang again?"

"I will talk," muttered van Aller, a broken soul.

He took the hand-mike and waited until Keen had snapped the switch. Then he called Heydemarck.

At first there was a torrent of abuse, which van Aller listened to with weary resignation. Finally he was able to speak and then he told Heydemarck the doleful news.

"You can try to get away, if you like," van Aller explained. "But you can't and you know it. If we return the ships, they can only hold us for smuggling diamonds. We're licked… beaten anyway. Our depot ship is done for and we couldn't get clear now, no matter what we do."

There was a jabbered appeal for a few seconds from the other *Monsoon*, and they turned and glanced out of the porthole. They saw the big flying boat start to turn away, but before she had made thirty degrees, four long scarlet and yellow fingers prodded out from above and forced her back.

"You see," warned van Aller. "You can't get away. You had better take my advice and follow us. You can't get away, Heydemarck."

With that, Keen flipped the set out again and nodded.

"Now then," he smiled, "while we are on our way back, will you please save me a lot of trouble and tell Mr. Lang just how the story runs. You know, your rockets that delivered the diamonds, and which the bland natives of Black Point thought were meteors; the details of your son's association with the Milford aeronautical plant; and just how you planned to disguise the *Monsoons* on the way to the Dutch East Indies so that you could produce two machines capable of carrying out the contracted schedules between Batavia and Amsterdam."

"What's that?" gasped the amazed Lang.

"He'll tell you," smiled the man they only knew as the Griffon, "and it will save me the trouble."

He reached over quickly then, took Lang's gun away from him, and stuffed it into one of the heavy leather holsters at his thigh.

"Just to be sure, Mr. Lang," he said with a meaning glance.

"Hey, wait a minute!" shouted Lang. "You can't leave me like that. Suppose this guy gets gay and tries to—"

"We'll just remind Mr. van Aller that he had something in that rocket idea—something that might come in useful to the United States someday. And if he uses his head and—well, it might help an awful lot. I don't think he'll try anything gay now, but I also want to make sure *you* won't, Mr. Lang."

Van Aller beamed at the prospects. Lang sat and glared at his captive, then took out his notebook and a particularly stubby pencil and sucked it in anticipation.

Keen took one look outside and saw that the *Black Bullet* had the other *Monsoon* by the tail, so to speak. Then he went back into the control cabin and took over the big wheel. He glanced out through his window, grinned and muttered:

"A special case of O'Doul's Dew for you when we get back, Barney."

THE TELEPHONE bell rang beside Kerry Keen's bed at 8 o'clock the next morning. Keen sat up and stared at Barney who stood at the foot of the bed with a lavish breakfast tray.

"I'll answer it," he smiled.

It was Lang, all of a bubble and a flutter.

"Hello Lang?" roared Keen. "Where the devil are you? I've been looking for you all over Connecticut."

"Yeh? Well, you can go back to bed now…. No, I mean you can come down here and see me if you get a chance today sometime. I got a story for you, you mug."

"I can't wait. Golly, you gave us a scare. I've been searching for you all over Old Lyme. What the deuce happened to you?"

"Yeh, I know. Scott told me about it, but I can take care of myself. I got nabbed, but I got away with it and scored the biggest snatch the Department has ever pulled off. You know those two flying boats that were stolen a few days ago? Well, I got those back, too, and the gang that swiped 'em. How's that for a dumb dick?"

"Amazing! No wonder I couldn't find you. I was searching all over Old Lyme for hours last night. I had about given you up. But I'll be right down. I can't wait to hear this one. You Secret Service men get all the fun."

"You come on down and I'll tell you a story that will make your hair curl."

"I'll be there for lunch with you," barked Keen hanging up.

"I think we got away with it," grinned Keen, taking the breakfast tray.

"If you did, pigs will fly," remonstrated Barney helping himself to some of Keen's toast.

"Well, get out my gray worsted spats, and all the doings, Barney. I'm going down and have a quiet laugh. You might run up to New London this afternoon and see what you can do about a cheap diving suit. We do a little underwater stuff in a couple of days, you know."

"Yeh, I know," growled Barney. "You'll have me doubled up with the bends, too, I suppose."

"Perhaps. But remember, Barney," smiled Keen. "There's nothing that won't respond to generous dosings of O'Doul's Dew."

Barney grinned widely: "Very generous dosings," he agreed.

WHEN Keen sauntered into Scott's office about noon, he was a perfect picture of a dapper young man-about-town. He provided a startling contrast to Lang who was still bearded, red-eyed, and generally bedraggled. Old Scott was not much better, but he had a cheery greeting.

"Sorry to have sent you on a wild-goose chase, Keen," Scott said, "Lang here seems to have been miles away from where we believed him to be."

"What the deuce happened anyway?" Keen said dropping into the only easy chair in the place.

"I ran into the Griffon!" Lang suddenly blurted out. "Sat with him in a plane—actually talked to him!"

"Now look here, Lang," remonstrated Keen. "If you're going to start that line again, I'll be off. I'm busy."

"But I'm telling you straight," Lang said. "Ask Scott here. He saw the guy I captured and he swears to it. I really saw the Griffon guy."

Keen lit a cigarette with a bored air, sat back and let Lang tell his story.

"And do you mean to say you were with him and you wouldn't recognize him if you saw him again?" demanded Keen completely huffed.

"Of course not. How could I? He was completely masked and spoke through some sort of a portable microphone so that you couldn't tell what his voice really sounds like."

"But *I'm* supposed to be the Griffon," argued Keen.

"Naw, that's out for sure now, Keen. This guy flew one of the flying boats back. You couldn't fly one of them! That's out. Besides, you were in Old Lyme looking for me, weren't you?"

"That's where Scott sent me. That's where you were supposed to be, wasn't it?" replied Keen. "But," he added, "what I can't figure out of your dizzy story, Lang, is how this guy, the Griffon, got away after you had brought the ships in with all those guys aboard like that."

"That's what I was wondering all the way in," said Lang. "I

wondered how he was going to get away with it, too. But he did, the clever devil."

"How?"

"Well, you see, this other guy who was working with him in this black plane, stayed over the other ship and made them follow us all the way to Milford. It was still dark, of course—somewhere between three and four, I think—and a few minutes before we landed he used the radio and put in a call for a Coast Guard cutter to hurry to a position about two miles outside of Milford, just off Stratford."

"But how the deuce did he get away?" demanded Keen.

"Take your time. Here's what happened: He put our boat down on the water and waited while the guy in the black plane simply sat on the tail of the other and made them plunk it down alongside of us."

"But how did the guy get away?" demanded Keen, sitting up straight.

"Say, you're an annoying cuss!" barked Lang. "You seem to forget what we have really accomplished. We cracked a big diamond smuggling ring and recovered two flying boats that are worth about half a million dollars. Yet all you worry about is how did this guy got away without us finding out who he was."

"That seems important to me," argued Keen.

"Well," said Lang with a guilty air. "I really intended to nab him somehow, before he got away, but the swine fooled me. Here's what he did: Once both flying boats were down and bobbing about while a Coast Guard cutter came up out of nowhere, this Griffon slipped back to where I was sitting with this van Aller guy and gave me a gun to hold the Dutchman down. Then he ran through the cabin, apparently climbed up on the seats, and went out through an emergency hatchway. The black ship which had been following us came down out of nowhere and this Griffon guy dived overboard. He timed his dive so well that before we could make out where he went he was climbing up on the floats… er, pontoons… of the black ship. And then they took off again."

"But you could have fired and held him," suggested Keen.

"Well, between you and I," confided Lang, "I tried to, but I found that the swine had given me a gun that wasn't loaded."

"So the man you call the Griffon got away," grinned Keen.

"Well, considering everything, he was entitled to," Lang said with a dumb look into nothingness. "But I would give a few bucks to know who he was."

"So then, to complete the story," broke in Keen, "the Coast Guard cutter came up with flags waving and captured the two flying boats and saved old Drury Lang."

"Even so," remonstrated the detective, "I think I did a pretty good job."

"Well," said Keen, "I think that you and that guy of mine, O'Dare, both drink the same liquor. He tells cracked stories, too."

And with that, Kerry Keen, the young ballistics expert, sauntered out—without even taking up Lang's luncheon offer.

Lang looked after him, then turned to Scott.

"Say," he grunted, "there *is* something goofy about that guy!"

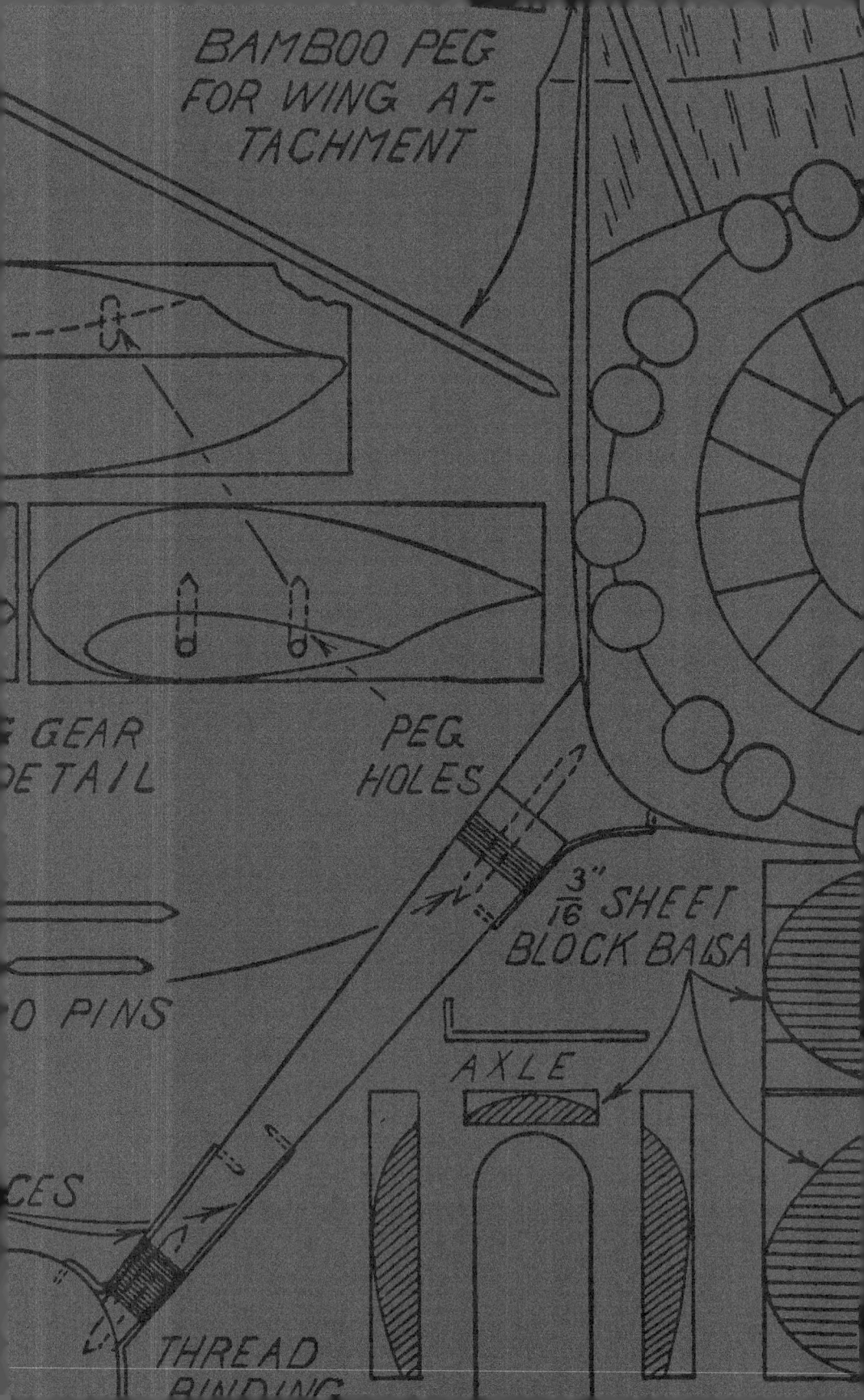

BAMBOO PEG
FOR WING AT-
TACHMENT

GEAR
DETAIL

PEG
HOLES

PINS

$\frac{3}{16}$" SHEET
BLOCK BALSA

CES

AXLE

THREAD
BINDING

Cavalry of the Clouds

THE BLACK BULLET streaked across the sky like a two-bladed knife hurled by some unseen giant. It dipped, swerved and turned, wheeling through its nocturnal gyrations under the skilled hand of the Griffon. Below, slashing alternately across the waters of Long Island Sound and the velvet black rollers of the broad Atlantic, the sword-blade shaft of light from the Montauk beacon brought out the indistinct outlines of surface craft below—a Boston steamer, a proud puffing tug, a palatial yacht.

Above it all, the *Black Bullet* raced against a stopwatch on the Griffon's wrist. It answered his every whim, sped through the full catalog of maneuvers demanded by the man in the scarlet mask. In the back seat, proud of his handicraft and his mechanical skill, Barney O'Dare, the Griffon's none-too-silent partner, likewise sat watching the black amphibian go through her paces after a thorough overhaul.

The Griffon turned to smile over his shoulder, then stiffened abruptly.

A grim, winged fortress was charging down on them from above. In the fraction of a second, the Griffon took it in completely, focused his camera-eye on its striking details.

It was a huge mid-wing monoplane powered with four massive engines of the in-line type. These motors were set in beautifully-faired nacelles. At the nose of the long, protruding fuselage was a movable gun turret flaunting a short, snub-nosed weapon that gleamed in the starlight and flare of the exhausts. It was larger in bore than the average machine gun and the Griffon winced at the thought of what might be hurled from that black snout.

Barney was doing nothing but stare. That was not like Barney. Usually he had to be restrained. He just sat hunched, peering out through the closed gun tray of the transparent coupe top.

The Griffon watched the flying fortress wheel, then gasped at its amazing undercarriage. This appeared to be a complete unit in itself. Instead of wheels, it had a complete set of caterpillar tractor treads.

"Whew!" whistled the Griffon. "If she needs something as strong as that, she must be heavy. What the devil sort of a bus is it?"

PUN-N-NG!

A flash of flame stabbed out of the nose of the monster with the strange silver body. A shell hissed past the *Black Bullet* and the Griffon screamed: "Get that guy in that turret, Barney!"

But Barney was not "buying" any. He simply sat back and stared with an insane glint in his eye at the thunderous bus that was pounding steel at them. He appeared to be strangely fascinated.

The Griffon threw the *Black Bullet* clear, curled into a climbing turn. Then he reached over, snatched at Barney's shoulder, and shook him. "Wake up, you dumb Mick!" he yelled. "What are you waiting for?"

Satisfied that O'Dare would finally go into action the Griffon returned to his front-office business and made ready for a general sally on the wide-winged, giant that was now below them.

Again that snorting big gun barked and another screeching shell slammed past and burst in mid-air above them.

BRR-OOOM!

The Griffon flew madly now, hurled the *Black Bullet* all over the sky, sought an opening to get a punch at the silver-bodied fortress below. Finally he worked the *Black Bullet* into a position dead behind the tail flippers of the big machine, preparing to give her everything he had up front.

"Get him on the twist, Barney, after I get through with her," the Griffon bawled over his shoulder.

He nosed down, gave the big Avia all she could take, and pressed every gun trigger in the office.

But before he could really draw a bead, something smothered him from behind. Two great arms were encircling him, constricting his own arms to his sides. The move caused him to draw the stick back and the *Black Bullet* went up the sky like a released rocket. For several seconds they remained at this angle and finally the Griffon's arms were released.

"Don't…. Don't…. Don't hit her!" Barney screamed into the Griffon's ear. "Don't…."

THE GRIFFON swore under his breath, turned his enraged attention to getting the *Black Bullet* back on an even keel. He had to ease her gently to prevent a spin. He had no desire to throw the ship about any too hard, for he did not know how much, if any, damage had been done to his own craft.

Finally he pulled her clear and hammered away to get out of range of the strange ship. He wondered why Barney had done that. He wondered what the Mick had seen to cause him to take such a strange attitude. This was a new one on the Griffon.

By the time he had cleared, the winged fortress was out of sight.

"What the hell?" he started to bawl over his shoulder. "What the deuce made you do that, Barney?"

He got no answer, so he twisted around farther, saw that Barney was still staring out of the side of the cockpit with unseeing eyes. He had not broken out the guns and he had no answer.

"Are you drunk?" the Griffon finally asked.

No answer.

"Oh well, there's no use sitting up here arguing. We'll have it out when we get down."

The Griffon turned the *Black Bullet* back toward the Long Island shoreline and rammed in the Skoda mufflers which deadened the roar of the big Avia down to a low purr. He throttled back and let her glide gently in.

She dropped on the water a few minutes after Keen had lowered the retractable pontoons and surged up with a minimum of noise to the flat, hard-packed sands in front of a boathouse. Then quietly, with no more noise than would be offered by a luxurious motor car, the *Black Bullet,* her pontoons tilted now for land movement, rolled past a heavy foliaged grape arbor and up a thickly-turfed lawn.

Barney slipped out, rammed his hand inside the fuselage, and the wings folded back snug against the sides of the fuselage. Then he moved forward, sought a sunken switch box at one end of a great rock-garden and in a few seconds the face of the garden mysteriously split open and folded back, disclosing a cavernous hangar.

The Griffon ran the ship inside and climbed out, prepared to get some explanation of Barney's amazing actions.

But Barney was nowhere to be found. He had disappeared completely!

Kerry Keen drew off his Griffon garments, let out a low whistle. Finally he turned on a light to inspect the damage done to the *Black Bullet,* and then, satisfied that she had suffered no untoward battering, he snapped the switch off and wandered, pained, puzzled and discouraged, upstairs to his snug den.

THAT was shortly before midnight; but it was well after 8 o'clock before Keen got up from his big desk where he had been working on a paper entitled *The Magnus Effect on the Spinning Projectile* which he was to read before the coming International Ballistics Commission conference. He had the weird quality of being able to completely throw his mind off past events to concentrate on the work at hand. By the time he was ready for his glass of warm milk, which Barney always had at hand by the time he was ready to slip between the sheets, he had to jostle himself to recall the incident of the flying fortress and the strange disappearance of the Mick.

"That's right," he said. "Now where the devil did he bust off to?"

He went through the great house, seeking his man, but he was nowhere to be found.

His room had not been entered since he had left it prior to going on the test flight. He was nowhere about in the sunken hangar. He was not in the wine cellar, nor were there any empty O'Doul's Dew bottles around.

Keen frowned, lit a massive, straight-stemmed briar pipe. He sat down again and pondered on the subject, wondered what was behind Barney's mind when he interfered with his diving on the great plane over the Sound.

There seemed to be no answer for it, so Keen sanely went to bed—to sleep on it, as it were.

NEXT morning, there was no cheery breakfast, no warm bath, no laying out of a neatly pressed morning suit. Keen, hair tousled and puffy-eyed, wandered about Graylands like a lost dog. He peered into rooms, sought evidence of Barney's return and even looked about for a note. There was nothing. And so, he made himself a light breakfast and continued work on his ballistics paper.

But by noon he could stand it no longer, so he ran out his sport roadster, a new Italian Renghali, and throwing a light top coat into the seat beside him, he started out for New York City. By three o'clock he was sitting in the dingy office of John Scott, Department of Justice agent, in the mid-town section of the city.

Drury Lang was there, looking even rattier than ever. Both Scott and Lang were working feverishly over broken sections of metal—something that looked like a battered taxi-meter and some sections of frayed wire.

"Trying to get London?" inquired Keen, with a smirk toward Lang. "Or is this something new in parlor games."

"You can get out of here as quick as you like. We're busy," growled Lang.

"Do anything for you?" inquired Scott a little more sociably, but businesslike nevertheless. "We've got a rather nasty job on our hands."

"Hmm. That's nothing. I've lost my man, Barney," exclaimed Keen, expecting to get some response.

"Drunk... lying in a gutter somewhere," mumbled Lang.

"You can get another man somewhere, can't you?" Scott added. "This isn't an employment office."

"But I want every hospital and police station in this section checked," said Keen. "Every one, understand?"

Both Lang and Scott looked up suddenly, Lang dropped the parts of metal he was studying and came over to where Keen was sitting. "What's up?" he said quickly. Lang had never seen Keen like this before.

"He disappeared last night from the house—about 11 o'clock. Just went, and he hasn't turned up yet."

"What was the matter? You bawl him out for something?"

"No, but I was going to. He disappeared before I could get around to it."

"Well, there you are, then," Scott said, throwing out his hands. "He must know the wrath of your tongue, and he was not having any."

"No, that wasn't it. I've bawled him out before, but it never leaves any impression. This time, I'm afraid, it's something serious. I want you to make a thorough search."

"Or what?" growled Lang.

"Or… or I won't tell the Griffon to do you any more favors," smiled the ballistics expert.

"Bosh! You've never even seen the Griffon," raged Lang. "I *have!*"

"So I've heard," Keen taunted. "But look here, I do want you to make an attempt to locate Barney. I do miss him you know."

"This ain't no lost and found department," Lang spat again. "Besides, I told you we're busy. Maybe," he added, "you heard about that taxicab business yesterday afternoon… in 84th Street?"

"No. What taxicab business?"

"That one that blew up, killing the driver and injuring about ten people who were nearby."

"Oh yes, another variation of the Wall Street explosion business wasn't it? I read something about it in the papers."

"This is what did it," said Lang with a proud gesture at the twisted metal on the desk.

"The meter?" asked Keen getting up and showing interest. "You mean to say the meter blew up? I've expected that before, the way those things run once you sit down in the back seat."

"Naw!" fumed Lang. "This was the gadget that set the bomb off. When it registered about $1.80 it touched off a fuse and blew the taxi up."

"What for?" inquired Keen. "A new taxicab war or something?"

"That's what *we* want to know," muttered Lang through his ratty mustache. "That's what we want to know. Why they went after this poor devil, an Alonzo Gabbritch, is more than we can figure. He was just a punk, a taxi-driver with no particular connections that we can figure out."

"You working on his background, Scott?" asked Kerry, showing real interest now.

"Haven't got the time, now," sparred Scott. "You see, a much more important case has just been laid in my lap. Believe it or not, some one has actually mislaid *this* thing." And he tossed a large glossy photograph across the table. On seeing it, Keen only just managed to stifle a gasp.

"Ever catch sight of anything like that?" asked Scott, turning around to fill his pipe.

"No.... What the deuce is it?" Keen finally managed to say, carelessly snapping a silver cigarette lighter and lighting a cork-tipped cigarette. "Looks like an airliner that has been crossed with a tank."

SCOTT turned around quickly, stared at Keen: "That's exactly what it is. How did you know?"

"Well, it has wings and a body, and yet underneath it has what looks like a tank of some sort. See, the tractor treads are quite plain."

"Have you ever seen this thing... anywhere?" asked Lang with a leer spacing his words carefully.

"There you go again, Drury," grinned Keen. "I know nothing about it. I have never seen it anywhere except on this picture. What's it all about, anyway?"

"Nothing," Scott said quietly, "only late yesterday afternoon this thing was stolen from a hangar outside Wright Field, at Dayton, Ohio. We don't know where it is—but we'd like to."

"Yes, I'd like to find Barney, too," said Keen quietly. And now what the deuce is this all about, anyway?" he said, indicating the photo.

"It's just what you said it was—a plane crossed with a tank. In other words, it's a bomber-fighter that is built to take a full-size Army tank into the air, and if necessary deposit it behind the enemy lines. They call tanks mechanized cavalry. Well, a corps of these things might be called cavalry of the clouds."

"Volunteers for the Winged Tank Corps, line up at the right—and no pushing," chanted Keen with a grin.

"Yeh, I wouldn't want it either, but someone in the Army has decided that it's a good idea, and strange to relate, the damn thing works. It has been tried out in secret. The plane simply rolls up with its wheels down and straddles the tank. Then an arrangement is dropped that fastens the tank in a depression in the body of the plane. The tank, you see, is a high speed machine and the men in the plane can use it to take off with. Into the air they go and fly behind the enemy lines. They land, release the tank to carry out its routine patrol, and fly off again on their own landing gear. After the tank's work is done, and provided conditions are favorable, the plane can return, pick it up again, and bring it back to its own side of the lines."

"The world gets dizzier and dizzier," Keen moaned. "So what?"

"Well, it has been stolen. Who did it and how, we don't know."

"Stolen yesterday afternoon? It must be half way to Japan—or Spain by now, eh?"

"That part doesn't matter. Everyone has had the tank-plane idea for years, but it took a young metallurgist in the War Department to put it over. No plane in the world, you understand, could pick up the average Army tank—I mean one big enough and armed enough to do any real damage behind enemy lines. It had to be made very light and still bullet- and shell-proof."

"A new metal?" said Keen, bending forward.

"That's it. A new light armor plate. It's called Avalin. And not only does it answer a great problem concerning this flying tank idea, but the stuff can be used in battleships, considerably lightening them and thus increasing their speed."

Keen had sensed all this long before, but he professed great amazement.

"So they not only stole a complete flying model of this tank-plane, but they have samples of the metal as well," he said, furrowing his brow.

"That's not quite the story," replied Scott. "It's true they have the tank, which is made of this metal, but the formula and the annealing process so necessary in its manufacture is another thing."

Drury Lang sat on the corner of the table and watched Keen like a cat watches a mouse. And now he could hold himself in no longer—

"How would you like to pick up that formula—for the return of Barney O'Dare, Keen?" he said with a snaky grin.

THIS new sally nearly caught Keen off guard. He hesitated, flicked the ash from his cigarette. "What the deuce are you talking about?" he finally managed to say.

"Just that. The formula and annealing process of the new metal known as Avalin was stolen a short time after they swiped that plane. We don't know where it is or who has it, but we can't have it out of the hands of the Government for more than forty-eight hours at the most."

"What's he talking about?" demanded Keen, appealing to Scott.

"That's it, Keen. They also swiped the formula, but as it is written in a special secret code, we know it would take them at least forty-eight hours to break it and find the real secret. And so, we might help you find Barney O'Dare—if you'll give us a hand on the Avalin formula."

"But what the deuce does Barney have to do with this?"

"Nothing," laughed Lang, "except that a man answering Barney O'Dare's description was the last fare to use the taxicab which was blown up yesterday afternoon. Do you happen to know where Barney O'Dare was yesterday afternoon about 8 o'clock?"

"No... no, I don't. He had the day off, and as far as I know he was in town mooching about, as he usually does, seeing his pet movie actress at the Palace Royal theatre. He goes for her in a big way, you know—autographs and pictures of her on his wall."

"Who's that?" demanded Lang, leaping off the corner of the table.

"Oh, this girl Doreen Yardley… she's playing in that new spy picture, *Whispering Wings.* Barney goes for her hard."

"*Whispering Wings!*" almost screamed Lang, charging for a newspaper. "There's a tie-up! Get it, John. That plot is almost the same as this mess. It's about enemy agents stealing a new bombing plane. What a tie-up!"

"Wait a minute," snapped Scott. "Gimme that paper!"

Keen sat back staring at the two Department of Justice men as they floundered about with the newspaper.

"Look here," Scott said with unvarnished alarm. "It says that Miss Doreen Yardley, star of *Whispering Wings* now playing at the Palace Royal, Broadway's newest and most luxurious movie palace, failed to turn up last night for her scheduled personal appearance. She had fulfilled one engagement in the afternoon, but after leaving the theatre in her appearance costume, she didn't show up again at her hotel, the Ritz Savoy. Later, about midnight, her car, an expensive limousine, was found abandoned on West Street near the Lackawanna Railroad ferry at Barclay Street. No trace of the chauffeur, one Pierre Gallante, has been uncovered either."

"Well, I'll be damned!" gagged Lang, peering over Scott's shoulder.

"What are you trying to make out of all these apparently un-related items?" barked Keen, selecting another cigarette.

"So your Mister O'Dare is missing, too, eh?" Lang gargled with a grimace at Keen. "When did you see him last?"

"About 11 o'clock, I should say, roughly speaking."

"Very roughly, I'd say. When did he get back from New York?"

"I don't know. I was out for a stroll and stopped in to see some friends for a cocktail until about five. Then I worked in my study on a paper I am to read before the International Ballistics Commission convention. Barney called me for supper some time after seven. He was around until about eleven or eleven-thirty, I'd say. Anyway, he was not about when I went to call him for some hot milk."

"Then you don't know when he came in, nor when he went off again?"

"I don't know when he came in, but he was around until well after eleven. As I say, I missed him about 11:30. I wanted some hot milk."

"If he got back in time to serve your dinner at seven, or a little after, what would be the latest he came in?"

"Well, I'm no cook, but I should say that it would have taken him half an hour at the least."

"Then he might have returned about 6:30. How long would it take him to get from downtown New York to your place?"

"With good connections, about two hours at the most," figured Keen.

"Then he could have been somewhere near where this taxi blew up just after three in the afternoon—and still get out to your place in time to get your dinner, eh?"

"Yes, he could," agreed Keen, trying to piece many things together.

"Now we are going to look for Mr. Barney O'Dare," clucked Drury Lang. "He might know plenty about Miss Doreen Yardley and the missing plane—and possibly the formula of the Avalin armor plate."

"You know, Scott," said Keen reflectively, "there are times when I am certain old Lang here is going off his noggin."

"I have felt the same way several times," agreed Scott much to Lang's dismay, "but somehow, this time, Keen, I feel that he is displaying a rare touch of perception. There may be a lot in what he says."

"Oh, my hat!" gasped Keen, getting up with a display of amazement. "Don't tell me he's inflicting his influence on *you!*"

"Boy, you'd better dig up Barney O'Dare," Lang crowed. "You'd better get him first, because if we get our hooks on him, we'll make him talk. We'll find out a lot of things, I believe, and many of those things will implicate a certain Mr. Ginsberg and a certain Mr. Pulski. Now will you go to work and see what you can do about a certain formula?"

KEEN had little to say after that. He realized that there were too many cock-eyed angles to all this. Could old Lang know that he had actually seen the tank-plane in the sky over Long Island the night before and that it had actually fired on him and his *Black Bullet,* he would never have been allowed to leave the office.

As it was, he sensed that he was in a tough spot. Suppose they did pick Barney up. Suppose they found him a trifle under the influence of O'Doul's Dew. Suppose they *made* him talk. Suppose Barney so forgot himself as to give the whole show away....

Reflections were terrifying, and Keen stared about for an out. There was only one. He must divert their attention from Barney and keep it focused on the missing formula.

"You say this tank-plane thing was stolen yesterday afternoon?" Keen suddenly nagged back at them. "How?"

"That we don't know. All we can get on it is that the ship was kept in one of the experimental hangars. There was some sort of a fire started in this hangar. The crew rushed the plane out quickly and then turned their attentions on the flames. While all this was going on, somebody slipped into the ship, and before anyone could do anything about it they were away."

"Clever idea, all right. Now about the formula. Where was that taken from?"

"As far as we can make out, it had been in Washington with one of the Technical Divisions where it was being transcribed into the secret code and bound. One courier brought it to New York by air... that is, into Newark and then to New York where it was to be turned over to another courier who was to take it on to Wright Field."

"How, by air?"

"No, the weather dropped down and it was decided to take it through by train. The case containing this bound formula appears to have been taken, by some deception, on the airline coach that was bringing the passengers through from the Newark Airport to New York City proper. They pulled the old duplicate brief case swap on the courier, and he didn't notice the change until he was in Grand Central Station."

"When was that?" inquired Keen.

"Yesterday afternoon about 3 o'clock. In other words, the courier must have lost it about 2:30 aboard the ferry that comes into 23rd Street."

"Didn't the airline car use the Holland Tunnel into the city?" asked Keen quickly.

"No, it appears that there was some sort of a tie-up at the New Jersey end of the tunnel, so the driver turned into Hoboken and used the Lackawanna Ferry."

"Lackawanna Ferry?... and Miss Yardley's limousine was found abandoned at the Barclay Street entrance of the Lackawanna Ferry?" Keen muttered aloud.

"Hey, there's an angle," said Lang, suddenly. "You're thinking now, Keen. That's an angle!"

"Just a tie-up of names," said Keen, trying to throw it off. "Probably nothing to it. But it does seem funny that that airline coach should take the Lackawanna Ferry instead of going through the tunnel. If someone snatched that case before the courier reached that point, he—the thief—could have left the coach in the Lackawanna station and taken the ferry that went farther downtown, while the coach took the uptown ferry. Why don't you try to check that time bracket?"

"Don't worry, we will!" blatted Scott.

The three men sat silent for some time. Scott puffed on a great briar pipe, Keen allowed long curling plumes of smoke to rise from his cigarette, and Lang picked at his brown tusks with the end of a match.

"Well, what are you waiting for?" demanded Lang after a lengthy reflection. "You only got a short time."

"This looks like a job for your friend, the Griffon," Keen said with a frown. "Why don't you put him on it?"

"I would—if I knew where he was or who the hell he really is," snarled Lang.

"Well, I'll be tootling," Keen added with a cheery air. "I shall be out at Long Island if you want me."

"You won't find much out there. It's all around here, some-where."

"What about the tank-plane. That might be one of the angles you know. Turn out the Army, the Navy, and the Air Service."

"Bah! It'll take more than that," Lang snorted, snatching at the paper again.

"Thanks, you certainly are reposing a special trust in me," grinned Keen, going toward the door.

"We'll trust you—until we get our hooks on that man Barney of yours," Lang hurled after him as he went through the door.

"Don't worry," retorted Keen. "He's probably miles away from here."

KEEN went out, closed the door quietly, then stared at a queer square of paper that lay on the floor at his feet. There was something strangely familiar about it—a label of some sort with a one-inch border gay with a Scottish tartan. The label from a whiskey bottle—O'Doul's Dew!

Keen picked it up quickly and went to the elevator humming a tune from an old time musical comedy.

> *Poets, guards and heroes true,*
> *Fighters, lovers, Churchmen, too,*
> *Crowd the chapters we go through.*
> *Then they scattered here and there,*
> *Causing trouble everywhere,*
> *What a lovely name, O'Dare!*

He got into the elevator without attempting to inquire if anyone had seen Barney. He knew that if the Mick had wanted to be seen, he would have arranged it. It was evident that he wished to lay low.

As the elevator started down, Keen turned the label over and read in a horrible scrawl: "Tonight… midnight… over No Man's Land."

For a minute or two Keen was unable to make head or tail of the crazy message. "No Man's Land?" he muttered when he got into the street. "What the deuce does he mean? He must be drunk."

But soon after he had started his car and was threading his way through the city traffic, it all came to him. No Man's Land was the name of a small island about 58 miles northeast of Montauk Point. It lay about ten miles out in the ocean, south of Martha's Vineyard. It was a lonely blot on the blue of the Atlantic inhabited by only a few hardy fishermen who were content to live much as had their forebears of two centuries before.

"Um," mused Keen as he headed for Long Island. "I wonder if they've got that bus hidden out up there? They might, hoping to contact someone—someone who might have that formula."

He drove on, his mind clicking as fast as the twelve-cylinder engine beneath the hood. He wondered now why Barney had stopped him from shooting at the tank-plane the night before. He wondered if Barney had seen something near the Lackawanna Ferry on the afternoon before that tied up with all this mystery. He wondered what the disappearance of Miss Doreen Yardley had to do with a secret military plane and the stealing of a secret formula for a light armor plate. He naturally wondered how Barney knew that something was going to take place that evening at midnight over the island of No Man's Land.

"What a lovely name, O'Dare!"

He sang at the top of his voice as he rolled through the beautiful countryside of Long Island.

THERE was no further news of Barney for the rest of the day and Keen contented himself with preparing the *Black Bullet* for any sort of action that might come up. He filled the tanks, checked the oil, and then went over the guns carefully, seeing that all belts were fully loaded. He might have been preparing the amphibian for a young war, for all the care he took.

At 7 o'clock, his task completed, he went back through the sliding panel that led into the wine cellar, selected a choice bottle of Heidsieck, wandered upstairs, and prepared his own dinner. He drank cheerfully by himself, lit a fine Corona-Corona, and sat back to enjoy a cheerful fire in his open fireplace. Then, satisfied with himself, he curled up on a great down-filled divan and went straight to sleep. At exactly 11 o'clock he woke up, took a quick shower, climbed into his flying kit, and went downstairs.

He started the Avia motor and turned on the high-speed ventilator system which took off all the carbon monoxide. After she warmed, he ran her out, closed the secret rock garden doors, then took her out on the water. Finally, he set the pontoons for a water take-off and purred away into the darkness.

In a few minutes he was well out to sea at 4,000 where he was now able to cut out the Skoda mufflers and let her run full out. With a last look around, he drew the pontoons up all the way so that they fitted snugly into their recesses and turned to the northeast for the island of No Man's Land.

Below, the water seemed warm and somehow luxuriant, and the moonlight streaking out from the rifts of cloud ahead seemed to give the land a warm cloak of moleskin. The golden flares of coastal signals lay like expensive brooches on a black satin pad. The towns along the Connecticut shore crouched like monsters with spangled scales as hide, and outside Hartford the tell-tale beams of airline beacons flashed in their ever-circling battle with the darkness.

It was all so enchanting that Keen found himself engrossed in the wonder of the night aloft—the undreamed-of paradise of flight in a night sky. The earth seemed more serene, more beautiful, more marvelous than it ever could under the blatancy of day.

But just as he discerned the outline of No Man's Land island, out of the west came a winged pack of opposition!

"Hello! Navy stuff, eh? They must have some idea, too."

Keen swerved to clear the first charge of the Voughts that were upon him. And now he felt a jangle of discordant battering upon his fuselage somewhere near the tail. He zoomed hard, gave her all the power she could take.

He felt his controls carefully; and sensing that nothing had been hit, he went to work to elude the Navy pilots. They were converging on him now with all forward weapons rattling. The sky, completely changed now, was streaked with tracer, alive with flaming-nosed fighters, and etched with grim smoke lines. Pennons of flame fluttered from the exhausts and riders of the night sky hammered away at the *Black Bullet*—a wraith they had sought for months.

"They're certainly after me this time. Wonder if the note on that label was a plant?" he muttered, as he turned sharply and sprayed a wild hosing of lead in front of the nose of one particularly offensive Vought. The leader of the Navy formation now turned to clear, and Keen swung high again, fought to get clear of a wild fanfare of lead that came up from four spitting Brownings.

He had to get away somehow. He could not turn on these Navy men, but neither could he be molested in this manner. Time was getting short and he knew Barney would be looking for him on the dot of midnight. He was cutting it fine now.

With one final lurch, however, he turned and hammered a long screeching burst through the center of the Navy formation, causing them to roll away. Then he screeched through with his Avia wide open in an ear-splitting roar, drew back sharply on the stick, and sent the *Black Bullet* straight up into the darkness, standing on her tail.

One or two gunners tried to get a burst at her before she disappeared into the darkness, but most of them were too amazed at the ship's performance.

That instant of hesitancy gave Keen his break. He eased out of the climb, rammed in the Skoda mufflers, doused every light aboard, and skuttled away before the Navy men could figure what had happened.

He raced out to sea making the most of his blinding speed and comparative silence and flew for about five minutes before turning back. It was already midnight and he had to take some rare chances, for the Navy planes were still in the vicinity, believing that he had returned to some base floating about somewhere on the surface of the ocean.

He lowered his pontoons and headed for the island which stood out stark and course. It had no particular shape at all, and there was not a light visible anywhere. On the eastern side there was the dull outline of something that might have been a large dilapidated building, perhaps an old lighthouse. He circled this side with the Avia well muffled and his flaps down slightly to cut his speed. He swung carefully, inspecting the land below; then he consulted a Navy chart he had brought along to check the depths around the island for landings.

There appeared to be plenty of water. He would be able to get down okay without fear of ripping the bottoms out of his pontoons.

Two pin-points of light then caught his eye—one green and two white lights blinking from a cove a short distance from the indistinct building. He glanced down again and once more they were flashed on.

"A green and two whites," he muttered. "That's Barney's old signal. Well, if he says so, it's okay with me."

He cut the forward speed of the amphibian and let her glide in and drop gently on the rollers about two hundred yards outside the cove. The green and white signals blinked again encouraging him to come in closer.

Keen took no chances, however. Cautiously he drew up his scarlet mask, tapped his big automatic reflectively, and eased in. Again the signal flashes flecked out.

"Pulski?" called Keen carefully.

"Please hurry, Mr. Ginsberg," a dulcet voice came back.

"Mr. Ginsberg?" repeated Keen. "What the deuce!"

By now the tide was swinging the *Black Bullet* dangerously close to the hard-packed sands of the cove. Keen took no more chances. He threw out a slim anchor, drew the line taut, and fastened it to a latch on the outside of his cockpit. Then he climbed out cautiously and stood on the wing.

"Pulski?" he said again.

"Please hurry, Mr. Ginsberg," the voice repeated. There was no question now. It was a girl.

KEEN was uncertain what to do, but he was interested in that voice. It was pleading in tone. There could be no treachery in a voice like that.

He dropped down into the swirling water and waded up the beach, his gun drawn and alert.

No sooner had he reached the edge of the rollers and started up the sand when out of a break in the rocks came a girl—a girl who was slim and stately. She walked with the unmistakable grace and poise of one who was used to acclaim. In a glance Keen took all this in. She wore a suede jacket and riding jodhpurs.

She was young, no more than twenty. She was blond with aristocratic features. She was strong, yet moved like a gazelle. But above all, Keen had to agree she was probably the most beautiful woman he had ever seen.

In a flash it came to him who she was—Miss Doreen Yardley, the heroine of *Whispering Wings*. The motion picture star whose name and photograph had been emblazoned across every newspaper in the country.

But Keen was not to be put off with the spell of beauty or motion picture prominence. He was on business and he was out for information.

"Where's Bar—Pulski?" he demanded as he approached the girl.

"They've captured him. You were late. I hid in the rocks."

"What's this all about, anyway?" Keen demanded.

"Didn't you come to get him and recover the book?" the girl asked. It was evident that she was plainly puzzled now. She pocketed Barney's flashlight, wrung her hands.

"Where's the tank-plane?" Keen snapped.

"It's over there, ready to take off. They have that formula book—and Mr. Pulski."

"What the deuce is this all about?" Keen inquired, eyeing the girl through his goggles and mask. "You're Miss Yardley, aren't you? Don't you know that the police of New York are searching for you everywhere?"

"I can't help that. We've got to get that formula back."

"How did they get it?"

"Through me—only I didn't know what it was when I first received it. You see a man named Anton Brassage, who used to be a scenario writer out in Hollywood, stole it from Captain Edward Hillary, who was—"

"—bringing it up from Washington," broke in Keen, "to take

it out to Wright Field. I know that much. But where does Pulski fit in with it all?"

"Well, this man Brassage changed the cases in the airline bus, got off in Hoboken, and took the Lackawanna Ferry down to Barclay Street. There he picked up this man Pulski, who was hanging around the newsstand there, and asked him if he wanted to make an easy five dollars."

"Go on," ordered Keen peering about. "Well, Pulski said he didn't mind, as long as it would not take him too long. So Brassage explained that he had a case that belonged to me—Miss Yardley, the motion picture star."

"Well," smiled Keen, "he picked the right man. Pulski has about twenty of your pictures scattered about his room."

A trace of a smile lit the girl's lips. "Anyway," she continued, "Pulski agreed to deliver the case to me direct at the Palace Royal where I was doing a P.A.—a personal appearance, you know. It was supposed to be my personal jewel case, and I hoped to wear some of my more expensive items at a special dinner party they were to give in my honor the following night at the Ritz."

"It doesn't make much sense yet," muttered Keen.

"I know that, but you see, Brassage did not dare keep that case in his own possession too long, for fear it would be missed and traced, so he used that idea to get it out of his hands and yet keep track of it."

"Do you know that the taxi exploded?"

"No, not until Pulski told me later. Anyway, I accepted the case and kept it in my dressing room with the idea of later taking it downtown to Benedict's—that's the big jeweler, you know—and have one of the clasps repaired. On the way down, my chauffeur took West Street owing to the heavy traffic on Broadway and near Barclay Street we were… well, we were simply held up, blocked off, changed into another car, driven downtown, and hustled into one of the warehouses facing the North River. There we were held as prisoners and later when it got dark we were put aboard a cruiser motor boat and brought here."

"You still thought it was a hold-up for your jewels?"

"Yes. You see, I had asked Brassage who was coming east, to

bring them for me. I naturally thought he had done so and had used this messenger because he was too busy to deliver them himself. At the time I realized that he had taken something of a chance, but I thought he knew this man Pulski."

"Well, it's getting clearer, but what about the taxi blowing up?"

"We must hurry, you know," Miss Yardley said. "I had a few minutes to talk to Pulski back there. Brassage drove up to the theatre with Pulski but did not come in, using some excuse about not wanting to see me until that evening. He induced Pulski to use the same taxi to return to the Pennsylvania Station where he could get a train to wherever he was going."

"And Pulski, still up in the clouds over having actually seen and spoken to his screen sweetheart," gagged Keen, "agreed."

"Well, I suppose you *could* put it that way," Miss Yardley modestly admitted, "but don't you see, it was just a plot to get rid of him after he had delivered the case. Brassage got out about a block from the theatre and left a newspaper covering a box of some sort. This, no doubt, was the contrivance he had devised to blow up the taxi."

"I'll be damned!" snorted Keen. "How did Pulski escape it?"

"He tells me he suddenly saw the box and told the driver about it. Then he says he suddenly remembered he had to get something at Macy's store and so he got out at 84th Street and Seventh Avenue. The driver said he'd turn the bag over to his office where it could be called for at any time. Then he drove away."

"And a few minutes later the bomb in the back seat exploded."

"Well, it exploded under the meter. You see, the driver had taken it from the back seat and had put it up front where they carry luggage."

"That explains some of it," muttered Keen glancing about again, "but there's still plenty to clear up. Now we'd better get going."

"We've wasted too much time; but I can see you are wondering what part I was playing, or where I fitted in this picture. It's all crazier than that thing I played in *Whispering Wings*," the girl said.

"I'm beginning to realize that," Keen said, hunching his shoulders. "But what about this place… and Pulski?"

"Oh, won't you please do something? We can explain all these things later. Don't you realize that they have Pulski in there and that they may get away any minute. They're only waiting for the word."

"Word for what?"

"I don't know… the word to go, I suppose."

WITH a last look back at the *Black Bullet* which was now riding easily at anchor, Keen nodded and started toward the higher ground of the island. They could just see the outline of the upper portion of the abandoned lighthouse which had been used as the headquarters of the gang. They climbed up the rocks together and tried to figure a way to approach it without being seen.

"How did you get out?" Keen suddenly asked. "Won't they miss you?"

He still felt uncertain about this young lady who seemed to have a reasonable answer to every question.

"Well, I was allowed a certain amount of freedom. After all, you can't run away from an island set out in the ocean miles from anywhere, can you?"

"No, I suppose not. Where was Pulski when you cleared out?"

"They had him tied up in one of the rooms. I don't know how he got here, but they caught him prowling around and Brussage recognized him as the man he had paid to deliver the case to me. At first he was scared stiff, for he believed Pulski had been killed in the taxi explosion."

Keen chuckled under his breath. But then there came a new tune out of the darkness—the bellow of engines and the scream of props.

"I told you!" the girl cried. "I told you! They're getting away! Look—they're taking off!"

Keen felt a wild surge of frustration. He started to run forward as the big four-engined bomber with tank attached rolled across an open stretch behind the abandoned lighthouse. He stood a moment watching it, then turned toward the girl and called: "Come on, show me the layout of that place over there!"

The girl came running up breathless and Keen suddenly snatched the flashlight from her hands. Quickly he twisted the colored lenses in the front and pressed the button switch. He directed it full at the climbing bomber and continued to signal, hoping that if Barney were aboard he would get an idea of what was going on.

The big plane circled the lighthouse twice, then headed off to the north. Keen and the girl raced for the lighthouse, swinging open its door, and ran down the white-washed corridor.

"Straight through," the girl shouted. "Into the big room beyond."

Gun in hand, Keen banged on the closed door, then wrenched at the door-knob. It gave under pressure and he lurched inside.

There was no one there.

The room was large with several murky windows looking out toward the sea. A large fireplace took up one of the narrow sides. The furniture appeared to have been salvaged from wrecks, for there were several ships' chests, boxes bound with iron, a massive table, and generous-sized swing-seat chairs. There was a dank mustiness about the place that indicated that it had not been lived in for some time. There was a fire still crackling on the hearth and the smell of tinned food struck the nose.

"This is the main room. There are several more above, in what was the light tower," Miss Yardley explained. "They had Pulski tied up in the room above."

"Quick, let's look up there. He may still be there," Keen said.

They went up the stairs and entered a small chamber with a narrow window at each end. There was a bed there, crumpled and drawn partly away from the wall. Keen took the lamp, went all over the wall near the bed. For several seconds he studied the dirty plaster, then suddenly concentrated on a murky spot near the head.

"Look," he said quietly. "It's just as I thought. They're heading for Newfoundland preparatory to a hop for Europe. That plane is intended for someone over there—probably one of the Spanish outfits."

The girl looked over Keen's shoulder and noted crude figures, drawings, and words indicating the intended course of the men who had stolen the great tank-plane. Barney had managed to scribble it there with a stub of a pencil before they had removed him to the plane.

"Well, there's no use trying to do much else here," Keen said starting across for the door again. "What are you going to do?"

"Do?... I can go with you, can't I?" she said puzzled.

"Not very well," Keen said quietly. "There's room, of course, but you'd be in the way."

"I wasn't in the way when you were sitting out there looking for a signal, was I?"

"No, but you see I've got to make time to catch them," Keen explained.

"I only weigh 110 and I am lightly dressed. I *might* be able to help… or are you going to warn the Navy to head them off before they pass Nantucket?"

"They are probably past Nantucket already, and besides I can't tip the Navy chaps off. They'd probably shoot the plane down— and Bar…. Pulski is aboard. That wouldn't do!"

"What are your plans to get him off?"

"I haven't the slightest idea. But I hope to warm one up before I catch them."

"Then you'd better take me along to help warm it up," the girl smiled.

"Wrap up in anything warm you can get on," Keen said crisply. "And let's be moving. I don't know what in Heaven's name I'm going to do with you later on, though. After all, young lady, I am the Griffon, a pretty ruthless character, you know."

"You don't sound ruthless," the girl said, selecting a short thick seaman's jacket from a peg on the wall. "I've heard of you, of course. Every once in a while your name appears in the newspapers. But I was under the impression that your name was Ginsberg—at least that's what Mr. Pulski said."

"You seem to accept unusual statements pretty calmly," Keen said. "I think you'll fit in all right, but I warn you that you'll be in for a warm evening."

"Did you see me in *Whispering Wings?*" Miss Yardley asked with a smile.

"No!"

"Well, let's go," the girl said with vigor. "After all, I have an interest in this expedition, you know. I still have my jewel case to pick up, and Mr. Brassage will have a lot of explaining to do."

"*If* we get them," said Keen holding the door open gallantly.

THEY hurried down to the cove again, and at the edge of the water they both laughed as they looked out to where the *Black Bullet* was swinging gently at her anchor.

"Well, there's no time for formalities," Keen said. "Do you mind?"

"Let's go!" the girl chuckled.

With that he lifted her in his arms and strode out to the plane. He placed her on the wing and gave instructions for getting into the rear cockpit while he released the anchor and turned the nose of the plane around.

The engine caught quickly and he kept her in close while the Avia warmed up. Then making sure the girl was secure, he nosed around into the wind. They were away with a rush and without bothering to gain altitude he headed her north after the stolen tank-plane.

He hooked Barney's helmet up with the phone set so that he could talk to the girl. "Just sit tight and hang on," he advised. "If trouble starts, we'll have to go through with it. You'll have to rely on me to get you out... somehow."

"Trouble?" the girl asked, once she had the bulky helmet arranged. "Do you mean from planes like those over there?"

"Planes? Where?" gasped Keen.

"Those over!"

Brat-a-tat-tat-tat-tat-tat!

For the second time that night, the Navy Voughts converged

on the *Black Bullet*. Keen just barely had time to roll out of the line of fire that spat at them, from the lead Vought.

"Holy Moses!" he exclaimed. "Here they are again."

"Who? Are they *really* firing at us?" the girl chattered.

"What do you think this is, a moving picture?"

"Good heavens!"

The Voughts bashed themselves at the *Black Bullet* again, and Keen swerved sharply and literally ran the gauntlet of the formation.

"Why they're ships belonging to our Navy, aren't they?" the girl cried as she peered out of the transparent coupe top.

"If they're not," Keen replied, "someone has done a swell job of painting."

Whatever it was the girl was going to say in reply was not heard, for two more Voughts came hammering at them again from opposite sides. Keen spotted them, stuck his nose down, and ripped the Skoda mufflers out. The Avia, gasping with backpressure, took up the load with everything wide open now. She bit in deeply and filled her steel lungs with gulpings of power. The terrific speed left the Voughts virtually standing still.

In a short time they were well in the clear again and heading on with the northern shore of Martha's Vineyard under their wings.

"*Now* keep your eyes open for the other bus," advised Keen as he settled back for the long run north.

THE MAN at the big control wheel of the tank-plane was surly, hard to talk to. He was staring ahead at the man who sat behind the 40 mm Madsen cannon, fitted into the movable turret set in the nose. The man in the right-hand control-pit seat was trying to soothe him down.

"We were saps to leave that jane," the pilot said. "We should have taken a little time to look for her."

"Forget her! What the hell can she do, wherever she is? We'll be over Cape Sable in no time. An hour at Nelson, and we're in the clear."

"Yeh, but I still don't like it. That broad can still sick the Navy guys on us, or even some of those Canadian Air Force guys. They got a station somewhere in New Brunswick; and if they're tipped off, they can still head us off from the fuel dump outside Nelson."

"So what? If it get's too tough, we can plant her on the water near the *Gontingen* and clamber aboard with the formula."

"Yeh, but we don't get paid for planting her on the water."

"We'll get the dough for the book, won't we?"

"Sure, but after all the trouble we took so far, I don't like throwing all this away. This is a swell boiler, Muggy."

"I know…. I know. But there's still a nice slice of jack in the book."

"Maybe you like the book. I like the boiler, and I think we was chumps to let that broad wander about like we did."

"Don't worry, she'll be mooching about that island for a week before anyone finds her. She'll get a chunk of publicity out of it and everything will look just like that—a gag. I tell you, Plunk, that was a swell idea. The cops won't give her a tumble. They run into a million gags by publicity-seekers like that every year."

"I still don't like it."

"Okay. What are we gonner do about it now? It's too late, and we had to get away quick, 'cause if that Griffon guy gets his hooks into us, we're goners."

"Well, don't let that Mick mug back there pull anything on you. He's a hostage, you understand? We may have to use him yet. I don't like that Griffon guy."

"I'd like to know how the hell the Mick got up there to No Man's Land," the man named Muggy growled. "Damnedest thing I ever heard of. He's the guy who took the case up to Yardley and was supposed to 'go up' in the taxi. I'll never forget Brassage's face when we dragged him in."

The pilot sniffed: "That's what gets me. He must have come in a boat, somehow, and hid the damn thing somewhere. You see, that's what gets my nanny. If that jane found that boat and got away, she could raise hell."

"Um," mumbled Muggy. "I'd like to go back and punch that Mick who says his name's Pulski, smack in the eye."

"Well," grinned Plunk Maheffey, "you got a good chance now. He's tied up tight as a drum back there."

JUST at that minute, however, Anton Brassage charged into the control pit. He was a sharp-featured man with long thin hands. He looked weary and haunted, and a full day's growth of beard did not help any. He was trying to talk, but somehow his mouth would not make any sound. Only his arms seemed to be able to indicate his terror.

"What the…?" Plunk Maheffey blarted out. "What's up?"

"It's that guy—the guy in the black bus. I just saw the plane a short distance below us. He's on us, I tell you."

"Well, what are you waiting for. Give him a packet from those lower turret guns."

Muggy Minturn, the co-pilot, slipped out of his seat, darted under the instrument board, and wriggled his way up into the forward gun turret. He warned the man behind the 40 mm Madsen to be on the lookout ready to give the black plane everything he could throw. Then he slipped back again and followed Brassage down the companionway past the small but compact radio compartment and came out in the main cabin.

"Where is he?" Minturn demanded, peering out a side window.

"You'll find out," laughed Barney from his uncomfortable position on top of a bomb locker. "If you guys got any brains, you'll turn right back and put this boiler down where you just took off from. You'll never get away from him."

"Shut up, mug!" Minturn snarled trying to peer back through the darkness.

"Look, there he is, climbing higher now," Brassage pointed. "See, there's the glare from his exhausts."

Minturn stood and studied the oncoming ship, then slipped back toward the upper-rear gun mounting. He climbed up on the dural platform, loaded the Browning guns, and waited. The gun was fitted to a cross-bar with a swivel attachment and the barrel fitted through a long narrow slot running through the center of the domed glass turret.

He drew a bead and let a wild screaming burst sing out toward the oncoming *Black Bullet*—only to see the flame pennons from the Avia's exhaust veer over and swing away.

"The swine!" he growled as he stepped back. Then he glared at Barney again. He stood thinking a minute, then whispered something to Brassage. For several minutes they consulted quietly and then Minturn went back to the gun turret and began dismantling the gun mounting. He then swung the revolving glass turret so that the opening was clear. The two halves of the dome folded down into slots in the side of the turret and left a normal open cockpit.

"Come on, mug," he said to Barney when he came back. "Up on your hocks. You're going outside for some air."

He yanked Barney up on his feet and steadied him while Brassage searched the side lockers for more rope.

Barney stood there, his mind thumping out ideas while Minturn released the bindings about his knees. The instant his legs were free he brought his knee up quickly and caught Muggy full under the chin.

"Gah-r-r-rg!" Minturn gulped and rolled over like a pole-axed steer.

Brassage stood terrified for a minute while Barney lunged at him, one shoulder down like a blocking back. Brassage yelled and went down in a heap with Barney on top of him. Brassage, terror-stricken, fought and clawed at Barney's face like a wild man and managed to gain time for Minturn, who had rolled over blinking, and bleeding from the mouth.

Barney's arms were still lashed behind him and he was fighting mainly with his knees and head. In no time he was a sorry mess of blood, but he still fought grimly.

"Muggy! Muggy!" Brassage screamed, as Minturn staggered to his feet. "Get him, Muggy!"

Barney got to his knees and poised for a crash at Muggy, but Muggy staggered at the last second and Barney, missing him, went crashing across the cabin to bash his head against a sharp dural girder.

Barney went out like a light, with a cruel gash opening across his forehead like a slowly grinning mouth.

Both Brassage and Minturn took a breather for a minute, then straggled to get the unconscious Barney to his feet. They managed to get him into the rear turret and then went back for another coil of rope.

Together they threaded the heavy rope through Barney's arms and brought the ends back into the cabin. Then hoisting him feet first, they rammed him up through the gun mounting and placed him outside, lengthwise upon the back of the fuselage. They laced him there securely and peered up at the black plane that hovered over them.

"There you are, guy," Brassage raged. "There's something to shoot at."

"You know," said Minturn, gasping, "I have an idea that bird up there might know who this mug is."

"I hope he does. He won't try any funny stuff then."

"But how the hell they worked all this I can't figure. You ran into a mug cold on West Street and kid him to deliver a bag to a doll in a theatre. You set him down on a ticker hoping to blow him to bits, but in about thirty hours he pops up again on an island about a hundred and fifty miles away. Not only that but somehow he manages to sick this bird on us again. There's something screwy, somewhere."

"Yeh? Well, how would you like to be tied up out there?" gagged Brassage.

"I still wish we wuz down okay at Nelson. Things have gone too smooth so far. It don't taste right to me yet, even though we got that egg trussed up out there."

"Well, let's go forward and put Jimbo to work with that howitzer of his. What the hell we got that cannon up there for, anyway?"

"I DON'T like this," the Griffon was saying through his phones to Miss Yardley. "There they are, but what can we do about it if Pulski's aboard?"

"It's certainly exciting so far. They'll have to come down for fuel some time, won't they?" the girl asked, peering ahead at the tank-plane over the pilot's shoulder.

"What do you think *we're* going to run on?" the Griffon asked with a smirk.

"I hadn't thought of that," the girl replied. "Look, they're firing at us again."

A shell from the 40 mm Madsen crashed near them, and Keen had to clear again. Then as he swerved away he caught the ominous outline of a figure lying flat on the top of the tank-plane cabin. Keen snarled, reached for his glasses.

"Here, snap those night-lens filters down and see what you make of that?" he said to the girl. But he had sensed already what it was, laying out there.

"It looks like a man—a body," the girl whispered. "Just a minute…. Yes…. It's Pulski. They've killed him and are trying to throw him overboard. Oh—!"

"Wait a minute," snapped the Griffon. "Wait a minute. He's not dead, is he? Look! His legs keep jerking up. They've tied him out there to hold us off, the dirty swine!"

"But look—that stain alongside the body. That might be blood. They've probably hurt him badly."

"They'd have to, to get him out there. I'll bet they knew they were in a fight," grinned the Griffon.

"But what can we do?" Miss Yardley pleaded. "We can't leave him out there."

"Sure! We'll just go down and clip him off. Nothing to it," moaned the Griffon, feeling helpless. "Just go down and clip him off. Any ideas?"

"Did you see *Whispering Wings?*" the girl said suddenly. "I wore this costume throughout most of the picture."

"No, I didn't see *Whispering Wings.* What do you think I am, a movie moron?"

"Well you really missed something. I'll bet I could pull it again."

"Pull what again?" said Keen still peering down toward the tank-plane.

"That mid-air change to get the plans of the Pacific fortifications the syndicate had stolen," the girl said with excitement.

The Griffon turned around sharply. "You mean to say you actually pulled something like that—no doubles?"

"Look here, young man," Miss Yardley said. "We can't get away with that these days. Most of that went out with the Keystone Cops. We have to do plenty of stunts. I had a parachute, of course, but it didn't show in the film because the action was 'shot' from the front."

"You think you could get down there and release Pulski?" the Griffon said hollowly.

"Why not? There's enough room on the back of that bus to stage a dance contest. Can you get me down there?"

"I can slip you into Pulski's vest pocket—if you've got the nerve," the Griffon said. "Here, you climb into my 'chute harness as soon as I can slip out of it. Then I'll drop my pontoons and give you something to work from. Take my gun and the one in the cockpit holster there behind you—and that big knife."

As he gave the girl these instructions, he was unfastening the straps of his harness and slipping his arms out of it. The girl took it and with a professional air adjusted the straps to fit her and buckled it over her suede leather coat and gabardine jodhpurs. Then she took the Griffon's kapok jacket and gun belt, slipped into them, and tucked the extra gun inside her jacket. The heavy hunting knife was slipped in a loop of the gun belt.

"Cut the ropes of his legs first," the Griffon advised. "Let him roll over a bit before you cut the rope that is holding him down. Understand?"

The girl nodded grimly and tightened the belt another notch.

"If you miss and go down, don't worry, I'll come down and pick you up. But don't cut him loose unless he is able to take care of himself."

"You watch me," the girl said gamely. "You didn't see *Whispering Wings,* eh? You think all pretty movie stars have doubles to take all their risks? Well, I'll show you, Mister Ginsberg-Griffon!"

"I'll swipe all of Pulski's photographs of you, if you get away with this one, baby!" beamed the Griffon, yanking the lever that lowered the pontoons. "I'll even go to see you in *Whispering Wings.*"

"Let's go!"

"Now look here. Once you make contact, I'll slam up front and blind them and give you plenty of time. If you get away with it, make them plant her down somewhere along the beach on Cape Cod, just this side of the Chatham Light, if possible. Then leave the rest to me."

"*You* leave it to *me*, Mister Griffon," the girl replied.

"All the best, sister!" the Griffon grinned, opening the rear portion of the cockpit top.

"Thanks. Here we go for *Whispering Wings* again," she smiled.

The Griffon steadied the plane while the girl clambered out onto the wing. He eased away from a long wild shot from the tank-plane's Madsen and watched her slip down to the pontoon. In a minute, her head appeared again just forward of the leading edge, and he knew she was crouching on the port pontoon where she could lower herself from the forward strut and drop to the back of the plane below.

Keen swerved around, dropped below the tail of the tank-plane, and slowly lowered his flaps. Then gradually he eased her forward well out of line from the tank-plane's front gun and crept up to the knife-like tail-fin. The seconds seemed to crawl by like hours, but suddenly he flipped his nose up to clear the fin and then eased back on the throttle. The *Black Bullet* seemed to hover a second, and a shot rang out from somewhere up front, sending a streak of fire hissing past the top of the black amphibian.

There was a slight jerk—and the Griffon knew Miss Yardley had slipped off. He rammed the throttle forward, the *Black Bullet* leaped away, and the Griffon pulled two levers.

One drew the flaps up and the other released a blinding cloud of black smoke that completely enveloped the tank-plane. He could hear the tank-plane's cannon barking at him somewhere behind. Streaks of saffron flame spat past him, but he had to stay there to give the girl a chance to release Barney and get him inside again.

He hung on as long as he dared, then swerved clear and climbed like a madman. He circled wide, came around again, and looked below. There was no phosphorus signal flare down on the water, neither was there a bound figure kicking on the back of the tank plane.

"Holy Moses!" he gasped. "She got away with it!"

MISS YARDLEY made a perfect contact, landed lightly on the tips of her toes, sprawled forward, and clutched at the recumbent Barney, who simply gagged: "What the hell?"

"You all right?" Miss Yardley husked into his ear.

"Swell! The air's lovely. What the hell?" Barney gagged.

Miss Yardley asked no more questions. With a quick flip she severed the cords that bound Barney's ankles. Then she hung on with one hand and helped him turn slightly with the other. Yanking the knife out of her teeth she slashed again and shoved Barney forward. He dropped down inside of the ship with a thud, and she plunged in after him.

She sniffed, still choking from the smoke screen that the Griffon had laid over the plane to hide their coup. Then she got to her knees, ripping out a gun. A figure charged at them and she pulled the trigger.

A report rang out, and the man stumbled forward, collapsed in a heap at her feet.

"You're still playing *Whispering Wings,* eh, Miss Yardley?" Barney gagged, as he clambered over the body of Anton Brussage. "Gimme one o' them guns and I'll join you."

He snatched at the extra gun she lugged out of her jacket and struggled forward. Muggy Mintern came out of the radio room and started to hurl a large bar of iron. Barney stopped him cold with a shot that spun him around twice and hurled him into a corner.

"Tie him up. Never mind the blood!" Barney yelled.

"Mister Ginsberg said to make them put it down along the beach this side of Chatham Light—on the Cape," the girl screeched.

"Okay! Where's that other guy?" yelled Barney, reaching inside the radio cabin. The girl heard a scream and a heavy thud, and Barney came out with the big automatic clutched by the barrel. He had clubbed someone into submission.

"And rope that bird up too," he barked, jerking his thumb toward the open door. "I'll send another through for you in a minute. A Mister Plunk Maheffey—an old friend of yours."

"He's no friend of mine," Miss Yardley grinned, "but I'll be glad to slip him a little attention."

Barney ripped the control-pit door wide, shoved his homely mug through.

Maheffey jerked around, glared into the muzzle of a big blue-black automatic.

"Okay, Maheffey. Lock them controls a minute and come out fer yer bindings. An' what's more, I'll relieve yer of the little black book—you know, that nice leather-bound book yer have tucked away in yer shirt there."

"How the hell—?" Maheffey started to say. But Barney suddenly spun quickly, fired toward the floor of the cockpit where Jimbo was emerging from the forward turret. There was a flash of flame in return from that opening below the instrument board. Maheffey let out a scream, plunged forward over the wheel.

Barney snatched quickly and pulled him off. He drew the wheel back gently and eased the ship out of her sudden dive.

"Too bad, Jimbo," he muttered, "but you were just a bit too late and you hit the wrong guy."

He held the wheel steady with one hand. Jimbo, the cannon operator, was now dead in the companionway that ran between the control pit and his front turret.

"Okay, Miss Yardley," yelled Barney. "They're all accounted for. We'll go down. There's Chatham Light." He fumbled with the controls for some time and finally found the touch. He reached over and jerked at the wave-length lever on the set near his left elbow and picked up the hand-mike.

"Okay, Ginsberg," he reported. "Where'll I set her down?"

"Along that stretch of beach just above Harwich there. How did it go?" came the reply from the *Black Bullet*.

"Swell. Didn't I tell you Miss Yardley had the stuff?"

"How do you feel?"

"Ouch! What a head! I hope you left that—that container in the locker, there."

"It's all there—except the label," laughed Keen. *"Put her down along that stretch and well-up to clear the tide."*

WITHIN ten minutes two planes slipped down out of the darkness and rumbled along the hard-packed sands toward the shadows thrown by the high cliffs. Keen was out first, leaving his engine ticking over. He hurried to the cabin door of the tank-plane.

"Come on! Move fast! Here comes a Coast Guard guy down the beach. We had better leave the tank-plane and get Miss Yardley back to—well, somewhere near a railroad station."

"They're all tied up in there tight as drums, those that are still alive. Here's the book they were all so keen about," barked Barney.

"Give it to Miss Yardley—and for heaven's sake, hurry!"

Reluctantly they turned away after giving the massive tank-plane a last look-over. Then they ran toward the *Black Bullet* and clambered aboard. Miss Yardley and Barney had to huddle together in the back compartment while the Griffon took off before the amazed eyes of the Coast Guardsman who had hurried up.

A short time later the *Black Bullet* dropped down on the darkened runway of the Providence, R.I., airport, ran along for a few yards, then hurriedly discharged a young girl dressed in jodhpurs and a suede coat. Then the black plane raced away again and disappeared into the darkness.

"BUT I tell you I have no idea who they were," Miss Doreen Yardley was saying to John Scott the next morning after she had freshened herself up on the ride down from Providence. "All I know is that they said their names were—"

"—Ginsberg and Pulski," broke in Drury Lang. "We know that part of it by heart. What we want to know is who they really are and where they come from."

"Ginsberg and—" Miss Yardley started again.

Drury Lang blew up.

"Yes…. Yes. But where did they come from? And where did they go to? That's what we want to know."

"Well, I first saw this man Pulski behind the stage at the Palace Royal that afternoon. He delivered what I believed to be my jewel case—it had been brought out from Hollywood."

"Hollywood? What the deuce was this guy Pulski doing out in Hollywood?"

"I don't know whether he was out there at all."

"But you just said your case came out from Hollywood and that this Pulski guy delivered it."

"Well he did. But he got it from a friend of mine named Brassage, who somehow has disappeared."

"Brassage? Why, that's the name of the guy who stole the case containing the formula—the guy they found dead in the tankplane last night out at Cape Cod. What the devil does all this mean?"

"Don't ask me. They told me to hand this book to you. I don't know what it's all about. But here it is."

"Look here, Miss Yardley," Scott broke in quietly. "Did you ever meet, or know, a man by the name of Barney O'Dare?"

"Who's that? Sounds like a character in a musical comedy."

"You never met a man by the name of O'Dare?"

"Never."

"All you know is that you were kidnapped, taken on board a cabin cruiser to an island off Cape Cod, and abandoned. Then you were picked up by a man named Ginsberg who flew a black plane of some sort. From there you were taken to the Providence airport and left in the middle of the runway. Then they gave you this book and told you to deliver it to me here in New York. Is that it?" asked John Scott, searching Miss Yardley with his eyes.

"That's it exactly."

"What's the matter?" said Scott slowly. "Your last picture, *Whispering Wings*, not going so well?"

"I think it's going swell. They're standing in line at the Palace Royal right now."

"Well, you don't suppose we're falling for any such story as that do you?"

"I don't care what you do."

"Well, considering that the plane was abandoned somewhere on Cape Cod, reasonably intact, and that we have recovered this important formula, we'll forget that publicity yarn."

"What about my jewelry?" Miss Yardley said. "Do you think I *threw* it away?"

"Some of you movie people would do anything for a headline. Besides, I suppose it's insured, isn't it. Let the insurance dicks worry about that. But if you ever meet a guy by the name of O'Dare, and you recognize him, you tip us off, and *we'll* get you some *real* publicity."

"Even if I could, I wouldn't pull a dirty trick like that," laughed Miss Yardley. "Besides, I'm going back to Hollywood tomorrow. Things are too hot here in the east."

"Yeh, ya can't get doubles to take the bumps for you out here, can you, Miss Yardley?" smirked Lang.

The girl went out with a joyous laugh in her voice, and Lang wondered what she meant when she said: "You're right, Hawk-shaw!"

"YOU heard what I said," barked Keen, as Barney suffered the first-aid ministrations to his forehead. "You're packing a bag at once and getting out of here as soon as you can get. Go any-where—fast. And lay low for two or three weeks. But send me a telegram, just so I can show it to old Lang. He still thinks you were mooching about New York when that taxi blew up."

"Well, he's right," gurgled Barney, gripping the neck of an O'Doul's Dew bottle.

"Sure, but we don't want him to know it. By the way, why did you stop me from firing on that plane the first time we saw it the other night?"

"I don't quite know now. Irish intuition, I suppose. You see, the day before when that mug was riding uptown with me to take that brown case in to Miss Yardley, he pulled out a wad of papers from his inside pocket to write her a note. With those papers was a photograph of the tank-plane, an' naturally I wondered what it was. I got a good look at it because it fell on the floor of the taxi and I picked it up."

"I still don't get it."

"Well, when I first saw that bus that night, I suddenly got it into my nut that Miss Yardley was a prisoner on board. When I left you after we got back, I went back to New York and tried to find out where she was—just a silly hunch. Then I saw the papers—all about her being missing, and the fact that her car was found abandoned down near Barclay Street."

"But what gave you the idea she was on board?"

"Well, soon after I got out of that taxi, I heard the explosion and hurried along with the mob and saw that it was the same taxi I had been riding in. I realized at once that something was queer. I didn't know what to do about it, and I figured that if I told the cops, they'd question me and finally they would ring Miss Yardley in on it."

"So you kept quiet to shield her. Cripes! You must be in love with her."

"Shut up! You know I don't like cops. Anyway, I cleared off, but I somehow couldn't forget the picture of that crazy plane and the more I thought about it, the more I figured that this guy Brassage was going to use it to kidnap Miss Yardley... for some cock-eyed reason."

"Well, you were only partly right. How did you find out that she had been held a prisoner and finally rushed away in a motor boat?"

"Gee, that was funny. When I found out about her being missing and her car being left down there on West Street, I took a wander down that way and saw the cops going over the car for fingerprints, and all that bunk. Then I cleared off again and further down West Street I ran into a drunk who had a dump down under one of the piers—a dock rat, if ever there was one."

"So what?"

"Well, he's sittin' there staring at a twenty dollar bill he said some guys had given him for letting them use his shed. I kinder gabbed with him for a while and then got the story. These guys had blown in late that afternoon and they had a girl with them who was dressed in men's pants. I got the idea at once that this was Miss Yardley, because she still had on the costume she wore on the stage—the same one she used in the film *Whispering Wings*. And then I really got hot.

"I found out that they had inquired about this island, No Man's Land, and how far it was. They had a boat come around and left about ten o'clock."

"Why didn't you call me?"

"I spent so much time getting it all straight with this guy and getting him drunker so that he wouldn't talk to anyone else. Then it was too late to call you. I did try once, but you didn't answer. Cripes, how you can sleep!"

"But the next morning?"

"I tried twice again, but you were out, I guess. So I tore about getting a boat and then I realized that you might go down to see old Scott. I saw you go in, but was too late to stop you. And I didn't dare call Scott's number."

"You were quite right."

"Anyway, I knew you'd be coming out, and the best thing I knew was to leave that note for you, and beat it, for fear you might be shadowed later. I got a boat and got up there, but they nailed me when I was foundering around in the darkness. Miss Yardley recognized me and I told her you would be there. I used your 'Ginsberg' name, of course, and slipped her my flashlight to signal you.

"Well, it all worked out okay but we were certainly taking chances."

"That's the fun of it, ain't it?" laughed Barney. "Now what do I have to do?"

"Get out of here. Take a train for anywhere about 500 miles away and then send me a telegram. Stay away for about two weeks until this gash heals a trifle and then you can ease back. But for heaven's sake act drunk when you arrive."

"That's easy," grinned Barney. "Wasn't I 'tanked' up for quite a while last night?"

"One more gag like that and I'll— Well, get the devil out of here. I've got a paper to prepare. But stay away from Miss Yardley—for you'll run afoul of Scott and Lang if you don't."

"What a gal! What a gal!" clucked Barney. Then he suddenly turned and pointed an accusing finger at Keen. "And by the way, a couple of my best photos of Miss Yardley are missing. Would you know where they are?"

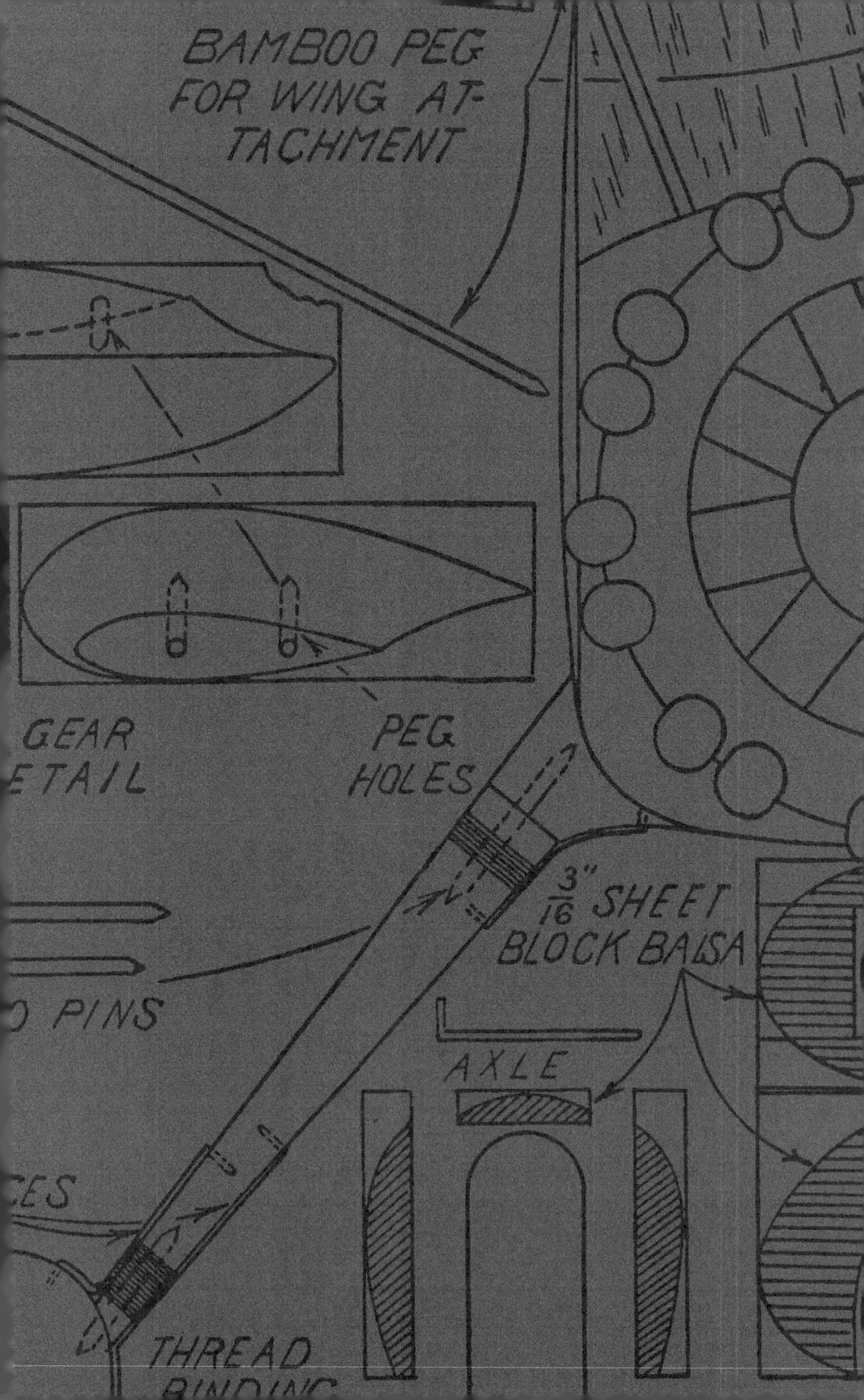

BAMBOO PEG
FOR WING AT-
TACHMENT

GEAR
ETAIL

PEG
HOLES

PINS

CES

3"/16 SHEET
BLOCK BALSA

AXLE

THREAD
BINDING

Twin-Engine Treachery

THE CLOCK in the Metropolitan Tower boomed the hour of nine. But it might as well have been midnight for all the life and movement that was to be seen in that drab, dirty Hell's Half-Acre under the Brooklyn Bridge. It was drizzling and bitter cold for the time of the year and the dirty unkempt figure huddled on a box against the corner of a tenement sniffled and drew his ragged clothes tighter.

Slatternly women, in coarse garb and clacking a coarser speech, shuffled on, ignoring the derelict. There were dozens of bums about at this time of night. The haggard fellow on the box only jerked his chin and winced as the last thud of the Metropolitan gong rang out. Even the tone of the bells seemed to grate on his torn nerves.

Hungry and cold, he continued to sit there, motionless—until a lone figure shuffled past, glanced his way for a second, then carelessly tossed away the best part of a cigarette butt.

For a few tense seconds the down-and-outer stared at the glowing butt, then abruptly he darted out, picked it up, ripped away the lip-dampened end. From the remainder of the butt, he drew a long and satisfying drag and exhaled with a sigh of contentment.

Then fingering the end he had carefully torn away, he slit the paper with his thumb-nail and drew out a strip of tissue that had been rolled inside. Spreading it out, he read: *"Caronni at Scallaci's."*

When the footsteps of the man who had dropped the cigarette died out, the derelict peered about, fingered inside his trousers waistband, and drew out a coin. With a low grunt, he got to his feet again and steadying himself, he wandered along the street, keeping well in the shadows on his right.

A DINGY dive with a bar, a few dusty brewery advertisements, and a picture of General Balbo—that was Scallaci's. There, at a small table in the back, sat Scallaci himself. He was a small fat fellow with a moon face, three chins, and enough hair for four men. It was said that he had never been behind his own bar, but from where he sat he could see the cash register and answer a wall phone without getting up.

A few seconds after the Metropolitan clock boomed nine, four men came in and sat down at one of the dirty round tables. Without instructions, the hatchet faced man behind the bar began to break the straw on a Chianti bottle and set out four glasses. Scallaci then took an envelope from his pocket and without moving, flipped it down the room, where it was caught by one of the men who had just arrived.

While the glasses were being brought to the table, the man opened the envelope and took out the small sheet of paper inside. The message was written in Italian. After a quick glance at it, the man handed it across the table and raised his glass.

He said something in Italian and nodded to Scallaci.

At that instant the door opened and a narrow-shouldered man with denim trousers, a leather wind-breaker, and a face that was covered with grease and dirt shuffled up to the bar. The four Italians glared at him and looked back at Scallaci.

"Gimme a double one, Tony," the newcomer asked. "Damned cold out on the river tonight."

"Yeh. What tug did you say you wuz on, mister?"

"The *Emily-K,* one of the Morton fleet. We just shoved four railroad barges around from the Jersey side to the Long Island slips."

"Oh yeh, the *Emily-K,*" said Tony. "One of the new ones, huh?"

"Yeh, a new one. Business pickin' up, I guess."

The door opened again and another man lurched in. Tony glanced at him, took a beer glass, and stood over the cheap tap. He knew his customers. The man drew his coat together with his dirty hand, put his fist down on the bar, and slowly opened his fingers. A quarter rolled out, and he said: "No, not that swill. Gimme rye."

Tony took the beer glass and set it behind him, then selected a quart bottle that had no label on it. He shoved it toward the derelict and turned to select a small glass. The derelict stared at the taller glass in the hands of the tug-boat engineer at his side.

The tug-boat hand, gave him a cold glance, then stared down at the quarter on the bar. He put his drink down and picked the coin up and stared at it, while the derelict watched him, a new cold fear in his eye.

"Hey, Tony," the tug-boat man said, dropping the quarter on the bar, "you ain't taking that clucker, are you?"

Tony grabbed the bottle before the derelict could pour out his drink and snatched at the leaden colored quarter. He weighed it in his palm, then turned to try it on the marble slab in front of the cash register. It replied with a dull leaden thonk.

"Beat it, monkey!" Tony spat. "What the hell you trying to shove at me? You gotter do better than that."

The derelict took the coin back, stared at it, then turned on the tug-boat engineer.

"Wise guy, eh? You got dough to buy a double, and you put the zinger on me. How about one for me?"

"You had more than your share already. Scram!" the tug-boat man snarled.

But with a quick movement, the derelict flipped his hand and the double whiskey went across the bar and splashed full in Tony's face. The barkeep let out a roar, covered his eyes with his hands, and began screaming. The raw liquor almost blinded him. He pawed at his face and saw the derelict duck a wild swing from the tug-boat man, then counter with a short hooking right that lifted the seaman to his toes. The boatmen let out a gasp, tottered back, and rolled among the Italians at the round table.

There was a quick scuffle, and Tony tried to leap over the bar with a mallet. But still half blind, he was not quick enough. The table was upset, drinks were scattered, and the Italians were on the bottom of a wild mêlée. By the time Tony was clear over, the two belligerents were crowding their way through the door. And by the time Tony got to the door, they were outside and had completely disappeared in the darkness and drizzle.

The Italians struggled to their feet, arguing volubly. Scallaci shouted into the telephone. One of the Italians was standing with a dazed expression on his face and an empty envelope in his hand.

"There ain't no such tug as the *Emily-K* in the Morton fleet," growled Scallaci as he hung up the receiver.

THREE blocks away from Scallaci's stood a blue Duesenberg roadster with the top and side curtains up. It was sheltered in the driveway of a trucking yard. The man in the denim overalls got there first and had the motor running by the time the derelict came shuffling up.

He let the clutch in even before the derelict closed the door; and they turned west, headed up First Avenue, and cut over to get on the Manhattan Bridge. Once well into Long Island, they let her out along the Sunrise Highway.

Neither spoke a word until they reached Jamaica. Then—

"Get it?" said the derelict.

"What, that sock in the jaw or the letter?"

"The letter, of course."

"In my side pocket. An' don't forget, next time, *I* do the socking. You get up these acts, but I'm always the fall guy."

The derelict did not answer but twisted and fumbled for the sheet of paper in his driver's pocket. He pulled it out, opened it under the dash light.

The driver glanced at it, and laughed aloud.

"Say, it's a good thing *you* went to school. What language is that?"

"Italian, which I don't know much about. But I can work it out when we get in. What's the time?"

"Nine-thirty."

"Step on it. It says something about midnight here."

The Duesenberg roared louder and hurtled past Freeport, Amityville, Babylon and Islip in its mad rush to the far end of Long Island.

But in spite of all the speed it was just after eleven before Kerry Keen and Barney O'Dare pulled into Graylands.

KEEN sweated with an Italian dictionary for nearly half an hour, but eventually he translated the message. He fretted over it while he climbed into another and much neater outfit. Then he wolfed two sandwiches and a bottle of ale while Barney sucked on a bottle of O'Doul's Dew and munched an apple.

"It's midnight over Block Island," Keen explained, reading his translation again, "and something about a 'pirate.' I can't figure that one. Which of those fellows was Caronni?"

"The shortest one. He's a speed pilot and is said to be top man over there with seaplanes. He brought them those two distance records."

"The whole thing sounds screwy to me," Keen argued.

"It did when I first overheard them talking to Scallaci. But I'm telling you, that boiler can't enter the race."

"Well, she's on tap for it nevertheless."

"Yeh, but there's two of them. One has three engines and the other has one. Look 'em up in *Janes*."

"No time now. Everything ready?"

"Everything. Let's get going. But remember, I'm not the fall guy this time if anything happens."

"You can be the first one out. How's that?"

"I'll bet I'll be losing. My jaw still hoits!"

"Quit squawking and get going," snapped Keen.

They were in full flying kit now, black coveralls, kapok jackets and parachutes. Barney led the way down the stairs and into the secret hangar.

The *Black Bullet* was a beautiful glistening thing when they turned on the lights. Barney stood aside while Keen climbed up on the step and climbed in. He started the big Avia motor and held her down with the Skoda muffler. They doused the lights, Barney yanked a hidden switch, and the front of the hangar folded outward, splitting the sham rock-garden and giving egress upon the wide lawn.

Keen drew his scarlet mask over his face, adjusted his helmet, and set his goggles. Then he let the Avia have it gently and the purring plane crawled out of the hangar and stopped in the shelter of the heavy grape arbor. Barney set the switch which closed the doors and darted out to the *Bullet*. Then while Keen checked the controls he climbed in and drew the cockpit cover back.

The *Black Bullet* stole quietly down the gentle slope on her amphibian gear and then crossed the narrow stretch of hard-packed sand alongside the boathouse. Slowly she eased into the water and Keen set the pontoons for a water take-off. She purred away silently, disappeared in the darkness.

As Keen cleared all possible traffic and was about to give her the gun he caught the sound of a motor somewhere in the sky above. He held her quiet, looked up. His eyes quickly caught the dim outline of a flying boat of some sort. It was hurtling along at high speed for a machine of that type, and Keen's eyes drew together in narrow slits.

"Better get going," Barney said getting his rear guns out from under the cowling.

Keen fed it to her and the *Bullet* hoisted herself up on the step. She caught beautifully on top of a roller and leaped into the clear. Keen held her steady and zipped across the top of the dark water until she had speed, then hoiked her hard and climbed like mad.

The strange seacraft was well ahead now and Keen flipped the flaps for climbing. He wanted height, the distance would come later. He checked everything, then realized that the seaplane was heading straight for Block Island. The clock showed 11:58.

Two minutes to midnight!

BELOW, the waters of Long Island Sound and the Atlantic were split asunder by the shining silver blade of Montauk Light. Could one slide along that beam for a distance of about fifteen miles when it was swinging out to the northeast, he would drop grace-fully on Dickens Point of Block Island.

But Keen avoided that betraying beam. He cut wide toward the open sea and drew every ounce of power out of the Avia.

"What are we in for this time?" Barney mumbled into his Gosport tube.

"You have as much idea as I," replied Keen. "All I know is that those thugs have some sort of a date with a 'pirate' at midnight.

If I only knew something about Italian," he mooned, peering about. "But say," he yelled. "There she is again. What the devil kind of a bus is it?"

"Looks like the German Dornier Monsun seaplane that's entered in the Lindbergh race. What's she doing up here at this time of night?"

"Probably getting in some night radio test work."

"Like hell! Look at that—*look!*"

Barney let out a choked bleat, and Keen turned, fully expecting to see the Mick toppled over with a bullet through his head. It sounded like that, anyway. Instead he saw his man pointing frenziedly and wrenching his guns out.

Keen tried to figure out what he had spotted. Then suddenly he caught a trickle of gunfire. The flying boat above had found a target—a speeding biplane of some kind which carried land-gear.

"Take it easy!" Keen called. "Let's see what's going on."

"Take it easy hell! That guy's firing on that Vought Corsair!"

"Corsair?... Corsair?" muttered Keen slowly. "Holy Maria! That's it....Corsair...'pirate'....That's what they meant. A Vought Corsair!"

But Barney was not figuring what anything meant. All he could see was a high wing monoplane flying boat that was hammering a wicked fire at a government biplane. His rear guns chattered as Keen tried to get into the fray. In reply the raider slapped two streams of lead back at the *Black Bullet* and Keen had to cut away and try for a position under her.

Meanwhile the Navy-marked Corsair was fighting gamely to get away. But its pilot was outgunned and the flying boat had speed to spare. Keen saw all this as he tangoed for a position.

"Look! Look! He's got the Vought!" yelled Barney as Keen swung around again to dive upon the flying boat. True enough, the withering fire had taken away the Vought's struts and now its top wing was crumbling. The pilot struggled in an attempt to get clear, but a gunner aboard the sea craft hammered a wicked blast broadside into the Vought and the Navy man slumped back.

"The dirty devil!" gasped Keen. "Did you see that, Barney? They wouldn't let him out to take to the silk!"

But Barney was trying to get a shot at the wildly stunting flying boat. And he was finding it difficult, for they were picking at him from all angles. The craft simply bristled with guns. Keen had to cut away again and watch the tumbling Vought spiral down to its finish.

"What sort of a crate is that?" Keen yelled.

"I don't know. It's got twin engines in tandem. But it looks like the Italian record-breaking Cant Z.501, though that bus only has one power plant."

"Well, never mind. Let's see what we can do for that poor devil. Wonder what they wanted him out of the sky for," Keen continued as he started to spiral the *Bullet* down, uncertain in his mind what course to take. He would have liked to have taken a real shot at that flying boat, but he wondered about the Navy pilot, and what was so interesting about him. He decided that the Navy man was more important.

The Vought was in a flat spin now and Keen breathed a sigh of relief. She would not hit so hard that way and there might be a chance if the pilot had not received a fatal bullet wound.

THE BLACK BULLET was circling down watching for the final smash, when suddenly from out of nowhere the flying boat came hammering at them again. A gunner was standing up in the bulbous nose with two guns ripping a fiery spatter across the sky. Another gunner, set in the center-section of the wing, added to the torrent of lead.

The *Black Bullet* took a wicked slamming about the wing tips, and Keen swore as he again curled away. They were getting nowhere with this baby.

Barney ripped out a volley of oaths that would have burned the brass knocker off a door. He sprayed the flying boat with a counter slam. But the flying boat came on and almost rammed the *Black Bullet* cold.

They had to clear once more and Keen now tried to figure out their tactics. They seemed to be stalling for time. They swung back again, losing height but still keeping up the fight.

With a lunge, Keen rolled the *Black Bullet* over and hammered full tilt at the flying boat, but he could only hold his dive a short time, for that nose gunner was putting up a curtain of lead that was no confetti party in any language.

Keen whipped up again and screamed over the flying boat which circled lower and lower. Off to the left, the Vought was just making her last three whirls. Keen kept clear and watched her slither in with a spray of foam and glint of wrenched metal against the glare from a fractured exhaust ring. Then, before either Keen or Barney could figure out what was happening, the flying boat darted down and circled low over the wreckage. Keen made a move to go after them and Barney yelled his head off to get closer so that he could take another poke at them.

But things happened fast from then on. The flying boat was down on the surface of the water, and a small searchlight was directed on the wreckage of the Vought.

"Wait a minute," argued Keen. "Maybe they're going to try to get the bird out."

"If they do," blarted Barney, "it won't be because they want to give the guy a break. He must have something they want aboard that boiler."

"You're in great form tonight, eh, Barney?" Keen remarked peering down. "You must have had several doubles of O'Doul's."

Keen then nosed their sleek ship down like a hawk. He directed the craft dead on the bobbing flying boat. Things were indistinct, but it was apparent that they were making some sort of a contact with the wreckage. They were after something.

The *Black Bullet's* guns now spoke and four streams of fire slapped the water around the flying boat. In reply the two gunners hammered back at the *Black Bullet* and again made Keen pull out. As he wrenched the black amphibian up, Barney smashed two more streams at them. But now they began to move quickly away. By the time Keen had the *Black Bullet* ready to engage them again, they were off the water and were heading around for Montauk Light.

Keen followed for a short distance, hammering away at the racing flying boat. But to all intents and purposes the ship was indestructible. Suddenly he turned back and decided to have a look at the Vought himself.

"We'll look that other baby up later, if he's the German Dornier entered in the Lindbergh race," Keen growled. "But I want to see what happened to that Navy man."

He drew the lever which lowered the pontoons again so that he could make a water landing. He could see the lights of a Coast Guard cutter racing up from somewhere off Fisher's Island. But he had to satisfy himself about that pilot in the Vought Corsair—and what he was carrying that was so important.

THEY nosed down fast and did a high speed landing that almost ripped the bottoms out of the pontoons. But Keen held her steady and let her skim down the side of a roller so that she came up gently within a few yards of the wreckage of the Vought. Keen was over the side and standing on a pontoon with a coil of rope and a grapnel hook. With a careful swing he caught the wreckage with the hook and drew the *Black Bullet* in carefully. The Vought was badly smashed up. One wing was off and had floated clear. The engine had somehow broken the main bearers and had rammed the forward portion of the body back so that it had crunched up the cockpit. The instrument board was badly cracked and most of the instruments had no glass in their dials.

The pilot was hunched over the back of the pilot's seat, in just the position he had assumed after that burst that had knocked him back into the cockpit. His hands were down and submerged in the water that nobbed about in the lower portion of the cockpit and fuselage. There was no one in the front portion of the cockpit, and it was evident that the man had been alone in the Vought.

Keen gave the man and his equipment a quick look-over. Nothing about his person had been touched. His coverall was buttoned all the way up. The pockets were still buttoned and there was nothing in any of them. Whatever it was they had been after, had evidently been in both a convenient place and a convenient form, enabling them to make a quick contact and a smart get-away.

A soggy, bullet-slashed map still hung in the clips. Keen ripped it out, stuffed it in his pocket.

Barney was yelling his head off! "Come on. The Coast Guard guys are hot-footing it for us. Get off that pile of old iron, will you?"

Keen clambered back on the pontoon. He shoved the *Black Bullet* clear, then ducked as a shell screamed over the top of the plane. Barney kicked the starter from his seat and Keen climbed in through the open top. Without wasting any time, they moved away as two more shells crashed over their cockpit. It was then that the blinding glare of a Navy searchlight caught them full in its beam.

"Lordy! Now they *have* seen us," gasped Keen. "Old Lang will be after the Griffon now for certain."

The Avia dug in and the *Bullet* took off as two more shells crashed too near for comfort. But they got away safely and raced out to sea again to cover their tracks before turning back toward their Long Island retreat.

"You were right, Barney," Keen remarked after a long reflection. "That thing must have been the German Dornier—the Do.18 which is entered in the Lindbergh race. She had two engines set in tandem."

"Yeh, but there was something funny about it. The Dornier does not have wing pontoons and this ship did. I saw them plainly. The German boat has two stub wings stuck out of the side of the hull from which the main wing is braced. But no wing pontoons."

"You might have made a mistake, depending on the angle from where you saw them," Keen added. "What sort of engines do you figure they were?"

"I couldn't tell. The front one was blotted out by the gunner who kept those damned pop-guns going so much. I could hardly tell what type motor they were using there, but the rear one certainly was an in-line of some sort."

"Well, if the rear one was a stationary in-line, it's bucks to bon-bons the front one is, too. It looks like the Dornier to me, Barney."

"I wouldn't bet on it."

"Well, let's get back. We'll be hearing from Lang in the morning."

"I'll bet we'll hear from him within ten minutes after we get in," Barney roared. "They'll be a swell stink about this."

"I'm afraid so. And the worst of it is that the Coast Guard actually saw us. They've never really seen this bus before. We'll have to watch our step from now on."

"Well, watch your step when you put her down this time. You almost bent her bottom on that last go-down."

KEEN was careful about his landing this time. From a height of about 3,000 feet he slipped in his Skoda mufflers and soothed the 1,000 h.p. Avia down to a lullaby purr. Then he set the flaps for a steep glide, eased the pontoons down again for a water landing, and checked every section of the Sound for traffic.

"Looks okay," muttered Barney, preparing to move fast.

"All set," agreed Keen.

The beautiful but slightly battered *Black Bullet* glided down, and Keen let her in with a minimum of slipstream whistle. He planted her carefully and let her purr through the night mists toward his boathouse.

Once he had her with her pontoons pressing the sandy beach, he adjusted the lever again and the tail end of the floats tilted upward and brought the wheel gear into position. Then he ran her up along the hard-packed sand and into the shadows of the arbor.

Barney leaped out, quickly pulled the king-pins, and let the wings fold back. Then he trotted up toward the false rock garden— and went sprawling on his face.

"What the—?" he gasped, leaping to his feet.

Then he hurtled quickly like a ferret and grappled with a man who lay on the grass. But almost at once he realized that the man was already either dead or badly injured.

He got to his knees, jerked the man to a sitting position.

In the half light he recognized the man's features and let out a gasp. He quickly felt his pulse and lowered him again.

"It's Lang—Drury Lang!" he husked into Keen's ear.

"Good Lord!" Keen gulped. "What the devil is he doing here?"

"Don't ask me. What shall I do with him? Chuck him in the Sound?"

"Don't be an ass! You carry him around to the front and prop him up on a porch chair. I'll put this tub away and will see you at the front. Are you sure he's 'out?'"

"He's got a lump just above his ear that would have made an elephant climb a tree. He's out, all right."

"That's a break, anyway. Push off with him to the porch, and don't talk if he comes to before I get around to you."

Barney went back, picked Lang up with a fireman's hoist, and staggered across the wide lawn with him. Meanwhile, Keen ran the *Bullet* inside, closed the doors, and quickly clambered out of his flying kit. Then he hurried to his room and with lightning moves began slipping into a dress suit. Within three minutes he was completely transformed from an airman to a dapper young man-about-town. He coolly lit a cigarette, sauntered out, and calmly made his way down the wide stairway that led to the reception hall.

With a last quick glance at himself in a long mirror, he allowed a hint of a smile to curl one corner of his mouth.

On the porch he could hear Barney talking quietly to Lang, but he was getting no answers. He opened the door after snapping a switch that flooded the veranda and stifled a gasp as he noticed that somehow Barney had also divested himself of his flying kit and stood bending over Lang clad in his neat chauffeur's livery.

"What is it, Barney?" Keen cried in a startled tone. "Who have you there?"

"It's.... It's Mister Lang, sir," Barney explained in mock anguish. "I found him laying out there on the lawn."

"On the lawn? How in Heaven's name did he get there?"

THEY soon had Lang laid out on a large sofa in Keen's study. Barney tramped off for some hot water and a first-aid kit, while Keen quietly examined the wound over Lang's ear. It was a bad one.

Barney returned with towels, hot water, a bottle of brandy and a complete first-aid kit. Together they went to work and dressed the wound, washing it carefully and sterilizing the gash. Lang began to shift about.

"Crack some ice and stuff it in that rubber ice-bag, Barney," Keen ordered. "Hello, Lang, how are you feeling?"

The Department of Justice man trembled all over, squinted a second or two then closed his eyes again.

"Lousy!" he muttered.

Keen made him more comfortable and Barney placed the ice bag behind his ear.

"When the devil did you get here?" demanded Keen.

"Where the hell were you?" Lang came back, "and what did you sock me like that for?"

"Me...? Me, sock you? Why you old fool, we just came in, and we found your car out front in the driveway. I didn't sock you."

"Who did?"

"How should we know. We saw your car and realized that you must be around somewhere. Barney went around outside after he put my car away."

"Your... car away? Why you damned liar, it was in the garage when I got here."

"That was the other one. I have two you know."

"Yeh?... That's funny. I only looked in the first section. Wow, what a noggin! Who socked me, anyway? You got any watchmen around here?"

"No, just Barney and I. We came in from town, saw your car down there, and—"

"Yeh, you said all that. But who the heck smacked me? I was just taking a gander about the dump when—well, all I know is that someone biffed me and I woke up in here."

"Didn't you hear our car?" asked Keen with a glance at Barney. They had to find out how much Lang had seen.

"Don't remember anything since I started around those bushes—until I woke up in here."

Behind Lang's back, Barney and Keen continued to exchange glances. How much of what he was saying could be accepted as the truth, and how much did he actually know about Graylands and the secret hangar? How long could they stall him off concerning the car? Would the effect of the blow keep him from uncovering the amazing game they had been playing for years?

BUT what was even more important was: "Who had smacked Lang, and why? And where was the man?"

All these and many more questions popped into Keen's mind as he carefully worked out on Lang.

"What the deuce were you after around here at this time of night?" demanded Keen, taking a new tack.

"Never mind that," Lang muttered screwing around to get a more comfortable position. "I was just keeping track of you. I'd been calling you ever since about six o'clock and couldn't raise you either here or in the city. Where the hell was you, anyway?"

"Oh, we popped into town to see some friends off on the *Georgic*."

"Who?"

"A very dear friend—Chief Inspector Sir Hubert Beamish, of Scotland Yard. He had been consulting me concerning some ballistics problems the British police have been encountering because of a flood of cheap Belgian automatic pistols that have been picked up in the Limehouse district."

"You said 'friends!'" corrected Lang with his theatrical leer.

"Of course," smiled Keen, "but one does have one's personal matters, doesn't one? As a matter of fact there was Sir Hubert's niece, the Hon. Cinthia Astridge, who was travelling with the Chief Inspector."

"A skirt, eh?" snorted Lang. "Well, that sounds like you, but I'd like to put a ship-to-shore call through to the *Georgic* just to make certain."

Keen smiled, quietly picked up his telephone, and handed it to Lang. "Just ask the operator to connect you with the *Georgic*. The toll is nine dollars for three minutes. I'll split fifty-fifty with you."

"You'd make a good poker player, Keen," Lang said, "but I don't like calling people out of bed like that. But I may do it tomorrow nevertheless. And say, gimme another drink," he continued while Keen drew a big chair up closer. "You know, Keen, you're gonner be too smart for your own good one of these days."

"You should know," laughed the ballistics expert. "You've been caught yourself too many times."

"Yeh, but I get caught on the right side. You'll get caught on the wrong side. Did you ever hear of a man by the name of Lieut. Commander Mario Caronni?"

"Good Lord, no!" Keen said like a shot. "What sort of a name is that?"

"Well this guy Caronni is an Italian airman of some sort. He has a plane over here that is entered in the Lindbergh Air Race from—from New York to Europe somewhere."

"Europe is a big place, Lang."

"Yeh? Well, they shouldn't miss it, eh? Anyway this guy Caronni has his plane docked at Three Mile Harbor, just north of East Hampton out here on Long Island. Now does the name mean anything to you?"

"Not a thing. What's it all about?"

"Just that this guy Caronni is making a squawk that his plane is being annoyed in the air and that his shed is being tampered with and he called on Scott to do something about it. He's a guest of the government, of course, and we're supposed to do something."

"So you come out here looking for me and get a sock on the pumpkin."

"Yeh, and that don't make any sense either. You see, Keen, there's always too many little things that somehow tie up whenever anything like this happens."

"So I'm trying to swipe his bus... his plane, or something, this time?"

"I wouldn't know anything about that, but you *are* interested in guns and things, aren't you?"

"So what?"

"Well, it wouldn't be above you to get into that shed and—well, just quietly lift one of the new Italian Breda-Safat machine guns that *happens* to be part of the regular military equipment that this Italian bus is carrying."

"Oh, I might," laughed Keen. "But what the deuce would they be carrying machine guns for if they're in a race. I should think they'd cut down on everything unnecessary to get as much fuel aboard as possible."

"You don't know *much* about aviation, do you, Keen?" Lang sniffed.

"Like Will Rogers, 'only what I read in the papers,'" replied Kerry.

"Yeh? Well, anyway, that's what I called about. I thought maybe you *might* know someone who *might* sorter forget himself and go that far."

"As I said before, I might," agreed Keen, "but I still don't see why they are carrying these guns."

"Oh, it's something about showing the world that they can enter a purely military type in such a race, with all the business aboard, and still show the rest of the world up."

"I get it," nodded Keen.

"You'll get something if that business up around that hangar doesn't quit," Lang snorted.

"Well, it's an idea," Keen taunted Lang again. "But I know plenty about the Breda-Safat gun anyway. I wouldn't have to go up and swipe one. I have one of the instruction manuals on the weapon. They can be obtained, you know."

"Okay. But why do I get smacked on the noggin when I come up here?" Lang groaned. "How do I know that you didn't do it? Either you or that bog-trotting Mick of yours?"

"Don't worry. If Barney had smacked you, you would have gone in all the way to your knees and if I had tried it, it would have been performed in a more genteel, but effective, manner."

Before Lang could answer, the telephone bell rang.

Keen took it up and answered. Then he handed the instrument to Lang. "Scott's calling, and it's for you," he said.

LANG grabbed the phone, grunted into it. He sat listening to the message for several moments with gulps of incredulity, monosyllables of amazement, and considerable activity of the one eyebrow that was clear of Keen's bandages.

"What's up with the old boy?" Keen asked.

"Shut up!" boomed Lang at Kerry, then he dived back at the mouthpiece and explained: "No. I'm talking to this slick gazabo here. Not you, Scott. Go on…. The Griffon, eh?… A black seaplane of some sort. Whew!"

"Say," cooed Keen. "What's the Griffon been up to this time?"

Lang made a wry face at him and continued to listen. Then he said: "Yeh, I'll get him down there first thing in the morning. I got plenty to tell you, too."

"What's up?" Keen asked again when Lang had hung up.

"Plenty. Your pal the Griffon again. They got him cold this time. And there'll be hell to pay."

"The Griffon? Why I'm supposed to be the Griffon, Lang."

"Yeh, and you were supposed to have been in New York seeing Sir Hubert Beamish off on the *Georgic*. But we'll make sure of that in the morning. What time did the *Georgic* sail?"

"Just after nine o'clock."

"Nine o'clock, eh? Never mind, you could still pull this one… somehow. It happened exactly at midnight, according to the Coast Guard."

"What's that?"

"Well, a young Navy commander, flying from Washington to New London with a complete model and the blueprints on a new Navy battle cruiser, was shot down by a black seaplane, and robbed of the battleship model and the blueprints."

"And you figure the Griffon was in the black seaplane?"

"That's the story. The Griffon guy. The Coast Guard cutter tried to get to the wreckage in time, but when they got there, they saw the black seaplane belonging to the Griffon down on the water near the wreckage. They drove him off with shell-fire, but they can't find either the blueprints or the model. The Griffon must have taken them!"

"Are those blueprints important?" asked Keen.

"Are they? Why this new cruiser type is one of the big secrets of the Navy. She's supposed to be a 35,000 tonner with nine 16-inch guns in a new turret arrangement, and there's some gag about the arrangement of the armor that all the navy designers all over the world would give their right arm for."

"Wow!" gasped Barney. And there was a strange expression on his face that made both Keen and Lang stare at him.

"What's getting into you, bog-trotter?" Lang said quickly. "Know anything about it?"

"Of course he doesn't," broke in Keen. "He was with me."

"One of these days you're gonner let him answer a question himself—and then you'll be in the soup!" Lang smirked.

"Quit kidding," Keen replied. "What does Scott say about it?"

"He wants us to come down to the office in the morning and talk it over."

"All right. But you'd better stay here tonight, Lang. You're in no shape to drive that distance."

"Thanks, I think I'll risk it… that is, I'll risk staying here. You'll probably bump me off right, this time."

"You haven't an earthly," smiled Keen, "See that a room is prepared for our guest, Barney. Select a nice haunted room, will you?"

"Nice guys," growled the Secret Service man. "I wouldn't put it past you."

THE NEXT morning they were all in Scott's dingy office in the mid-town section, listening to the story of the missing blueprints and the model. While the conversation progressed, Lang stepped into a private room. It was at this time that someone knocked upon the door.

Scott, weary-eyed and badly in need of a shave, frowned, then got up to open it. Keen was trying to listen to what Lang was telephoning about in the next office.

Then, to Keen's surprise, Scott came back with a chunky black-chinned man in a foreign uniform, a fellow who was gesticulating excitedly and talking like a machine gun.

"This is Lieut. Commander Mario Caronni, Keen. He's the chief pilot on the Italian seaplane that is entered in the trans-

Atlantic Lindbergh Race. And this is Mr. Keen, who is something of an expert on ballistics, Caronni."

With the formal introductions thus dispensed with, Caronni went back to his excited explanations.

"It is terrible, Mister Scott," he said. "Again last night while we were in the air, making what you… you call a test on avigation instruments, we were attacked in the air by a black seaplane. You can see the bullet holes all over the plane. Can't you do something about it?"

"What time did it happen?" asked Scott.

"Time? I would say about… let me see… about midnight."

"That's very interesting. Did you see any other planes in that area? You say you were working off Montauk Light and taking cross-bearings on the Coast Guard station on Cape Cod."

"Other planes?… No. No other planes, Mister Scott. Only a black devil… firing guns."

"I asked this, Commander," Scott tried to explain, "because we lost a Navy plane in that area about that same time. Do you suppose you could have been mistaken for someone else? By that I mean, do you suppose you could have first been mistaken for the Vought, and then later the men, or man, in the black plane discovered his mistake and fired on the Navy job?"

"I do not see how my Cant flying boat could have been mistaken for a Vought. The Vought has one engine and wheel gear. We have one engine also, but a flying boat hull."

"*One* engine?" snapped Keen. "But I thought that one of the conditions of the Lindbergh race was that the planes entered had to have two or more motors. The German and French entries all have multi-motored ships, haven't they?"

"Ah yes, that is right, Mister Keen," Caronni replied, somewhat flustered. "But you see we are not entering for the prize, but for the honor of winning and to show the world what our military ships will do."

"But Italy has several types of planes with two engines," Keen said, trying to fathom all this. "You have another Cant type with three engines, for instance; and then there are the Savora Marchetti and Macchi C.94 boats."

"Ah yes, but you forget. The Cant Z.501 has flown 3,080 miles non-stop. She is most suitable for our desires."

"How do you know all this, Keen?" Scott suddenly asked.

"I was interested because a few nights ago I was talking to a noted American airman, whose name I will not mention, and he was complaining about the two-engined business and said that the sponsors of the race had drafted the rules to suit their own country's craft. He was particularly bitter about it because he has a single-engined ship that is capable of that flight but is automatically eliminated because of the rules."

"Perhaps your friend would like to race the Cant?" Caronni suggested oilily.

"Perhaps. When are you starting?"

"We plan to leave tonight—shortly after dark. You see, there is no particular reason for waiting until the rest start, as we are not officially in the race."

"But I'm afraid my friend wouldn't be able to prepare his plane in time for that. However, he's a resourceful chap and I might be able to kid him into it. You will, of course, select reasonably decent weather?"

"True. But we have already been advised that it will be most suitable for a take-off tonight."

"Well, I'm afraid that's a little too soon for my man, but you can't ever tell. I'll see him. You have an idea," he added, "who I am talking about?"

"Of course. The young man who recently established a new trans-continental mark. I am sure we would relish a race with him. It would add a little spice to the event."

"On the other hand," Keen continued, "there may be an obstacle in the way. You know the government is interested in his plane as a possible basic type for a new high-speed single-seat fighter. So there is a possibility that they would not care to have the plane leave the country for some time."

Caronni's eyes sparkled. Keen knew there was a new angle to

it now. "I am sure we would like to… to see your friend and his plane in Rome. We would be interested in it. I am sorry we cannot hold up our start. But unfortunately we have received orders to get away as soon as possible."

"Well," grinned Scott, "the quicker you get away, the safer we'll feel, considering all the trouble. But I would give something to know who was flying that black plane last night. Anyhow, Commander, we'll see that you get plenty of protection out there until you get away. You say you're leaving tonight?"

"We hope to start about nine o'clock."

"I'll get all the men you want out there to make certain you are bothered no more."

"Unless, of course," Keen broke in, "this chap in the black seaplane decides to race you across."

"I'm afraid he does not have the courage of your friend," smiled Caronni. "He does not like Breda-Safat bullets."

"And who does?" laughed Keen. "Well, best of luck, Commander," Keen said, extending his hand.

"Yes, best of luck," Scott added.

Caronni turned to Barney who had stood in the background taking it all in but saying nothing. "And you, my friend?" he asked.

Barney rubbed his hands on his trousers and said: "Put it there Commander, but I'll bet you a buck you don't make it."

"Barney!" cried Keen, amazed.

"Well, I mean I bet he don't get across in the shortest time," the Mick explained lamely.

"A fair bet, my friend. You can send the 'buck,' as you call it, to me in Trieste," said Caronni, handing Barney his card.

"I'll bet you another buck it won't reach you," snarled Barney.

"What can one do?" Caronni asked, throwing out his expressive hands.

"Try and get across with that one-engined Cant, that's all," Barney said. "That's a fair bet."

"Sit down, you Mick," growled Keen. "Good-bye, Commander."

"Yeh, good-bye, Commander," Barney added with a grin.

"What the heck was that all about?" Scott said when he came back from seeing Caronni off.

"I don't know. Barney takes the craziest dislikes to the strangest people."

"Yeh?" broke in Drury Lang coming out of the other room, "and we're taking the craziest dislike to you, Keen. I just had Sir Hubert Beamish on the ship-to-shore phone. He said he has never even seen you. And as for you seeing him off, he said he went aboard quietly early in the day and was sound asleep when the ship sailed."

Keen smiled and said: "You know, the Chief Inspector is the strangest man and says the strangest things at times."

"Maybe. But the Hon. Cynthia Astridge denies that she has ever heard of anyone with your name," Lang added. "Now where were you two last night between 8 o'clock and when you socked me on the napper about 12.30?"

"Did you say that there were some blue-prints and a model missing?" asked Keen in a new tone of voice.

"You heard us, Keen," Lang snapped, "and unless they are returned damned quick, you're gonner go into the cooler—until you tell us *where* you were. I'll hold you on personal assault."

"Come on, Barney, I'll have to see my friend who has that fast plane. We'll see you tomorrow, Lang. So long, Scott. Just remembered something."

And with that Barney and Keen darted out of the door.

"This is the screwiest case ever," Scott barked. "What the devil are those two up to this time?"

"You tell me who socked me on the konk, and I'll tell you the rest of the story," moaned Lang, holding his head.

"**HOW** many engines did that tub have last night, Barney?" Keen asked as they drove back to Graylands.

"I saw two props. That I'm certain of," Barney mused as he sat beside Keen.

"But you were not sure whether they were both the same type?"

"No. The front job looked like a radial of some sort and from the shape of the nacelle, it looked as though they were using some sort of an in-line motor in the back. But that don't make sense."

"I'm not so sure. You know those Italians did some things with that Macchi-Castoldi seaplane racer which everyone said could not be done. But they did it."

"You mean bolting two twelve-cylinder motors together and running two props in opposite directions? That had me fooled for a time, too," agreed Barney nodding to himself in the reflection of the dashboard instruments.

"And what's particularly wrong with mounting a radial up front and an in-line tandem behind it? Golly, you certainly could get a real streamline nacelle out of that."

"Yeh, but this egg Caronni says they don't have two engines."

"And if they *had* two engines they would be eligible for the Lindbergh Race prize—if they won it. That doesn't add up right, either."

"Here," said Keen suddenly, "get over here and drive. I'm getting off at East Hampton. I'm going to have a look at that baby."

Barney took the wheel and Keen plunged about in the car's rear locker and found some old clothing. There was a pair of brown overalls, a dirty gray pull-over sweater, a blue flannel shirt, and a pair of laborer's brogans.

While Barney hurtled the Duesenberg out of Southampton, Keen made a quick and startling change. He folded his business suit up and tucked it away in the locker hidden behind the front seats.

"Let me off at the Three Mile road just outside East Hampton, and be back and pick me up about six o'clock."

AN HOUR later, a cheery but roughly dressed hobo wandered into the boathouse of Jed Summers on Three Mile Harbor and bought a package of cigarettes. He lit one and stared about the shack, casually inspecting a rack of surf rods that stood along the back wall.

"Any fishing going on around here?" Keen asked the man behind the tobacco showcase.

"Uster be, but since them Italians came up here with that

seaplane, yer life ain't safe out there any more. Be glad when they shove off. Bad for business, you know."

"Eh?… Oh yeh, that seaplane thing. She's a big one, eh?"

"Pretty damn big to me," Jed agreed.

"Makes a lot o' noise, eh?"

"Hell of a lot for one engine. Now you take them little ships they use up at the country club—they ain't so bad. But this big brute raises hell."

"She only got one engine?"

"That's all. They got it stuck in a thing that looks like a bath-tub upside down on top of the wing. Craziest looking airplane I ever see, but I don't know much about 'em, I suppose."

"You sure she's only got one engine?" Keen asked, picking his teeth, rustic fashion. "That ship they got down at North Beach has two."

"Yeh, so I heard. I ain't seen her yet. She must make a hell of a lot of noise. What I can't make out is how these guys expect to race against them other ships what have two engines. That don't seem fair to me."

"I can't figure that either," said Keen, peering out the dirty window, "but I don't know nothing about 'em, so what do I care. What do you charge for a boat, Mister?"

"Well, I get two bucks a day—with a five deposit. But you can take that green one down at the end of the dock without a deposit."

"What's the matter with her?"

"Nothing. Just one of the old ones, and business being what it is I can't be choosy these days. Want to borrow some tackle?"

"That's an idea."

The formal transactions were completed and with a small can of live bait, a rod and reel, Keen pulled away and headed out toward the middle of the harbor. Keen looked about, saw which way the wind lay, and selected his course.

"Look out for that seaplane if she ever comes out and starts churning about," Jed yelled.

"Don't worry, I will," Keen said to himself as he waved a cherry acknowledgement.

THE NEW metal hangar at Three Mile Harbor was bolted tight. Only the small side door was used for passage to and from the interior. At this door stood two heavy men in black overcoats, derbies, and hefty-soled shoes. They were doing their best not to look like plainclothes men.

Inside on a massive wheeled cradle lay the Cant seaplane with half a dozen Italian mechanics in cream-colored coveralls swarming all over her from the engine to the tail surfaces. Two worked on the 850 h.p. Isotta-Fraschini engine mounted in the upper center-section while another sat in the upper wing turret and overhauled the two Breda-Safat guns mounted on the moveable ring. Behind him the nacelle smoothed off as neat as the prow of a small racing yacht.

Both Keen and Barney had been fooled about that engine. It *looked* like a radial because of the circular radiator which covered the W-type front. It actually was an eighteen-cylinder job. They were to find that out later.

Lieut. Commander Caronni stood off to one side talking to a fellow who answered to the name of Rufus Gould. Warrant Officer Francesco Vittorio, the Cant's co-pilot, stood nearby listening carefully to all that was being said.

Gould was a small man who wore clothes that were too large for him. He had a cold, lifeless face and a long thin nose through which he sniffed continually as he spoke. He frequently glanced about like a haunted man, and now he brought out two cablegram forms and showed them to Caronni.

"You must get away tonight, Caronni," he kept saying. "I'll see that suitable (sniff) explanations are made (sniff-sniff). We are taking too much of a risk letting it go any longer. I won't rest (sniff-sniff) until you are safely in Rome. And in contact with the Society," he added in a whisper.

"But I do not like this hurry business, Gould," Caronni argued. "It does not look right."

"You won't look right either (sniff-sniff) if you are stopped and your plane taken over. That business last night at Scallaci's (sniff-sniff) you know."

"Yes, but we are covered," Caronni whispered. "Did you see the latest reports on it?"

"No, what do you (sniff) mean?"

"Well, just before we finished that Navy man off, he managed to get a radio report off. The Fire Island Light operator caught it and made a report to someone in New York."

"What (sniff-sniff) did he say?"

"He reported that the Dornier seaplane was attacking him. You see he was completely fooled. That fake shaft was a brilliant idea," smiled Caronni. "What do you say, Vittorio?"

The little dark-complexioned Warrant Officer just smiled.

"Well, that's a break (sniff). But I still don't like that business in New York last night."

"You are partly to blame, remember. It was your idea in the first place. And you should have been sure of that man on the lawn last night."

"But I figured we could trust Scallaci (sniff-sniff) to cover us."

"He played his part all right, but we were a little careless. I should have sensed something wrong."

"What I can't (sniff) make out is how they knew," Gould muttered. "You say there were two of them (sniff-sniff) and that they were apparently working together? There was only one at that Graylands place."

"Are you positive? But hello... what now?"

Gould cringed at the expression on Caronni's face, then turned to where he was staring.

The two plainclothes men were shouting through the doorway.

"Hey, you fellows got a boat of some sort? A guy's drowning out here!"

Caronni led the pack to the doorway and raced out to the concrete ramp. There, about 200 yards off shore, was a floundering green row-boat with a man hanging to it and shouting for help. Gould came puffing up to Caronni's side and stared out with the rest of them.

"What's the matter with him?" he demanded forgetting to sniff in his excitement.

"He's in bad shape. His boat's sinking or something. You got a boat over there. Go get him in," the plainclothes man ordered.

Gould shoved his hand into Caronni's ribs and whispered.

"Yeh, go get him in (sniff). This looks fishy."

Caronni caught the look in Gould's eye, nodded coldly.

WARRANT OFFICER VITTORIO and two mechanics went out to rescue the man with a boat they used for servicing the Cant when she was anchored out off the concrete apron. They found their man struggling to hang onto the boat which was almost submerged. They dragged him clear, put a line on the boat, and brought him to the hangar. For several minutes the man struggled to get his breath and continued to argue about saving the boat and the fishing tackle, as he did not own them.

"What happened?" one of the plainsclothes men asked when they finally got him quiet and helped him inside the hangar. Gould and Caronni asked no questions, simply stood off and listened.

"I was fishing out there and hooked into a flounder or something. I stood up to handle him when suddenly my foot went through the bottom of the boat and a plank went out. She filled right away, and I had to hang on while I drifted."

"Where'd you get that tub, anyway?" demanded the other plainclothes man. "She was about to fall apart anyhow."

"I just hired it at Jed Summers' place down the line. He charged me two bucks for it, an' I nearly get drowned. A hell of a note."

"You'd better get out of them duds and get dry. Maybe you can hammer a hunk of wood back on there later and get her back. You're a lucky guy. Good thing you was near the shore."

Caronni, who had been peering at Keen—for Keen it was—suddenly stepped up and said: "You'd better come in here, my man. I think we can find you a drink that will warm you up. Must be frozen, eh?"

"Yeh, about frozen, mister. Thanks."

Caronni and Gould led the way to a small rear office. Vittorio followed, trying to fathom the strange grimace on Caronni's face. As they crossed the hangar floor, the dripping man just glanced up at the plane a second or so, then completely dismissed it. Caronni had been watching for that move, but he was not yet sure of his ground.

"Take him inside," Caronni said to Gould. "I'll go and get him a drink. He looks as though he's going to have a heart attack."

"You think so?" husked Gould, sniffing.

"I don't *think* so. I'm sure of it. I've seen this fellow… somewhere."

"Well, don't make any mistakes."

"I'll never make another."

They led the disguised Keen into the office and helped him get out of his wet clothes. Someone wrapped a blanket about him and he sat down before a small electric heater.

Caronni ordered the plainclothes men back to their posts at the door and then went into a small equipment shed. He came out a few moments later with a glass brimming with a brownish liquid.

"You're a lucky man," Gould was saying when Caronni came in with the drink. "But you don't look (sniff-sniff) any too good yet. You'd better get something warm into you… and get a little sleep."

"Yeh, I guess I need something warm and some sleep," repeated Keen, eyeing Gould carefully.

"Here you are," Caronni boomed. "Get this inside you before you get a real chill and wind up with pneumonia."

Keen took the glass, noted that the liquid it held was not very clear.

"That's the best Italian cognac— something of a rare vintage in America. We brought that all the way across with us. Drink it down, you look pretty well done up."

Keen eyed Caronni before he took the glass and fumbled with the big blanket with one hand. Then he took the glass, still twisting about with the awkward covering.

"Cognac is brandy, ain't it, mister?" he asked, passing it under his nose.

"That's right. A form of brandy."

"Kinder smells different from any other grog I ever drank."

There was a strange smell about it, and Keen was on his guard.

"Never mind how it smells," Caronni laughed. "You'll find it has plenty of heat. It'll pull you together quickly."

"Well, here goes," Keen said, as he started to raise the glass.

But suddenly the blanket began to shift off his shoulders and he made a quick move to draw it up again. Somehow the glass changed hands and disappeared amid the sudden folds of the blanket. Then before either Gould or Caronni could figure what had happened, Keen seemed to have suddenly gulped it down, from a position in which the glass hand was shrouded by the blanket.

"That's very good," he said smacking his lips and blowing out to indicate that it possessed plenty of power. "That ought to do the trick!"

Caronni took the empty glass, peered into it as though he was not quite certain what had happened. He threw a quick glance at Gould and got no satisfaction there. But when he turned back, the man in the blanket was rubbing his eyes and bending over.

"Come on now," Caronni ordered, "you'd better lie down now and try to get some sleep while your clothes dry out."

But Keen did not reply. He lurched forward with a low groan and fell sprawling on his face like a dead man.

"He got it all right," Gould said quietly.

"I thought he put one over on us for a minute," Caronni observed.

"Lord, that stuff certainly took effect quickly," Gould puffed as he helped get Keen over onto an old Army cot.

"Yes, but we'll make sure. Just to be sure," Caronni muttered with a grimace.

He quietly drew a pin from the lapel of his uniform jacket and with a quick movement jabbed it under the nail of Keen's forefinger.

Keen let out a low cry and his hand recoiled against the painful jab.

"I thought so," Caronni raged, hauling Keen to a sitting position. "You thought you could fool us with that old game, eh? Well, when you pulled that face just then, you gave yourself away completely. I remember you now. You're one of the men who staged that party at Scallaci's last night."

And before Keen could get into a position to defend himself, Caronni whipped out a massive automatic and brought its butt down on his head. That was all he remembered.

GOULD flew to the door, bolted it. His face was yellow and he now sniffed twice as fast. He glared down at the slack form of the man Caronni was covering up in the blanket.

"What did (sniff-sniff) you do, Caronni?" he husked. "Kill him?"

"Not yet, but we'll have to, you know."

"But you can't do it like that—in (sniff-sniff) cold blood!"

"Why not? You had no objection to me giving him arsenic."

"But that would have been (sniff-sniff) different. We could have said that he died of a heart attack. You can't kill him now."

"No? Well what are *you* going to do with him? Leave him here?"

"No. I suppose he knows too much, But we can't murder him. It's all right for (sniff-sniff) you. But I have to stay here and they'll question me about it. Besides (sniff-sniff) there's the other man somewhere, and he might turn up, too—and make things worse."

"Well, talk fast, we've got to do something with him somehow."

"Let's leave him for a while. He'll (sniff-sniff) be out for some time, won't he?" Gould asked with a cowardly grimace.

"How can we leave him? Those policemen at the door will ask questions."

"Damn the man, anyway!" sniffed Gould. "I suppose we had better (sniff-sniff) get rid of him now. But how?"

"I'll get rid of him," snarled Caronni going to the door and peering out. "The minute it gets dark, I'll order a short test flight and we'll take him along. In the meantime, you stay here, Gould, and watch him. Keep this gun and don't let him move. I'll make arrangements to have those plainclothes men relieved at 6 o'clock."

"You're going to throw him overboard?" Gould asked.

"That's the way to get rid of devils like him," Caronni nodded. "There's no mistake that way."

"Well, don't let's (sniff-sniff) have any mistakes," Gould said, taking the gun.

AT 6 O'CLOCK, which was about three hours later, Caronni returned to the small office and looked for Gould. But Gould was nowhere to be found. The man on the cot was still bundled up in the blanket, and the Lieut. Commander smiled as he noticed that Gould had carefully roped the ankles securely and had covered the man completely with the blanket.

"Where's Gould?" he asked of Vittorio who was standing outside watching movement of the big Cant across the floor.

"He's been about. He went around that way looking for you. Didn't you see him?" Vittorio asked.

"No. I've been taking care of the relief of those damned Secret Service men. I want Gould to help me get this man aboard for the test flight. Can you give me a hand?"

"Gladly. What's it for?"

"You'll see, Vittorio," smiled Caronni. "Come on before those Secret Service men get nosey."

This conversation, of course, took place in Italian. The two airmen now crept into the dark room and carefully tied the blanket tighter around the snuffling and groaning man. Then satisfied, they lugged the shapeless bundle out, skirted the darkened side of the hangar, and made their way toward the flying boat which now teetered gently in the breeze on the wheeled cradle. They cut over quickly before they were noticed and quickly shoved the blanket-wrapped bundle into the lower compartment behind the control cockpit.

Then stepping out again, they gave their orders for lowering the flying boat down to the water. They explained to one of the Secret Service men that they were going for a short night test hop to check their avigation instruments again and would be back in a short time.

"Oh," the Secret Service man said. "I thought you were checking out without waiting for a clearance. You got to get that, you know."

"Oh, yes, we understand. Mr. Gould is probably taking care of that now," Caronni smiled. "We'll be back in twenty minutes. Then we'll fuel up and be away."

In exactly twenty minutes the big Cant flying boat came back. Both Caronni and Vittorio had that weird Cheshire-cat look about them as they climbed down and dropped into the small boat brought out to the side of the hull.

"Where's Gould?" Caronni asked as he came up the apron. "Has anyone seen him yet?"

"Who's Gould?" asked one of the Secret Service men.

"Rufus Gould, our public relations man. He's supposed to be here now," Caronni snapped with a vile scowl.

"A fellow in a brown tweed suit, who sniffs all the time?" the Secret Service man said. "I saw him mooching about, blowing his nose and acting like a guy with a bad dose of hay fever. He went down the road there."

"Well, if you see him again, will you please ask him to come into the office and see me. We're hoping to get away shortly after 9 o'clock."

"You'd better get those clearance papers first," the plainclothes man advised.

Warrant Officer Vittorio was strangely silent as he followed Caronni back into the hangar. Where could Gould have gone down that road? They had no connections down there. They could do all the outside business they required direct from the hangar.

"What's Gould up to?" he asked Caronni. "He should be here now if he wants to get that package aboard."

"Don't worry about clearance papers, Vittorio," the Commander eased. "The papers should be on their way here now, and if Gould is not on hand, that will be his look-out. I have the package."

"But he should be here," Vittorio argued, staring about as if he expected to find Gould dodging about in the hangar. "There's too many chances of a slip-up. I'd hate to be held up just as we were getting away."

"Don't worry. We won't. We still have plenty of armament aboard; and once we get off the water, we'll be on our way. Remember that the Society has *real* money awaiting us in Italy. And the Society has contacts with several great powers who will be interested in the contents of that package."

"One cannot forget that," the little Warrant Officer smirked. "We were told that often enough."

"Still," agreed Caronni with a slight smile, "I *do* wish we knew what had become of Gould. This is not quite like Gould."

"Look here, Commander," Vittorio said with a quake in his voice and thinking now of the fortune that awaited him. "I think we ought to take no more chances. Unless Gould turns up by 7 o'clock, we ought to get away, papers or no papers."

"I'm beginning to worry about it myself now. He wouldn't disappear like this for no reason."

"We have everything here. The crew is on hand and they will have completed the fueling by that time. We must get away. Every minute is dangerous now."

"You are right, Vittorio. I'll see what I can do. I think we can entertain our Secret Service friends with a glass of Italian cognac, eh?"

"I wouldn't know what you mean," smiled Vittorio. "But I will go and supervise the refueling… just in case."

AT THAT very minute a Duesenberg automobile, with the engine purring idly, stood outside a large hardware store in East Hampton. The man behind the wheel was plainly agitated about something, for he continued to consult first a heavy turnip watch he carried in his pocket and then the jeweled clock mounted in the dashboard.

There was no satisfaction in any of them. Both time pieces said 6:27. So Barney did what he always did when he was perplexed.

He drew the cork out of a stubby brown bottle, took a long swig, and rubbed his mouth with the back of his hand.

No sooner had he set the bottle down in the folds of a steamer rug than from somewhere behind the car a drab figure in brown tweeds slid up to the door, yanked it open quickly, and said: "Thanks for the drink. I need one."

It was Keen, chalk-faced and plainly weary from much exertion.

He slipped into the seat beside Barney, drew the cork from the bottle, and said: "Home! and quick!"

"Where the hell you bin?" Barney argued at once. "Old Lang has been calling for you for hours."

Keen took two more long drags of the liquor, replaced the cork, and dropped the bottle on the floor between his feet.

"What's he want and what did you tell him?"

"I told him you'd gone to take a look at the Statue of Liberty, or something."

"Swell idea. I've never been there. You know, that's a funny thing about New Yorkers, Barney."

"What?"

"Darn few real New Yorkers have ever visited the Statue of Liberty or the Empire State tower. You know, if I were a thug I'd hide in the Statue of Liberty or the Empire State tower. But home please... fast!"

"What happened to you, anyway?"

"A sock on the pumpkin and—well, almost a 'ride.'"

"Whose outfit you got on now?"

"A gentleman by the name of Gould owned it."

"Owned it?"

"Yes, you see, he went for a ride in my place. We switched outfits. I had a blanket, and he, he had little choice. They hadn't hit me as hard as they figured."

"Where is this Gould?"

"That I wouldn't know. I didn't go with him, but in all probability, he's somewhere at the bottom of Long Island Sound still wearing my blanket."

"Whew!" gasped Barney, stepping on it as they reached the open road between Nepague Beach and Hither Hills State Park.

"What's the news from Lang?"

"They're holding the German Dornier outfit. That Navy pilot managed to get a call through to Fire Island Light and said he was being attacked by the Dornier."

"He was fooled, too, poor devil," Keen said, still fighting a splitting headache. "Know what, Barney?"

"Sure. That Cant is powered with a water-cooled W-type engine that has a circular radiator which makes it look like a radial. I looked it up when I got in."

"Right. But I learned more. They used a shaft fitted into a spline at the rear end of that motor to another prop that can be fitted to the rear of that gun-turret nacelle. I saw the shaft and the prop. It was a smart wheeze."

"Wow! So that's how they fooled us, eh?"

"Yes, but I fooled them. And they're going to get another shock the minute they get far out. We're going to play a dirty trick on them, Barney."

"Who is?" asked Barney becoming suspicious.

"*We* is."

"Oh, I had an idea that *I* was, as usual."

"No, we'll pull this one together. Did you say that I had gone to see the Statue of Liberty?"

"That's right. The first thing I could think of."

"Well, that was a bright idea. Have a drink."

Barney took the bottle, gulped a long swig, and grinned.

In another ten minutes, which was covered in silence, they pulled into the curving driveway of Graylands.

THERE was no reason for Keen to ask whether the *Black Bullet* was ready for another adventure. He knew Barney would see to that. He knew she would be spotless and all her wounds carefully patched and painted over. The tanks would be filled with carefully filtered fuel and the gun boxes crammed with gleaming rows of bullets in silver metallic belts.

Keen carefully dressed his head wound, then got out his flying clothes in preparation for another aerial adventure.

Just then the telephone bell rang, and he made a move to pick it up; but seeing Barney coming in bearing a tray of food, he signalled to the Mick and said: "If that's Lang again, I'm still not here. Pump him all you can. Before you hang up, I'll tell you what to do."

Barney took up the receiver, grunted into it.

There was a long spell between his "Hello" and the time he got another chance to speak. Then he said with a weary smile: "No, he's not back yet. I guess I'd better come into town and look for him. But he did say something about the Statue of Liberty."

Another long splutter of words from the other end and Barney pantomimed a long harangue. Then he said. "Well, he might know something about it. He knows all about guns, I suppose."

Then while Lang carried on again at the other end, Barney clamped his hand over the mouthpiece and whispered: "They got some of the bullets out of the Vought and they want you to identify them. They have no record of any like this. Breda-Safat, eh?"

Then as Barney listened patiently to Lang's further details, Keen caught a new sound above. It was the roar of an airplane engine. Quick as a flash he husked to Barney: "Ask him where he is."

"Where are you, Lang?" Barney asked, watching Keen scribble something on a pad and shove it under his eyes.

"I'm uptown at the office of the Italian Consulate General, 626 Fifth Avenue," the detective came back.

Barney repeated that aloud and Keen grinned.

"I see," Barney fenced, listening with one ear to the airplane engine above and the other to the phone. "Well, this may sound crazy, Lang, but I figured I'd better tell you about it. I just found a message out on the lawn near where you fell. It's signed 'The Griffon,' and it says: *There's a strange package on Bedloe's Island, and the Statue of Liberty is holding it in her hand.'* "

"What the hell does that mean?" barked Lang. " 'The Statue of Liberty is holding it in her hand.' That don't make sense."

"Nothing makes sense when the Griffon pulls it," laughed Barney, "but that's what's written here."

"Wait a minute, you can go up inside the hand of the Statue of Liberty, can't you?" Lang cooed. "I remember you could years ago. But they shut it off some time ago because it was getting shaky, or something."

"Well, you figure it out," laughed Barney.

"But I can't get there tonight. The ferries have stopped running by now."

"Well, if it means anything, you could get there some way," Barney laughed. "Personally, I think it's all nuts, though."

"You do, eh? Well, I'm going down there the minute I can get away—if I have to charter the *Queen Mary* to get across from the Battery. That Griffon guy is up to something. Why, I bet he's the gink who cracked down on me. What's more, the facts begin to indicate that your Mr. Keen certainly is the Grif—"

"Best of luck," Barney roared, slamming the phone down and racing after Keen who was already on his way down to the hidden hangar.

"HEAR what went over?" demanded Keen, climbing in and starting the Avia engine.

"Sure. The Cant. They must have cleared quick."

"Something went wrong, somewhere. Or else they found out."

Barney had the doors open and Keen rolled the *Bullet* out without waiting for much of a warm-up. The wings were drawn out and locked and Barney clicked the hidden switch that closed the fake rock-garden over the entrance. In a few minutes they were rolling down the sand and into the water. The thunder of the Isotta-Fraschini could still be sensed off in the distance. Caronni was undoubtedly heading out on a Great Circle route, secure in his feelings that they were well away with their booty.

Keen quickly set the pontoons for a water take-off and ran her, well muffled, out into the blackness of the murky night.

Then gently hoiking her to her step, he gave the Avia full gun and she was away, clipping the tops of two rollers and getting space under her pontoons. They were after the Cant and the valuable package she was carrying out of the country.

Keen flipped off his strip map cover, selected the chart he wanted, and quickly drew a Great Circle course out of Montauk that cut directly for the Banks off Newfoundland. He felt confident that he knew the course Caronni would set for his getaway, so he quickly cleared the Skoda muffler and let her roar with the prop set for climbing. They headed past Block Island and hammered the atmosphere for Nantucket.

"There they are," boomed Barney into Keen's ear, as he held up the night glasses. "They certainly have been taking it easy."

"They don't want to take a chance on that motor after making such a quick getaway," said Keen. "They'll have to run at three-quarter throttle for about an hour. It's a long way to Tipperary."

"What do you know about Tipperary?"

"Nothing. Neither do you, you Houston Street Mick."

"No, but some day when you get over your night gadding, I'm going over and find out what it's all about."

"Fine! I'll go with you. But right now we'd better get out the lead-slinging apparatus. All set?"

"Been waiting for hours. Let's go."

"Now don't do her up too badly, remember. Try the motor first."

"Getting choosy, eh?"

"We've got to get that 'bundle of washing' off safely."

"Let's go."

THEY overtook the Cant a few miles due south of Nantucket—caught her cold.

Keen jumped her from about 5,000 feet with a burst of lead that punched great holes in the wide-spread wings. As he zoomed up and fluttered through a weak return-fire, Barney leaned out and sprayed a wicked hurricane of lead at them that battered the engine cowl to bits.

Keen wheeled around again and came at them full tilt broadside and swept the Cant rear gunner out of the play with heavy bursts from his Darn guns. As they roared over the floundering flying boat, Barney directed two more streams of lead at the engine and they saw the steel blades of the prop flash in a glare of fire that seeped from the battered exhaust ports.

The blades, cut by the fire, ripped themselves out of the three-way hubs and with a screaming flash, dug deep into the control pit below. Barney never knew it, but one of the blades went through the back of the cabin and pinioned Vittorio to the three-ply floor of the space that led through to the front gunner's pit. He never moved after that. He was skewered to the floor like some gigantic insect specimen mounted for inspection.

Caronni, realizing what was going on for the first time, tried to fight her down. He now felt alone, terribly alone. The throttle meant nothing. The engine responded in a choking manner, but there was no forward response.

He could see the black seaplane hurtling at him again and with a low cry shoved her nose down. The black seaplane poured burst after burst at him, but the damage had been done now. Caronni yanked levers and pulled wires with metal handles on them. The fuel escaped through the dump valves and rip-seams so that possibility of fire was greatly lessened. He looked up and back and saw the black seaplane coming down on him again, but this time they did not fire, realizing that they had to give him a chance to get down.

Caronni tried hard to get away, but he realized that his chances were hopeless. He had to get down safely first of all, then hope for a break in some other direction.

But Keen and Barney were taking no chances on him now. They poured fiery bursts past his nose and indicated that they wanted him to go straight down. There was no time for much fooling and the minute the Italian pilot tried to turn toward the shore of Nantucket they blasted a burst past his cabin that gave him other, and better, ideas.

In a few minutes Caronni planted the Cant down on the black waters of the Atlantic and sat there helpless. He reached inside a locker set under the control-pit dashboard and drew out a long narrow parcel which was carefully wrapped in water-proof paper, tied with heavy cord, and securely sealed with large red gobs of sealing wax. For a moment or two he sat there, pondering on his next move as he saw the black seaplane come in toward him, displaying her pontoons now and easing up slowly.

Caronni wanted to throw the incriminating package away, but something told him to hang on to it. That something was a cradled gun in Barney's arms. Caronni simply stared helplessly at the menacing weapon and watched the masked men ease the pontoons up to the disabled Cant.

Keen let the *Bullet* ease in, tossed a light grapnel hook that caught the front gun ring, then stepped out on the wing root.

Caronni gasped as the slender masked man ordered him to stand up.

"You have a package, an official U.S. Navy package, aboard there, Caronni. I want it, complete and undamaged. If it has been touched, you go the same way that you sent Gould."

"Gould? What do you know about Gould?" clacked the Italian.

"You threw Mr. Gould overboard from a great height, didn't you, Caronni?"

"Gould?... No, I didn't throw anyone overboard. What are you talking about?"

"The package, Caronni. I want that package you have there—and quick."

"But Gould? What did you mean when you said I threw Gould overboard from a great height."

"Just a mistake on your part, Caronni. You didn't know you were throwing Gould over—but that's what happened. A case of mistaken identity, I think they call it. Now the package, please. I see you have it. You were going to hand it over, of course."

Caronni, white and quaking, now threw the package forward and Keen caught it and studied the seals carefully. They had not been touched and he sensed that Caronni had had orders to deliver it sealed, just as it had been taken.

"That will be all, Caronni. You're on your own now."

"But you can't leave me out here—alone."

"No, you'll be taken care of in a short time. We'll see to that. You can tell them that you were on your way home, heading for a new record, when you were shot down by… the Griffon. Good night, Caronni. I'll remember you to Mr. Scallaci, one of these days."

"You… you dirty Yankee fiend!" was all that Caronni could cry.

Keen laughed aloud, swished the grapnel line, and cleared the hook skilfully. Then pushing the *Black Bullet* clear by holding the wing of the Cant, he stepped back inside and took the rear pit while Barney, still covering Caronni, edged forward and kicked the starter.

Once they were well clear of the Cant, Barney dropped into the front seat and took her off. Keen now grabbed a pad and scribbled a note:

Pick up Italian flying boat seven miles south of Nantucket. Hold Lieut. Commander Caronni for investigation concerning loss of Navy Vought Corsair off Block Island. Believe bullets found in Vought will agree with those fired from Breda-Safat guns aboard Cant boat. Check use of false shaft and prop which made flying boat look like German Dornier Do-18.

—The Griffon

This note Keen carefully slipped into an official Navy message streamer and then directed Barney to fly toward a Coast Guard cutter that was steaming along off Martha's Vineyard.

They headed for it and Keen, daring a short fusillade of fire from a one-pounder, dropped the message precisely on the deck of the cutter. That sealed the fate of one Lieut. Commander Caronni.

THE NEXT half hour was a hair-raiser. For Barney, following Keen's orders, hammered the *Black Bullet* in a southwesterly direction at top speed. They screeched across Block Island again, continued on for Montauk Light, then hurtled down Long Island Sound.

Keen adjusted his parachute, belted the package tightly to him, then gave Barney his final instructions.

"Circle the Statue of Liberty at 1,500 feet. Give me time to check the wind and once I clear, you beat it back and play your little game with Lang. Then come to town and get me in the morning. Understand?"

"I get it. You really are going to plant that thing in her hand, huh?"

"It's as good a way of getting it to him as any."

"I wish you luck."

"Thanks. I'll need it."

Twenty minutes later, Keen was out on the wing root, poised directly over the Statue of Liberty. He gave Barney a signal, then dived headlong into the night. The glorious Bartholdi monument on Bedloe's Island held up its giant torch, as if directing Keen's course.

The black parachute flapped in the chilly night, but this sound was sufficiently muffled by the whistles, foghorns, and sirens of the lower bay traffic. Handling his shrouds carefully, Keen dropped like a cat on the Jersey side of the lawn surrounding the base of the Statue.

He quietly slipped out of the parachute harness and crept across the grass toward the heavy granite base of the great pedestal.

All was quiet, but he took no chances. There was a caretaker on the island and a small dock where tiny ferries brought visitors across from the Battery. Quietly making his way around one side of the pedestal, he found the wide main door. Then with a swift movement he opened it and darted inside. He could hear a man talking somewhere into a phone. He listened a minute and caught the words: "…very irregular, Mr. Lang. But if you say so, I'll come across and get you with my boat. Yes, you can get up that far, but we do not allow the public up there now."

Keen realized what was going on, and he darted for the stairways and disappeared in the gloom.

EXACTLY one hour later, he was changing into full evening clothes in his 55th Street apartment penthouse. His other clothing, still dripping and cold, was carefully hidden away in a secret closet under his study desk. He had had to swim from Bedloe's Island to the Jersey shore against a particularly swift current. But he made it with comparatively little effort and huddled away for a few minutes in a freight yard where he wrung out his clothes as best he could. Then he hurried into Jersey City where he found a taxi and ordered the driver to rush him to New York City.

Jersey City taxi-drivers are a race apart. They accept their fares and ask no questions. After all, many strange characters frequent the wharfs and docks along the Jersey side of the North River, hence a cabby is never quite certain whether his fares are members of the Port of New York river police or simply mysterious characters from the dry-docks, warehouses, or basins that line that section of the river.

All he knew was that he had picked up a fare who wanted to go to New York City. He took him to a tenement on 54th Street, and was paid. So what mattered? A fare's a fare.

KEEN was just inspecting himself in his long mirror when the bell rang. He went to the door, casually smoking a cigarette, and found that Drury Lang was his caller. He quickly noted that Lang had a long package under his arm which was tightly sealed and corded.

Keen nodded cheerfully, invited him in.

"Where have you been all day long?" Lang demanded once they were inside. "Your guy O'Dare has been trying his best to get you."

"I've been a New York tourist today, Lang. I've been seeing the things every true New Yorker should see before he dies."

"What are you talking about? And where did you get that sock on the dome?"

"Well, after I left you this morning, I visited the Stock Exchange, Brooklyn Bridge, Trinity Church yard, the Museum of Natural History, and finally the Empire State Building. And would you believe it? On top of the Empire State Building a fellow swung one of those fixed telescopes too abruptly and banged me on the head with it. Purely accidental, of course. Interesting, eh, Lang?"

"Yeh, very." Lang smirked. "But that's all the bunk. I've got the dope on you. You're the Griffon, and you smacked me on the head at Graylands and left a note there on the lawn about a package at the Statue of Liberty."

"The Statue of Liberty?" gagged Keen. "Well, I *had* hoped to complete my sight-seeing by going there today. But after getting this crack on the head at the Empire State Building, I didn't feel quite up to it. But say, what's all this business about a note?"

"Well," answered Lang, "your man, Barney, told me about it."

"Sounds goofy," replied Keen. "Are you sure Barney wasn't under the influence?"

"Well, he sounded like that, only…."

"Only what?"

"There *was* a package up in the hand of the Statue of Liberty. Here it is."

Keen frowned and took it. He inspected the seals and wrappings. "What is it? Something important?"

"Yeh, very important. It just happens to be the package and model that was stolen from that Navy guy last night. Come clean, now. You're the Griffon and you wrote that note. But how did you know the package would be there?"

"I didn't. How could I?"

"I don't know either, but there it is."

"Do you mean to stand there and tell me you actually went to the Statue of Liberty tonight because a drunken servant of mine told you a crack-pot story like that?" Keen demanded. "If you did, you're sillier than even I believed."

"But the package… the package!" Lang argued. "It was up there in the small compartment inside the hand of the statue. There is a compartment up there, you know."

"No, I didn't. I understood you could only go up to the gallery set inside the coronet around the head."

"You didn't know, huh? But the package was up there, Keen!" Lang argued, beginning to feel himself slipping. "Let me see your shoes. You probably took it there yourself."

Keen squinted, then exhibited his neat evening pumps. Lang stared at them and wagged his head.

"No, this guy had big brogans with rubber heels that had the word 'Catspaw' marked on them. The dust down there was thick enough to take a good impression."

"Guy? What guy?"

"The guy who went up those stairs into the hand and left this package up there with my name on. You got any heavy walking shoes here?"

Keen directed Lang to his shoe closet and for several minutes the detective inspected the footwear on the neat rack.

"I can't figure it out," he said finally. "But some guy with big shoes with special rubber heels on them went up that arm staircase and left this package—and your man Barney told me that the Griffon's note said a package was up there... and there it was."

"So what?" laughed Keen.

"I don't know, either."

"Well, I certainly did *not* steal that package in the first place," Keen said.

"No? Wait a minute. Here, these bullets. What are they?"

Keen took the slugs from Lang and inspected them closely.

"They are Italian bullets, and the kind usually fired from a Breda-Safat gun," Keen said after a short deliberation. "This unusual cartridge ring marking identifies them clearly."

"Well they were found sunk in the dashboard, or whatever you call it, on that Navy plane. They're from Caronni's flying boat, eh?"

"Well, that is the only airplane in this area that carries such guns."

"But the Navy guy, before he 'went out,' reported by radio that a two-engined Dornier was attacking him. They picked his message up at Fire Island Light."

"What about the time bracket?"

"The Dornier *was* in the air at that time. But the German flyers claim she was out along the south Jersey shore. And what has us stumped about Caronni and his outfit is that they left suddenly around 7 o'clock without clearance papers. What's more, two Secret Service men, Davis and Meyers, were found dead in the shed out there at Three Mile Harbor."

"Whew!" gasped Keen. "Then Caronni and his boys must have faked a two-engined ship somehow and escaped with the plans and the model," Keen said with a particularly dumb look.

"But I'm telling you, Keen, that the plans and the model are right here in this package. I found 'em up in the hand of the Statue of Liberty. Can't you get that into your thick nut?"

"No, I can't. It seems to me, Lang, that this time *you* are trying to put something over. You appear to have found the plans and the model and are trying to pass me off as the Griffon in some cock-eyed way. Griffon, my eye! Why you, yourself, really solved this one. No, Lang. You can't drag either him or me into it."

"Well," agreed Lang, "I have been working on the thing from several angles, and of course I had my own ideas on it. But I was trying to figure if you could have been in it anywhere. You're a queer guy, you know, Keen."

"Don't be silly."

JUST then the telephone bell rang and Lang grabbed the phone. "Yes! Yes!" he cracked. "All right, Scott. Yes, he's here. What's that?... They've found the Cant flying boat shot down and Caronni is a prisoner? Wow! *What?* He said he was shot down by a man who called himself the Griffon? How can that be? *I* have the plans and the model, Scott. I picked them up on Bedloe's Island.... No, I am not nuts! I have them all right, but I can't figure that Griffon guy. I guess we're all crazy!"

He hung up, perspiring. "You hear that?" he asked.

"You were right, then. The Cant *was* masquerading as a two-motored job, eh? You know, Lang. I think you know a lot more about aviation than you admit."

"Well, I'm not so dumb as I may look. I know a thing or two, when I need to. But I still can't figure out that business about the package up in that hand."

"I think you and Barney were *both* drunk."

"I'm not so sure myself now, and for the life of me I can't remember just what it was he *did* say that note said. All I know is that I went to Bedloe's and there it was."

"You tell a good story, Lang," laughed Keen. "But you can't cover up a smart bit of detective work with a story like that."

"Well, you know," smirked Lang. "It don't do to tell *all* you know in cases like this. But I'll have to shove along now. See you later—and you needn't say anything about this to Scott, eh?"

"No, of course not," laughed Keen. "But Sir Hubert Beamish *does* really know me, doesn't he, Lang?"

"Beamish?... er, well, I suppose so, But he didn't remember you this morning. Hey—wait a minute—"

But with a hurried "good night," Keen had already shoved him out of the door.

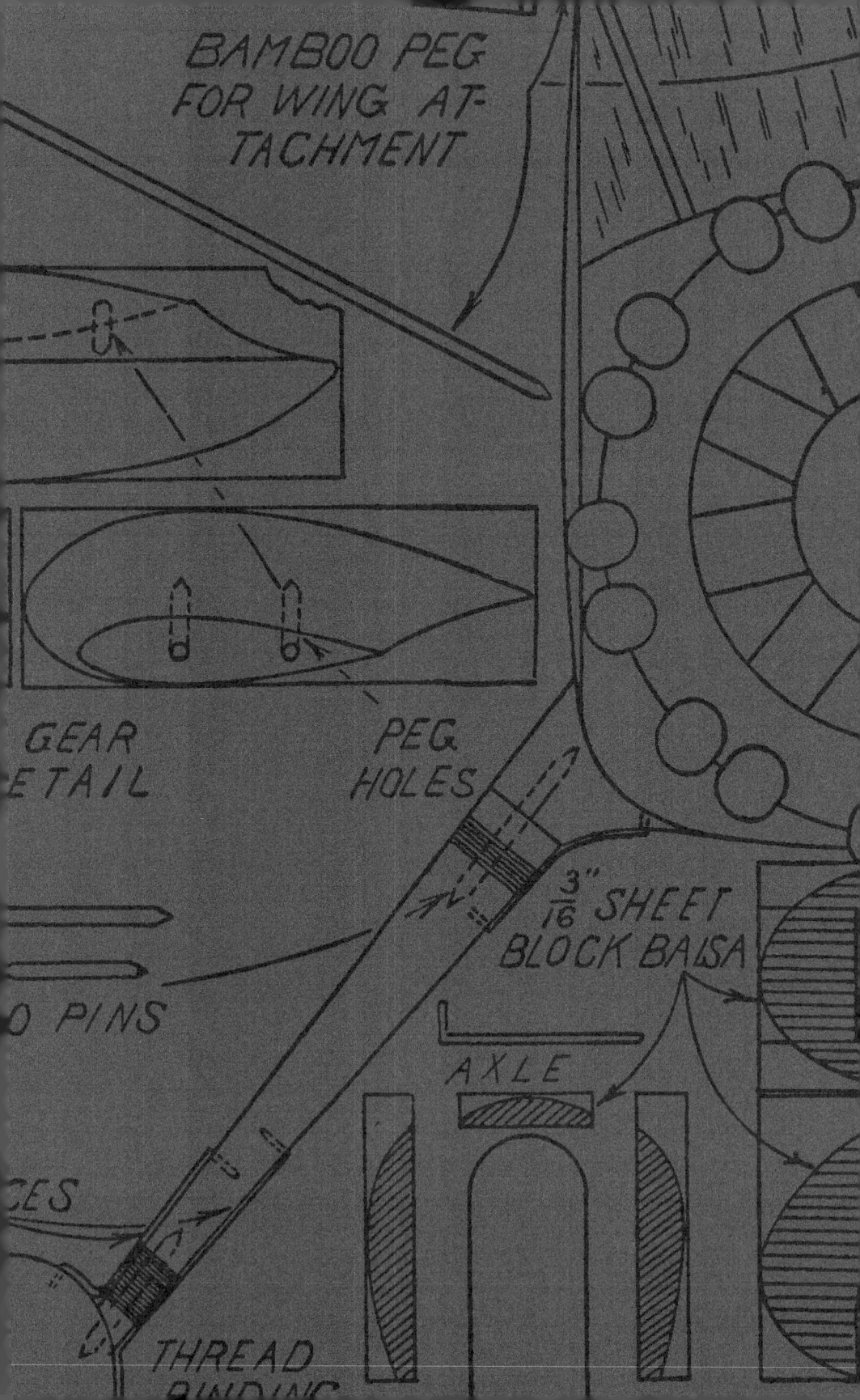

BAMBOO PEG
FOR WING AT-
TACHMENT

GEAR
ETAIL

PEG.
HOLES

O PINS

$\frac{3"}{16}$ SHEET
BLOCK BALSA

AXLE

CES

THREAD
BINDING

Test Pilot Terror

"**I**F you could see this guy's face, you wouldn't believe your own eyes," said Barney O'Dare, twisting the cork of an O'Doul's Dew bottle, while Kerry Keen, the young ballistics expert, sprinkled some pepper over his meal.

"Where did you meet this bird?" Keen asked, sniffing the aroma of the condiment.

"I stopped in at the Half Moon Hotel bar on the way back. And there he was, drinking stingers. I'm telling you, I could hardly believe it—he's a spittin' image! Yep, a dead ringer."

"You saw him before you had any drinks?" Keen asked quietly.

"I'm telling you!"

"And I'm listening. But you say he thinks there's something queer about it all?"

"Two crashes in a row on 9-G dives—when the bus has done over 11-Gs in preliminary factory tests. It don't add up right, according to this bird."

"He knows something about the ship?"

"He designed it originally, but his brother, Hubert, raised the dough, got government backing somehow, and took over the old Jordan Aircraft factory outside Farmingdale. They built four to start. There was some idea of using the basic form for high altitude fighters, ground strafers, general cooperation, and possibly as a Navy fleet fighter.

"They were covering a lot of ground. A ship that could be built to fit all those conditions would be worth a lot of dough—to anyone.

"And this guy—I wish you could see him. You'd get the shock of your life." Barney raged on.

"Never mind his looks. Go on with the fable."

"Anyway, this guy is certain that something is being put over. He says the first one blew up somehow at about 16,000 feet."

"Pilot get out?"

"No. It blew him to bits. The second lost a wing—clipped off by heavy caliber bullets after it had climbed out of sight, passed 20,000 feet. It came down on a high-tension tower and burned up."

"So that about finishes the sleek Salisbury *Salvo,* eh?" asked Keen.

"That's what I said. But this fellow says no. The Army Materiel Division guys know the ship's tops and they want to give it another whirl. They're getting a Navy test pilot from San Diego, a guy named Chunk McGuire, to bring her down tomorrow."

"Wait a minute!" said Keen suddenly. "If the Army is giving these birds a *third* chance, this Salisbury bus *must* have something. And in the meantime, some one who knows what this ship has, is seeing that it is not bought by the U.S. Army Air Corps, Barney."

"That's what this guy argued, but he can't figure who to blame. They have a picked outfit working there—half a dozen Army specialists have been working there for about a year."

"Umm," Keen mused. "This Alton Salisbury invents a new fighter type. He has no money, but his businesslike brother, Hubert, raises the dough and in addition gets Army engineers to assist in developing the job. Does this Alton Salisbury fly?"

"Sure. He's been out on the trans-Pacific business for Pan-American. He only just came East—blew in tonight."

"Then he's never even seen one of the ships he designed?"

"He hasn't. When I left him he was just on his way to his brother's place. No, wait a minute. He was waiting for this guy McGuire, and he and McGuire were going to stay at his brother's place until the final tests were finished."

Keen was no longer interested in his food. He sat staring out of a side window at nothing. Barney poured himself another drink. He knew when to keep quiet.

Finally Keen got up and went into his library. From a shelf he took down two books and began fingering through them. At last he selected a column in the first carrying names beginning with "S" and finally found the item he sought. He read it and smiled. Then he went over the second volume, read for several minutes, and nodded grimly.

"So that's it!" he mused aloud. Then he called: "We take the air the minute it's dark, Barney. There's a gentleman down at the Salisbury plant who will have to be shoved around a little—either that or the U.S. Air Service stands to lose a swell ship."

The cork squeaked again in the O'Doul's Dew bottle. Barney wiped his mouth with the back of his hand, grinned, and went downstairs.

Keen then consulted a map and checked the position of the Salisbury field. This done, he called up a man he knew on the New York *Times*. By nine o'clock he had all details of the mysterious crashes of the Salisbury *Salvo*.

After that he took down a volume on the history of Irak and folded up comfortably in a large leather chair for some recreational reading.

IT WAS well after 10 o'clock when Barney came up again and aroused him. Keen stared at his Mick mechanic for several seconds, then said: "Oh yes, the Salisbury show."

They went downstairs and into the wine cellar, where Barney reached up and pressed a dummy Chablis bottle. There was a low whine and a portion of the shelf rack slid open to reveal a narrow corridor. Keen went through first, and Barney drew the rack back into position and snapped on a light. There Keen drew on a black coveralls, parachute harness, and helmet. While Barney busied himself with his own flying gear, Keen adjusted a scarlet silk mask over his face.

Without another word they went into the underground hangar. The *Black Bullet*, gleaming and smart, stood on the turntable in the center of the floor.

Keen climbed into the control seat while Barney doused the lights. The 1,000 h.p. Avia engine was started and the mufflers cut in. Then Barney snapped the switch that raised the great doors bearing the rock-garden camouflage. Keen let her run out gently, let her purr into a warm-up. Soon Barney was drawing out the folding wings and holding them steady while Keen snapped in the king-pins.

Barney climbed in and snapped the hatch shut, and Keen ran her down past a thick arbor, onto the hard-packed sands of the beach, and into the water. In a few minutes they had crept out into the darkness of the ocean and wheeled around for a take-off. And presently they were in the air, clicking along at 4,000 feet three miles outside of Fire Island beach.

Keen studied the sky above and the water below for some time, then he turned off his course and cut inland over Fire Island Light. He climbed to 6,000 feet, observed the ground around Farmingdale, then switched in his Skoda mufflers again.

With a nod over his shoulder to Barney, Keen cut the engine to idling speed and let her go down in an easy spiral for the Salisbury field below. In two minutes the ghostly black plane dropped on the far side of the field without a light or a rumble. Then with no more noise than would be made by a high-priced sedan, it nosed around and stopped in the dead center of the field just off the broad concrete runway crossing.

HUBERT SALISBURY was a bony faced man with skin like mouldy parchment. His eyes, which were very close together, peered past a long thin nose that had a grayish discoloration along one side. His dress was neat, almost dapper, yet there was something distasteful about him. He smelled of strong soap, Turkish tobacco, and hair tonic, and he had the peculiar nervous habit of always jerking his head to the right before he spoke or moved.

It was Hubert Salisbury who, within the operations office, was talking into a telephone fitted with a metal box that silenced his voice to anyone in the room. Another man—a small, pudgy fellow with a blue scar along the lower half of his moon-like face—sat opposite restraining a cruel smile. He was sucking on a black cigar as Salisbury barked into the metal-box mouthpiece.

But while this stubby man could not hear what Salisbury was saying, nevertheless there was a mysterious man in black outside the building who could. For this new, phantom-like character who had come upon the scene had clipped a pair of steel claws about two wires and was listening in.

Salisbury was bellowing into the phone: "I told you to stay out on the Coast until this thing was cleared up. I know what I'm doing. You keep out of it."

While Salisbury talked, the pudgy man watched. As he puffed contentedly on his cigar, he had visions of a smiling bank teller in Paris—a teller who would give him a fistful of crisp bank notes.

"No, you've got the story all wrong," Salisbury was saying. "There *is* something the matter with the ship, and you can't blame them if they won't take it. I don't know what it is, but that's the story. And take it from me, you'd be better off away from the field until we get it over. If you blow in now, these Army guys will shove you up against a drawing board and you'll have to redesign that whole wing fitting again. Yes, I know. There's nothing wrong with it—except the wings come off. That's all." And he hung up.

Salisbury now turned to the pudgy man and indicated a leather dispatch case on one end of the office table.

"Okay, Elbikon," he said, "you'd better grab them now and get going. This mug brother of mine may spill this thing yet. You can call me tomorrow the minute the test is over."

The little stubby man picked up the leather case with a greedy grasp and stuck it under his arm. Then he reached inside his coat pocket, drew out a long envelope, and proffered it.

"Until we get the rest," he said.

At that instant the door opened and a scarlet-masked man in black stepped inside and covered them both with a heavy black automatic.

"That's all, Elbikon!" the newcomer snapped. "You can put the case back where it was. I'll take care of it."

"What the devil! Who are—"

"My card," the man in black said, flipping a small white oblong on the table.

Elbikon picked up the card gingerly, stared at the name on the face of it.

"I told you! I told you, Salisbury!" the little fat man screamed. "Look!"

Salisbury edged over, picked up the card.

"The Griffon!" he husked.

"The Griffon, is correct, gentlemen. Just in time, too."

"How did he know?" Salisbury demanded of his stubby companion.

"Some one must have talked," came the snarled reply.

The Griffon now stepped up and took both the leather case and the long envelope. There was a warmth to the crackle inside the latter.

But as he lowered his gun to slip the envelope into his coverall pocket, both Salisbury and Elbikon made quick moves. Salisbury snatched a gun from somewhere just as the little fat man dived for the Griffon's gun arm. There was a shot—and Elbikon fell face down on the table.

"You did that!" screamed Salisbury. "You did that!"

"Ah, no, Salisbury. My gun was not even fired. *You* did it. You have killed a man—several men, from what I gather. But if another dies in the test of the Salisbury *Salvo* tomorrow, I'll quickly see that you are apprehended for the murder of Emil Elbikon."

And with that the man in black backed through the doorway, still covering Salisbury as he went. The convulsed body of Emil Elbikon rolled off the table, hit the floor with a thud.

NO SOONER was the Griffon gone, when Salisbury flipped the light and darted for a side door that led into the main hangar. Moving with the speed of a panther, he rolled open the huge doorway, then climbed into the pit of a sleek single-seat plane that stood in the center of the floor. A Twin-Row Wasp opened up, blarted in rising tempo.

Salisbury could not contain himself. He rolled the trim *Salvo* to the open doorway long before she was fully warmed. Then as he slewed onto the concrete apron, he saw a man running across the open turf toward the center of the field where the three broad runway ribbons crossed.

"You devil! You swine!" blazed Salisbury.

He gave the *Salvo* the gun, and as she leaped ahead, he rammed the stick forward and hoiked the tail up. Then, as the man in black, handicapped by his heavy equipment, hurried on, Salisbury fanned his rudder, brought the nose of the ship around, and pressed his triggers.

Brt-rt-t-t! The guns spat, and four streams of yellow-flecked death fingered out for the man in black. Jets of dust spurted up, sparks flickered off the concrete, and ricocheting slugs spanged off in wide parabolas.

Still the man in black stumbled on along his uneven path.

Salisbury held her as true as he could, fired another volley—and the man before his guns went down in a shapeless heap just as he lifted the *Salvo* clear of the black amphibian that suddenly loomed ahead of him on the runway.

The *Salvo* went up with a loud scream. And as the ship hung on her prop, Salisbury stared back to see what it was below him. He saw that the man in black was again stumbling along toward the black amphibian.

Over went the *Salvo* again, and once more those four guns spat and screamed. But the man in black had reached the machine now, had quickly thrown himself upon the port pontoon.

Salisbury pulled up sharply as he saw the black amphibian dash away. He tried to get the *Salvo* around to pound another burst at it, but the black amphibian was already screaming over the hangars.

"Damn!" spat Salisbury.

He whipped the *Salvo* around in a flat turn, again tried to get his nose on her; but the black amphibian suddenly flipped over in a snap roll and came back at the *Salvo* returning the fire with plenty to spare.

Salisbury screamed, rolled over giving the Wasp all she could take, and cleared. The black amphibian now flashed past him into a tight turn, and Salisbury peered up to see the man in black—the Griffon—straddling the pontoon with his grasp upon the forward leg of the landing gear.

With an oath, Salisbury jerked his stick back, treadled the rudder pedals, and jerked the *Salvo's* nose up. He held her there long enough to get a short bead on the black amphibian, then he let drive with every barrel aboard.

Brt-rt-t-t! His fire spat out and sprayed the *Black Bullet* with a bath of liquid fire. He could see the man in black huddle down in an attempt to gain cover. Brt-brt-rt! Across that narrow pontoon a leaden pattern of death stitched toward the scarlet masked figure that clung there.

But then the *Salvo*, held on her tail too long, let out an ominous sigh, slipped back, and nosed down into a stall.

Salisbury fought her for two turns of a spin and only finally drew her out about fifty feet above the field. By then, the black amphibian had disappeared.

THE BRIGADIER-GENERAL stood stiff and silent at the long pine board table set up in front of the Salisbury Aircraft Company's hangar. It was early afternoon the next day.

"I didn't go through West Point to do this sort of thing," he muttered to a Marine Captain near him.

"Testing is worse than war, sir," the captain replied.

"Yes, the War was cleaner. You knew what to expect," the Brigadier snapped, fingering his sword chain nervously. "Why should test pilots, engineers, and research men be tortured this way?"

The Marine Captain held his tongue and simply stared at the gleaming Salisbury *Salvo* that stood out on the concrete. She was deep bellied; yet at the same time she was sleek and beautiful. The Marine Captain liked her, wondered why so much tragedy could be wound into the history of anything so splendid.

"Two skilled test pilots die in crashes that never should have happened. Another man is murdered for no apparent reason at all. And who is this Griffon swine?" the Brigadier demanded.

"I'd give three years of seniority to know—and four more to blast him with a bullet," muttered the Captain between his clenched teeth.

A corps of Army engineers was swarming all over the Salisbury *Salvo*, jotting down figures on long cream-colored sheets. They had been counting the rounds in the wing-gun boxes for the third time. They had computed the fuel to the last gill. They had weighed and tested every bit of equipment on board.

Eight dummy fragmentation bombs were in the belly racks. The heavy caliber Brownings under the hood gleamed and sparkled as the Aviation Armament Major made a last check of the releases and detonator fins.

The *Salvo* was ready for her final 9-G dive test!

There was a lull in activity, a strange silence of expectancy. The mechs stood off, staring at this beautiful killer. "She's a sweet-looking ship, sir," the Marine Captain said for the tenth time.

"So were the other two," snapped the Brigadier. He wiped his long thin fingers across his eyes and added: "One hit the top of a high tension tower at Pinelawn. The other—well, they just shoveled the dirt over the hole where she went in."

John Scott and Drury Lang stood behind the table trying not to look like cops. All they knew was what they heard—something to the effect that two Salisbury *Salvos* had cracked up in mid-air while doing 9-G dives for the Army officials. A man named Emil Elbikon had been murdered, too. And the Army was pretty much baffled.

The Brigadier explained: "Now one ship *could* go wrong like that. Understand, Scott? And there is a possibility that the second might. But considering the fact that both machines had already done better than 9-Gs in preliminary factory tests, there was no excuse for it."

Neither Scott nor Lang had a very thorough idea of what the Brigadier was talking about, but they looked solemn.

"You must understand, Scott," the Brigadier continued. "We, of the technical division have done all we can. There is no reason in the world why these planes will not stay together in T-V work—in terminal velocity dives, that is," he added, by way of explanation. "They have been stressed far beyond that point, and we know it."

"Then why try to put them through again?" John Scott asked.

"You are not in the Army, Scott," came the reply. "Salisbury cannot sell us ten cents' worth of equipment until the *Salvo* actually withstands a 9-G dive under *official* observation."

"But you say she *has* done," Lang insisted.

"Under factory tests, yes. But not with the Material Division looking on. That's the trick. The minute this test pilot lands and shows us that his accelerometer has registered 9-Gs, we'll sign for the delivery of two hundred of these *Salvo* fighters."

"At about $40,000 apiece," muttered Lang. "That's a lot of skins."

"We can't get them quick enough," the Marine Captain chimed in.

"So you're gonner send another test pilot up to see what happens *this* time?"

"Right! And that's why we called you Secret Service men in. We know that some one is tampering with these ships, somehow, somewhere. Hence, we want you on hand to see if you can spot anything we are muffing. After all, we're only technical men. We're not detectives."

So that was how Scott and Lang—who appeared about as much at home as a pair of Chinese laundrymen at a rodeo—were on hand for the third attempt to put a Salisbury *Salvo* through a successful 9-G dive.

SOME one started the 1,100 h.p. twin-row Wasp and let her purr for about ten minutes. Scott and Lang looked on, studied every man who went anywhere near the plane. The table was littered with charts, binoculars and slide-rules, and at one end a meteorologist was adjusting the spring cradle of a barograph.

Then from the hangar which was surrounded by a group of factory officials, there stalked a man dressed in heavy black leather. He walked stiff legged, for to both of his thighs were strapped small portable instruments. Moreover he was weighted down with the cumbersome harness of a parachute.

Under all this the test pilot, a strange character by the name of Chunk McGuire, wore a heavy suit of thick underwear. And over the underwear had been strapped wide strips of adhesive tape to take the terrific strain his muscles would have to undergo in the pull-out. His stomach was also wrapped with a heavy rubber circlet, and a broad leather belt similar to those worn by motorcyclists gave further reinforcement.

A stout corduroy suit came next, a few woolen scarves, and

then the shapeless ghost mask that carried a reinforced rubber tube to connect to his oxygen tank.

"Who is this guy?" Lang asked. "Know anything about him?"

"Named McGuire. A crackerjack. But like a lot of these fellows, a little queer."

"Whatya mean queer?"

"Very quiet. Doesn't mix much. Won't let anyone touch him while he's dressing. They'll never slip anything over on McGuire. He takes no chances on anything," the Marine Captain explained.

"What's he doin' in this racket then?" asked the doleful Drury.

"He says it's the only way he knows how to make a living without working—if you can get the idea."

"I don't get it."

"Anyhow, that's the reason McGuire gives for taking these jobs. And of course he makes about two grand a shot."

"He can have it."

Scott and Lang moved away from the table and sauntered about among the men who were still buzzing about the *Salvo*. They watched McGuire climb in, then they paced about. The test pilot sat studying the instrument board and jacking in his muzzle mike connections and the tube to the oxygen tank. He flipped the stick and checked the movement of the controls, then he pulled the cowling panels together, fingering them as he did so to make certain he could open them again quickly if necessary.

"This bird knows his stuff, I'll bet," Lang said out of the corner of his mouth.

"We'll find out, if he comes back with all he took with him," Scott said. "I hope—"

RR-R-R-R!

Whatever it was Scott was about to add was cut off with the roar of the Wasp. The test pilot gave her a run-up and let her down quickly. He nodded with a jerky movement, waved both hands, and rolled away from the hangar.

In two minutes the *Salvo* was out at the end of the runway and the Army engineers sat down near the portable radio receiver mounted on the table to listen to the routine check reports from the man in the fighter.

Then with a cheery, "Okay! Let's go!" the pilot let her out. The *Salvo* roared, flipped her tail up, and bellowed down the runway. In twenty yards she was fighting to get her wheels off, and in thirty they were clear and hanging grotesquely at the ends of their cantilever struts. Then with a final bellow, the *Salvo* hoiked up in a crazy climb.

"I NEVER saw McGuire take off like that before," the Marine Captain said.

"What was wrong?" asked Lang. "Looked all right to me."

"Yeh? Well, if his motor had conked then, we'd be ordering a new section of concrete runway."

"Well, he's away okay now," Scott said, watching the *Salvo* climb into a gossamer veil of cirrus.

"One goes with a time bomb in the fuselage," muttered the Brigadier. "The second had its wings chewed off by machine-gun fire and hits a high-tension tower. And the pilot burned up."

"Is that what really happened?" asked Scott hollowly.

"Nothing else but."

"Then why didn't you give him some sort of protection. You could have put some other ships up there to keep anyone away."

"It could be done, yes. But it might be dangerous to have other ships around when he starts down. We have ordered the area kept clear for two hours. That should be quite enough leeway."

"Yeh, but how can you be sure at twenty or thirty thousand feet?"

"Do you know how many planes in this area can fly at 30,000 feet?" demanded the Brigadier.

"Most all the Army planes can, can't they?"

"But you're not suggesting that an Army plane is shooting down a ship that is being tested for the Army, are you?"

"I should think that it would *have* to be an Army plane of some kind if it is carrying guns," said Scott with a simple face.

"But man alive! We can check every Army plane in this part of the country. No one could get away with that."

"But some one *has!*" snapped Lang defiantly.

The Brigadier took off his hat, wiped his brow with his handkerchief. "You're right," he said. "Some one has."

There was no further chance for conversation, for the routine check reports were coming in from the *Salvo:*

"*Six thousand feet in 1:58… top speed now 257… r.p.m. 2,200… no, cheek—r.p.m. 2,300…. Okay?*"

The Brigadier barked back an affirmation.

They got another check at 10,000 feet, which was reached in 2.7 minutes. And the top speed in level flight was given as 277 m.p.h.

As the checkers jabbed these figures down on their long sheets, their faces showed their amazement at the performance. The Brigadier allowed himself to smile across at Hubert Salisbury, who was walking up and down tearing cigarettes into quarter-inch lengths.

More checks and reports came at 15,000—and then a loud, unholy cry burst from the receiving set. A radio man leaped to adjust the dials, but he stopped as the cry was repeated.

"My Lord! Again!" the Brigadier said in a low tone. "Listen, Scott!"

Again a scream came through the speaker. Then after an abrupt thudding sound, the radio went dead, leaving a ring of chalk-white faces staring despairingly.

Then from the sky there came a low whine like the wail of a distant siren. Ever louder and more strident grew that whine. And those on the ground turned slowly like silly automatic dolls in a tableau, stared upward without moving the positions of their feet.

The *Salvo* was on its way down, one wing fluttering back over the tail. The wail now became an ear-piercing scream. Then the doomed ship abruptly lost its original spiral dive as the broken wing went away with a high-pitched metallic clank and the distorted fuselage jerked up like a hooked tarpon.

"Why doesn't he get clear?" demanded the Brigadier. "Jump,

man!" he cried, as though he believed the wretched flyer could hear him.

"We'd better get clear ourselves," raged Drury Lang. "That mess will be right here on the table in a minute!"

The wreckage, sending forth a new wail as the nose came down again, now whipped into a wider spiral. The motor roared in mad spurts, then the other wing folded back.

C-CR-RACK!

She continued down, spiraling tighter and tighter. The rage of her death wail now pitched even higher—and then she nosed into the ground a few feet off the runway with a terrific smash. There was a mushrooming billow of dust, a clatter of chunks of dural, and a final gush of smoke. Already the mournful bleat of a siren sounded as the wreck-car dashed toward the crash.

"Everybody back!" ordered the Brigadier. "Only Captain Blaine, Mr. Salisbury, the two Secret Service men, and I will approach the wreckage. I will call if we need any other assistance. Those are my orders!"

Salisbury stood half-blubbering, still nervously breaking up cigarettes. He followed the Brigadier and the Marine Captain out as though he were being towed by some unseen wire. Scott and Lang approached almost on tip-toes.

The wrecked fuselage was telescoped over the motor which had gone in about four feet. The coupe top had been wrenched open by the force of the impact, and there the pilot lay in a heap, his back against the instrument board. It was evident that he had tried to the finish to get clear—but something had held him.

They reached in from both sides, tried to pull him clear. His helmet and face mask, already loosened, fell away.

"What on earth?" gasped the Brigadier. "Look, Captain. This isn't McGuire! I say, who—"

"Look! Look!" cried Drury Lang. "That card in his hand—the one with the glove off!"

John Scott reached past the Marine Captain, snatched at the card. But he knew already, what it would say.

"The Griffon!" husked Lang.

"And that's not all, Lang. Look again. Who is that man?"

"My Lord! It's Kerry Keen!"

THEY roped the wreckage off. Then piece by piece they dismantled the *Salvo* and checked every section of it. Salisbury would not go near it. He stood off lighting cigarettes, taking short puffs, and throwing them to the ground where he crunched them into the turf with his heel.

Drury Lang went over to him. Salisbury seemed stricken with fear and started to walk away.

"Wait a minute, Salisbury," Lang snapped. "Is that the guy who blew in here last night and bopped off this man, Elbikon?"

"I… I don't know. The murderer was… was masked. I never saw his face," Salisbury stammered. "I… I never saw *that* man before," he added with a nervous nod toward the wreck.

"You mean—but wait a minute," snarled Lang. "You saw him before he got into the ship—when he dressed in there, didn't you?"

"I saw Chunk McGuire—the Navy test man. But that isn't McGuire!"

"Did you actually see McGuire dress and climb into his clothes?" asked Lang.

"No, not actually. You see—"

"I know. I know. McGuire is a queer guy who won't let anyone assist him in his dressing. What really happened, then, is that you met McGuire when he came in, then he went to dress for the test. Actually, you never saw his face again, because of the helmet, goggles, and the oxygen mask."

"McGuire came in and they all spoke to him. He went over the details of the ship in the hangar and then lay down on a couch in my office. I was busy with the Army men. Well, when I came back, McGuire had left the office and I presumed that he had gone down to my locker room to dress. The next time I saw him was when he came into the hangar all decked out."

"I get it," observed Lang, rubbing his whiskery chin. "But what happened to McGuire, then?"

"I don't know," replied Salisbury slowly.

At that moment the Brigadier came out from the tangle of wreckage, his uniform streaked with blood, flaked dope, and oil.

"Shot down," he said coldly. "Same bullets, same caliber as those used on you by that black plane last night, Salisbury. They got him with about ten in the small of his back. His spine went and he couldn't move. Another burst took the wing root out. That's all."

"That's plenty," added Lang. "It means that this black ship that fired on Salisbury last night, shot this machine down today, eh?"

The Brigadier nodded, wiped his hands with his handkerchief.

"But wait a minute," broke in Scott. "That doesn't make sense. If this Griffon guy escaped on the pontoon of that black ship last night, why would the same ship shoot him down today when he was aboard the *Salvo?*"

"You don't expect anything to jibe where the Griffon is concerned, do you?" demanded Lang.

"Regardless," snapped the Brigadier, "there's one *Salvo* left. And we're going to put it through a 9-G, if I have to bring her down myself. There's something queer about all this, but still I'm going to get to the bottom of it."

"You will," smirked Lang, "if you try to dive one of these babies."

"The other *Salvo* will be thoroughly checked," the Brigadier snapped. "Everything will be arranged for the dive test tomorrow afternoon, the same time. Is that clear, Salisbury?"

Hubert Salisbury jerked. He had been staring at the man who had been lifted from the wreckage. He was white and trembling, and his lower jaw sagged.

"No... No! Not tomorrow, sir," he pleaded. His hands were outstretched, pleading.

"Why not? Why not tomorrow?"

"You... you can't. You see, I can't be here."

"Why not?"

"That... that—" He was pointing to the dead pilot they were lifting to a stretcher. "That... that man is my brother—my brother, Alton. He's dead."

The Brigadier stood transfixed. He turned finally and stared down at the heap that had once been a man.

"Your brother? The man who originally designed the *Salvo?*" he managed to get out.

"Yes… Alton. He came in last night, from the Coast."

"But… but that's Keen—Kerry Keen, the ballistics man," argued John Scott. "I'd know him in a million!"

"Look at his right forearm," husked Salisbury.

The Brigadier kneeled beside the stretcher, pulled up the leather coat and coverall. There in a dull bluish tattooing was the design of an Army Air Service badge with the initials of A.J.S. beneath.

"Whew!" gasped Drury Lang.

"Even so," snapped the Brigadier, getting up, "the last *Salvo* will be tested tomorrow."

LANG waited no longer. He raced into the hangar, he leaped a low barrier, plunged into Salisbury's office, and snatched at a phone. Breathless, he called a number.

"Hey you, Mick," he barked when his call was completed. "Where's that dandy of yours?"

"Who you talking about?" demanded Barney.

"Keen—that bullet-chaser you feed and bed down. Who do you think I mean?"

"I wouldn't know," answered Barney from Graylands.

"You wouldn't know what?" Lang spat.

"Neither!"

"Neither what?"

"Neither who you meant, or where Keen is," Barney taunted.

"Don't stall for time, you bog-trotter. Where's Keen?" Lang ranted again.

"He's not here," Barney tried to explain, still stalling for ideas. "Where is he?"

"He went out just before lunch. I think he took a walk. He's digging in to do a lecture and he's not fit to speak to."

"Where was he last night?" Lang suddenly blarted.

"In bed."

"How do you know?"

"I ought to. I put him there."

"Listen, you damn pig-stealer, if I don't get a straight answer out of you in a minute, I'm gonner.... Holy Heaven! What the—"

Lang forgot Barney completely. He put the phone down on its cradle, stared as a man came staggering toward him from a door at the far end of the office.

The newcomer was of medium build, freckled and ginger-headed. He had shoulders as broad as an ox. He walked like a man who is punch-drunk and carried his massive chin in one cupped hand.

"Who hit me?" he demanded, glaring at Lang.

"Who the hell are you, and where did you pop in from?" Lang countered.

The man sat down heavily, rubbed his chin: "Some one conked me when I went in there to change. What happened, anyway?"

"You Chunk McGuire?" snapped Lang.

"Yeh, McGuire. I was to test that *Salvo.*"

"You're lucky, getting only a sock in the mug. The other guy's in the meat wagon."

"I don't get it," said McGuire, letting his chin drop.

"Neither do we—but that's what happened. The guy who took your place came down with his wings off."

"Not in that sky boiler. I looked her over."

"No? Well go outside and look her over again."

"But who was it that took 'er up?"

"Salisbury's brother, Alton—the guy who designed it."

"I thought he was out on the Coast?"

"That's what Salisbury thought, too."

McGuire sat staring at Lang, then he cocked his head on one side like a dog listening. "Wait a minute," he said after a few seconds. "Wait a minute."

"Think fast, kid," encouraged Lang.

"No, I guess there was nothing to it. I mean, when I got here just after lunch, I threw my flying gear on a bench in the hangar.

And when I came back I saw a guy—I think he was one of those oil-tank drivers. Anyway, he had some sort of a jumper coat on with Richfield, Socony, or something like that, stitched on the pocket."

"Yeh? Go on."

"I sorter shooed him off from my stuff. I don't like anyone messing around with my gear. But when he was gone, I found a card stuck on one strap of the glove."

"A card?"

"Yeh, just a card. On it was printed—"

"The Griffon?"

"That's it. But how did you know?"

"We found it in Alton Salisbury's fist when we pulled him out."

"Did you read what was written on the back of it in pencil?" asked McGuire.

"On the back? No. What was it?"

"It said: *'Test pilots have to shoot straight—or else.'* I didn't think anything about it. This racket has its nuts just like any other."

"What do you think it meant, though?"

"Nothing at all, I'll wager. Just a nut."

"I don't think so. I'm gonner trace that oil-tank guy. You stick around. And I think you got the test job for tomorrow, McGuire."

THAT night the Brigadier General sat at a long table in the hangar with Salisbury, Scott, Lang, Captain Blaine, and two engineers of the Army Air Corps Materiel Division. Chunk McGuire sat by himself in one corner smoking cigarettes and reading a magazine.

The Brigadier was testy and anxious. The Marine Captain, still somewhat shaken, was silent. Salisbury looked like a ghost with clothes on, and John Scott sat staring at nothing in particular.

"We don't know what we can gain by this," Lang was saying, "but I'm playing a hunch. You, Salisbury, will get the shock of your life when you see his face, but don't let it get you. Act as though nothing had happened."

"One more shock won't make much difference," Salisbury muttered.

Lang busied himself with a display of small metal slugs and a few other articles of evidence which were set about on the table. Then there was a rumble of a car and a door slammed. Lang sat up, listened, then gave the crowd the nod.

"Here he comes," he husked. "Take it easy, Salisbury."

A side door opened and Kerry Keen, dapper and neat in a black top coat, a smart dark fedora, and a white scarf under his chin, came in and stared about as though he was uncertain of his bearings.

"Okay, Keen. Over this way," Lang ordered.

Salisbury let out an audible gasp, gripped the edge of the table. The Marine Captain steadied him quickly and Salisbury sat back and turned his eyes away.

Lang made quick introductions and a short explanation. Keen nodded and sat down, loosening his coat and displaying a well-cut dinner jacket.

"We're glad to see you, Mr. Keen," the Brigadier opened. "We need your assistance. No doubt you have heard of the trouble we have been having here."

"Trouble?" queried Keen, staring about with a mystified air.

"Trouble—and plenty! We have been attempting to complete a test on a new military plane built here by the Salisbury firm."

"Oh, yes. I remember reading about that now. Two bad accidents, I believe."

"Three, to be exact. We had another this afternoon."

"Another? Then there must be something radically wrong with the plane, eh?" asked Keen.

"There's nothing wrong with the plane, Mr. Keen. It's something much more serious Now you, I believe, are something of an expert on ballistics—"

"Yes, my main interest—especially small arms stuff," Keen explained. "But what has that to do with air crashes? I'm not a flying man, you know."

"We *don't* know," snapped Lang. "If we did, maybe we'd jug you, Keen."

The Brigadier looked at Lang puzzled. But he went on:

"What would you say these three slugs were, Mr. Keen?" he asked, shoving three copper-colored bullets across the table.

Keen picked them up, weighed them in his hands, then inspected them with a small pocket glass.

He put them down after a moment and put his glass away.

"Chatelleraults—about 13.2 slug, I'd say off hand," he said selecting a cigarette from his gold case. "One of their new weapons for high speed fire."

"And these three," the Brigadier asked, shoving over another set.

Keen blew two plumes of blue smoke through his nostrils, gave Salisbury a sidelong glance, and picked up two of the slugs. He gave them the same close inspection.

"Same type slug, same caliber," he muttered.

Salisbury got to his feet quickly.

"Then the same man—or men—who fired on me last night, shot my brother down this afternoon. The very same man who came in here and killed Emil Elbikon—The Griffon!"

He was about to raise his hand and direct an accusing finger at Keen. But Keen made a slight move with his eyes and Salisbury hesitated.

"I wouldn't know anything about all that," Keen said quietly. "But these three slugs were not fired from the same gun as the first three."

Lang jerked, almost rose to his feet. The Brigadier shoved his cap to the back of his head, tugged at his crisp mustache.

"Are you sure, Mr. Keen?" the Brigadier finally managed to get out. Keen's statement had completely disrupted their well defined explanation for the crashes.

"Positive! These three slugs were fired from a different gun. Look at them yourselves. There's five rifling grooves marked on them. On the other three there are only four. Entirely different guns, you will agree, gentlemen."

They all examined them and counted the grooves carefully, then sat back helpless. Keen lit another cigarette.

The Brigadier tried another tack: "The Chatellerault is a French gun, of course, Mr. Keen?"

Keen nodded, continued to eye Salisbury.

"Are there any in this country—that you know of? I mean…. Oh, I don't know what I mean."

"There might be a few at Ordnance Headquarters in Washington. And there might be one or two somewhere in the hands of collectors."

"Do you have one, Mr. Keen?" Lang growled.

"Oh, yes. On the wall in my study there's a war-time Chatellerault, Mr. Lang," replied Keen, bowing.

Lang had no answer for that.

Keen turned to the Brigadier: "Well, sir. Now that we have solved this ponderous problem concerning the slugs, I presume I may be on my way?"

"Mr. Keen," the Brigadier answered. "Sit down a minute. You appear to have a pretty good mind, and Mr. Scott is quite impressed with you. I wonder if you could offer any suggestions in this matter?"

"But I know nothing about it—only what I have read."

"Good! Then you have no preconceived ideas on the case. I'll outline it all as far as we know."

KEEN sat down and listened to the story from the time the first *Salvo* crashed. But he did not show much enthusiasm until the Brigadier brought up the matter of the startling likeness between himself and Alton Salisbury, the pilot who had been killed that afternoon.

"This Salisbury knocked out the Navy man and took his place?" asked Keen with a frown. "Then it is obvious that he suspected something and tried to make certain himself that the test would go off okay."

"What do you mean, he suspected something?" demanded Hubert Salisbury, rising to his feet, his face a mask of rage.

"Just that," replied Keen coldly. "The blueprints of the plane have been stolen from you, haven't they?"

"Are you suggesting that I—I who saw this thing through this far—am mixed up in a plot to prevent the *Salvo* from passing government tests?" blazed Salisbury.

"The Brigadier simply asked me what *I* thought," reminded Keen coolly. "I'm telling him. My opinions may mean nothing; but he asked for them, and so he's getting them."

"Go on, Mr. Keen," the Brigadier ordered. "What you say is interesting, at least. Particularly since no one had mentioned—"

"I'm just a dreamer, I suppose," Keen broke in, with a smile at Salisbury. "But suppose the *Salvo* does *not* pass specifications?"

The Brigadier threw out his hands, "Well, I suppose that will be all there is to it."

"So that after the government has spent considerable money and lent the Salisbury firm its best engineers, they'll get nothing in return?"

"Well, you might put it that way?"

"So if the *Salvo* should fail to pass just one particular test, the Salisbury concern would be free either to sell the plans and its remaining ship to any firm—or to any nation that saw fit to purchase it. Is that so?"

"That could happen," agreed the Brigadier.

"It has happened," Keen suddenly barked. "Where are the all-important blueprints? And who was this man, Elbikon, who was so strangely murdered here by an almost fictitious character known as the Griffon?"

The Brigadier stared at Salisbury, who in turn glared at Keen with deep hatred.

"Aren't those pretty serious charges, Mr. Keen?" the Marine Captain broke in. "How did you know—"

"They're *not* charges! The Brigadier simply asked for my opinions," Keen replied.

The Brigadier was now distressed, seemed unable to find anything to say.

"Emil Elbikon," Keen went on, "was supposed to be an expert on flush riveting, wasn't he, Salisbury?"

"He was," Salisbury snapped. "He was to take charge of that department when we went into production."

"But then a man known as the Griffon murdered him, you say?"

"Shot him down in cold blood and got away with the blueprints," Salisbury grated through his teeth.

"What were those important blueprints doing out of a safe at that time of night?"

"We had been going over them again to see if we could find any fault in the wing structure."

"That's very interesting, considering the fact that Emil Elbikon was actually a representative of an important European aviation concern. I happen to know that Elbikon was particularly interested in American machine guns. He had corresponded with me on several occasions, and had asked for certain details on new American guns, which I felt I could not give out."

The Brigadier and the Marine Captain both sat with their mouths open, staring at Keen, who was getting up again and adjusting his muffler about his throat.

"Just a few opinions, gentlemen," Keen said, pushing his chair back. "And now, if I may...."

"Wait a minute," broke in Chunk McGuire, coming out from the corner shadows. "You don't work for an oil company, do you? You ain't the guy I caught messing about with my gear this afternoon, are you?"

"Work?" Keen replied with a distasteful grimace. "My dear man, I don't believe in even taking a hand at manual labor. If you ever do, they make you keep at it. You know, I once had an uncle who gave me the finest advice in the world. He used to say, 'Look here, Kerry, my lad. Don't ever take your coat off—they'll never let you put it on again.' And I never have."

"Even so, you look a hell of a lot like the guy—"

"Who was pulled out of the *Salvo* this afternoon. The Brigadier told me all about that. Funny, two fellows looking so much alike," smiled Keen. "And now, if you don't mind, gentlemen, I have an engagement at the annual meeting of the Foam Combers Club. You'll excuse me, I'm sure."

"Yeh," said Lang. "I'll see you to the door myself, Mr. Keen."

Keen waved a cheery good-night toward the table and left, with Lang at his heels.

"What is it, sniff-hound?" Keen said, when they were out of earshot.

"So you don't know anything about this business, eh, Keen?"

"Not a thing!"

"No? Well, let me tell you something. Only a few of us knew the blueprints were missing. And here *you* just mentioned it. How did you know?"

"The Brigadier said—"

"He never even mentioned it. We were keeping that quiet."

"But I was under the impression that they were stolen."

"They were," Lang sneered. "But you're in deep this time, Keen. There's only one way out, too, you know."

"What are you driving at?"

"Just this, Mister Keen. That *Salvo* over there has to do a 9-G dive tomorrow and come down with her wings on. Not only that, but she has to be delivered with those blueprints. Get it?"

"You're away off this time, Lang," Keen came back.

"Not so far off as you, Mister Keen," Lang smirked. "You certainly pulled a bloomer that time."

"Or did I?" Keen said, buttoning up his top coat.

"Whatya mean?"

"Don't worry about me. You keep that beady eye of yours on the man who killed Emil Elbikon—he'll bear a lot of watching between now and the time they take that plane up."

"Who do you mean?"

"You don't believe for one minute that the Griffon killed Elbikon, do you?"

"Salisbury said he did."

"All right. Then why did the Griffon kill Elbikon and not

Salisbury? And why, if Salisbury is on the up and up, did his brother try to do the dive test?"

"Say, you got something there—but what about those blueprints?"

"Sorry, but I've got a date at the Foam Combers, old lad. You watch Mr. Salisbury. Good night!"

KEEN returned to his Duesenberg which was purring quietly outside the airport office. Barney was still at the wheel, his homely face grave and anxious.

"Do me a favor, will you?" Keen said, as he opened the door. "Step outside here a moment and plant that fist of yours on my button—for about a count of seven."

"Get in, you're groggy now. What happened?" asked Barney.

"I guess I spoke out of turn. And Lang caught me," muttered Keen. "But now step on it!"

He explained what had happened as they raced back to Graylands. Barney listened thoughtfully.

"You know what that lug Salisbury is going to do, don't you?" he finally said without any comment on Keen's boner.

"I'd like to be sure," Keen replied.

"That mug will try to get away with that sky boiler tonight, somehow."

"Give yourself a dime, Barney. I have the same feeling myself."

"So what?"

"Well, we've got the blueprints."

"And the dough," Barney gurgled.

"I ordered three more cases this afternoon."

"Only three? Practically an abstainer these days, eh?"

"All we need now is the *Salvo*... and—"

"And the chance to put her down for 9-Gs. But say! Wait a minute. That cigar store over there. I've got to call up Lang."

Barney frowned but pulled up to the curb outside the cigar store. They had reached Patchogue. Keen darted in, flipped a coin into the slot, and called Lang at the Salisbury plant.

"Lang," he said. "This is—well, Floyd Gibbons, if anyone asks you. Get it? Okay. This is Keen. Tell me something, will you? On the quiet?"

"Okay, Gibbons," Lang replied, "but don't run anything until I give you the word."

"Good stuff, Lang," replied Keen. "How near is that *Salvo* ready for the test?"

"She's ready now. They worked all afternoon on her."

"Are all the test instruments in? All-up weight aboard and the accelerometer set?"

"All they have to do is to take her up—and bring her down."

"Fine. Now get this. Forget Salisbury...."

"But you said...."

"Never mind what I said. Forget him any time after 11 o'clock. He'll try to get away with something, but let him. You know—enough rope and he'll give himself a necktie party."

"I don't get it... er, Gibbons."

"Keep close to him until about 11. After that, let him go to the hangar if he has any excuse at all. But keep the Brigadier and his mob somewhere handy... just in case. Get it?"

"I don't... but I'll do it. What's it all about?"

"I have a hunch Mr. Salisbury wants to do the dive test himself, so give him the chance, eh?"

"It sounds loopy, but if you say so, okay!"

"Thanks, old son. On to the Foam Combers, and the devil take the hindermost!" laughed Keen.

"You're nuts!" spat Lang, hanging up.

IT WAS well after 10 when Keen and Barney got back to Graylands. The Mick rushed downstairs and went to work getting the *Black Bullet* ready for an amazing adventure. Keen kept his dinner clothes on, but selected a new black coverall to slip over them. Finally he made a few telephone calls, then glanced at the clock and raced upstairs to a small room in the upper part of the house. The clock on the stairs clanged the half-hour as he slipped inside a door and sat down before a broad slate panel fitted with dials, adjusting screws, switches, and recording instruments. He jammed a set of headphones down over his ears and began a systematic search of the air. Above, hidden from view inside a small crypt on the roof, two loop aerials turned in response to Keen's movement of the direction wheel below. His right hand worked the rheostat knob and brought in the sounds picked up by a set of delicate microphones carefully hidden in a movable chimney shield.

For nearly a quarter of an hour he sat tense and expectant. Then gradually he caught a sound that electrified every fibre of his nervous system. He drew it in carefully with his detector, amplified it, and directed it through the filter for clarity. He worked a cross bearing on the sound until he was confident of its location.

He listened for some time, moving the direction wheel slightly and tracing small marks on a map before him. The marks moved from out over Long Island Sound, cut in across Mt. Misery Point, and headed down the North Country Road toward Smithtown.

Keen listened a few minutes more, checked the sound carefully.

"No mistake," he muttered. "That's a Gnome-Rhone, or I'm a Dutchman!"

He snapped the switch of a desk speaker-phone, barked: "Run her up, Barney. We're leaving at once!"

Then he ran down the stairs, completed his dressing for the flight, and lastly selected a carefully wrapped package tied with stout cord.

Then he climbed into his black parachute harness and hurried through the house and down the cellar stairs. He slipped through the secret panel in the wine cellar and found that Barney had the *Black Bullet's* motor ticking over quietly.

They doused the lights, opened the hangar doors, and Keen ran the ship out. Barney took care of everything on the ground, then climbed in the rear pit while Keen took her on down the turf to the beach and slipped her into the water.

They were away in a jiffy with their pontoons tucked up into the recesses along the body. Keen muttered a few instructions to Barney as they climbed over Southampton.

"She'll probably be an all-metal Dewoitine, Barney," he explained, "so you'll have to give her everything. That guy has two Chats in the wings and two more weapons of higher caliber in the nose somewhere. I traced him out of Connecticut. He crossed at Mt. Misery—and he'll wish he hadn't."

"How did you find out about this Dewoitine?" the Mick asked, as he scanned the sky.

"One of my gunnery friends who works down at the Custom House traced a shipment of ammunition 'for experimental' purposes to a jerk-water gun factory outside Hartford. A couple of guys who had worked at the Colt plant for a few years figured they could make a lot of money quick if they could build a gun involving all the best parts of the Browning, Colt, Chat, and Vickers. Quite a large order! Anyhow, Elbikon used them as suckers to get his stuff in after he had brought the Dewoitine through on the excuse of entering it in the National Air Races."

"But they actually used the plane to shoot down *Salvos,*" Barney added.

"Exactly! Now this bird is going to find out how it feels to go down with *his* wings off. But we've got to be lucky. Damned lucky!"

They climbed, and it got colder and colder. Below them stretched the full outline of Long Island, gleaming with its varied necklaces of lights and flickering baubles that marked the towns and villages like jewel-encrusted brooches. But they failed to sight the guerrilla ship, though they circled back and forth carefully between Patchogue and Bay Shore, watching the sky and ground below for any movement of aircraft. They cut in once toward Farmingdale and circled the Salisbury field at a height of about 8,000 feet, but Keen had kept his Skoda mufflers cut in and their presence was not detected from the ground.

They were watching the Salisbury field below with the aid of powerful glasses and were utterly oblivious of the danger that came hammering out of the sky above.

A sleek, dull silver high-wing monoplane with a cat-fish nose came down at them from the darkness above. Keen first caught the glint of tracer flame in a reflection from his instrument dial. Quickly he flipped the *Black Bullet* out of line.

"Wow!" gasped Barney. "What was that?"

He hung on while Keen threw the *Bullet* all over the sky, then he waited with his guns poised for action.

THE SILVER Dewoitine wheeled out of its zoom and Barney poured a quick burst at it. The pilot continued to climb fast, however, and Keen turned under him and gave Barney another shot from below.

The French pursuit flipped its wings twice, screwed away.

"Keep on him. Don't let him get away!" Keen yelled.

Barney waited again, and as he set himself, the Dewoitine suddenly whipped over, hung for a second in a roll, and came down like a winged hurricane. Lead spattered past them, and Barney, huddled behind his gun mounting, slammed lead back.

Keen waited until the last possible second. Then, instead of flipping off to one side, he took the play into his own hands and nosed up sharply. His guns barked, spewed death.

The Dewoitine pilot tried to get clear, but he jerked out too hard and seemed to beat up into a fluttering stall. Barney took his chance and pasted a long wailing double burst at the floundering pursuit—and suddenly one of its wings trembled ominously. There was a loud crack and the Dewoitine fluttered. Barney poured another long burst into her while Keen screwed the *Black Bullet* around again to give him a wide angle of fire.

The Dewoitine seemed to stand still, as if getting its breath. Then it nosed down slowly as its broken wing folded back. Keen watched it, and Barney held his fire as they saw a man scrambling out of the cockpit.

"Give him a chance," Keen bellowed.

The wretched flyer managed to fight his way clear and poise himself on top of the fuselage. He held there a moment, raised a menacing fist, then hurled into space, tumbling grotesquely head over heels into the semi-darkness below.

They watched and sensed the "plop" that marked the opening of the parachute. They could just discern the white of the canopy as it drifted away toward the Mannetto Hills.

The falling wreckage had taken on a dull glow now, and they watched it twisting down toward the junction of the Melville-

Road Hollow roads. The flame of the wreckage gradually brightened and spread itself into a broad-bladed spear-head of gold and scarlet, slashing down through the night.

It twisted tortuously for about three thousand feet, then blossomed to its fullest as it went to its doom. As it hit the earth, the glare blazed up brightly and illuminated the whole area about the Salisbury Field—just in time to show Keen and Barney the outline of a racing single-seater that was streaking across the concrete-slashed field. It was the *Salvo*.

"Just as I figured," smiled Keen. "Here comes our man!"

"If he only knew what he was in for, he'd nose her over right now," Barney grinned.

KEEPING his Skodas in, Keen nosed down after the racing *Salvo*. He moved fast and was soon in a strategic position below and behind the Salisbury ship. He fired two short indicating bursts past both sides of the *Salvo* and caught the pilot's attention.

The *Salvo* pilot tried to get away, hut Barney, standing up with his guns clear of the coupe top, added more warning tracers.

They wheeled to one side a moment, and Barney, catching the *Salvo* pilot's attention, pointed upward. The man in the *Salvo* cockpit stared in amazement. The glow from his lighted instrument board brought out every line in his face.

"It's Salisbury, all right," Keen remarked. "Make him go upstairs!"

Barney took the orders over his Gosport headset and again pointed upward with one hand while he threatened the *Salvo* pilot with his guns. Now they cut in close again, and they could see that Salisbury was in bad shape. He was flying sloppily.

"He'll never do it," snarled Keen. "The swine hasn't got what it takes."

"He's *got* to do it," Barney raged, pointing upward again.

"He *won't!* He'll wreck it yet. You'd better flag him down. Make him land just beyond where the Dewoitine lies. It's still burning and ought to give him enough light."

Barney gulped, stared at Keen and said: "You crazy nut!"

"Flag him down!"

Keen zipped the *Black Bullet* alongside the *Salvo* and Barney pointed ahead and down. He trained his guns on the *Salvo*, and they saw Salisbury nod anxiously and slow the *Salvo* into a glide. The fighter cleared a tangle of telephone wires and zipped over the railroad tracks that separated the Salisbury field from the meadow land of an industrial school. They saw Salisbury drop her down with a series of metal-wrenching bumps and finally roll to a stop.

Keen had dropped his amphibian pontoons to a ground landing position, and now he quickly landed the *Bullet* near the *Salvo*. He leaped out, automatic in hand, and raced across to the fighter.

He was well masked and strode straight up to the *Salvo*. Salisbury had already raised the cockpit covering.

"Get out, you rat," Keen snapped. "I thought I'd get you to take her upstairs and bring her down for 9-Gs. But you're lily-livered!"

Salisbury, now a pathetic figure, tried to climb out with his hands raised. Keen yanked him clear, caught him as he fell over the edge. With a low mutter of disgust, he pushed him away.

"And when you get back to the hangar, tell them who killed Emil Elbikon—and who Elbikon really was. Tell them about the Dewoitine that was shooting down your *Salvos*. And tell them why, or I'll be back again—tonight!"

Salisbury picked himself up, staggered a few steps, then ran bawling like a madman into the darkness.

Keen shot a quick signal to Barney, climbed into the *Salvo*, and closed the cover. Barney gave the *Bullet* the gun and raced away with Keen following him in the captured *Salvo*.

Together they climbed high into the air and circled over the Salisbury field which had suddenly blossomed out with square lines of light. A floodlight had splashed its gleam across two runways. Men, looking like frantic ants, ran in all directions.

Keen carefully inspected the *Salvo's* cockpit. Then he took up the small microphone and checked the switch of the sending set. He flipped it to "on" and made a test call.

"Calling the Salisbury field," he started, disguising his voice. "Calling—" He glanced about the cockpit and sighted the card set above the Western Electric set. "Calling WTEV…. Calling WTEV… pilot aboard *Salvo,* calling WTEV."

"Go ahead, Salisbury," a voice came back. *"What are you doing?"*

Keen half sensed the voice of the Brigadier General. He replied still maintaining his voice disguise.

"Pilot aboard Salisbury *Salvo* 3,000 feet over field. Am going to carry out test dive, as per schedule. Can you take altitude, time, and check reports?"

"Test dive? At night, man? You're crazy! The strain is that much greater in heavier night air. Come down! I order it!"

"Start taking checks," Keen ordered. "Time 11:20… altitude 4,000 feet in 1:20… top speed at level flight now 256…. R.P.M. 2,300…. Okay?"

"You're mad! But go ahead, Salisbury," the voice finally answered resignedly.

"Six thousand feet in 1:52…. Top speed 259…. Temperature 36…. R.P.M. 2,300…. Check?"

AND SO it went all the way up to 23,000 feet. Keen, his voice completely disguised, made his routine reports every two thousand feet and the amazed dockers jabbed the figures down on the prepared check sheet. Lang and Scott stood wide-eyed listening to the reports as they came through. They stared about as if they expected to wake up any minute.

"I still think there's something queer about all this," Lang barked.

"Shut up. You *always* think there's something queer about *everything,*" Scott answered testily. "Give the man credit. He's suddenly decided to clean up the whole business himself. You've got to admire a man like that."

"I still think there's something screwy," Lang growled.

Abruptly the radio blared: *"Twenty-five thousand feet in 8 rain. 27 sec…. Top speed 252 full throttle…. Coming down-n-n-n-n…."*

"Check!" the Brigadier bawled into the transmitting box.

And with that they all raced outside into the half glare of the hangar mouth, stared upward, and listened. Somewhere above, they caught the first dull wail of diving speed. It increased in tempo and violence and they stood still, hardly daring to breathe.

"He can have that job," muttered Drury Lang. "I'd sooner be with Keen at the Foam Combers Club."

KEEN had sucked in his breath as he whipped her over into a half roll and let her nose down. He pressed his stomach against the broad belt, shoved the throttle forward. The air-speed needle wavered, crawled around the dial. All of the instruments seemed to grow hazy, and Keen found the many indicating needles dancing around—cake-walking across the board.

He tried to draw a breath, but his teeth seemed cemented together. His eyes sought the top of the stick, but instead he saw only the center bracing bar of the coupe top. The dials appeared like dizzy figures in a cartoon comedy.

Keen caught himself shaking, then pulled himself together. His stomach felt as though it were constricted in some unseen chain device and his feet seemed glued to the rudder pedals. His brain whirled. Somewhere he thought he heard voices—the voices of Elbikon, Salisbury, and the Brigadier. They seemed mixed with the strains of a song that was all out of tune. Then everything went black before his eyes and he fought to see. He found himself screaming, fighting against unseen hands with tendons of steel that forced his arms back. He struggled to make his wrists move. His head swam.

Kerry Keen—the Griffon—was doing a 9-G dive in a *Salvo!*

He made a last superhuman effort through the tornado of blasting sound and terrific pressure to get his sight back so that he could see ahead. He forced his head up with a slow curling movement, and finally saw a criss-crossed design in dirty yellow, planted on a blackish-green counterpane—the field was just below him!

With a gasp, he stiffened, fought the stick back.

The *Salvo* came up and out with a grinding of control rods and levers. She cleared with very little to spare, ripped up with a mad wail and a scream of frustration, and shot back into the blackness above.

Automatically, Keen fingered the throttle. Then still flying automatically, he brought her around, zipped over the hangar, and let her float down on the long concrete runway that ribboned away from the apron. He let her roll, and pulled himself together quickly.

He whirled her fast on one braked wheel, flipped the cover back, slid out of the belt, and fastened the catch again. Then he carefully dropped the looped belt over the stick, so that it lay back slightly off neutral. Then he set the throttle so that the *Salvo* would rumble back at low speed toward the hangar. Finally, he darted away into the darkness.

THE CROWD stood spellbound in the mouth of the hangar. No one moved as the *Salvo* landed and rolled away into the darkness at the far end of the runway. They heard the engine jazzed on as the ship was turned around for the taxi back to the hangar. Then everyone seemed to speak at once.

"My Lord!" gasped the Marine Captain.

"Whatever is registered on that accelerometer," the Brigadier said, wiping his brow with a handkerchief as big as a tablecloth, "he certainly let us *see* him yank her out. That was the finest—and the craziest—piece of flying I have ever witnessed!"

"I quit," muttered Chunk McGuire. "This business gets tougher every—"

"There's something screwy," Lang broke in, finally getting his breath.

They watched the handful of mechanics wander out to take the wing tips as the *Salvo* came up slowly—ever so slowly. Automatically, the men took their positions; and without realizing that the plane was empty, they carefully guided it up to the hanger. But when it continued on, they let out a concerted yell, and braced themselves so that the *Salvo* wheeled. Then the light of the hangar flooded down on the plexiglass cockpit covering—and they saw that there was no sign of the pilot.

The Marine Captain acted fast. He leaped up on the root, ripped the hatch up, and snapped the switch. Then, bending over lower, he fumbled around inside and tried to find the pilot. Then, and then only, did he realize that the stick had been carefully fastened back and the throttle set for slow running.

He turned with a blank stare and said to the ring of faces below: "No one here! There's no one in the cockpit!"

"I told you there was something screwy," Lang bawled. "Look for a Griffon card. I can feel it in my bones."

"Never mind any cards," the Brigadier yelled. "Get the accelerometer out carefully. I want that report."

"There *is* a Griffon card," the Marine Captain gargled, "stuck... stuck in the deviation card bracket. Look!"

"Yeh, look!" howled Lang. "And say, there's Salisbury now!"

INTO the ring of figures staggered a slobbery-lipped man. He was ragged, dirty, and drenched to his knees where he had floundered through unseen mud and brooks to get back to the hangar. He tottered into the arms of brawny John Scott, then stared about like a wild man.

"I... I did it," he gagged, pawing at his mouth with dirty, trembling fingers. "I did it. But he made me. It was an accident.... The Griffon!"

"What the devil?" the Brigadier barked, one hand in the fuselage wall where he had been reaching for the barometer and the accelerometer. "What are you talking about?"

"I did it by accident—killed Elbikon. I didn't mean to. Accident... like... I tried to shoot the Griffon.... He took the blueprints. I didn't mean to."

They stood in a stunned ring, watched Hubert Salisbury fold up with a last gasp and slump in John Scott's arms. They started to drag him inside.

"Wait a minute," the Marine Captain said suddenly. "Here's a package of blueprints here on the seat. All tied up. Are these the ones he means?"

No one took much notice. They were staring down at Salisbury.

"Bum ticker," explained Scott, lifting the man bodily. "He's done."

"These *are* the blueprints of the *Salvo*," said the Marine Captain, still standing on the wing root. "How the hell—"

"It still sounds screwy," Lang growled. And then, noticing a grinning man approaching, he made a quick dive.

"Keen… Keen, you silly-looking devil! Where did you come from?"

They all turned and stared at Kerry Keen who had come out from the open hangar beating time to an imaginary jazz band with a short smooth white celluloid blade, generally known as a bartender's baton. He was dressed in his dinner coat with his white scarf fluttering in the light breeze. His hair was hanging in careless disarray under a somewhat battered black fedora, but his white shirt front still gleamed immaculately.

"What's going on… making all this bother… this time of the night," Keen said slowly with a somewhat thick tongue. "S'going on?"

"Where the hell did you come from?" demanded Lang, with a beady eye, taking in every bit of Keen's clothing.

Keen blinked, steadied himself. And then with a rare flourish, he presented Lang with the strip of celluloid and said: "Froth Combers Club, my man…. Froth Combers Club…. Lovely gentlemen in Froth Combers Club, Lang…. You musht be my guesht some time, eh?"

Lang took the white strip and read:

"You are a member of the Froth Combers, Brother. Cut yourself a piece of froth!"

Lang read it, stifled a grin, and said: "You punk, you're drunk!"

Keen nodded with dignity, bowed from the hips, and said: "First qualification for membership, Mr. Lang."

"An' it didn't take yer long to get that skinful, did it?"

"Second qualification," gagged Keen.

"How'd you get here, anyway?"

"My drunken driver… left me outside and trundled off in the chariot to find some O'Doul's Dew…. Nasty man, my driver. Never make the Froth Combers, eh?"

Keen's tongue was getting thicker and thicker, and Lang gave it up.

"Stick around, mug. We got a beaut for you to figure out. The

Griffon guy swiped the *Salvo* from old Salisbury, took it upstairs, and—believe it or not—brought it down again—"

"In an 11-G dive," broke in the Brigadier, his eyes blazing at the accelerometer!

THERE was plenty of excitement for nearly an hour. They had to get Salisbury examined and taken away. The Brigadier and the Marine Captain sat down and made a quick calibration of the test. They were more than satisfied with the dive, even though they had no idea who had brought her down. Keen stalked about like a man in a dream, poking at things with his celluloid strip and asking dumb questions.

"Why don't you buzz off home?" demanded Lang after a time.

"Where's Barney… my drunken driver?… Oh, yes, he went for a bottle of O'Doul's Dew…. He'll be back."

"If he ain't back you walk the rest of the way," gagged Lang, turning away. "I never knew you to get yourself in a state like this before."

"Oh, I've had a very large evening, Mr. Lang," said Keen with a solemn wag of his finger.

"You sure have, but I'd give ten bucks to know how *you* knew that those blueprints had been stolen, just the same. If I hadn't seen things happen here tonight, just as they have, I'd jug you on general principles."

"Jug?… Jail? What happened, anyway?" asked Keen thickly.

"You're too drunk to understand. Oh, there's your man…. Here, you drunken Mick. Take this Foam Comber home. He's getting in my hair."

Barney came in swaggering, holding the neck of an O'Doul's Dew bottle in his fist, and chortling bravely. He staggered up to Keen, waved the bottle in front of his half-closed eyes, and lugged him away.

The Brigadier stood off and watched the show, his hands on his hips.

"I'd like to have those two birds in the Army for about two months," he rasped. "I'd straighten them up."

"Yes, sir," wagged Keen, waving his celluloid strip. "And right now, Corporal, we'd like to have you in that *Salvo* for about ten minutes. We'd straighten you out, too. Go'night, sir. Sappy landings, sir."

Lang stood speechless for several seconds and then he said: "Drunks say the damndest things!"

And as Keen went through the doorway to the Duesenberg he said: "For the love of Mike. I thought you were never going to get here, Barney."

"How long do you think it takes to fly from Farmingdale to Montauk, anyway?… And then drive back here?"

"I wouldn't know. I've been to the Froth Combers Club."

"An' what the hell is that?"

"You've got me. Give me a drink."

"Wait a minute, I haven't had time for one myself."

"Funny guy, old Lang," smiled Keen, as he took the bottle and wiped the neck off with his palm. "Sometimes I think he likes me."

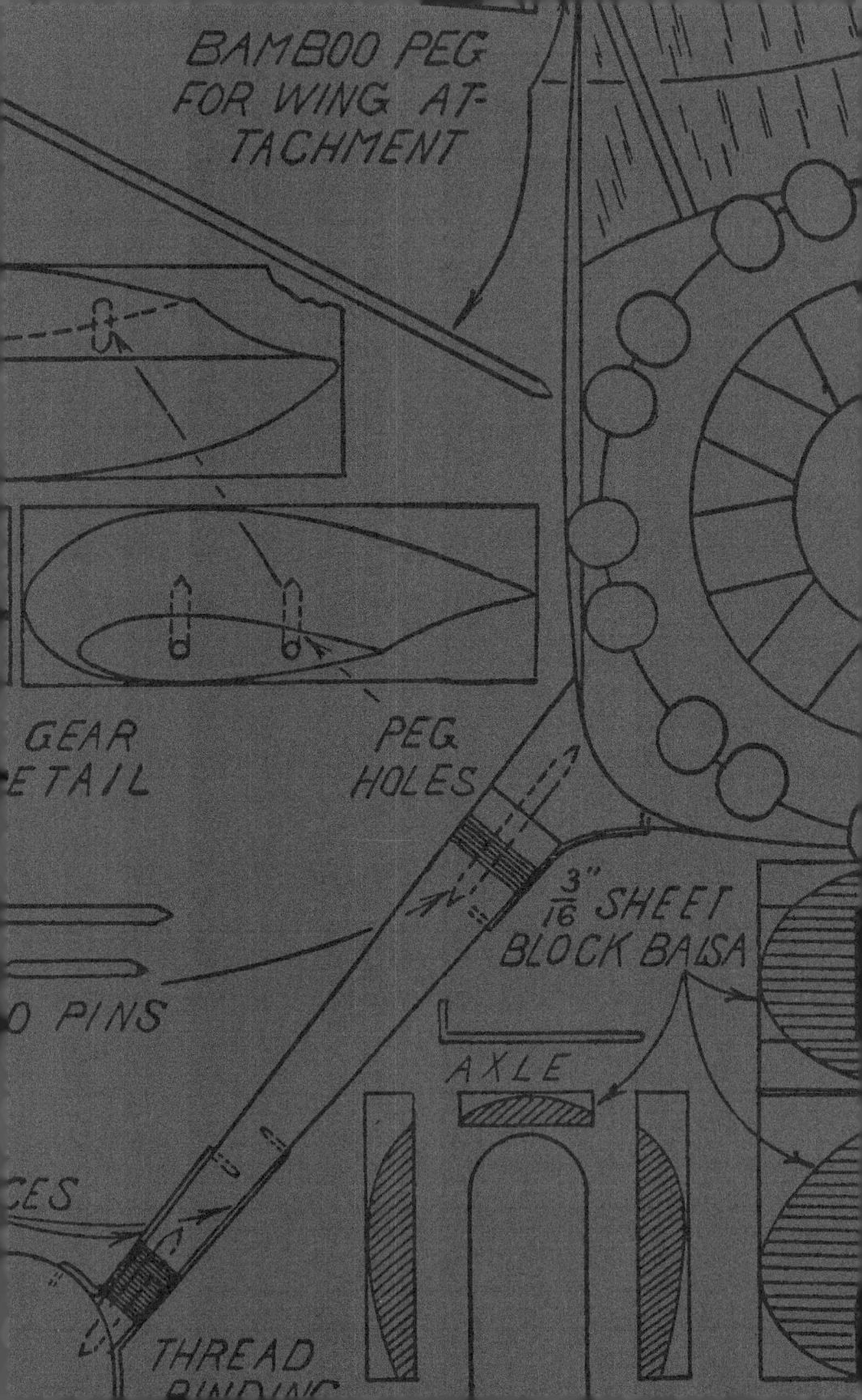

BAMBOO PEG
FOR WING AT-
TACHMENT

GEAR
ETAIL

PEG.
HOLES

O PINS

$\frac{3"}{16}$ SHEET
BLOCK BALSA

CES

AXLE

THREAD
BINDING

The Carrier Coup

KERRY KEEN lay on his back idly blowing tiny darts through a slender tube. His target was a speck on the ceiling. Barney O'Dare, his chauffeur and right-hand man, sat in a corner suffering the tortures of the damned. Togged out in his white service coat, stiff collar, and polished shoes, he was listening to the seventy-fourth episode of Spook Night, a gory radio thriller coming from a West Coast station. A chill voice came from the speaker—

"The bony hand reached out from the battered coffin and clutched at the fallen weapon. Sleek Slyne saw the fingers coil around the mother-of-pearl handle and suddenly jerk the muzzle up. The forefinger of the hand creaked as it drew the trigger back and—"

Barney made a leap across the room, snapped off the switch. He stood there, streams of perspiration marking his homely mug.

"Saved! Saved in the nick of time by the daring of O'Dare!" chuckled Keen. "Saved by a Mick on a switch three thousand miles away. Say, where was all this coffin stuff supposed to be happening, O'Dare?"

"A place called Ogbania, wherever that is," said Barney, rubbing a handkerchief across his brow.

"Ogbania?... Ogbania?" mused Keen after directing another dart. "Ah, yes! Ogbania is a small but compact little kingdom situated near the principality of Inkumsplash. Its chief products are Georgian princes, funny hats, and a gosh-awful beverage known as Blerk which is usually served with oysters and a strait-jacket."

"Which reminds me," answered Barney. "A beverage is what I need right now after all that."

He reached for the bottle of O'Doul's Dew hidden behind a typewriter table, then poured himself a tremendous snort.

"There should be a law against that sort of thing going out over the air," he gulped after he caught his breath again. "'Tis enough to scare the life out of a man."

"You say that every week—and then go right back and listen to it again," laughed Keen. "I have an idea you really believe in ghosts."

"Ghosts? Not me, Mr. Keen," Barney said, wiping the back of his hand across his mouth. "But look here, do you think a hand could come out of a coffin like that and fire a gun?"

"Certainly. It's been done hundreds of times. Comes under the head of the perfect crime. Only the guy who does it has to be dead anyway, so there's no one for the D.A. to prosecute after it's all over."

Barney jerked, darted back to the radio, and snapped on the switch again. He had to wait for the tubes to heat up and then got—

"...tune in again at the same time next week for further adventures of the Phantom Glazier. Who stabbed Maria Moccasin with the Blood-stained Putty-Knife? And who dug up the body of Toothless Hank? All these and more thrills will be offered in next week's great install-ment. This program comes to you...."

Barney snapped the switch again and swore under his breath.

"There ought to be a law against cutting a fine thing like that off in the middle that way. Now I don't know whether that corpse killed Sleek Slyne or not."

"I'm worried pink, too," agreed Keen, puffing another dart.

Barney took another gulp of Scotch and sat down adrip with perspiration. "But ye don't mean, do yer, boss, that *you* believe in ghosts, do yer?"

"Of course I do. What's left otherwise? I'd hate to think that when my time comes I can't canter all over the place at night clanking chains and spitting sparks. Look at all the fun I'll have with old Lang."

"Ye'd better have another drink yerself. Yer not feeling yer best, are ye?" Barney asked hollowly. He reached for a bottle of Musigny and popped the cork. Keen took the glass, nodded, and sipped.

"Of course there are ghosts, Barney. Where there's smoke there's fire. People don't just make these things up, you know."

Barney, completely flattened, sat back and mopped his head.

"For instance," Keen continued unmercifully, "I'm certain there is a ghost of some sort out at Graylands. Do you know that my Great-Aunt was strangled with a fish line in the very room you use back there?"

Barney let out a gasp—and his perspiration poured!

"They tell me she often gads about the place trying to get someone to untie the knots and cut the lead sinkers loose—her ghost, I mean. You've never run across her, have you?"

BARNEY answered with a queer noise in his throat and again reached for the bottle. But he was interrupted by a loud knock on their door. He gulped, pulled his shirt front down, and went to the door.

It was Drury Lang, the Secret Service man.

"There you are," roared Keen to Barney. "Speak of ghosts and they're sure to appear—this time a ghost carrying hand-cuffs."

"Shut up!" smirked Lang, peering about and then suddenly reaching down behind the table after Barney's bottle.

"Lang looks happy," remarked Keen. "We're in for trouble, I'm afraid."

Lang grinned with satisfaction. "Not yet, Keen. You're still in the clear, somehow. But I thought I'd find you in, here at 55th Street, so I dropped around to let you know that this time I'm going to do a job on my own."

"Let's ring the bells and put out some flags," Keen said, shooting a dart.

"We've got a beaut this time, Keen, and we're going to solve this one ourselves. Of course, you'd love it, but you're to keep your hands out of it, understand?"

"Don't worry. Barney and I are preparing for a vacation."

Lang stiffened, but regained his composure. He went on:

"Two battleships were attacked and badly damaged a few miles off Newport last night. The attack came from the air."

"Not interested," said Keen, fixing another dart in his blow pipe.

"The new aircraft carrier being built at the Brooklyn Navy Yard was bombed and damaged an hour or so later," Lang went on.

"How interesting!"

"And that's not all! A phantom aircraft carrier has been seen discharging a number of fighters and bombers a short distance off Long Island."

"Phantom aircraft carrier?" gasped Barney. "A ghost ship?"

"Yeh! And what are you so scared about ghosts for, O'Dare?"

"I've just been telling him about my Great-Aunt Sibby," broke in Keen. "Aunt Sibby was strangled with a tennis net."

"You said it was a fish-line," snapped Barney.

"Did I?" asked Keen. "Go on, Lang. Let's hear the rest of your story."

"Oh, that's all. I'm just telling you so that you will keep out of this affair, Keen."

"Thanks," answered Keen.

Abruptly the telephone rang and Lang leaped up. "That's for me," he said, quickly grasping the instrument. Then he spoke into the mouthpiece in monosyllables, and neither Keen nor O'Dare were able to follow the trend of the conversation.

Soon Lang came back with a bland smile.

"I was explaining to Barney that I believe in ghosts," said Keen unconcernedly. "My Great-Aunt Sibby—"

"Was it a fish-line or a tennis net?" moaned Barney. "There's no sinkers on a tennis net."

"Maybe it was a fish net," returned Kerry. "Yes, I'm sure, now that you mention it. It *was* a fish net. Anyway, you'll know for sure one of these nights. She'll be along worrying you to untie the knots...."

"Hey! Wait a minute, you guys," Lang burst in. "What *is* this ghost business? I got enough worrying about a ghost aircraft carrier without you ringing in your Aunt Sibby."

"Great-Aunt—on my father's side," corrected Keen. "And say, who was that on the phone, Lang?"

"Oh, this is not for you. But just to keep the record straight, I'll let you in on the fact that they just bombed the Lakehurst hangar. A swell mess, too!"

Keen sat up, stared at Lang.

"That's the first real clue," continued the detective. "These guys are probably disgruntled Germans who think someone over here set fire to the *Hindenburg*. It's beginning to shape up now. And as for the ghost aircraft carrier, we'll get a boat and go out and look for it. There ain't no such thing as a ghost, Keen, and you know it. If those Coast Guard guys saw that thing, it must be there."

"Or else the grog in the Navy is getting better," smirked Keen. "But just what means does one take in getting a boat to look for a ghost ship?"

"That's our business," grinned Lang, stuffing a shapeless pipe full of Navy plug. "You're not in this, Keen. You couldn't get a Coast Guard cutter to get out there. This is official stuff."

"It certainly sounds like it. When are you going, Lang?"

"Oh, I guess I'll pop along any minute now. I just dropped in."

"Nice of you," agreed Keen. "Now do you mind just dropping out? We're tired and would like to get some shut-eye."

Lang, contented with his small victory, got up. "I can see I'm not any too welcome tonight. Suppose you feel a little out in the cold, eh, Keen? Well, this is one time we'll have to dispense with your services. Well, I'll be toddling. Good night!"

"Okay, Mr. Secret Service," said Keen with a low snarl. Then he gave Barney a quick wink.

"Good night, Mr. Keen," called Lang as he closed the door.

"And now, let's move fast," whispered Keen to Barney. "We'll get out of here on the wire."

BARNEY was already climbing out of his house-man makeup and was pulling on a pair of heavy denim trousers. Keen was getting into a tweed suit and a light pair of shoes. They worked systematically and finally nodded that they were ready. One by one the lights were doused, then together they hurried to Keen's bedroom, quietly raised a window, stepped out on the roof, and hurried through the shadows of the penthouse to a point on the buttress where the fire-escape ladder crawled over.

"I'll go first," said Keen. "You lay doggo!"

They went down the fire-escape for two flights, then stopped. Keen drew a pair of gloves from his pocket, then fumbled around the corner of the building and unhooked what appeared to be a radio aerial cable from a heavy white insulator. He tested the strength of this steel line, then climbed up on the rail of the fire-escape. Finally with a quick movement he kicked himself out into space.

There was a low swish, the arc of a swinging figure. Barney watched Keen thus attain the open space on the roof of the adjoining building on 54th Street. Then O'Dare waited a minute, caught a low call, and steadied himself. There was a new swish and the end of the line came back across the open space between the two buildings. Barney caught it. A weight fastened to the end of the steel cable had brought it back.

And now Barney mounted the rail himself and kicked himself clear. He quickly swung across and joined Keen. Then after fastening the steel cable to another insulator, the two bent down over an open trapdoor on the roof. A dim light from below brought out the tense lines in Keen's face.

"Come on, Barney! Old Jarrett is just about to go to bed."

"Where we ought to be, too!"

"Shut up, Barney. We're after ghosts."

"Ay, and ye can have 'em."

They hurried down the dusty stairs to be greeted by a sleepy-eyed old man.

"Did you bring the bottle?" Keen asked Barney.

"He niver comes without it, Mister Keen," old Jarrett replied with a toothless grin. "Thank ye me bhoy, Barney. Thank ye."

And Jarrett then wished them a cheery good-night and backed away with a bottle of O'Doul's Dew.

Keen and Barney hurried on down and out into the street. Together they looked around, and then walked quickly to the garage where Keen kept his car. In ten minutes the Duesenberg was purring its merry way out to Long Island.

WHILE Barney prepared the *Black Bullet* for a night flight, Keen took out a map and several charts and studied them carefully. Then he grabbed a copy of the New York *Times* and went over the shipping news.

He pored over the latter for fully fifteen minutes, then suddenly came upon a unique name in the "arrival" list. He pondered over it for some time, then drew down a nautical volume and went over the details of an illustrated ship for several minutes. Frowning, he went back to the shipping list, studied it closer, then muttered: "Oh, I see! She's just been in for stores and supplies. She's working back and forth between New York and Gloucester in hopes that the industry may be revived in this area. Now this begins to sound like something."

With that much information gained, he climbed into his black coverall, pulled on a helmet, scarlet mask, goggles and gloves. Then he went downstairs to their secret hangar and found Barney waiting for him. The *Black Bullet's* Avia engine was already ticking over. Keen climbed in, and Barney doused the lights and pulled the lever that opened the great doors. Keen ran her out with the Skoda mufflers cut in.

Once outside in the shelter of the heavy grape arbor, Barney let the doors drop back and the exterior of the secret hangar took on its normal appearance of a rock garden. Then the plane's folding wings were drawn out and locked into position and she was allowed to purr gently down the lawn and across the hard-packed sands to the water. Keen adjusted the pontoons for a water take-off and they were soon out in the clear and on their way.

With her pontoons retracted into their recesses, the speed of the sleek ship mounted as Keen headed quickly out to sea. Barney made himself comfortable in the back seat, checked his Browning guns, and otherwise saw that their armament was ready.

"Where you heading?" he asked Keen through the Gosport headset as he eyed the horizon.

"Looking for a ghost," replied Keen.

Barney argued. "You aren't gonner start that again, are you?"

"You can never tell," Keen replied, peering high out of his covered cockpit. "Funny things happen at sea."

"What's the straight story on your Aunt Sibby?" Barney started again. "Is that on the up-and-up?"

"Anything that Great-Aunt Sibby had anything to do with had to be on the up-and-up."

"Yeh, but what *was* she strangled with?"

"I told you."

"First you said a fish-line, then a tennis net, and then you changed it to a fish net."

"I never said anything of the sort. Great-Aunt Sibby was strangled in a clothes-press."

"I can see this is gonner be a great night," moaned Barney.

"Hello! Look at that, Barney! Look down there!"

"I don't want to look. I've had enough for one evening."

"You're missing the sight of a lifetime. Here's our phantom aircraft carrier!"

Barney jerked himself into position, peered down. They were now about ten miles out from the Long Island coastline. But Barney saw nothing at first.

"Look ahead down there," Keen insisted. "Just off our port gun muzzle."

Barney looked again and at last caught a glow of something. There was no doubt of the carrier now. They could see the broad deck as plain as day. It was a medium-sized craft somewhat off the order of the new *U.S.S. Ranger.* They could see ships taking off from the deck—strange ships of some foreign make.

Keen stared at Barney. This had upset his plans completely. He had been figuring along another line.

"Look! It disappeared!" Barney yelled.

Keen twisted, again stared down toward where the phantom aircraft carrier had been sending off those strange fighters. Yes, the ship had vanished completely. Only a thin mist could be seen there now.

"What the deuce do you make of that?" Keen said with a sour grimace.

"Your Great-Aunt Sibby has been making game of us," Barney answered. "But I saw it as plain as daylight."

"That's exactly the point I don't understand. Why should they put on a show as bright as that—if they are trying to put something over? They had that deck lit up like Coney Island."

"Who?" asked Barney with a simple stare.

"Who? Why those birds down there."

"What birds? I thought it was a ghost ship. You don't really believe that carrier *was* down there?"

"Oh, I suppose you figure it's a mirage."

"Maybe we'd better go home, eh, boss?" said Barney peering over the side again. "But Holy Mother o' Moses. There it is again!"

Keen twisted, looked once more. Sure enough! The phantom carrier was back where it had been before. The fighters were taking off again in regulation style.

"Maybe we'd better go home," replied Keen in a serious tone. "Old Lang was certainly kidding us… somehow."

"If this is kidding, I hope he never gets serious," O'Dare exclaimed.

THEY circled a minute, then Keen suddenly drew his throttle back and started a fairly steep dive. "I'm going to find out what this is all about or know the reason why," he said.

But no sooner had he nosed down than from somewhere above and behind came the tell-tale streaks of tracer. Keen kicked the *Bullet* over into a tight spiral and Barney opened the gun rack behind him. He was in action in no time pouring burst after burst at the unknown bus that hammered out of the sky at them.

Keen tried to get his engine open again, but somehow a terrific back-pressure had been developed and she simply chugged. He fought with her for some time and finally yanked the Skoda mufflers out. She spat, spluttered, then finally sang out again with full power.

By this time, Barney was having the devil's own trouble with the attacker. He tried to drive it off, but it came on closer and closer. He was able to see that it was a trim biplane flying boat with a racing hull and some sort of a water-cooled engine mounted in the upper center-section.

"She's an Italian bus of some kind," he panted, reloading his guns.

Keen was still holding the *Black Bullet* in her spiral.

Barney now returned to the fray, and again the two machines hammered at each other with tracers flying all over the sky.

The enemy pilot sat well up front and appeared to have two heavy-caliber guns mounted high in his hull. He was using them with a vengeance, too. Barney seemed unable to stop this hellion, even though he was hammering everything he had at it.

"Take it easy!" Keen yelled. "Fake it and let's give him the old Backbiter!"

Barney then dropped down into his pit, and Keen brought the *Black Bullet* out of her spiral, made a wide turn, and appeared to head for the mainland. Barney was actually using a sight set in the hump of the fuselage which was directed aft past the port side of the vertical fin. He waited while Keen slowed her up and let the raider flying boat get dead behind him. It was a tense moment, a deadly period.

The flying boat swayed back and forth to get into position for the kill. But the instant she got dead behind, Barney tugged at a ring fastened to a steel cable.

Instantly from under the *Black Bullet's* tail came the rattle of a high-caliber Chatellerault. A shattering torrent crashed dead into the center-section of the flying boat. Struts cracked, the raider's top wing crumpled, and with an ear-splitting screech, the lead-ruptured motor tore from its supports, leaving a dead man at the controls.

Then Barney yelled at Keen and the *Black Bullet* went over on one ear and just cleared. The gun hidden in the empennage under the tail-wheel housing had done its job well.

They watched the wretched biplane drop in a slow spiral. It nosed down, boot-laced, then dropped with a dull plop onto the water. Keen and Barney now staged about for the carrier—but it was nowhere in sight.

"Come on," barked Keen. "Let's go down and have a look at that lad."

"I don't like this business," growled Barney. "That carrier thing."

"Who does? But it's a good idea," said Keen, holding the *Black Bullet* in an easy spiral while he lowered the pontoons for a water landing. "It's the best idea we've run into in months—if it works as I think it does!"

"What do you mean—works? It's a phantom—a banshee battle-wagon."

"Great-Aunt Sibby couldn't have said it better," remarked Keen. "But what the deuce sort of flying boat was that, Barney?"

"You've got me. A biplane job with its 'coffee-grinder' on the top wing. There's the wreck of it right below us now."

Keen glanced over the side and quickly drew the *Bullet* into a position for her glide. He was surprised at how low they had been operating. Now they were zipping over the velvety rollers toward the tangle of wreckage that had once been a beautiful plane.

It had hit nose first. The portions of the wings that still remained were badly battered and the hull was splintered near the tail assembly. Still there must have been a few air compartments holding, for the broken ship floated fairly high in the water. There were two pontoons under the lower wing tips that seemed to be intact.

"An Italian job," said Keen, as he eased the *Black Bullet* in close. "Take over, Barney. I'm going down on the pontoon and have a look."

The *Bullet* nudged into the smashed plane and Keen cut the engine, shoved his cockpit cover back, climbed out over the root of the wing, and dropped down on the pontoon. He threw a grapnel line to the wreckage and drew it close. Then he clambered down over the shattered hull.

He looked into the cockpit and made out the body of but one man—that of the pilot huddled in a heap against the small windscreen. It was obvious that the gaping wounds in his head had been fatal. Keen straddled the cockpit, reached in for the maps, and went through the man's pockets. He snapped a flashlight inside and saw two Italian Safat guns mounted so that they fired forward through small ports in the nose.

The light also fell on the metal plate on the instrument board that read: "*Costruzioni Meccaniche Aeronautiche, S.A... M.F.10. Fiat A.30RA... Marina di Pisa.*"

He jabbed this information down on the back of a map, then worked his way back to the rear cockpit. It was a normal affair for Naval spotting work. But there was no observer inside.

SUDDENLY Barney gave a warning cry. Keen ducked back, took a card from his coverall pocket and quickly slipped it into the hand of the dead man in the front cockpit. Then he hurried back to the *Bullet*, clambered onto the pontoon, and shoved clear of the wreckage. Seeing anxiety scrawled across the Irishman's mug, he cried, "What's up?"

"Plenty. Look!" And Barney pointed out to the east.

"The carrier again?"

"No.... Look.... Over there, coming dead at us!"

Then Keen caught the object of Barney's fear. A high-prow motor boat was coming toward them with the speed of the wind.

Barney had the big Avia motor hammering by now and the *Black Bullet* was well on her way. Keen took over and zig-zagged the plane as a stream of bullets slammed at them from the motor boat.

The *Bullet* took the air after a series of mad jumps. Barney was huddled over his double-Brownings, drawing a bead on the thundering boat below.

"Hold it!" warned Keen as he reached down and drew the retracting gear lever back to draw up the pontoons. "I want to take another look at that boat before we beat it."

The *Black Bullet*, under Keen's expert hand, swung over in a series of startling maneuvers until the gunners below were off range. Then Keen suddenly nosed down, sent the *Black Bullet* at the boat with the speed of death. When almost upon her, Keen zoomed and peered over the side. The full details of the craft were brought out in high relief.

"Get it?" Keen yelled.

"I'm getting it," answered Barney, plastering the boat with Browning lead.

"No, I mean do you know what it is?"

"Niver saw anything like it before."

They hoiked away under a desultory fire from the motor boat below.

"Well, it's an Italian Coastal Motor Boat known as the Tipo Veloci type. They do about forty knots an hour."

"What's it for?" asked Barney, as he directed a dirty look down toward the craft.

"They carry a torpedo and are supposed to be the terror of the Italian Navy."

"Look wicked enough. What do you suppose they are doing out here?"

"It's all part of some game. That ship we knocked off was an Italian Navy M.F.10 flying boat. It can be catapulted or launched direct. Yes, that was a swell job we broke up."

"I remember it now. Has a 600 h.p. Hisso and does about 185 top. But what's this all about?"

"You tell me. I'm completely in the dark."

"So's that ghost carrier. Where did *that* go to?"

Keen wheeled the *Black Bullet* around and went back to the spot where they had last seen the phantom carrier. They then cruised about at various altitudes, but they could find no trace of the craft. There were a few smoky tramp steamers crawling out from beyond Ambrose Light, a trans-Atlantic liner, agleam with lights, plunging out of the northeast and headed for quarantine, and a weary string of garbage barges. But there was no aircraft carrier.

KEEN was frankly puzzled. Nothing was working out as he had expected. He felt strangely afraid and unable to cope with the situation. He had seen the carrier, of that much he was certain. He had seen the ships take off from the deck, had seen the carrier disappear and then as suddenly appear again with all activity going on, as though nothing untoward had happened. At the start, he'd had an idea about it all. But now—?

He sensed that Lang had something this time, realized now that his visit that night was a come-on of some sort. He knew that Lang suspected something of his nocturnal activities, but so far the detective had never been able to place a finger on any of them. He knew that Lang had told him all this in hopes that he would work on the case. Just how much Lang really knew, he had no idea.

But the eerie carrier!

That was the exasperating point of it all. What was it all about? Actually there could be no ghost ship. In spite of all the lurid tales of the Flying Dutchman, that was impossible. But there *had* been a ghost ship! They had seen it on the surface below discharging trim fighters.

But what aircraft carrier was it? Keen tried to recall the details. It was a normal sized vessel, carrying the usual elevated deck. Umm! He had it now—it was the British *Courageous!* And as for the airplanes that had left that deck, they looked like fighting biplanes.

If so, what had happened to them? Where had they gone, and what new hellish games were they up to tonight?

There were no answers to any of the questions, so Keen decided to return to Graylands. Barney still kept a watchful vigil over the tail, expecting any minute to find a flight of unknown fighters pounding down on him. He was frankly relieved when Keen turned back.

They whistled across the night sky at well over 200 and sought their hidden base. The last they saw was some activity around the wreckage of the flying boat. They wondered whether the Italian coastal motor boat had drawn up beside it or whether some other craft had come upon the downed plane.

Finally, the *Black Bullet* dropped down on the water off Keen's boathouse, and under cover of the Skodas, they ran it up on the beach, across the lawn, and into the shadow of the arbor. Barney leaped out, folded the wings back, and opened the rock garden doors.

Once the plane was inside, they called it a night. Keen went upstairs and crawled out of his togs and dropped into a large club chair. Barney came up in a short time and reported that the *Bullet* appeared to be sound and not seriously damaged anywhere.

"Now do you believe in ghosts?" laughed Keen.

"I don't believe what I saw tonight."

"Neither do I—but that carrier was there."

Barney turned on the radio, and they waited for the tubes to warm. Then a torrent of words, excited and high-pitched, sprayed out of the loud-speaker.

"...has attacked again. Tonight, less than an hour ago, a number of mysterious planes suddenly appeared over Newark Airport and bombed the Air Corps hangar. Several small sized bombs seriously damaged the new Lorenz system for blind landings. Another group of planes in attempting to bomb the main control station killed several engineers in the dispatcher's tower. Two National Guard Douglas planes, which were in the air on routine night operations, were shot down in flames when they tried to drive off the unknown raiders. Few details of the attacking planes are available, as they approached from a considerable height and used some new kind of smoke-screen for protection. Further bulletins on this frightful affair will be broadcast as they are received."

A stand-by dance orchestra took up where the announcer left off.

"We certainly missed something tonight," said Keen. "Anyhow, you get to bed. We'll have to be back in New York early in the morning. Old Lang will be pottering around."

Barney trudged off and Keen called after him: "And if my Great-Aunt Sibby turns up, ask *her* what she knows about it."

Barney halted in his tracks, looked up the dark stairway, then came back into the room. Without a word, he peeled off his coat, trousers, and shoes, and curled up on the lounge. Keen laughed and took down a copy of *Brassy's Naval Almanac* and prepared for a long night.

THEY were on the road shortly after six o'clock, returning to New York. Keen had managed to get about two hours of sleep, a cold shower, and a quick but substantial breakfast. They slipped quietly into the 54th Street garage and put their car away. Then Keen wandered on toward the apartment with all the air of a man who has been out for an early morning walk. He sauntered in, nodding to the doorman who had just come on duty and remarking that it was lovely in the park this morning.

"You must have been up before breakfast, Mr. Keen," the elevator man smiled as he reached the penthouse.

"I can't resist these early summer mornings," Keen replied.

Then he entered his apartment—and received the shock of his life!

Drury Lang sat dozing in a big chair. He awoke when Keen walked toward him.

"Where the hell you bin?" Lang demanded, rubbing his eyes.

"First off, how did *you* get in here?" Keen came back.

"I can get in anywhere. You didn't want me to stand out in the hall all this while, did you?"

"How long have you been here?"

"Long enough—about two hours, I guess," Lang answered with one eye on his watch. "I repeat, where you bin all night?"

"Just out for a walk,"

"That's funny. No one seen you go. What's your game, anyway, Keen?"

"Just an old family weakness. Just couldn't sleep after that crazy yarn you told me last night."

"Sleep? Why you never even went to bed!"

"Of course not. That's why I went out. No use me trying to sleep when my mind's disturbed like that."

"It ain't so good sleeping on a cell cot, either. Where's the Mick?"

"I don't know. Probably down at the garage—or maybe just lounging about somewhere reading a paper."

"Well, he'll have plenty of time to read—unless...."

"Unless what?"

"Unless he tells a straight story," smirked Lang.

"Thou speaketh in parables, Brother Lang," Keen smirked back.

"Yeh? For the last time—where were you two guys last night? Come clean."

"Well, I'll tell you. I sat up for a while trying to figure out your story—you know, about that ghost aircraft carrier. I was so absorbed in it, I found out it was almost morning—time to get up. So I just took a walk."

"Yeh? Well, what about the Mick?"

"He sat up, too. Ghosts, you know. Never can sleep after his dish of radio banshees. Slept in that chair, as a matter of fact. He went out about the same time as I did."

"What a yarn! I suppose you expect me to believe that. You know what happened last night, don't you?"

"Sure. The ghost carrier steamed up the Hudson, did two loops over the George Washington Bridge, and put on a fireworks display for the Fourth."

"They bombed Newark Airport and raised hell!" snapped Lang. "What do you know about it?"

"I was there. I steered the carrier and had a deuce of a time figuring out which was the Hudson and which was the East River. I can never—"

"Cut it out!" Lang spat. "You say you sat up all night figuring it out. But do you know anything about it?"

"Me? No! You told me to keep out of it, and I knows me place as a gintleman should," Keen minced.

"That's enough. Do you know that an Italian biplane of some sort was shot down last night a short distance off Long Island and that when the Coast Guard got to it, they found—"

"I know.... I know. They found a Griffon card stuck in the pilot's hand. The Coast Guard *always* finds a Griffon card in someone's hand. Must be quite a printing bill on those cards."

"How did *you* know?" demanded Lang, selecting a vicious-looking stogie from an inside pocket.

"You always say that, Lang. It's an old story."

"No older than yours, Keen. And now, what's it all about. You've got some ideas on the subject. That carrier just ain't ghosting out there for fun, you know."

"I should think it would be. Is there *really* a ghost carrier?"

"It's been seen by two Coast Guard cutters. The *Megantic* reported seeing it off Ambrose Light last night and several freighters, including the Swedish whaler, *Wrangel,* report having seen it heading up the coast."

"The what?" queried Keen. "What Swedish ship?"

"The *Wrangel*—a whaler of some sort. Why?"

"Nothing. I was just interested."

"Hmm," breathed Lang with a gleam. "You *do* have an idea, don't you, Keen?"

"Maybe, but I've been told to keep out of it, remember."

LANG did not reply at first. He was watching Keen closely. He knew the young ballistics expert had something up his sleeve, but he was uncertain as to the right method of approach. He had tried one tack, and he was not certain how well it had come off. He could bluster and threaten, but at the moment he had nothing with which to threaten Keen. He might plead and call on the ties of an old friendship. He knew Keen was expecting all these now, so he used the only weapon he had left.

He drew out his old pipe, packed it with Navy plug, and smiled.

"Ah," he said, "you tell a good story, Keen, when it comes to guns and bullets. But you'll admit that this time you haven't the slightest idea what this is all about, huh?"

"Well—" Keen started to say.

"No 'wells' about it. You have no idea at all what it is, do you?"

"Still, you were very worried about my movements last night," Keen taunted.

Lang felt that he was slipping now and clutched frantically.

"I don't care where you were. I've got to find out something about this business and I don't care where I get the information," Lang suddenly stormed.

"Is that an invitation?"

"Take it how you like. That Griffon guy knows something about it, I'll bet."

"I should say he does. You say he shot down an Italian flying boat last night? What does that have to do with it?"

"That's what you had better find out. You must know who the Griffon is."

"*I* know?" replied Keen with an amazed stare. "Why I—"

"Listen, Keen. Quit stalling. I hear your pet charity—well, read this story in the paper. They need a lot of dough."

Lang tossed over a newspaper and lit his pipe again. Keen glanced down the columns and caught what Lang was getting at.

He read it, frowned, then looked up.

"How much can a man get—working on the side—straightening that mess up?" Keen asked.

"Enough!" explained Lang. "You can get that much—for some real dope."

Keen read the article in the paper again.

"I'll see you here this time tomorrow, eh, Lang?" he said with a grin.

"You'd better. They won't hold that dough for a reward long, you know."

"Get out of here now. I'll see that you get some dope on it somewhere. Leave me alone in the meantime, too. Any annoyance, and I'll call it off."

"Yeh? And what about those crippled kids?" Lang snorted.

"Keep them out of it. I'll take care of that. Now get!"

And Lang, rubbing his big hands together, got up, and "got."

Keen called Barney at once and prepared himself for a heavy day. He put on an old denim outfit of overall trousers, a thick woolen shirt, and a dirty peaked cap. Barney took one look when he came in and without a word went into his room and soon came out looking even more disreputable.

Keen made a call on the telephone and got an okay on a proposition. Then he called once more and held a lengthy conversation with someone connected with the Barge Office in New York City.

With automatics tucked away, both Barney and Keen went downstairs and hailed a cab. Keen gave the address of a downtown pier. The taxi-driver gave one good look at the bill Keen proffered, then set out at breakneck speed. Finally, they pulled into a partly-covered wharf where a tall gaunt man with a chin beard awaited them. He was built like a typical seaman and had the eyes of a man who had stared across vast wastes for years.

He nodded to Keen and led the way to a narrow, creaking gangway that was thrown across to a pot-bellied tug. Both Keen and Barney looked the tug over quickly, then went up into the wheelhouse. A whistle split the air, the gangway was shoved clear, and the tug *Estelle* churned out to midstream and headed down the bay.

IT WAS a beautiful morning, but Keen had no eyes for the sea. He huddled back in the wheelhouse on a creaky chair and perused a handful of newspapers. The headlines blarted the news of the night before. An imaginative artist had created a scene in which the jagged skyline of New York City had been bombed to a mere saw-toothed tangle of wreckage. A fleet of giant bombers were depicted releasing a load of destruction, and the caption read: "Who Is Our Unknown Enemy?"

"That's what we'll soon find out," said Keen grimly.

He turned the pages and got the story of the latest bombing. There were the pictures of Newark Airport which showed the damage to the control tower, the wreckage of the Air Corps hangar, and the pathetic tangle of two burned Douglas observation ships. Huge gashes had been blown out of the airport runways, and the faces of the men caught by the camera were strained with terror.

There were other photos showing the great hangar at Lakehurst with a section of its great door blown fully two hundred yards away. The mobile mooring mast lay on its side like the skeleton of some great animal. As for the damage at the Brooklyn Navy Yard, details had been carefully censored. It was admitted, however, that several bombs had fallen in the main graving dock and that a number of the Navy personnel had been killed.

Keen tried to piece it all together. Starting with the first attack, he worked out the distances between the points which had been bombed and the spot where he had seen the phantom aircraft carrier. Yes, if there *was* an aircraft carrier out there, all these attacks could have been carried out from that point with ease. But Keen was confident that the planes that carried out the bombing were not operating from that carrier. He was certain in his own mind that there was some sort of a trick to all this. He had seen what purported to be an aircraft carrier—yet he could not help but feel that the "four" of this problem was arrived at by other than the common "two plus two" method.

Barney was standing behind the man at the wheel taking in

the beauties of the Lower Bay. The sea was churned to a froth with the movement of saucy destroyers operating in small groups. A number of light cruisers had passed them heading out to sea to take up their posts, hoping in some way to stand off these phantom raids. And already a flotilla of warships was stringing out in line between Cape Cod and the mouth of the Delaware.

A formation of Army observation planes now hammered down the bay, turned outside the quarantine markers off Rosebank, then thundered away across the forest of masts that lay at anchor. A short time later they were followed by a broad-winged patrol of Navy flying boats.

"Bet there'd be plenty of action if they could find something to pick on," said Barney. "Where we going, anyway?"

"Out to take a look at the ships," said Keen, without looking up.

"We'll get torpedoed out there," Barney laughed. "There's enough big stuff about to film the Battle of Jutland for Hollywood."

"I wouldn't be surprised if we *were* torpedoed," Keen said, looking up at the chart on the wall. "Our quarry stands off about here, Driggs," he went on to the tug captain.

"I figured that myself. I seen it in the shipping news," the Captain answered through his massive teeth which held a pipe as big as a carpenter's hammer.

"Well, that's where we want to go. There might be some fun, but I'll see that you get paid for your trouble. Remember now, you're supposed to have been sent out to deliver a casting. You've got that cylinder head, haven't you?"

"Sure. It's up front there in that crate."

THERE was little else to do now but watch the activity of the Coast Guard cutters and the destroyers that were slashing their way through the water and heading out to their posts. So Keen turned on a small portable radio while they bumped and thudded along.

He listened to further details of the raid of the night before. The death toll was mounting hour by hour. Already there were signs of mass panic in the sections of New York City, Newark, Jersey City, and Brooklyn which the people figured contained the best targets for the raiders. All National Guard units had been called out. Boy Scout troops were at work distributing leaflets advising the terror-stricken population what to do and how to act during possible gas attacks.

There was a loud hue and cry because there were so few gas masks available. There was a question of food shortage and already the government had issued a preliminary warning concerning the conservation of all staples. Then, too, the Croton Reservoir might be damaged, hence an order went out that as little water as possible should be used during the next week or ten days until something definite could be ascertained as to the operations of the unknown enemy.

FOR ANOTHER two hours the tug plunged on, headed north-east-by-east. Then finally Driggs nodded to Keen.

"There she is," he said. "That big bruiser over there."

"What is it?" asked Barney who thus far had been very patient.

"A Swedish whaler," said Keen studying her through Captain Driggs' glasses.

"A whaler? As big as that?" gasped Barney. "I thought—"

"The old days of Moby Dick were over long ago. This is a 1937 whaler, Barney."

"They catch, kill, and bring them aboard direct—then do every job right there on hoard, from boiling the blubber to drying the whalebone," Driggs said out of the corner of his mouth.

"Begorrah, she's a big ship, though," Barney argued. "And say, what's that strange bump in the back?"

"She has a long hollow tunnel opening at the stern, and going all the way up to midships," said Keen still studying. "They pull the whales up the tunnel direct from the water."

"I'm beginning to get an idea," said Barney, his eyes drawn to two narrow slits. "I'm beginning to smell a rat."

"You may smell plenty worse than that when we get a little closer," laughed Keen, "because they don't use Lifebuoy on dead whales."

And now the *Estelle* drew up alongside the whaler *Wrangel* and a line of squarish hard faces looked down on them from the rail above.

"Ahoy, *Wrangel!*" boomed Captain Driggs.

"Ahoy, below. What do you want?" a big bo'swain bawled back.

"Have a casting—cylinder head casting for the *Wrangel* from the Mayhew ship yards. Can you pass me a line?"

"Cylinder head casting? Wait a minute, Captain. Must be some mistake. Stand by, will you?"

"Sure, stand by," whispered Keen. "Let her drift back to the *Wrangel's* stern a little. I'd like to take a look up that tunnel."

Barney, now taking in everything, was giving the seamen above plenty of inspection. Keen allowed his eyes to run along the strange bulbous sides of the craft. He sniffed, tried to pierce the heavy odor of whale blubber.

The *Estelle* slipped back with the easy current, and two of the tug's deckhands began to put rope buffers in position as the tug moved closer to the whaler.

"Keep clear back there," someone yelled. "We have screws well away from our stern posts, you know."

"I know. I know," roared Driggs. "I'll keep clear."

The *Estelle* flobbed around sidewise, then slid back faster. Keen tried to see through several of the portholes, but they all seemed to be painted over on the inside. Then at last they were in line with the stern of the boat. And as the tug flobbed still farther back, they managed to get a view up the inclined whale tunnel all the way through to the upper deck. It appeared to be fully twenty-five feet wide all the way up. There was a set of narrow-gauge rails in the base of the huge chute over which a fair-sized truck could be run. At intervals up the incline could be seen covered boats, possibly fishing dories or power dinghies of some kind used in the work.

Keen looked the boats over carefully and was interested in their general outline. They certainly did not have the lines of fishing dories or dinghies, he found on close inspection.

"Come on, Barney," whispered Keen. "Let Driggs argue with them as long as possible. We've got to get aboard."

Driggs watched them slide out of the door of the wheelhouse and crawl unnoticed along the side of the superstructure of the ungainly tug. They slipped over the side into the milky-white churning of the tug, drew long breaths, and swam under water. Soon they were grasping the rusty end rails of the tunnel tramway. No one had seen them, so they drew themselves up onto the metal ties that held the rails apart.

"Wait here until the tug gets around to the winch boom again," Keen ordered. "They'll all be so busy leaning over the side, we'll have some chance of getting aboard."

"Aboard what?" grunted Barney. "We're already aboard."

"Aboard one of those boats up there—for the time being at least. Come on."

THEY now darted across the slimy tunnel floor to a space between two of the tarpaulin-covered boats. They huddled there for some time, listening to the bellowing above about the casting.

"It's a mistake, I tell you," the Swede bo'swain was yelling. "We haven't ordered that cylinder head. We don't have that kind of engine, I tell you."

"But I was ordered to deliver it," Driggs argued back. "I didn't say it was for your vessel—but I was ordered to deliver it to you. Pass me a line, will you?"

"We didn't order it, and we're not accepting it! Shove off, Captain!"

"You don't have to pay for it. It's paid for. I've got my orders."

"An' we're not accepting something the Chief Engineer didn't order."

"All right. You try to make radio contact with your brokers in New York. I'll stand off for a signal. You'll find I'm right."

"You'd better go back to your rat-eaten wharf, if you know what's good for you," a new booming voice ranted.

"My papers are all clear and I'm standing by until you leave— or until you accept this crate. Is that clear?" demanded Driggs.

"Shove off!" the big booming voice ordered.

"He'll shove off," grinned Keen, as he loosened the ropes that held down one of the covers. "But he won't be far off."

They huddled behind the boat and made arrangement for a quick entry into it if the occasion arose.

"Get it?" said Keen. "Another one of these Navy torpedo motor boats."

"Not the same as the one we saw," said Barney.

"No, this is a smaller version—the kind used in the Swedish Navy. It carries machine guns, a smoke-screen apparatus and one torpedo. It does about forty knots."

The clatter on the deck had subsided by now, so the hands were returning to their posts. A few came down the tunnel and went to work on one of the high-speed motor boats. A young officer in a dirty blue coat took up his watch at the lower end of the tunnel from where he had a good view of the sea.

"What's the game now?" Barney asked.

"You stay here. Get inside this boat and find out what it's all about. Then, if you get a chance, see what possibilities are of getting her launched quickly. I'm going to buzz about a trifle. Don't worry."

"I won't," grinned Barney. "I can see I'm gonner have my own troubles to worry about."

Keen looked about, saw that the men were busy at their tasks. He looked over his automatic, saw that it was dry again, then started up the tunnel incline, keeping well behind the row of boats. Half way up he found a doorway leading off the tunnel. He drew the heavy iron handle down carefully and eased the door back carefully. It moved without a creak and he looked in.

He was not particularly surprised at what he saw there, but he was somewhat amazed to find such a well-organized set-up. There, between the wall of the tunnel and the outer hull of the whaler, stood a line of M.F.10 flying boats with their wings folded back! There must have been at least a dozen on this one side alone; and Keen figured that if the vessel were built the same on the other side, it meant that there were at least twenty, and perhaps twenty-five, of these machines on board.

"Just as I thought," he muttered to himself. "They have been launched down the whaler tunnel and sent off on the raids."

But still this did not settle the argument of the phantom aircraft carrier. There must be an answer to that somewhere. What was it all about?

Keen closed the door, moved cautiously about. The machines were clean and in good repair. He carefully inspected the first one, saw that it was exactly the same as the one he and Barney had shot down the night before. But this one not only carried two forward guns but was also fitted with special wing racks that accommodated four sixty-pound bombs of heavy demolition type.

"Whew!" gasped Keen, after glancing along the lines of wings. "These babies can do some real damage. And there'll be hell to pay if they get off again with 'em all loaded!"

HE STOOD hesitant for some time, then made his way carefully forward until he came to a section of the hold that ran across from the port to the starboard side. He studied it for some time, saw that he was in a lathe and machine shop which was fully equipped for all sorts of exacting work. He looked about farther, then spotted a large steel pillar that came up from somewhere below and continued on through the ceiling of the shop.

"I get it," Keen said. "That's the mast. I wonder...."

He dropped to his hands and knees and crawled along under the benches, passing very close to two men who were working at a lathe. He reached the mast—and realized that his impression had been right. It was hollow and no doubt had steps going up inside. He crawled around it and found a small metal door. He opened it, slipped inside, and peered up. There was a set of iron steps set in a spiral up through the mast, and at intervals, he noticed narrow slits of light that indicated small openings at various heights. The top one would open out on the crow's nest.

Keen slipped inside, drew the narrow door shut, and reflected on the situation. He had learned much. But he would have to get plenty of additional information to be able to give Lang something to work on. And he would have to work fast to prevent any more night raids.

He pondered for a minute further, then started up the steps. He wondered whether there would be anyone in the crow's nest while the *Wrangel* was at anchor. There was only one way to find out.

He passed the first narrow doorway and peered through the slit. The door opened on a level with the booms that ran out to the bridge wings.

Then he continued on up until he reached the opening to the crow's nest. He was very cautious now, but finally he took a chance and opened the door. There was no one there.

Quickly, he slipped out of the mast and crouched down in the canvas sheltered lookout station. He could see the whole layout from this lofty perch. The *Estelle* was standing a few points off the port bow. Keen watched her for a few minutes and smiled. He now peered down on the *Wrangel's* deck and noted that there was plenty of activity under way. A winch began to whine and wheeze, a great chain clanked somewhere, and heavy voices barked orders.

"Hello!" Keen husked to himself. "Now I've done it. We're getting under way. They must have decided there's an Ethiopian in the wood pile."

Men appeared on the wings of the bridge, and now a plume of steam swept from the whistle. The *Wrangel* was under way.

Then Keen tensed. Once under way a member of the watch would take his post in the crow's nest. That plastered the situation completely.

Keen peered down the ladder inside the mast and gulped. The man was already on the way up! Keen waited with his automatic in his hand. He drew to one side and waited. The clump of heavy boots resounded inside the metal mast, then the door clanged open. A head came through—and Keen quickly selected a convenient spot at the back of the man's head.

THONK!

The butt of the gun came down and the man fell forward with a low groan. Keen caught him gently, then hurriedly slit the man's heavy dungarees into long wide strips and tightly bound and gagged him. Lastly he stripped off his heavy blue turtle-neck sweater and drew it down over his own blue flannel shirt.

From the bridge came the clang of the watch bell.

Keen hesitated, stared about, then remembered that the crow's nest was supposed to answer. He reached up, grabbed the bell cord, and answered, repeating the watch bell signal.

All he got was a snarling growl from the watch officer below— for being so tardy with his signal.

But Keen was too busy to worry now. He took the fallen man's shapeless navy cap and pulled it down over his own head, then ruffled his hair to complete the masquerade. Then he went down the ladder again, rubbing his greasy, rust-stained hands around his chin until he looked like a dirty seaman badly in need of a shave.

He went all the way down until he came to the repair shop again, then boldly walked out through the benches and lathes, keeping well away from the men who were working there. He went through the companionway to the tunnel, and sauntered casually around the tarpaulin-covered boats. He stopped at the end one and peered in. Barney had a gun ready. Keen whispered to him just in time.

"Hold on. I've just made a capture up in the crow's nest," Keen grinned.

"How the devil…?"

"Can't explain now. Stand by and be ready to chop this boat loose. We may have to do that, you know. But I want to look about a bit more first."

"Don't worry, I've got this boiler all set, if we have to get running."

Keen made his way back up the tunnel and noted that most of the men were still looking over the side toward the *Estelle*. Keen wondered what was going on, then suddenly he sensed that something had been released—somewhere. There was a low cough, a hissing choke, and the big whaler seemed to shudder from stem to stern. Keen climbed up the curved side of the tunnel, clambered over some dunnage, and peered out of a dirty porthole. He got there just in time to see a whitish streak fang out from below the *Wrangel's* water line and slash like lightning toward the little tug *Estelle*. Keen watched it, helpless. Then before he could make a move there came a dull flash and a terrific explosion. The *Estelle* leaped clear out of the water. He saw her go up several feet, hold an unbelievable mid-air position for a second, and then completely disintegrate. The tall funnel did a smoky flip-flop, a man seemed to climb through the air after it, then the roof of the wheelhouse slapped him down as though it were a giant fly-swatter. A forked splash of flame followed—and the *Estelle* was gone.

The men aboard the *Wrangel* had torpedoed the little tug!

Keen bit his lip, gripped an iron rail, and swore. He closed his eyes knowing full well that not a man could have lived through that explosion. He also knew that the radio operator aboard the *Wrangel* would simply report seeing an unknown tug blow up with the loss of all hands. Keen hated every man connected with this fiendish pirate vessel.

He rammed his hands into his pocket and gripped the gun there for comfort. Then he ducked his head and went through two more doors until he came out on the main deck. He moved forward, ignoring the dumb stare of a man who came out of the galley with a large basket of potatoes. He turned in a companionway door and stood staring up a set of white stairs. One last glance about, then Keen hurried up and slipped into the chart-room, fixing his scarlet mask as he went.

Two men sat there, peering out of the window at the frothy spot that marked the grave of the *Estelle*.

Keen walked up quickly, jabbed his gun into the stomach of the first man, a big fellow whose uniform bore gold braid, and growled: "That's the last vessel you'll ever torpedo, Captain Trondheim. You are Captain Trondheim, of course."

The big officer wheeled around, gasped, and sat down. The tall man with him was dressed in Navy togs but wore no rank insignia. He was a strange figure with a high forehead, small piercing light-blue eyes, and a cropped mane of yellow hair. This second man started to get up, but Keen's gun made him wriggle back.

"Who are you?" Captain Trondheim bawled.

"Not so loud, Skipper. I do not wish to be disturbed," smirked Keen tossing forward a card.

THE TALL man took it, and blanched. He tried to skip it across the table to the Captain. But his attempt at nonchalance was blunted by fear. The card fell on the floor.

Trondheim picked it up with a grunt and Keen saw that he had a cruel scar running from under his left ear to a point just above the eye on the same side. He was a massive compact man, but too fat for his own good. He puffed as he squinted to read the card, then let his jaw drop like the lower lip of a tired bulldog. He tried to say something, but his throat would not answer his command. He just gurgled and put the card on the table.

"What do you want?" the tall man finally managed to say. "I understand that every man has his price."

"I have mine, yes," replied Keen. "And it is not too high—considering."

"We are prepared to pay," the tall one said. "But how did you know?"

"Never mind. I'll ask the questions. You sit still and answer them. And don't try any funny business. If anyone comes in here, you are to act as though you were simply interrogating me. If anything slips up, you two are getting my first two bullets—and I might add that I am not alone on board. I have someone very near."

The two men stared about as though they expected to see other strange faces in scarlet masks peering at them.

"I'll tell you this much," Keen rasped on. "Unpleasant international complications, diplomatic rot, and all that, may be avoided. But I do want to satisfy myself on one or two matters mentioned in papers I found on the man I shot down last night."

The two men both looked at the menacing figure in the scarlet mask. They were puzzled and uncertain.

"You needn't worry," continued Keen. "The Griffon never lies. He gets what he goes after—but you can rely on his word. Now then, you, sir, are really Prince Vincente Alvarez Capdevilla, are you not?"

The tall man nodded gravely.

"You are head of the Navarro Council for Monarchy, and one of your aims is to place a member of the Navarro family on the now-vacated Spanish throne. Am I right?"

The man nodded again.

"You have been staging carefully-planned raids on the east coast of the United States and attempting to leave the impression that they were carried out by planes launched from a foreign aircraft carrier. Is that not so?"

Captain Trondheim and Prince Capdevilla exchanged glances, and the man in the scarlet mask knew that his verbal thrusts had scored with telling effect.

"You hoped, by these means," Keen went on, "to embroil a certain European power with the United States. And under the cover of this conflict, you planned suddenly to take your place at the head of a new Spanish government—a position you have not dared to assume under the present set-up in Spain."

Prince Capdevilla shrugged his shoulders: "There are more ways than one of skinning a goose," he admitted.

"Agreed! Then my findings have been correct, so far. You had hoped to cause trouble between, let us say, Italy and the United States. On the other hand, you apparently desire to cause a rift between Great Britain and the United States; for though you are using Italian bombers to make your under-cover raids, you have also been attempting to give the impression that a British aircraft carrier has been discharging raiders a few miles off the coast here. As a matter of fact, I saw what looked like the *H.M.S. Courageous* out there discharging Hawker Nimrods, whereas, I have since learned that the *Courageous* is actually on duty off Gibraltar. As for your Italian M.F.10 bombers, you smuggled those out of Spain."

The Prince smiled and pressed his finger-tips together. Then there came a knock at the door.

Keen gave both men a quick glance. He shoved his gun into his pocket while Captain Trondheim barked an answer. Someone outside answered and Trondheim started to speak.

"In English, Trondheim," Keen husked. "No tricks, or I'll blow your liver into that chart rack!"

"We will continue on the pre-arranged course," Trondheim called gruffly. "I am to be advised if naval vessels of any sort attempt to make semaphore signal contact with us."

The man outside clumped away, and Keen eyed the Captain through his scarlet mask.

"All right," he said finally. "Now let's go on from where we left off."

Prince Capdevilla lit a cigarette, settled back with a strange air of satisfaction.

"I'm still not quite sure of this set-up, however," Keen went on. "I'm uncertain what your game is."

Prince Capdevilla smiled. "You most certainly don't expect us to tell you, do you?" he breathed.

"You saw what happened to that tug out there," Keen snapped. "The same thing could happen to the *Wrangel*."

Trondheim and the Prince exchanged puzzled glances.

Keen continued: "The same thing *could* happen, you know—and just as mysteriously. But we are wasting time. The Navarro Council hopes to obtain certain port and harbor concessions in the Mediterranean—strongholds which would be particularly offensive to Britain and France. Am I right?"

The two men before him did not answer.

Keen went on: "This move could be blocked by France or Britain, which have attempted to limit the war in Spain to the Spanish borders. But, your move has been to provide outside problems for these two countries so that they will not be able to police the situation in Europe. Your plan to involve Britain has been particularly well carried out."

Both Trondheim and Capdevilla frowned, and Keen knew he was on the right scent.

"I'm not quite sure what angle you will adopt to involve France. But what I want to know now is the secret of your phantom aircraft carrier," Keen hammered on.

"You have been very clever so far," taunted Capdevilla, "I see no reason why we should spoil your findings. I'm afraid you'll go to your end without ever finding out."

Capdevilla had hissed the last sentence, and Keen instinctively stiffened in his chair. Something told him he had been tricked. He peered about as something creaked behind him. Quickly he turned, drew his gun, and fired with lightning speed. A man in dirty blue fell forward, dropping a great automatic from his hand. There was another report, and a slug hammered past Keen's head with a crash. For a fraction of a second, Keen was stunned by concussion. There was a loud cry from somewhere behind him, then Prince Capdevilla fell across the chart table with a great gash in the middle of his throat.

He had taken the bullet meant for the Griffon!

TRONDHEIM let out a bull roar as a second man came through the door and leaped over the fallen seaman. Keen backed to the wall, fired again and sent the newcomer's gun smashing against the paneled wall. The seaman grabbed at his wrist which spurted blood and stared with wide eyes at the weapon which clattered across the floor.

"Get over there," Keen bellowed, indicating a position behind the fallen Capdevilla with the muzzle of his gun. "So you got a signal through, somehow, eh, Trondheim? Well, now you're going to get what I promised you."

"You'll never get off this vessel!" Trondheim screamed.

"I will—but *you* won't," taunted Keen, backing toward the door through which he had entered.

The body of Prince Capdevilla now rolled off the chart table and hit the floor with a thud. Trondheim made an impulsive move to pick him up; and as he did so, Keen suddenly darted back and grabbed a black log book that had been lying on the chart table. Then he shot through the doorway.

Down the companionway stairs he raced, diving headlong through two lard-faced seamen who stood at the bottom unable to make sense out of it all. One went flat with a split skull as Keen brought his automatic butt down hard. The other screamed and started crawling up the stairs on his hands and knees. Keen was out on the deck now and men were standing in small groups uncertain as to which way to turn.

They saw Keen and let out yells. He turned, raced forward, climbed the rail under the bridge wing, and pulled himself up to the derrick-boom cradles. He climbed up them like a cat, ran along the booms toward the mast. A shot rang out, sizzled past his head, and chugged into the sea. Another and another—but he had already reached the small door in the hollow mast and wrenched it open. Two bullets spattered inside just as he dropped clear and hurried down the iron steps.

Once below, Keen again made his way through the machine shop that led to the hidden hangar section. And now he was out in the sloping tunnel.

Men were running in all directions, shouting and attempting to answer orders. Keen crawled along the row of coastal motor boats and found the homely mug of O'Dare peering out from under the tarpaulin.

"Enough to wake your Aunt Sibby," Barney bawled. "What the hell's the matter?"

"This has got Aunt Sibby beat a mile, Barney. I've upset a lovely little wasp's nest. Can we accomplish a launching?"

"All we need is a bottle of O'Doul's Dew to bust on her beak," the Mick said. "How will you have it?"

"The quickest way possible. What's the layout?"

"She's on a small cradle fitted to a set of tracks. She'll run straight down, once we cut her loose."

"Go out and breathe on her prow. That ought to be enough."

They cut the ropes that held the tarpaulin and shoved it clear. Keen crawled back in and Barney started bashing at small chocks with a heavy hammer. The speed boat creaked, rolled slightly, and then the Mick put his shoulder to the prow and she started down the incline. Barney pulled himself over the nose, clambered in, and ducked under the armor-plated cabin roof.

Keen huddled down as the boat gained headway. Shouts went up somewhere above them, but the boat was now racing down the inclined rails. And now the shouts were drowned out as Barney started the Thorneycroft engine.

The speed boat slipped into the swirling water at the stern of the *Wrangel* and they were tossed about like a cork for a few seconds. A rattle of gunfire from the deck of the *Wrangel* made Keen huddle down closer, but somehow the boat cleared, leaped over the milky rollers like a greyhound, and raced away. Barney was at a wheel, grinning broadly, as they plunged through another storm of lead. The *Wrangel* gunners were getting their range.

"Pull that black handle over there," Barney yelled.

Keen stared about, then pulled the handle indicated. Instantly, a heavy plume of black smoke belched out, hid them behind a velvet screen. They charged away, and Keen now lay back and inspected the general arrangements on board.

"You want to have a smack at them? We got a tin fish on board, you know," Barney yelled.

"No, let them go. The gauge here shows we haven't enough fuel to chase them. Besides, I've still got to find out one thing—and we'll never find it out that way."

They were well away now, so Keen shut off the smoke screen and then gave the cockpit a closer inspection. He was puzzled at all the gadgets, especially by a handle on the other side exactly like that which had produced the smoke screen. The only difference was that this one had a white handle. He squinted at it, tried to figure what it was for. Meanwhile Barney kept the boat headed for the Long Island shore, a few miles away.

Finally, Keen could stand the temptation no longer. He pulled the white handle and turned to the stern.

A new smoke screen bloomed out—this time a white one!

Barney was too engrossed to worry about smoke screens of various colors. He was steering clear of all vessels and was keeping a weather eye peeled for Coast Guard cutters.

Keen shut the white screen off, sat back and pondered. Then he reached out for the big black log book that he had tossed into the boat when they cut loose. He turned to the most recent pages and for several minutes studied them. Then finally he breathed a deep sigh of relief.

He had solved the mystery of the phantom aircraft carrier!

"Home, James!" he gurgled, lying back with a smile of satisfaction. "I think we'll go to the movies tonight."

"What? And let those guys get away?" roared Barney.

"I said we'll go to the movies," smiled Keen. "It'll be a pleasant change."

Barney gave his boss a queer look, spat over the side, and turned back to his wheel.

"You're slug-nutty," he growled.

LATE that afternoon, a Coast Guard cutter picked up an abandoned coastal motor boat drifting off Montauk Point. It carried no markings. But on close inspection, it was found to be a naval vessel of some sort carrying a British torpedo, a number of French machine guns, Italian instrument dials—and a card stuck in the compass bracket which simply said, "The Griffon."

It was towed to the Newport submarine base and carefully inspected. Attempts were made to link it with the mysterious explosion which had sunk a tug boat known as the *Estelle,* and before night was well on its way, the newspapers were screaming new headlines of the menace that was now facing American shipping—high speed coastal motor boats.

Lang called Keen up about 7 o'clock that night.

"He's at it again," he opened. "What *you* bin doin'?"

"Who, me?" gurgled Keen. "Why just loafing around trying to think."

Lang blatted on: "That Griffon's using some sort of a coastal motor boat now. Blew up a tug boat off Fire Island Light somewhere about noon today. The Coast Guard found his speed boat drifting off Montauk Point. What do you make out of that?"

"Nothing. What do *you* make out of it? And what does that have to do with the aircraft carrier they're all jittery about?" Keen replied.

"It just jerks the reward up to about fifty grand, my friend. What are you going to do tonight?"

"Nothing much. Go to the movies for a change, I guess. I got what you might call an invitation for a special showing."

"*Movies!*" exploded Lang. "Movies! What the hell…? How you gonner get anything for me? You promised to, you know."

"Oh, something will turn up. It always does. And fancy our old Griffon having a game with a coastal motor boat!"

"We'll give him game, if we ever get him," snorted Lang. "He's up to something rare, I wouldn't be surprised if it wasn't some trick to pull the Army and Navy guys away from New York so that they can pull another raid somewhere tonight."

"That's what I'm afraid of, Lang," said Keen seriously. "I'd warn those service fellows to keep a close patrol over New York, or maybe even the Newport submarine base."

"That's an idea, Keen. I'll see what they think about it."

"Fine! I'll be seeing you tomorrow."

"You'd better—if you want a cut of that fifty grand."

"A cut? Say, I want the whole lot!"

"THIS is a hell of a way to be going to the movies," growled Barney that night as he worked over the *Black Bullet* in the hidden hangar. "Where you gonner park this boiler?"

"The girl at the ticket office will check it for us. They hang them up in the lobby now. Nothing like service, you know," Keen grinned as he reached inside a long pine box. "We'll take a few of these along, too. Always assures one of a seat." He pulled out a long bullet-like finned projectile with a shiny steel nose. "Yes, we'll take all the racks can carry. We may need several seats."

"Yeh, we might even get one for your Great-Aunt Sibby," Barney grunted, pouring a can of oil into the tank.

"Oh, she'll be there—with the rest of the ghosts," Keen said disinterestedly.

O'Dare let out a low moan and returned to his labors.

The radio set in the wall continued to blart away with all the latest horrors of the mystery raids. Already the police were attempting to break up wholesale emigrations to the interior. Railroad stations were crowded with swarms of terror-stricken humanity. The roads were choked with cars, trucks, and wagons bearing frantic-eyed citizens to safe retreats in the mountains of Pennsylvania.

Life in the cities along the coast had taken on a new tempo. A few financial houses suffered serious reverses. A mob stormed a New York radio station, took over the transmitters, and bellowed insane warnings and advice. The police and National Guard charged the building and more than a dozen men were killed in the fighting. For hours, patrols of fighting ships continued a systematic search of the coastal waters between Boston and Philadelphia.

The most maddening thing about it all was the comparative blindness in which they all groped. Navy pilots flew back and forth without knowing what they were looking for. Sleepless hours of intense search, holding tight formations, put strong airmen on the verge of collapse. Those who still retained their strength threw out their arms and pleaded for action.

The newspapers virtually declared war on everyone from Great Britain down to the Republic of Cuba. Hundreds of innocent public officers were rushed off to Army posts and questioned for hours. Spies were rounded up by the dozens and three were shot while resisting. Wild stories of wholesale shootings were circulated by disgruntled men in the minority political groups.

Yet Kerry Keen dare not tell what he knew until he was able to expose the phantom carrier. That demanded that he establish incontrovertible proof of his theories. In the meantime, the slightest bungling might involve America in an international catastrophe.

THE NIGHT fell on the most hectic day in American history. More service squadrons arrived from the West and took over areas between New York and the Canadian border.

And under cover of the dark of night, the *Black Bullet* crept out of her secret hangar and raced off into the east.

Keen in his black coveralls and parachute pack was at the controls. Before him was propped a special hand-drawn chart spattered with dotted lines, circles, and crosses. He had special night glasses at hand, and every gun and bomb rack was loaded.

Checking his flight every two minutes, he climbed to 6,000 feet. Barney, behind him, sat watching the sky, sighted the night patrol of destroyers swarming out of New York harbor. There were no planes of any kind in the air over the ocean, for they had all been withdrawn to shore patrol lines.

Keen was tense, plainly excited. Silently he flew on, following the strange dotted course indicated on his chart.

"A foine way to go to the movies," Barney grunted every five minutes.

Then suddenly action broke around them like a storm that floods out of the thunder-heads gathered around high mountain peaks. A tight, three-ship formation of fighters swept down on them from somewhere above, slashed the *Black Bullet* with their leaden scourges.

Barney was on his feet in an instant and returned the fire with his Brownings. Keen gave him fine assistance with his splendid flying. The nerve-taut tension was broken now and their maneuvers went off like clockwork.

A flying boat slammed at them, and Barney caught it full in the snout with a close-range double burst. There was a low boom and the raider exploded like a Fourth of July star shell full in the path of another M.F.10 flying boat that had swerved in to get a wide-angle shot at the *Black Bullet*.

Keen let out a yell as Barney tried to batter off the third raider.

"There's the carrier!" Keen yelled. "I told you we'd go to the movies, Barney!"

The Mick had no ears for him, however. He was engaged in a bitter duel with the third flying boat.

The sky was now decorated with tracer streaks, smoke streamers, and burning debris. Barney slammed a full burst at the oncoming M.F.10, saw it screech up, roll over on its back, and throw away its tail section. A man leaped clear, toppled head over heels, then drifted down under his parachute.

Barney watched it flutter away, then saw a large chunk of dural drop down on the open canopy. The tangled mess went toward the water like a stone.

"Look, Barney, look!" Keen was screaming. "There it is again! The phantom aircraft carrier!"

The Mick stared forward for a few seconds, then spat: "That ain't the same one!"

"What do you mean?" Keen shouted.

"It's a different one. Remember, the other looked like the British *Courageous*."

"I think you're right, Barney," Keen said finally. "Wait a minute—that's the French carrier *Bearn*. They've given us the French tie-up I was wondering about!"

Ahead and below them the ghostly aircraft carrier plunged on through a weird light. It was an island type ship, but the superstructure carrying funnels, control tower, and bridge, was more offset, giving full width to the flight deck. The vessel was shorter and stumpier, and its flight deck appeared to be raised on skeleton girders so that it did not present the smooth hull lines of American carriers.

As they watched it, a number of small French fighters of the Levasseur and Nieuport 140 C2 naval bomber-fighter types raced down the white guide line on the deck.

"We're nuts!" announced Barney.

"No, not that bad. Let's go!" And Keen nosed down and felt around for his bomb toggles.

"What's the idea? You gonner bomb a *ghost?*" Barney asked.

"Never mind about that. You keep the M.F.10s off our tail. You're going to see some real drama."

The *Black Bullet* plunged down with a screech. Keen held her in the dive under a bitter fire from another formation of flying boats that came up from nowhere. Barney plied his guns while the flying boats attempted to stop them by hurling themselves directly at the amphibian.

The Mick belted one after the other while Keene hammered his way through the winged defense. Down they went—and the details of the aircraft carrier became clearer.

Keen set his sights, aimed at a point a short distance short of the aircraft carrier, and yanked twice. Immediately there came the cough of anti-aircraft guns. But then came a belch of flame from below and the thunderous bellow of an explosion.

Kerry Keen's bombs had found their mark!

The aircraft carrier ahead wabbled like a badly handled screen projection, then suddenly disappeared. In its place was nothing but a milky-white veil!

"Holy smoke!" gasped Barney. "What the deuce did you hit?"

"I told you we'd go to the movies. I just blew up the projection room!" Keen yelled back. "That was the *Wrangel*. They went in for ship-board movies, you know."

Then with a whirl he snapped the *Black Bullet* over sharply, nosed down toward the source of the white smoke screen, and opened his front Darn guns. Barney had to battle three more flying boats that again came down on them from above. Keen's fire bit into a racing coastal motor boat that tried to turn sharply. He held his fire on her hard, and the coastal reeled, rolled, and suddenly swung over on her back, leaving her bronze screws whirling in the light of the flame from the burning *Wrangel*.

"That's the end of the phantom aircraft carrier," grinned Keen.

THEY had to fight like mad after that, for the air was full of flying boats that were intent on their destruction. But Barney was equal to it. He kept hammering lead into the enemy sky raiders, fought off every attack.

Keen was not satisfied, however. He hurtled the *Bullet* after the *Wrangel* and strafed the deck gunners with storms of Darn lead and Chatellerault fire. He yanked more toggles, and long, pencil-like bombs lanced through her decks and blew great holes in her hull.

Nevertheless, the *Wrangel* gunners stood their ground and punched back with three-inch stuff. The sky was aflame with explosive, burning flying boats, and the red streaks of exhaust.

Two more small coastals tried to get away, but Keen was on them like a banshee. His heavy gunfire fanged into the cockpits, hurled men overboard. With dead men at the wheels, the boats raced about aimlessly. One of them finally crashed into the sinking *Wrangel*.

"Beat it! Here come the Navy!" Barney suddenly screamed.

As Keen nosed up sharply, three Navy Boeings came out of

nowhere and set upon the remaining flying boats. The *Black Bullet* was now headed out to sea at top speed, and Keen climbed her to about 12,000 before he turned her back toward Graylands.

They were safely home in less than an hour after they had set out, with Keen explaining what had really happened to the mystified Barney.

"You see, Barney," he went on as the Mick prepared a couple of sandwiches, "they were using motion picture films through a projector fitted with a special infra-red light which, of course, cannot be seen. For a screen, they used the white smoke put up by the coastals.

The phantom carrier idea, you see, was a blind to cover the take-offs of their flying boats. That's all there was to it. I didn't get the idea until I discovered that those motor boats were fitted to discharge both black and white smoke screens. The white smoke, I might explain, contained some sort of chemicals which made the infra-red projection rays invisible when they hit."

"I think there's a lot of your Great-Aunt Sibby in you," Barney observed as he pulled the cork of an O'Doul's Dew bottle.

AT NOON the next day, a sleepy-eyed Lang called on a very dapper Kerry Keen at the latter's penthouse apartment in New York City.

"Where were you last night?" Lang opened as usual.

"I told you I was going to the movies, didn't I?" Keen grinned. "Well, I did."

"See the papers?"

"Rather. Very interesting, too. They say this Griffon bloke was in rare form last night."

"But what's it all about?" asked the perplexed Lang.

"First, where's the fifty grand?" smiled Keen.

"The what? Say, you weren't out there last night." Lang spluttered.

"Of course not. How could I be? But you remember our arrangement. I was to solve the mystery, then you were to get the credit and I was to get the filthy lucre."

"But what do you know about all this?"

"Enough to make you a pretty big guy in the Secret Service, old scout."

"But how did you find out anything?"

"Now, that wasn't in the agreement. But if you must know, the Griffon tipped me off."

"Now wait a minute. The Griffon was out there last night shooting down planes by the dozens. For some cock-eyed reason, he also bombed and sank a Swedish whaler. If you were at the movies, how did you get all this dope?"

"What about the fifty grand?" taunted Keen.

"Don't worry. I'm ready to give you a credit slip on the Department of Justice for the amount. But first you've got to come clean."

"Then I guess we're all through. You go and solve your mystery yourself," Keen snapped.

"I'll run you in the jug!"

"All right. Let's go right now. But, of course, that won't solve the mystery of the phantom aircraft carrier."

Lang snorted, drew out a narrow check book, and scrawled across the top leaf. Then he ripped out the draft and tossed it across the table to Keen. The latter picked it up, read it, and wrote something on the back.

"I'm endorsing it for the Tenement Camp Fund," he said as he folded it and slipped it into his pocket. "As for your mystery, I've got the dope you need. And never mind how I got it."

"Get on with the story," grunted Lang.

"All right. Here it is: The whaler *Wrangel* was actually an aircraft carrier of a sort operated surreptitiously by the Navarro Council— an outfit you can check on through the State Department. The planes—Italian high speed flying boats—were hidden aboard and were launched down the long whale chute. A modern nautical book will give you full details on this ship."

"What about the aircraft carrier?"

"There wasn't any."

"But—but several persons saw it!"

"They *thought* they saw it. Actually, they only saw a motion picture thrown on a white smoke screen from a large projector mounted aboard the *Wrangel* and which used a form of infra-red ray as light. This light projected pictures of aircraft carriers in action without the usual white beam. Thus the launching activities of the *Wrangel's* flying boats were covered."

"Holy smoke!"

"It was un-holy smoke while it lasted. The smoke screens were put up by the coastal motor boats—"

"Run by the Griffon?" broke in Lang hollowly.

"Of course not. They were operated by seamen from the *Wrangel*."

"But the Coast Guard found one of those boats, and it had a Griffon card on it."

"I wouldn't know anything about that," smiled Keen. "But there's the story of your mystery aircraft carrier in a nutshell."

"Yeh, but how can you prove it?"

"That's where the great Drury Lang comes in. He will go before the U.S. Navy Department with the log of the *Wrangel* under his arm. He will stand before all the brass hats and gold braid and turn page after page outlining the complete activity of the phoney whaler. He will even show them where the projector was fitted and how the flying boats were launched. In short, he will pull the greatest coup in the history of the Secret Service."

"You mean he would if he had the log book," muttered Lang.

Keen walked across the room, opened a wall safe, and took out a black book. He handed it over, and Lang stared at it amazed. And when the G-man turned the cover, a card fell out.

Keen displayed astonishment. The card read:

With the Compliments
of
The Griffon

With a quick gesture, Lang tore the card up and threw it into the fireplace. "Like hell!" he snapped. "That guy ain't gonner crab my act. But where'd you get this book?"

"It's not a matter of where *I* got it, Lang. You'll have to figure out some way of proving where *you* got it. You will have to have a better story than mine."

"Yes…. Yes," mumbled Lang, "I'll have to tell them where I got it. Yeh, and where *did* I get it?"

"Well, you might have found it in the wreckage of the *Wrangel*. Or you might have had it mailed to you from Newport by the Griffon for he might have found it in that motor boat. Moreover, you'd better find a way to deposit that fifty grand which I get for solving the mystery of the phantom aircraft carrier," smiled Keen.

"But how *did* you get this book?"

"I've already told you. I just went to the movies," Keen came back.

"I've got it! I've got it!" suddenly cracked Lang. "Why, say, Mister Keen, I can explain this thing for you myself! You said that you got an invitation for a special movie showing. You know what? Sure as shootin', the Griffon sent you that invitation in order to get you into a dark place where he could pass you this book. I'll bet that crook wanted to square himself for some of the raw stunts he's pulled. And you found the book on the seat next to you, huh?"

"Well—" began Keen.

"Yeh, that's it!" broke in Lang without waiting to hear any more. "And I coulda bin at that movie house myself. The Griffon coulda passed it to me just as well as to you, couldn't he?"

"Sure thing," said Keen. "I don't think it would be much of a lie to say that the Griffon passed it to you. And now, so long, Lang. I'm a busy man," continued Keen, moving toward the door. "You won't forget to make that deposit, will you?"

"N-no," sniffed Lang as he backed away. "Of course, you *did* go to the movies, didn't you, Keen?" he whispered as though he needed one final word of encouragement.

"I *sure* did!" said the young ballistics expert as he shoved Lang out.

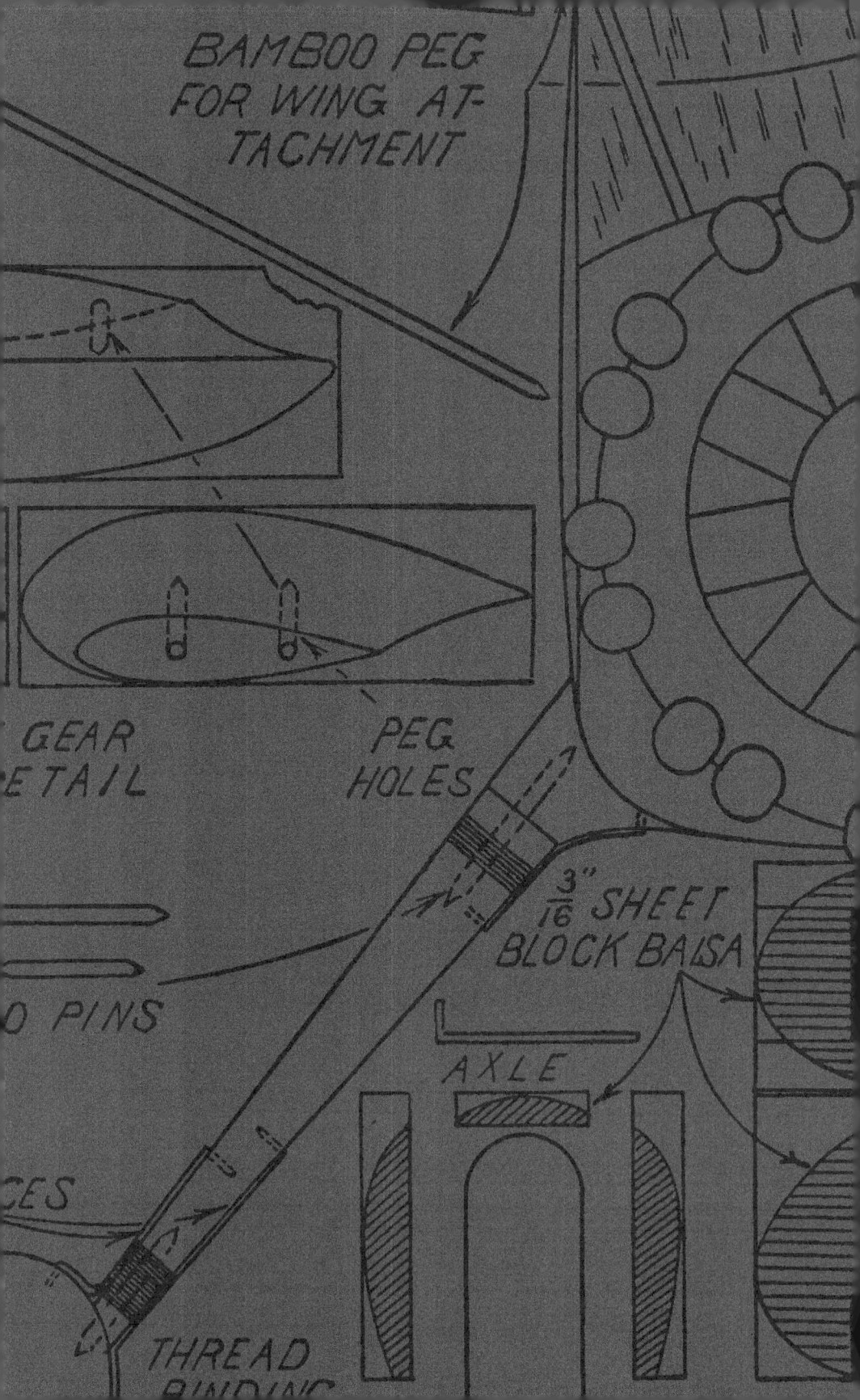

BAMBOO PEG
FOR WING AT-
TACHMENT

GEAR
ETAIL

PEG
HOLES

PINS

$\frac{3"}{16}$ SHEET
BLOCK BALSA

AXLE

CES

THREAD
BINDING

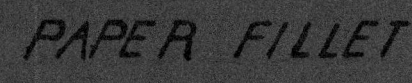

Scourge of the Sky Brood

THE BOX was about two feet long and about nine inches across at its widest point. It was a strange, ungainly box, obviously difficult to carry. Only the carefully screwed, black angle iron at its corners offered contrast to its steel-gray color. The woman who bore it seemed to show it all the tenderness of one who cuddled a first-born. Yet she cast furtive glances over her shoulder as she hurried with painful steps along the dimly lit street—for she was old and this precious box was to be her salvation. Her long walk had wearied her and now a cool Fall wind had sprung up to whip her ragged skirt about her thin, bony knees.

Yes, the box meant life and a certain degree of ease. She had risked her all to get it.

"Two thousand dollars, that's what the man will give me," she mumbled to herself for the fiftieth time. "Two thousand dollars, all in five dollar bills. I could go back to County Tipperary with that—and have some left over."

She had been trudging on now for more than two hours, always heading north and east. She could have taken a streetcar, a subway, perhaps. But she was taking no chances on any public conveyance.

"Ay," she muttered again. "It'll be County Tipperary for me when I get this over. Two thousand dollars in five dollar bills! That's a powerful lot o' money!"

The wind, stronger now, whistled down the street, and the old woman clutched the box even tighter, even though her old bones ached where the sharp corners of the box cut deep into her flesh.

She stopped at a corner, peered up at the blue and white street sign under the light. Finally she made out the letters. Mumbling them over in her toothless mouth, she nodded and hurried on. She was right, now. In a few minutes she would find the man—the nice young man who promised her two thousand dollars in five-dollar bills.

Those visions of County Tipperary were sweet to this old scrub-lady who had worked for years to keep body and soul together in the great New World metropolis. Two thousand dollars took on the proportions of a magnificent fortune after sixty-five years of toil that had brought no material reward.

She paused at the next intersection. Then hugging the box closer to her, she bucked the wind and made for the opposite corner.

"Two thousand dollars," she muttered again. "In five—"

But that was as far as she got. A long black car suddenly purred out of the darkness, flashed its headlights on once, then flipped them off again. There was a thud, a low choked scream, then the dull retch of brakes. The old lady never knew what hit her. She rolled toward the gutter, still clutching the steel-gray box.

"Nice work, Tony," a voice said with a cruel chuckle. "Hold it a second."

The man who had spoken darted out of the darkened car, ran to the fallen woman. He took one look at her, kicked brutally at her twisted leg, then yanked at the box.

A voice abruptly crackled out of the gloom, and the man turned sharply, drew a blue-black automatic, and fired three times.

Then with the box in his arms he leaped for the black car again and the door slammed behind him as the gear went in with a clash of metal teeth.

Into the dull night the car crashed and lunged. It was impossible to get the license numbers.

" *'AV ALL* the filthy jobs," the man who now hurried up said. "To kill an auld lady like that just to steal her groceries. That's what it looked like anyway. An' thin, begorra, he tries to kill me, too!"

He crouched at her side. Doors were opening now and windows creaked upward. Faces and heavy bare arms appeared.

"How are ye? Are ye much hurt, mother?" the man said, lifting her head around with crude tenderness.

"...thousand dollars in five-dollar bills," she said between gulps. "He said he'd... give me... two thousand dollars. And then I could go to County Tipperary."

"You from County Tipperary, m'am?" the man asked. He knew she'd never get back there. "The devils hit ye—and ran off."

A crowd gathered around. The man tried to make her comfortable. He dragged her to the sidewalk, then noticed that she held one fist clenched. He fumbled with her shawl, carefully opened the fingers, and drew out a small slip of paper. He quickly stuffed it in his pocket as a bluecoat shoved his way through the crowd.

"She's done," he told the policeman. "A big black car—a Lincoln, I believe—hit her and cleared off."

The cop leaned over with a bored professional air. He'd seen so many of these things. He reached out, yanked a tattered bed quilt from the top of a refuse can, and drew it across the body. Then brushing his hands together with a gesture of finality, he said:

"Nut'in' you can do about it. Them hit-run guys will be miles away by now. Stick around while I go in that store over there and call up the wagon."

But the man who had taken the paper from the old lady's hand was nowhere to be found when the cop came back.

EXACTLY twenty-four hours later, Kerry Keen and Barney O'Dare were enjoying an evening at home. Both had pipes going and the study was tinted a pleasant blue. Keen was working on a chart of internal ballistics on several new machine guns; he planned to display it during his coming lecture before the Army War College. Barney was wrapped up in a gaudy-covered adventure novel set in darkest Africa. Already he had consumed more than half a bottle of O'Doul's Dew and the book was getting more exciting by the minute.

Finally, the Irishman could stand the tense thrills of the yarn no longer. With a glance at the clock, he stepped over and flipped on the radio switch.

"Ah! That's right, Barney. Let's find out what's going on in the world," said Keen, looking up. "Time for the news, eh?"

"Where's Africa?" asked Barney without glancing up.

"South of Europe—most of it," answered Keen. "What of it?"

"Ever been to a place called Angola?"

"No, I haven't. But why?"

"Well, I was just reading a story about how the cannibals down there light fires on yer stomach when they catch you, and—"

But the radio tubes were now warm and the voice of the announcer came in gradually:

"*...most amazing crime story of the year. A United States Secret Service man named Layton Beale was mysteriously murdered aboard* *a Bermuda bound Clipper plane this afternoon. Beale was found stabbed to death in his seat a short time before the plane landed in Hamilton Harbor. He was found by the plane steward, George Blott. Government officials in Bermuda are investigating the case. We hope to bring more news of this amazing affair later in the broadcast.*

"And here's another item of interest: The mystery surrounding the death of Mrs. Margaret Kennedy, who was knocked down and killed by a hit-run driver last night, is still attracting the attention of police and government officials. Mrs. Kennedy was a cleaner in the Brooklyn Navy Yard office buildings and no one seems to be able to account for her being in the Maspeth section of Long Island at that time of night. She lives in a small furnished room in central Manhattan."

"Wait a minute," Barney suddenly growled. "That name—that George Blott guy."

The radio continued on with less interesting news while Barney fumbled about in his pockets. Keen watched with mild interest, unable to figure out what Barney was getting at.

"Yes, that's the same name," Barney suddenly said, peering at a crumpled piece of paper he had extracted from his coat. "Look, 'George Blott.'"

He handed the paper over to Keen, who read:

Mr. George Blott
The Waterford Cafe
64th and Grand Avenue

"What's it all about?" Keen said.

"This paper was in that old woman's hand when I got to her. I saw her knocked over, you see. But the guys got away before I could get their number."

"The woman you were talking about last night when you came in?"

"Sure! That's the same woman. She had this paper in her hand. The guys who hit her, grabbed her groceries or whatever she was carrying."

"And this George Blott is the steward on the Clipper who found this Secret Service man dead?"

"That was the same name—but listen!" The radio had taken up the subject again:

"We have just learned that Beale, the Secret Service man, was stabbed through the heart with a strange Indian knife, believed to be a Ghoorka weapon. Bermuda officials have studied it and have found definite fingerprints on the handle. But strangely enough none of the prints fit any person aboard the plane! This is the most unusual murder mystery that has come up in years."

"Whew!" gasped Keen. "That is a beauty! A man is murdered with an Indian knife aboard a plane some 4,000 feet in the air. The knife carries fingerprints—but they don't fit any person aboard the plane! How do you like that?"

"I don't like it," muttered Barney. "It all adds up to—"

THERE was a sudden plunk of feet outside the apartment. Then the bell rang. Both Barney and Keen exchanged smiles. They knew it would be Drury Lang.

Barney let him in, first stuffing the piece of paperback into his pocket.

Lang shuffled across the room, spotted the O'Doul's Dew bottle, and headed for it under draft. He took a long swig, wiped his mouth with the back of his hand, then sat down. The radio blared on. Lang leaned over, snapped it off.

"What do you think of that Kennedy woman case?" he asked finally.

"Anything missing?" spoke up Keen.

"What made you ask that?" Lang said, sitting bolt upright.

"A perfect set-up. Old lady who works in the Administration Building of the Navy Yard goes tramping across Brooklyn late at night—to be knocked down by a car."

"Go on," said Lang. "You're getting warm."

"I read the story in this morning's paper. She was knocked down on a fairly quiet street and they took a package she was carrying, according to an eyewitness. There was some shooting, too."

"Well, there is something missing," Lang said, peering about.

"But we're not broadcasting it. No, it ain't the design of a new battleship, or anything like that."

"No? What is it?"

"A model of the *U.S.S. Saratoga*, incorporating a working model of a new flight-deck arrester gear. Only a few men in the Navy know how it works, and every other naval power in the world would like to get the dope on it."

"What's it do?" asked Barney.

"Arrests planes coming in for a landing on the flight decks of the Navy aircraft carriers," answered Lang with a sniff.

"What do they want to arrest them for? They ain't done nothin', have they?"

"My gosh, how do you live with a guy like this?" Lang exploded. "How could you arrest a plane, you dumb Mick? They don't arrest—"

"But you said they did," argued the irrepressible Barney, with a twinkle in his eye.

"I mean arrest the ships," spluttered Lang.

"Oh, the battleships."

"No—the planes!" came the screeching reply. "They arrest them...."

"You just said they didn't. That you can't arrest planes."

"It's an arresting gear, that—"

"Oh, a mechanical police system. Ain't the cops smart enough any more? Do they have to...?"

"Will you shut up while I explain? It's a... a thing, something to stop the Navy planes from running off the deck when they are landing—that sort of an arrester. Cripes! I used to think you knew something. But I give up," Lang moaned, shaking his head.

Keen broke in at this point to get Lang started again. "I know what you mean, Lang. Go on with the story."

"I'm glad some one knows something about something. To think that I came up to this funny factory to get some help."

"We don't know nothin'," scowled Barney.

"You don't know nothin'," agreed Lang. "But this mug over here knows plenty," he added, indicating Keen.

"Here comes the 'Griffon' gag again," laughed Keen.

"I suppose it was the Griffon who killed the Secret Service man on that Clipper ship. Find any cards yet?"

"Shut up! I might be the next one," Lang said. "I got to go down next trip and get him."

"What are you talking about? Get who?"

"Beale was on his way down to bring back a former Navy guy—a Commander Hugh Stanwick, who was wanted by the government for selling Navy secrets. Now I got to go and get him."

KEEN'S mind was working fast now. Things were beginning to jell—the old lady from the Navy Yard... the man named George Blott, who was a steward aboard the Clipper ship... the missing model of the aircraft carrier arrester gear... and the murdered Secret Service man.

"The British," Lang continued, "nabbed Stanwick down there and we got extradition papers on him. Beale was to go down and bring him back."

"But what about that model?" Keen suddenly asked.

"Does that case hook up with this Clipper business?"

"I never thought of that," said Lang, pensively. "You know, Keen, you got a good mind. You ought to be in this racket."

"But where is the model now?"

"I thought you might have an idea. There's some real dough in it if we can get it back."

"You're going down on the Saturday Clipper to bring this man, Stanwick, back?"

"Yeh, but I don't like it."

"Um, and you'll be going down on the same plane and with the same crew that took Beale?"

"Hey, take it easy, will you?" pleaded Lang. "You could go by boat, you know."

"Sure. But it would take too long. Besides, they need me on the arrester-gear model business."

"I see," said Keen. "But don't forget what I said before. This man Stanwick may be connected in some way with the stealing of the arrester gear. He might even have it in Bermuda."

Lang sat and studied the design in the Chinese rug for some time. Finally, he wagged his head solemnly and agreed.

"That's right! Stanwick is reasonably free. He's out on some sort of parole, being a U.S. Naval officer and all that sort of thing."

"You'd better be sure he is clamped up somewhere. If the man who was going down to pick him up was killed—murdered—it should be pretty obvious that this guy Stanwick is a pretty important character. Desperate, too, by the looks of things."

"How about you, Keen?" Lang asked after another period of solemn contemplation of the rug.

"I mean, what are you doing for the lecture to reel off before the War College and I'm working on a lot of research stuff. Why?" Keen asked. He knew what Lang was after.

"We've got to get that model back," Lang said through his browned teeth. "I wish I knew where to get hold of that Griffon guy. I can't figure him out yet, Keen. I'd like to contact him, somehow, and make a dicker with him."

"Maybe the Griffon was in this thing at that. It sounds like the sort of mess he cooks up," said Keen with a serious grimace.

Lang looked at his host, unable to make out just what he meant.

"Come clean for once in your life, Keen. You know who the Griffon is, don't you?" he queried, lighting a cigarette and looking around for the bottle.

"But how would all this business interest the Griffon?" Keen asked, avoiding Lang's question.

"There's plenty in it—for the guy who can get that model back. More than you'll get for spouting about ballistics before a War College crowd," Lang replied, equally as evasive, but pointed in his inference.

"So you still think I'm the Griffon," Keen said with a low chuckle.

"No, I don't. But—"

"Well," interrupted Keen hurriedly. "Regardless of all that I think I'll let you get bumped off on the Clipper trip. You're becoming a nuisance, Lang. You bother me with your trifles. Yes," he added slowly, "I think

I'll let you go and get yourself bumped off."

"Tripe!" Lang blarted out, jumping up. "You can't scare me that way. I'll go to Bermuda and I'll bring Stanwick back. And then I'll come back and go to work on you—and the Griffon!"

"No, you mustn't forget the Griffon," grinned Keen.

"And don't forget the model of the aircraft carrier arrester-gear. That's very important."

"I won't forget," Lang continued to storm. "I won't forget you, either, when I get back."

He barged out of the door, clucking like an insulted hen.

"If you do get back," Keen hurled at the closed door.

"WHAT did you mean by that?" queried Barney after they heard the elevator doors clang.

"That man's in real danger, Barney," Keen said as he gathered his papers together. "He'll get into trouble as sure as shooting— or knifing—if he goes after that egg Stanwick."

"You worrying about him?"

"In a way. I'd hate to see the old guy shoved off. He keeps us prime. I don't know what we'd do without him sticking his beak into everything. No, we can't let old Lang go like that. He's too valuable. He's ready money any time we get down on our uppers."

"I can see that we're in for something hot tonight, eh?" Barney grunted. "Who gets hit this time? Me, I suppose."

Keen did not answer. He was scotched on the corner of his big desk, fingering a yellow pencil. "The old lady had the box last night," he mumbled, talking to no one in particular, "and they got it before midnight."

"So this guy Blott, who she was looking for, probably took it to Bermuda on the same Clipper carrying that G-man Beale," offered Barney.

"Maybe," Keen said frowning. "And yet Blott would be taking an awful chance doing it that way. No, the box was not on board that trip, or they wouldn't have bumped off Beale. They got rid of Beale to keep Stanwick free a little longer. Because, you see, they want to hand Stanwick the box so he, in turn, can deliver it over to some one in Bermuda and get the dough he needs to get out of this mess."

"But suppose Blott did take the box down," argued Barney.

"He couldn't have," persisted Keen. "He knew that if Beale was to be killed, there would be a thorough check of the ship, and then the box would be found. It's going down on the next trip."

"That lets us out, then," Barney mooned. "They do a daylight show all the time."

Keen nodded at that, then took a new tack: "It is evident that the box is somewhere here—or out on Long Island near Port Washington, the Clipper base. But there's no use in trying to get it here. We must wait until we are certain of its position, and we can't be sure of that until Blott's plane leaves on Saturday. Then we'll know for certain that it is aboard, and we can work from that point on."

"Wow! Then old Lang *will* be on board with it all the time!"

"Yes. But he won't know it. He'll be so scared waiting for someone to stab him, he won't be able to figure out anything."

"Neither would I," said Barney.

THAT was Wednesday night, and Keen and Barney went to bed and slept on it. By noon next day, however, they were out at Graylands, Keen's small estate out on Long Island. There they checked maps, charts, and the tanks of the *Black Bullet*.

At 6 o'clock Barney took his dilapidated flivver and headed back toward the city, but when he was certain no one was following him, he turned north at Mineola and headed for Port Washington.

He was back again before ten o'clock. Keen listened to his story, made a quick decision. "Okay," he said quietly. "Get something to eat. After that we're heading out."

Barney lunched on a cold leg of lamb, a dish of cold spuds and a bottle of beer, while Keen muffled himself up in his black coverall, helmet, and parachute harness. When the Mick had his fill he pulled on his flying gear slowly and went downstairs with half a bottle of beer in his hand, flicking out lights as he went.

Below, in their underground hangar, Keen was swinging the *Black Bullet* around on her turntable so that her nose was pointing out. He climbed up into the covered cockpit, kicked over the Avia starter, and the big 1,000 h.p. engine roared into life. He set the Skoda mufflers, then nodded down to Barney. The latter snapped off the lights, moved up to a master switch box, and drew a red handle down.

"Make it snappy," Keen called over the side. "We've got to make it fast before daybreak."

The great doors of the sunken hangar silently swung outward and Keen ran the amphibian into the velvety darkness outside. Barney flicked the switch again, darted outside before the doors closed.

"Those suitcases were put aboard, weren't they?" Keen husked over the side.

"Sure. Everything's aboard—enough to start a circus," Barney grunted, more to himself than in an answer. Then he drew out the folding wings and Keen pressed the king-pins down with his feet. At last they were ready, so Barney climbed aboard and took his position in the rear cockpit.

Keen let the *Black Bullet* roll down the hard turf, past the thick foliaged, grape arbor, and into the shadow of his boathouse. The engine was throttled back to a low purr as she rolled across the hard wet sand and settled on the water. Keen drew back the levers which set the pontoons for a water take-off, then ran the plane out away from the shore. Once in the clear, he opened the Avia, whereupon the *Black Bullet* leaped up on her step and fought herself free of the light rollers.

Now she was away, climbing like a hawk. Keen settled back and waited until he was at 4,000 feet before he cut off the mufflers and let her roar. He finally shot her out toward the sea after turning to take a point on the Montauk Point light.

"Bermuda, next stop," he grinned.

HARDLY had he spoken the words, however, when Barney turned sharply in his seat and reached under the cowling for his gun.

"What's up? Keen queried. They were in communication through their helmet phones now and could talk with little trouble.

Keen hunched his shoulders, turned back to his job. But in a moment, Barney jerked again and peered about. This time Keen took no notice but went to work checking his chart.

"I don't like it," Barney finally said.

"Get out and walk," was all the satisfaction he got from Keen.

"But there's something going on, somewhere. How's she flying?"

"Beautiful! What's eating you, anyway?"

"I don't know… but something's screwy on this show."

"Sure—no one has shot at us yet," cracked Keen, getting on with the business.

"No, not—"

But before Barney could finish his remark they were both deafened by a series of sharp explosions that crashed all about them. The *Bullet* staggered as she plunged through the concussion. Chunks of screaming metal wailed all about them.

Barney ducked down. This was more than aerial gunfire. He sensed that this was heavier stuff.

Keen threw the *Bullet* all over the sky, tried to get a sight on the source of the trouble. As he swerved away, turning out to sea again, he almost ran smack into a giant flying boat which seemed to be in as much distress as themselves.

There were strange flashes coming from its control cabin windows just below the giant wing.

CR-RA-SH! CRR-ASH!

Another salvo of fire now exploded all about them and the *Bullet* tangoed in waves of concussion. Keen climbed her hard, sensed that Barney was breaking out his rear guns.

"No! No! Take it easy. It's not that flying boat!"

Barney turned, stared at Keen amazed. "Not that boat? Where is it from then?" he barked.

"I don't know. But look! The flying boat's getting it, too."

They both stared at the floundering transport as she took the beating from the explosions that rent the sky.

"What is it—a Clipper?"

"No, a Short Empire job."

"But the Imperial Bermuda ship is not due here until Saturday when the Clipper goes out," Barney argued.

"That's what's funny about it," Keen said as he cleared and ran into a thin patch of clouds.

"I think she was firing at us," Barney said, letting his lower lip fold over the upper. "I saw flashes."

"Just Aldis lamp signals from the control pit. They were trying to signal some one."

"Sure, but who? I didn't see anybody."

"I give up, too," said Keen. "But let's buzz off."

They were in the clear now. The firing had ceased and the silver Empire boat was somewhere well below them heading for Port Washington.

They raced away into the darkness on a southeast course, settled down for a four-hour run. All the way they saw nothing but the stars, a few straggling surface vessels, and the lights of that majestic liner, the Queen of Bermuda.

It was nearly 4 o'clock Bermuda time when Keen finally swung her around over Port Royal Bay. The straggling fishhook of land known as Bermuda lay 6,000 feet below.

"Well, we're here. What are you gonner do with this boiler?" demanded Barney.

"You'll see," said Keen. "I've been here before. It's perfect for prowlers like us."

"If the British Coast Guard doesn't spot you," added Barney.

The *Bullet* sped on for a mile or so, then Keen snapped in the Skoda mufflers. Finally, he carefully turned her back and let her glide gently toward Church Bay. Watching carefully ahead, he let her clear the Southwest Breaker Bar, then suddenly switched her around at right angles, headed for Great Whale Point, and with careful S-turns finally brought her down on the silent waters.

Keen snapped an order.

Quickly, Barney slipped out of the cockpit and stood on the wing root.

Keen eased her in quietly, released the wing king-pins, and the Mick folded the airfoils back. Then like a wraith the *Black Bullet* slipped inside a black slit in the rocks and disappeared.

EIGHT HOURS later, two men in neat white linen, with well shaven chins and the early flush of a tropical sunburn, trundled black enameled bicycles along Front Street in Hamilton. They stopped in at Arundell's, had a drink, and made a few discreet inquiries. Yes, these men were Keen and Barney. Finding a newspaper, Barney quickly scanned the headlines. "They are still working on the knife theory," he whispered to Keen. "And say, how's that Planter's punch?"

"Lovely! But what about the knife?"

"Says they have made another examination of all aboard the plane and again proved that none jibes with the prints on the handle."

"Maybe he was murdered in New York City and he walked out to Port Washington with the knife in his chest without anyone knowing it," said Keen colorlessly. Then he added: "There's something screwy about that knife business. I'd like to see that weapon."

"Let's ask the Governor-General," smirked Barney, folding up the paper.

"Oh, it can be done," Keen snapped. "Drink up and pop along with me.... No, that's no good. You'd better stay here and see that that bartender keeps the Planter's up to snuff."

Barney readily agreed to that, and Keen went out, threw a leg across his bicycle, and pedaled away. In a few minutes he arrived at the Council Chamber buildings and got directions to the Island Police Inspector's office.

With the aid of several cards and letters he had carefully fixed up for the event, Keen was able to get inside and ask a few questions concerning the murder of Beale. The Chief Inspector, a ruddy, bacon-faced Britisher, was brusk at first, but he gradually warmed up as he talked to Keen. Keen, however, had adopted the name of Ginsberg for the occasion, as he usually did under such conditions.

"It has left us somewhat flat," the Inspector admitted, trying to adjust the name of Ginsberg to Keen's profile. "This knife business, you know."

"That's what I was interested in," Keen added. "I'm something of an expert on weapons of that sort and I'd like to see it. I have a theory about it."

"Of course you may see it. Anything to get on with it, you know."

The Inspector led Keen into a smaller room, nodded to a young man in civilian clothes who was working at a chemistry bench, and showed Keen the exhibits of the case. The knife was among the most prominent.

At first Keen simply stared at it without touching it. But then the Inspector spoke up.

"You can pick it up. We've done all we can with it."

Keen smiled, took the knife in his hands, and with a quick underhand movement suddenly drew the handle off the knife and handed it to the Inspector with a smile.

The Inspector was amazed. He took it gingerly, fumbled with it for some seconds. "But I say, it never came off before. It was on tight."

"They all are—until you shove this curved section of the small hilt guard down with the knuckle of your first finger. Like this— see?"

Keen demonstrated for the Inspector's benefit.

"This is a Ghoorka knife, all right," Keen explained, "but it is small—a woman's knife. They carry them for many things, and one of their features is that they can use them for sticking in pieces of meat for smoking or cooking. You see, they remove the handle until they are ready to take the meat down. But it never had the same ceremonial standing as did the regular fighting knife of the men."

"But what does it mean?" the Inspector asked, puzzled.

"Only one thing. Beale was killed on board the Clipper all

right, but the handle of the knife was changed, and this one put on with a lot of misleading fingerprints on it. But hello! Look here!"

Keen was holding the knife in his hands and putting the blade back and forth inside the handle. As he fingered with it in this manner, the handle end of the blade disclosed a small piece of folded white paper.

Keen picked it up off the floor where it had fallen and examined it. He unfolded it—and they both stared at a portion of a Clipper menu.

"Get it?" said Keen.

"Not quite, except that it might have been fitted into that particular handle to make the tang of the knife fit tight at that end."

"Right! But who put it there?"

"You have me… unless…."

"Of course. The steward—Blott. He would have used one of the printed menus to make the tang fit, so that it would be tight after he had changed the handles. Had it been loose, you might have stumbled over that trick catch idea and realized what you know now."

"Then Blott's our man. I'd better wire New York right away," the inspector said anxiously.

"But you can't arrest him on anything as flimsy as that," Keen said in feigned horror. "You might have him traced, or carefully watched. But he'll be down here again tomorrow afternoon. I'd wait and have him apprehended here."

"I suppose you're right," the inspector said. "Besides, I believe a Secret Service man is on his way down on that flight to get—"

"I know—to get Commander Stanwick," broke in Keen. "And there's another point, Inspector. You have charge of Stanwick, haven't you?"

"In a general way, yes. He's under some sort of parole until he goes aboard the Clipper on Sunday. Navy chap of some sort, and it's messy, that parole business."

"Your men, of course, keep a fairly good tab on him, eh?"

"As well as we can."

"Then you would know if he has received a wooden box—a special steel-gray box, well braced, and all that sort of thing. As a matter of fact, it's a U.S. Navy box of some sort. Between you and me, Inspector, it's lost—and I have a hunch that Stanwick is to get hold of it somehow."

"I'm almost certain he would not have received anything like that without our knowing it. We keep a close tab on him, you know, as far as his post and communications are concerned."

"All right. Do you have a man on the island by the name of Haageman—a Professor Haageman?" Keen asked suddenly after another examination of the knife.

"Haageman?... Professor Haageman? Of course! He's a guest of the Governor-General. It's said he's got something to do with a German munitions syndicate."

"Yes. I read about him being down here—and I just wondered."

"I think I understand."

"Thanks, Inspector. So if you run into this gray box, it's to be returned to the U.S. Navy—unopened. You understand that, too, eh?"

"I think we understand one another, Mr. Ginsberg. By the way, where are you staying?"

"I'm with friends—aboard a yacht. I'd rather keep that quiet, too. I'll keep in touch with you during the next few days, but don't take a chance on Blott yet. He may slip out of your fingers."

"Thanks for your assistance in the matter, Mr. Ginsberg. I hope you'll come in again," the grateful Inspector replied. "I'll have Blott watched."

"I know a better plan. I'll have him watched. I'll have someone aboard the Clipper watch him. How's that?"

"I'll leave it up to you, sir," the Inspector said.

Keen went out, found the government post office and wrote a telegram to Drury Lang. It read:

KEEP YOUR EYE ON THE CLIPPER STEWARD STOP
HE MAY BE THE GRIFFON
—GINSBERG

And with that he hurried back to Arundell's and joined Barney who had picked up more interesting information.

THEY chatted quietly in a corner, watching the colorful tourist crowd mill in and out as they talked.

Across the street, the Monarch of Bermuda creaked against the piles of the dock. About them was the clean spicy smell that only Bermuda can provide.

"Well, what about it?" Keen finally asked. "Anything doing?"

"I got a boat and I think I can get the 'juice' later on this afternoon. I had to pay a buck a gallon, but it's aviation stuff."

"What is it in—four-gallon cases?"

"Sure, export stuff. But we got to haul it ourselves."

"Don't worry. No one will be in on this. When will it be ready?"

"I take the boat around about 4 o'clock and tie it up to a small pier on this end of Morgan's Island. Then we go back after dark and clear it. I have the boat until noon tomorrow."

"That means we've got to run through Seeley's Narrows to get out on the south side of the island," Keen said reflectively as he glanced up at a lithographed map of Bermuda that was framed on the wall. "Well, that's the best we can do, I suppose. It'll work out, I hope."

They split up again after that. Keen went to a nearby hotel and ordered dinner while Barney clambered on his bike and pedaled away.

KEEN met Barney again that night at the end of a bicycle path that ran down from the main road to the sands on Burgess Point.

Barney was at the oars of a light skiff and together they rowed across to Morgan's Island, which lay about a mile away.

They found the boat Barney had hired and climbed aboard. Below under neat tarpaulins were stacked a number of boxed cans of aviation fuel. They looked them over quickly, saw that there was enough for what they would require, plus a few gallons of oil into the bargain.

"That Limey thought I wanted it for a motor boat," Barney

laughed under his breath. "He said: 'You won't 'art be able to splather abart wiv this stuff in yer tank, mate!'"

"I hope he keeps on thinking that way," Keen answered. "And now, let's go."

The boat was an American job of a popular type. Barney had no trouble starting it and getting it under way. They shot westward at high speed and headed for Seeley's Narrows that slit Somerset into two chunks. They carried all riding lights and Keen even turned on all cabin lights to stimulate the impression that they were on a typical tourist holiday outing. For about an hour they carefully picked their way through the Narrows on a chart Barney had wisely borrowed. Then they eased out on to the ocean side of the island and turned south to make their way to the hidden cave that sheltered the *Black Bullet*.

"How did you know about the place?" Barney asked, showing interest in it for the first time.

"Funny, all right, how I remembered it," Keen replied. "It actually belongs to a very close friend of mine who is in New York at the present time. The cave has been there for years and probably was used in the old days as a hide-out by the pirate trade, but few enter it today owing to the morays that infest the water."

"Morays? What are they?"

"Why, they're a form of giant eel, and they are absolutely ferocious—have teeth like razor blades. If you fell in the water there, you'd have a rather bad time for a while. For they will attack a human being with all the vim of a barracuda."

"Oof!" grunted Barney. "You sure pick the spots."

"It's a good one. You can bet no one will go in there. No, it's a swell place for what we want."

And with that explanation they settled back for the four-mile run to their lair. Barney was at the wheel and Keen sat in the stern and enjoyed the night. They kept well outside the Great West Breaker Bar then turned toward Great Whale Point.

The headlands were ahead of them now, and Keen, deciding to play safe, doused the riding and cabin lights. Barney throttled her back and let her skim along with hardly a sound. They were riding thus when Barney suddenly sat bolt upright. He peered about, cut the engine down even more.

He turned and looked at Keen who had caught it, too.

"Where the deuce did that come from?" Keen said in a husky whisper. "It wasn't there a few minutes ago."

"It came up out of the water," Barney said quietly. "Must be a submarine."

"There's no British submarines in these waters. I checked that this morning. Look, it's got German markings on it."

"I didn't know Germany had any submarines," Barney husked, watching the long gray wraith come out of the water.

"Lay low! Look, there's a boat out there."

They let the motor boat ease along quietly, then saw a small boat run up to the deck of the dripping submarine. Two men climbed out and got aboard the submersible. Keen and Barney watched it, their hearts in their throats.

"Beat it!" screamed Keen. "They've spotted us!"

Barney rammed the throttle up the quadrant, shot the boat up on its step. Almost at the same instant two shots rang out from the submarine and threw up two jets of water in front of them. Barney jerked the wheel back and forth, rolled the boat over on her side. Back she went like a Gold Cup chaser. Two more shots rang out, but they were well past the mark.

From his crouched position. Keen watched the activities aboard the sub. The boat was quickly taken aboard, folded up, and stowed away in a metal slot along the base of the conning tower. The men, indistinct figures, clambered up the ladder and dropped down the hatch.

A few minutes later the submarine disappeared below the water again.

"Well, there goes Commander Stanwick and Professor Haageman," Keen said as Barney throttled her down and turned back for their original destination. "From now on, anything can happen."

In a few minutes they were easing the motor boat through a narrow gash in the rocks and guiding her by shoving against the damp rock wall. Inside they could see the *Black Bullet* high and dry on a platform of rock that was now out of the water, owing to low tide.

They worked fast unloading their fuel crates and in another hour the plane was completely refueled. They checked her carefully and prepared her for a quick getaway in event of an emergency. While they worked, hungry morays slashed about in the black waters below, snapped at chips of the crates.

Giving the craft a last careful look-over and turning her so that they could run her out with little trouble, the two conspirators now climbed back into the motor boat and eased her out into the open again.

"Yeh, let's get back. I'm afraid those Planter's punches won't hold out against the thirsts of those American tourists," moaned Barney.

They made their return trip uneventfully, but noticed that several government cutters were speeding up and down outside the Great West Breaker Bar.

"Those shots aroused someone," Keen reflected. "Don't stop unless you have to—and remember, we didn't see or hear anything. We have just come from around Elbow Beach way—a bathing party."

"Yeh. It came near being one," growled Barney.

But they were not bothered, since there were too many light craft racing about for them to be selected.

They got back through the Narrows and returned to Morgan's Island without hindrance. Finally they skiffed over to Burgess Point, picked up their bicycles, and cycled back to town.

HAMILTON was at fever heat in excitement. The newspaper, the *Bermudian*, had ripped out an extra, the first since the Armistice.

The story was a strange conglomerate affair concerning the escape of Commander Hugh Stanwick, an American Naval officer who had been held on parole until the arrival of Secret Service men from the States.

It seemed that Stanwick had slipped out of his hotel window

by the use of a rope, had dropped down on a small cottage nearby, and had escaped. Then there was the mysterious disappearance of one Professor Haageman, a German munitions man who had been a guest of the Governor-General. The Professor's room had been left in complete disorder. The Governor-General's private study had also been raided, several important portfolios of papers being missing. And to top it all, there was the report of movements of a submarine of some kind off Great Whale Point.

Keen sipped his punch, read the reports, and smiled across at Barney.

"Oh, what fun we shall have tomorrow," he grinned. "Old Lang is in for a tough day, but he'll have to go through with it now."

"He'll never make it," Barney muttered. "Somehow they'll pinch that Clipper—and there will go Mister Lang and the box of tricks." And Barney leaned back and let out a loud guffaw.

Keen frowned, stared at the ice in his drink. "That isn't so funny. It's too true to be funny. What time do they start tomorrow from Port Washington?"

"About noon. They'll be here about 5 o'clock—if they get here."

Keen sat gritting his teeth while Barney ordered two more Planter's punches. Keen was making plans for stopping the German submarine from getting away.

"We can do it," he muttered. "But it sounds too easy. There's a dark gent in the kindling somewhere. They are not just working with a submarine alone. There's too many chances to take. No, we've got to be ready for almost anything."

When the Mick came back, Keen mulled over the whole mess again to see if Barney had any more good ideas. They knew, for one thing, that old Lang would be on his way down on the Clipper the next afternoon, because he would want to check up on Stanwick's escape. They were certain, too, that Blott, the steward, was the killer. And in all probability the man would have the box containing the secret model of the aircraft carrier arrester gear somewhere on board.

"As a matter of fact," Keen said, "the best thing we can do is to give them a chance to show their cards. In that way we shall be sure of several points jibing up. Haageman and Commander

Stanwick are no doubt aboard the sub. Blott will have the box with him. And if we pull the right strings...."

"Or press the right triggers," grinned Barney, "we can nab a lot of birds with one rock."

Keen nodded, packed a new briar with some pungent shag, and applied a match after due contemplation of the whole situation.

"But there's something in all this, somewhere, Barney, that worries me. They're not relying simply on the submarine. There's some other angle to it somewhere."

"Well," agreed Barney, torching a massive black cigar, "we'll find out what it is—later on. For now, let's worry about that bartender."

THEY checked out quietly the next noon and had their light bags taken to a point near Gibbs Hill lighthouse and left with a cottager. They had lunch in Riddle's Bay, rode around the Warwick Camp, and watched the Sherwood Foresters winding up their morning maneuvers. Then they picked up their bags, quietly cycled away, and headed for the scrubby gorse that sheltered the pathway down to the rocks that hid the cave where the *Black Bullet* was sheltered.

It was well after one o'clock when they clambered down inside and worked their way up to the amphibian. Using small flashlights, they changed into their black flying kits, being particularly careful now to put on full length face masks under their helmets. Then they eased the plane down into the water, started the engine, and guided her out through the narrow opening and into a small cove outside. Barney quickly opened the wings and Keen jabbed the king-pins in. They held her there a few minutes until the engine warmed completely, then they took off with a roar and a milky wake before anyone in the vicinity could figure out what had happened.

Keen hoiked her up fast, climbed her to 4,000 feet, set the throttle for cruising speed, and went to work on his avigation. Bermuda fell away fast as they headed northwest toward New York. Barney was twisted in his seat in such a way that he could watch the water below and still keep a close watch on anything above and behind.

The *Black Bullet* gleamed like an evil thing in the glare of the mid-day sunshine as it raced to keep a rendezvous with crime.

THE BERMUDA CLIPPER left Port Washington dead on the clang of noon. She carried sixteen passengers and a crew of five headed by Captain Marty Strack, First-Officer Pete Blumenthall, and Avigator Jerry Mundin. Eric Lawrence was the radio-man and George Blott the steward.

The passenger list was a typical tourist crowd that included two honeymooning couples, three school teachers, several middle-aged couples of the comfortable class, and a number of unassuming men who were obviously on "tired-business-man" trips.

Drury Lang was not one of these; for while he was tired and not a little worried, he was making no effort to get into the snatches of conversation that was bantered back and forth across the cabin. He made no effort to change his seat at any time but simply sat near the window in the compartment aft of the Steward's pantry. Across the aisle, three men in business clothes started some sort of a card game that Lang could not quite understand.

As they headed out to sea, Lang pondered on the strange message he had received from a man named Ginsberg who was in Bermuda.

"To think that that guy turned up again. I thought we were through with the Ginsberg and Pulski business. I wonder who Ginsberg is, anyway."

Then he sat thinking about the business of the escape of Stanwick, the mysterious rumors about a German submarine and the disappearance of Professor Haageman.

"I wish Keen was here," he muttered. "All this would make sense to him, the lug. I don't even know why I'm going down now that Stanwick is on the loose. Still, I don't see how the guy can get off an island like that."

The Steward now came along the gangway and dropped a printed menu on Lang's table which had been drawn out of recesses in the wall. Lang took it without looking up, then watched Blott as he moved across the cabin and handed out three more.

In a few minutes Blott came back and Lang ordered soup, cold chicken, vegetables, and coffee. The men across the aisle gave their order, too, without breaking up their card game. From farther down the aisle, gay laughter could be heard in the other compartments, and Lang wished he could find something to laugh about.

Blott stood in the doorway, consulting his watch. Then the three men in Lang's compartment quit their game and the Steward began serving the first course.

For the next half hour, Lang was occupied enough to quit worrying, and as Blott carried his dishes away and inquired whether there was anything further he could do for him, he relaxed into a comfortable position, let his chair fold back a trifle, and took it easy.

He did not know that the three men across the aisle were watching him carefully, even though they had returned to their three-handed card game.

After the ship had been on its way for about ninety minutes, Marty Strack turned the wheel over to his co-pilot, dropped down the narrow companionway, and walked down the aisle to see how his passengers were faring. He was amazed to find that practically every one was sound asleep.

"Hmm! What a lullaby trip this turned out to be," he remarked to Blott who stood near his galley doorway. "I thought we were having an easy, quiet flight, but I never saw them cork off like this before. You'll have to wake them all up to get them unloaded."

"How far out are we?" Blott asked casually, turning back into his pantry.

"We're about here, last check," Strack said, pointing out the position on the lithographed chart on the compartment wall.

The three card players, sleep having not as yet won them, glanced up and saw where the Skipper had planted his forefinger. They exchanged glances, stared across at Lang. The Secret Service man was actually snoring.

Then before Strack could sense what was happening, he felt a gun rammed in his ribs.

"All right, Strack. Take it quiet now and sit down."

Amazed, the Clipper Captain turned, saw that all three men had dropped their cards and were carrying big black automatics. Strack stuck his hands up, then suddenly brought them down fast, in an attempt to grab one of the guns. But Blott quickly stepped up and smacked his Captain with a short brown leather billy. The Skipper grunted, folded up at the knees, and went down. They dragged him clear of the aisle and rammed him into one of the seats they had vacated.

Blott turned and stared at Lang. That worthy had stopped snoring and was twisting uneasily in his chair. Blott went over, gave the sleeping man a solid smack across his hair part with the billy. Lang slipped farther down into his chair.

The three men now worked fast. While Blott ran through the compartments to make certain his doctored lunch had done its trick, the others clambered forward into the control section. First, young Lawrence, the radioman, was caught cold and tied up well away from his instrument panel. Then Mundin was jerked away from his chart table, rammed against a bulkhead, and tied to the wall.

Two of the men with automatics eased up alongside Blumenthall and displayed their hardware.

"All right, Blumenthall, it's a stickup and you can live a long time if you keep your nose clean."

"What's the idea? We've got passengers aboard this boiler," young Blumenthall argued.

"Sure, you got passengers, Blumenthall. An' you want to get them to Bermuda, okay, eh? Well, act smart. We only want to go down on the water a few minutes and do a little business. We won't bother you after that. What do you say?"

"What about the Captain?"

"He's all right. He's just got a headache for a while. He's back there, okay. You'll get your name and your picture in the papers, Blumenthall."

"Yeh? In the obituary pages, I guess. What's the gag, anyway?"

"See that gray streak ahead there about two miles ahead? Well, that just happens to be a submarine. And all you got to do is to put this boiler down alongside her. Simple, eh?"

"And then what?"

"Well, after that you just get rid of us guys who don't want to go to Bermuda, see?" the beady-eyed gun-man grinned. "That's all there is to it."

"I'll put her down—but no monkey business with my passengers, remember."

"Now you're acting smart, kid. You put her down and hold her as near to that tin-fish as you can. They'll come out to get us."

Blumenthall stared ahead, saw the distinct outlines of the submarine. He eased back on the throttles and let the four big engines tick over gently.

"What country runs that sub?" Blumenthall asked.

"Never mind. Get this flying boat down—fast. But say, what the hell is that up there?"

Blumenthall looked ahead and above. He could see the distinct lines of a fast black plane. He frowned.

"So you're gonner shoot us down again when we take off?" he started to argue.

"That must be one of their jobs," one thug said to another. "They said they'd have a couple nearby—just in case."

"Yeh. But that ain't one of them," the first grunted. "Get her down fast, Blumenthall."

The big Clipper nosed down steeper and the co-pilot curled her around sharp into the wind and let her glide toward the long gray submarine which was now well out of the water. The crew on the forward deck of the sub was breaking out the folding boat and three men stood before an A-A gun which came up through folding deck plates.

"Yer see, Blum, they ain't taking no chances. So don't try anything funny."

KEEN climbed the *Black Bullet* higher as he spotted the Clipper coming on. He had been watching for it for the past hour. Apparently he had timed his approach beautifully.

"There's the sub," he muttered and Barney stood up and peered over.

"Yeh," the Mick muttered moving fast. "There's the sub and here's some more trouble. Look above us."

Keen jerked his head up and spotted three silver-gray fighters bearing down on them from above. Two were Arado seaplanes with narrow, racy pontoons that looked like long torpedoes. The third, likewise a seaplane, was a Focke-Wulf biplane.

"I get it. They've got one of those depot ships somewhere in this area, eh? I knew there was something else to this game. They're taking no chances on this gag failing with Professor Haageman aboard the sub. Let 'em have it, Barney. I'm going down for the sub—in a minute."

Barney opened fire at once and the two Arados replied in a wicked dive. Barney slapped it at them with his Brownings while Keen held his dive until the proper time. Below, the Clipper was on the water and churning up close to the submarine.

The enemy fighters fanned out and Barney took them on one at a time as they hammered at the *Black Bullet*. He finally clipped one of the Arados. Pummeled by a second terrific burst from his Brownings, it twisted as though in torture. They saw the pilot stiffen, jerk up into an almost standing position, then go head first out of the cockpit and over the wing. Out of control, the plane fell away in a spinning dive. It finally hit with a terrible smash that sent up a climbing spurt of bluish-white water. A rosette of steam followed and blotted out all signs of the craft.

"That's the stuff, Barney," yelled Kerry Keen. "Hold them off long enough for me to time my dive."

Keen was now circling the submarine below and watching the Clipper ease toward her. The sub's small boat had already been launched. It was headed for the big Sikorsky.

"Hang on—and get ready to take a passenger," Keen barked.

Then they went down, hell-for-leather, toward the submersible. To repulse them, the gun crew opened fire from the deck of the undersea boat, pounding through a salvo of three-inch stuff that deafened them with steel throated screams. A concussion high above them added to the din. But Keen held her there. He would not pull out until he could read the small markings on the side of the conning tower.

Down… down! But now the fighters were on them again. Barney spewed out another burst at the Focke-Wulf, then watched the second Arado skim past their wing tips with but inches to spare. As it went by, the Mick poured a double stream of lead into her vitals. That was the deathblow. The raider's right wing crumpled and she plunged downward in a tight spiral.

It was at that instant that Keen pulled his bomb toggles. He yanked twice, and the *Black Bullet* jerked as two slim, armor-piercing projectiles flicked out of the belly compartment. They went down flashing and spinning, and Keen had to hoik out of the dive fast.

As they whipped past the submarine's deck, Barney swung his guns around, poured lead at the gun crew below, and watched two men roll away and struggle to grip the scupper rail.

Then the whole scene blanked out in a curtain of garish flame and smoke!

The *Black Bullet* was hurled over on her back by the force of the explosion. Keen fought to get her back, and as he eased the throttle he saw the Focke-Wulf hurtle down through the smoky haze and disappear in the mass of wreckage.

"We must have nicked the sub's magazine first shot," he screamed at Barney who stood stock-still, uncertain what to do now. "That Focke-Wulf slammed smack into the middle of it. The concussion was too much for it."

"Look! Those fellows are trying to get back to the Clipper," Barney yelled.

Keen dived at the folding boat now and poured a long burst ahead of it. The men in the boat eased up on their oars. They saw the Clipper start to move away.

"That's right. Clear off, Clipper," grinned Keen. "Cover them, Barney, while we go and do a little picking-up on our own."

Barney kept a short series of bursts battering the water around the submarine's folding dory and they saw two sailors, a man in a white mess jacket, and three other men, huddled aboard.

Keen dropped the *Bullet* on the water after he got his pontoons down and eased up to the boat while Barney covered them with his Brownings. They sat tense, white and plainly frightened. One of the sailors was mopping at a bad gash on his forehead with a large dirty handkerchief. One of the men in a dark business suit was standing up holding a white handkerchief by its corners in the form of a flag.

"They give up," grinned Barney.

"What now?"

Keen eased the *Black Bullet* up close to the bobbing boat and opened his cockpit hatch. He raised himself a trifle and yelled:

"We want George Blott—Blott, the Steward aboard that Clipper. We want him aboard here at once and he must come with the U.S. Navy box that was stolen from the Brooklyn Navy yard. Is that clear?"

They saw the men in the boat turn to the man in the white mess jacket and expostulate.

"You've got two minutes to get him and that box aboard. So make it snappy, or I'm sinking the lot of you. Move fast now!"

There was another hasty discussion and finally Blott leaned down, picked up the gray box from somewhere, and with reluctance moved toward the prow of the boat. Keen edged the *Bullet* in close so that Blott could step onto the port pontoon and steady himself with the leading edge of the wing. Finally he shoved the box ahead of him and climbed up. Keen took the box, noted that the seals had not been broken. Then he ordered him to get in beside Barney.

Blott was terror-stricken and obeyed orders like a whipped dog. Barney made him sit down and stood over him still covering the boat.

"What do we do now?" someone in the boat yelled.

"Don't worry! We'll see that you are picked up. The Queen of Bermuda will be along shortly. We'll tip them off about you and see that you are taken care of—well taken care of," Keen added.

The small boat then bobbed away through the streaked oil

surface of the sea while the Clipper stood off and awaited developments.

Keen rammed the *Black Bullet* through the water and came around on the windward side of the Clipper. Then he took out a megaphone and hailed her.

"Ahoy, Clipper!" he called. "Carry on with your trip. I'll see that Blott is taken to New York and turned over to the proper authorities. Is Mr. Drury Lang aboard?"

"Yes—but he's unconscious. Any other message?" came back from Blumenthall in the control pit.

"No, that's all. Pleasant voyage—and my respects to Mr. Lang."

"Thanks, who shall I say left that message?"

"The Griffon!" bawled Keen. "He won't believe you," he added, "but you tell him anyway."

"The Griffon?" gasped Blumenthall. "You're the Griffon? Thanks!... Thanks! You did a swell job on that mob."

"The same to you," laughed Keen, "so long, and all the best. And will you advise the Queen of Bermuda to pick the rest of these thugs up?"

"I sure will. Thanks, again!"

And with that Keen threw them a cheery wave and raced the *Black Bullet* away and over the rollers into the sky. Barney, in the meantime had shackled Blott's hands behind him and had fastened him securely to a cross-bracing rod.

IT WAS about three o'clock before they got clear, leaving the small boat bobbing about on the surface of the Atlantic, and the Clipper churning a white wake in her take-off. They had to kill several hours before they dared attempt to get into Long Island, so Keen headed her northwest again for an hour, climbing to about 7,000 feet.

"I hope that guy aboard that Clipper don't try to have us checked," Barney muttered.

"Don't worry. He's got his hands full bringing the Clipper in. But keep your eye on Blott there, and see that he don't try any monkey tricks."

"He won't. He's tied up tighter than a drum."

Keen pondered on his new problem—Blott. Then he decided to head for the long stretch of beach running north out of Cape Hatteras. There were several long dunes in that area where they could hide away for several hours until it got dark. That would give Keen time to question Blott, also, so that he could get the inside story on what actually happened.

In another hour and a half they landed again, ran the *Black Bullet* up out of the water, and hid her away between two high sand dunes. Barney crawled out on top, lay flat, and acted as a sentry, just in case some prowling fisherman might stumble on them. Keen released Blott and gave him a chance to stretch his limbs. Then for about three hours they rested and Blott was induced to tell his story.

Keen took notes and stuffed them away in his pocket. Barney came back and they shared their light meal with their captive, then they carefully blindfolded him, stowed him away on board again, and took off for their flight north.

By ten o'clock they were back at Graylands where they led their blindfolded captive through the hidden hangar, up the hidden stairs, and into Keen's study. All this time neither Keen nor Barney had removed their masks and only spoke to each other with the use of the names Ginsberg and Pulski.

Barney fed Blott while Keen typed out a full report on the case, explaining how the aircraft carrier model had been stolen from the Navy Yard, and how the Secret Service man, Beale, had been murdered with a knife having two handles. He also explained Blott's tie-up with Commander Stanwick, who, he learned, had once got the Clipper steward out of a jam when both were in the Navy.

"He wasn't such a bad guy," Blott had argued in a subdued manner. But Keen pointed out from behind his mask that, after all, Stanwick had been in the Navy and pledged in the service of his country. Blott agreed sullenly that there was something to that.

"But anyway, I liked him and he was good to me," Blott doggedly continued. "I wasn't gonner let that Secret Service guy get him if I could help it. Sure! I bumped that Beale guy off, an' the knife had two handles. I had one handle in a saloon with me the night we knocked off Old Lady Kennedy—to get it daubed up with fingerprints from fellows at the bar. I changed the handles after I drove the knife into Beale's heart. I handled it with a tissue paper napkin to keep my own fingerprints off it."

The rest was clear to Keen. He completed his report and then jerked Blott to his feet.

"All right, Pulski," he growled at Barney. "Clap the bandages on him again. Let's get him out of here."

In a short time they were racing down Long Island for New York City. Once they got rid of Blott they returned to their 55th Street apartment and went to bed.

BOTH Keen and Barney slept soundly for a full twelve hours' for they were physically exhausted by the time they had completed their job. It was well after 3 o'clock on Sunday afternoon before they were up for a meal. After that they sauntered out, entered a motion picture house on 50th Street, and sat through a two and a half-hour show.

"Well, let's get back and see what happened," Keen said. "He's had plenty of time to blow in by now."

They sauntered back to their penthouse and entered just as the Paramount Building clock showed the hour of seven. There, just as they expected, was the raving Drury Lang, pacing up and down the corridor.

They looked at him in mock amazement, squinted at the bandage that capped his head.

"What did you do—fall out?" Keen inquired.

"Never mind me—where the hell you guys bin?" Lang demanded. "I bin here half an hour."

"How's Bermuda?" demanded Keen, ignoring the question.

"You look like you bin there yourself. Where'd you get that sunburn?"

"On Long Island. The sun still shines out there, you know," Keen parried. "And now, what happened?"

"I got slugged on that Clipper—just as you said I would. Say…

you weren't on that Clipper, were you… under another name, or something."

"Don't be silly. Get on with your story."

"Well, we got the guy who got Beale—and we got the arrester-gear model back."

"Good work! I was wondering about that business. How did you do it?"

"I didn't! Last night old Scott got a call to meet a guy named Ginsberg at his office—that is, Scott's office. Well, when Scott got there, he found this mug Blott tied up in a chair with the Navy box on the table in front of him—and a typewritten report of the whole thing."

Both Keen and Barney acted surprised. Neither spoke for several minutes. Lang got sore at that, too.

"Don't look at me like that. It's right enough. There was the guy—tied up tight as a—"

"But how did Blott get there?" Keen broke in.

"I don't know. It's all screwy. But he said that two guys—and get this, two guys named Pulski and Ginsberg—brought him there."

"But.… But Blott went to Bermuda on the Clipper, didn't he?"

"Yeh, he did—and so did I. But they took him off, swiped his box, and brought him back by plane. So that lets you out, Keen. And once they landed somewhere down along the coast near Hatteras. He doesn't know what else happened to him because they kept him blindfolded."

"Who gets the dough for the arrester-gear model, Lang?"

"Nobody. We can't figure out how Blott got there, but this guy Ginsberg was in Bermuda, too. He tipped off the Police Inspector down there how Beale was killed. If we could find Ginsberg, maybe we could get somewhere."

"Ginsberg? Ginsberg was in Bermuda, too?" gasped Keen.

"Sure. In fact, he tipped me off to watch out for Blott." Then Lang mournfully told the story of the business aboard the Clipper and how he was put to sleep while the gang captured the ship and forced the co-pilot to land alongside the submarine.

"Then Ginsberg might be the Griffon," suggested Keen.

"No. The Griffon was the guy who blew up the submarine and took Blott—but say, maybe you're right! The Griffon nabbed Blott and the box, brought him back to New York, and planted him—" But Lang then gave up, wiped the perspiration from his nose, and reached for Barney's bottle.

"Then the Griffon is entitled to the reward, eh?"

"Sure! But who the hell is the Griffon?" moaned Lang.

"Ginsberg," suggested Keen.

"Pulski, maybe," added Barney, grabbing the bottle back.

"You know, a funny thing happened here last Friday night," Lang went on. "One of the trans-Atlantic flying boats coming down from Montreal—one of the British test boats—reported something queer."

Neither Keen nor Barney flicked an eyelash.

"Funny, in a way," Lang went on.

"The Army was doing a special anti-aircraft show on Governor's Island, and the Empire boat had not been warned. They flew smack into the restricted area. They got out of it for a time, but landed and said that they had been fired on by a strange black plane of some sort."

"They were laughed at, of course," Lang went on after another drink, "and the situation was explained to them. But the crew insisted that they had been fired on by a black plane."

"So what?" demanded Keen.

"Don't you get it?" beamed Lang. "That black plane was the Griffon going down to Bermuda to snatch Blott. They just happened to be in the air over that anti-aircraft display at the same time."

"Well," agreed Keen with a stifled sigh of relief, "I suppose that's as good an explanation as any."

"Sure, and that's why I went to Bermuda, even though I knew that Stanwick had escaped. I figured I'd nab the Griffon myself."

"Boy! That was close—only you were asleep all the time the Griffon was nabbing Blott," laughed Keen.

"Never mind. I'll get that guy yet!"

"Sure! But when you do, don't forget you owe him the reward for getting Blott and the arrester-gear model."

"Oh yes. But I still wonder who Ginsberg and Pulski are," muttered Lang as he sidled toward the door.